NINJA BASEBALL
Kyuma!

1

STORY & ART BY
SHUNSHIN MAEDA

HOW TO READ MANGA!

Hello there! My name is **Kyuma,** and this is my very first book - **Ninja Baseball Kyuma**! It is a comic book originally created in my home country of **Japan,** where comics are called **manga.**

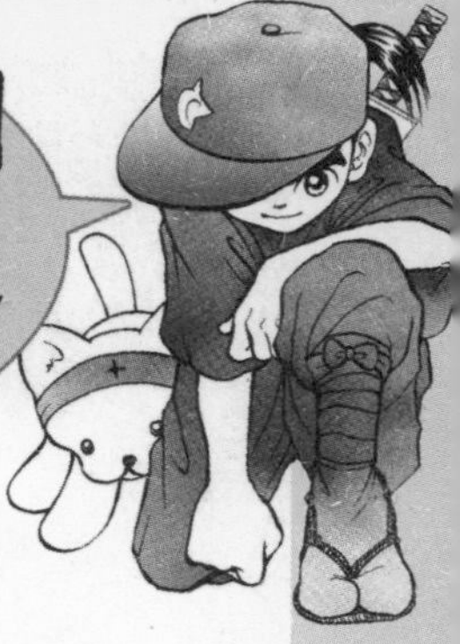

A manga book is read from **right-to-left,** which is **backwards** from the normal books you know. This means that you will find the first page where you expect to find the last page! It also means that each page begins in the top right corner.

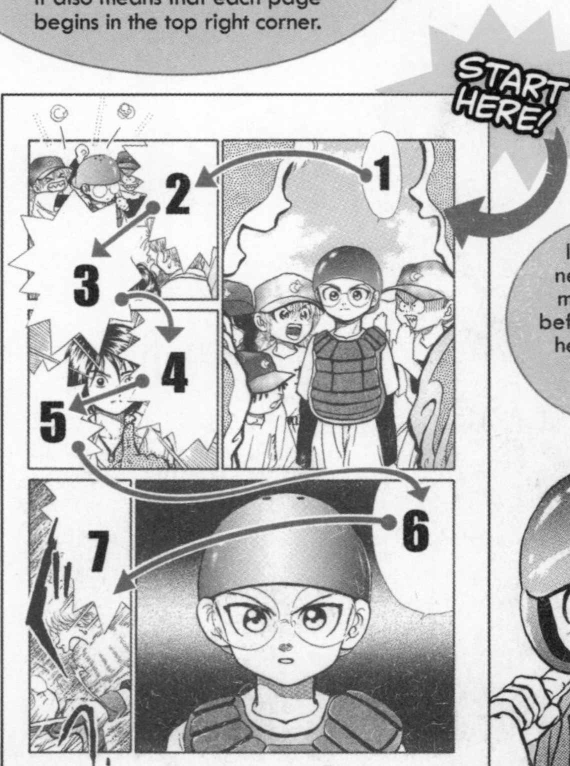
START HERE!
1
2
3
4
5
6
7

If you have never read a manga book before, here is a helpful guide to get you started!

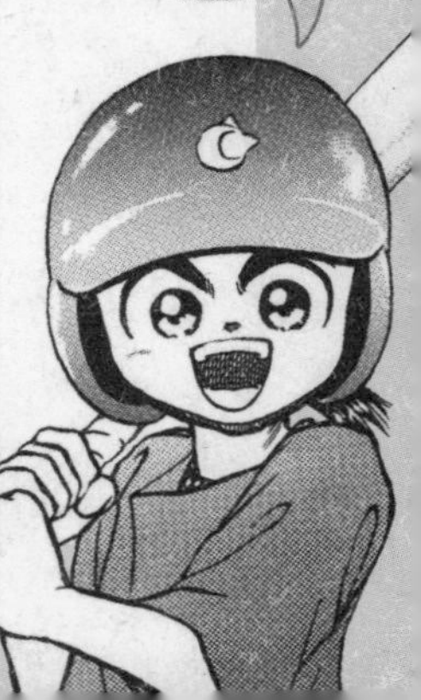

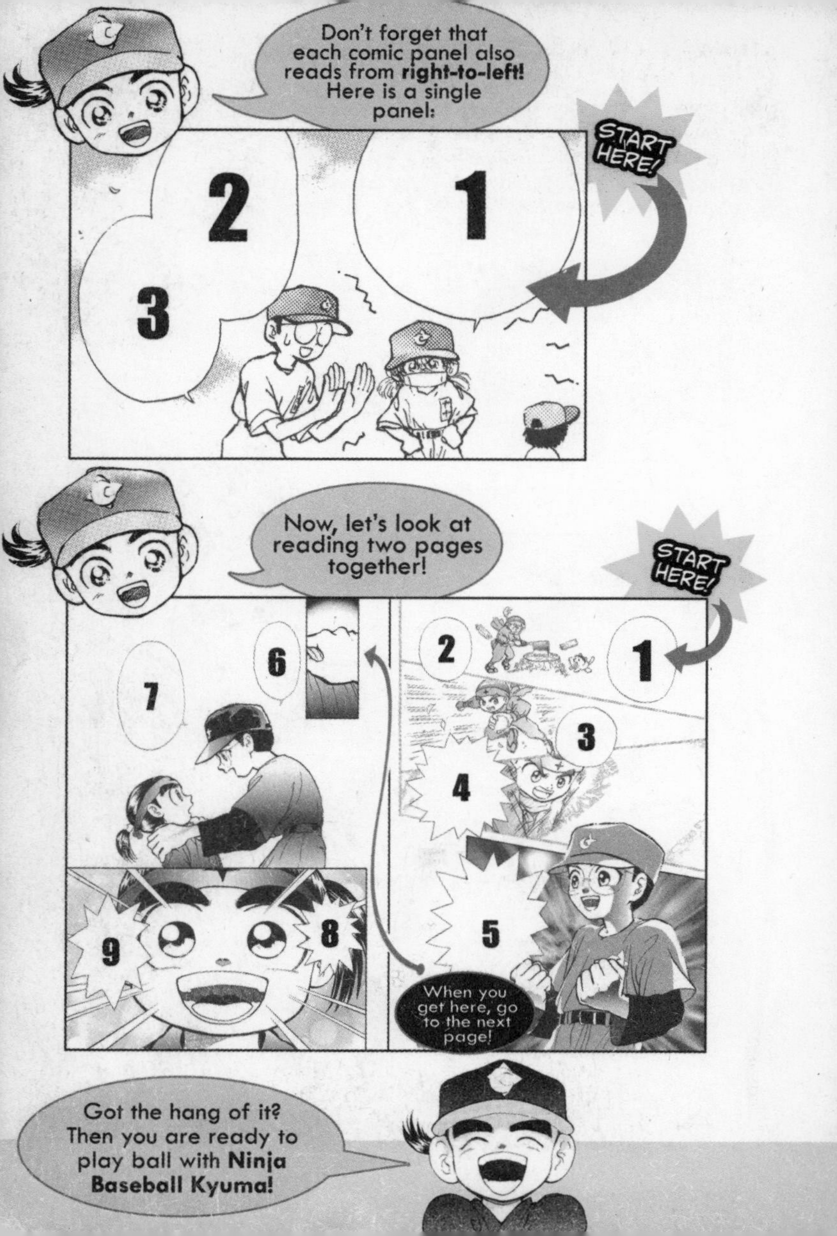

Don't forget that each comic panel also reads from **right-to-left!** Here is a single panel:
START HERE!
1
2
3
Now, let's look at reading two pages together!
START HERE!
1
2
3
4
5
When you get here, go to the next page!
6
7
8
9
Got the hang of it? Then you are ready to play ball with **Ninja Baseball Kyuma!**

CONTENTS

PITCH 1
A BASEBALL GENIUS LIVES IN THE MOUNTAINS!

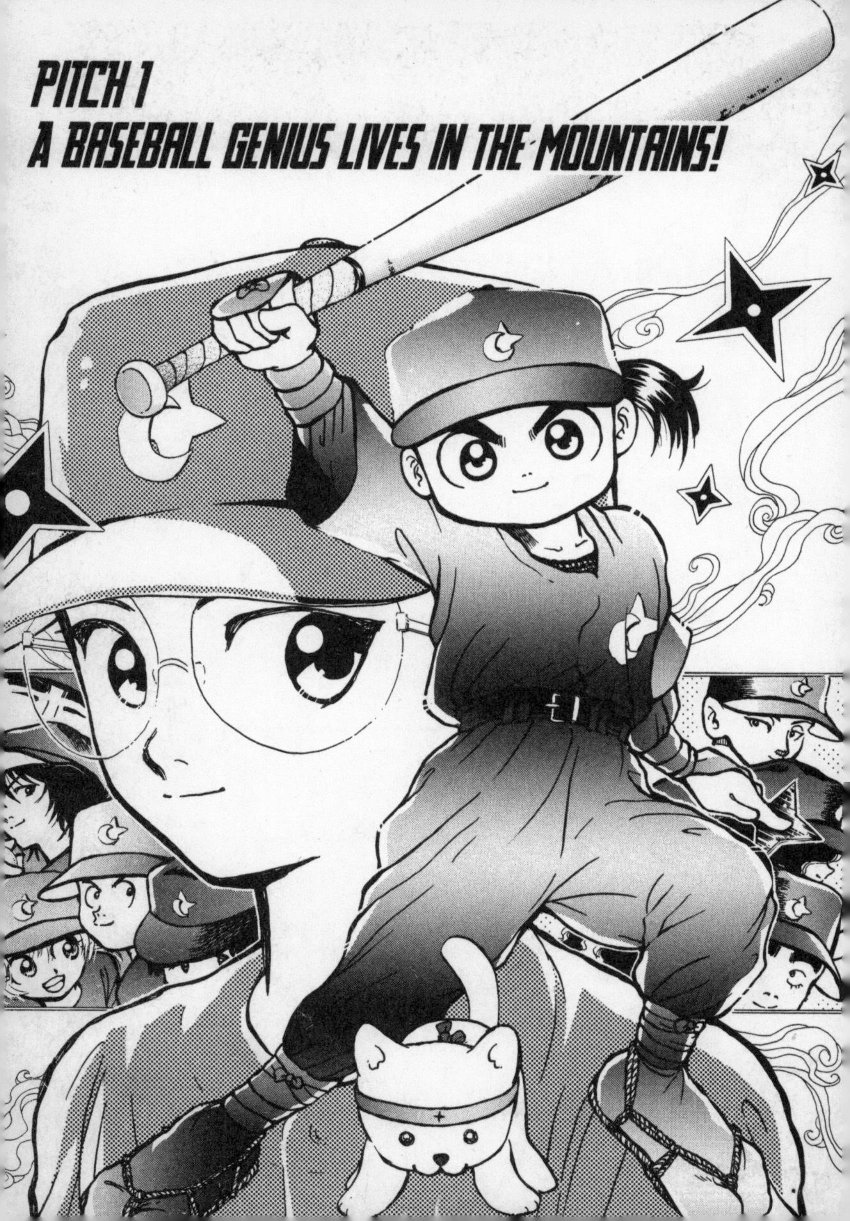

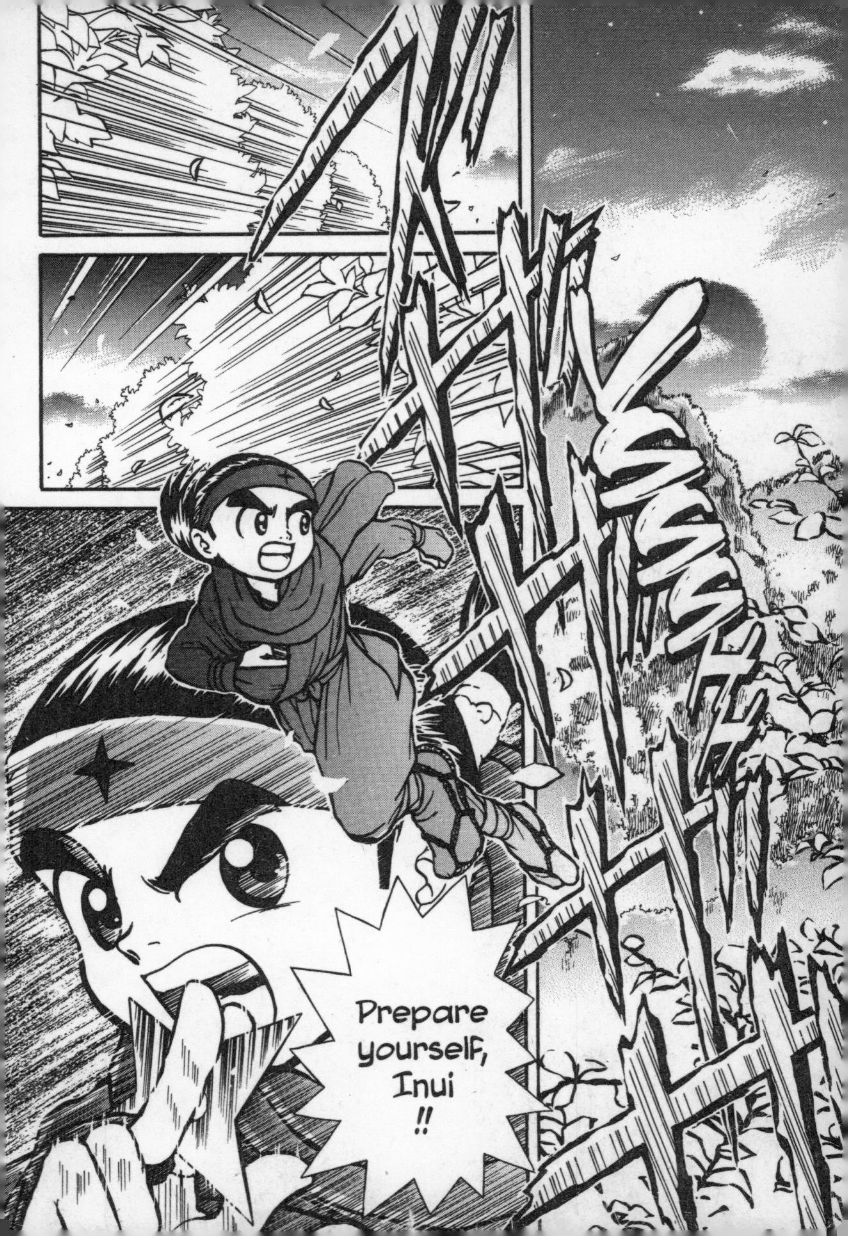
Prepare yourself, Inui !!

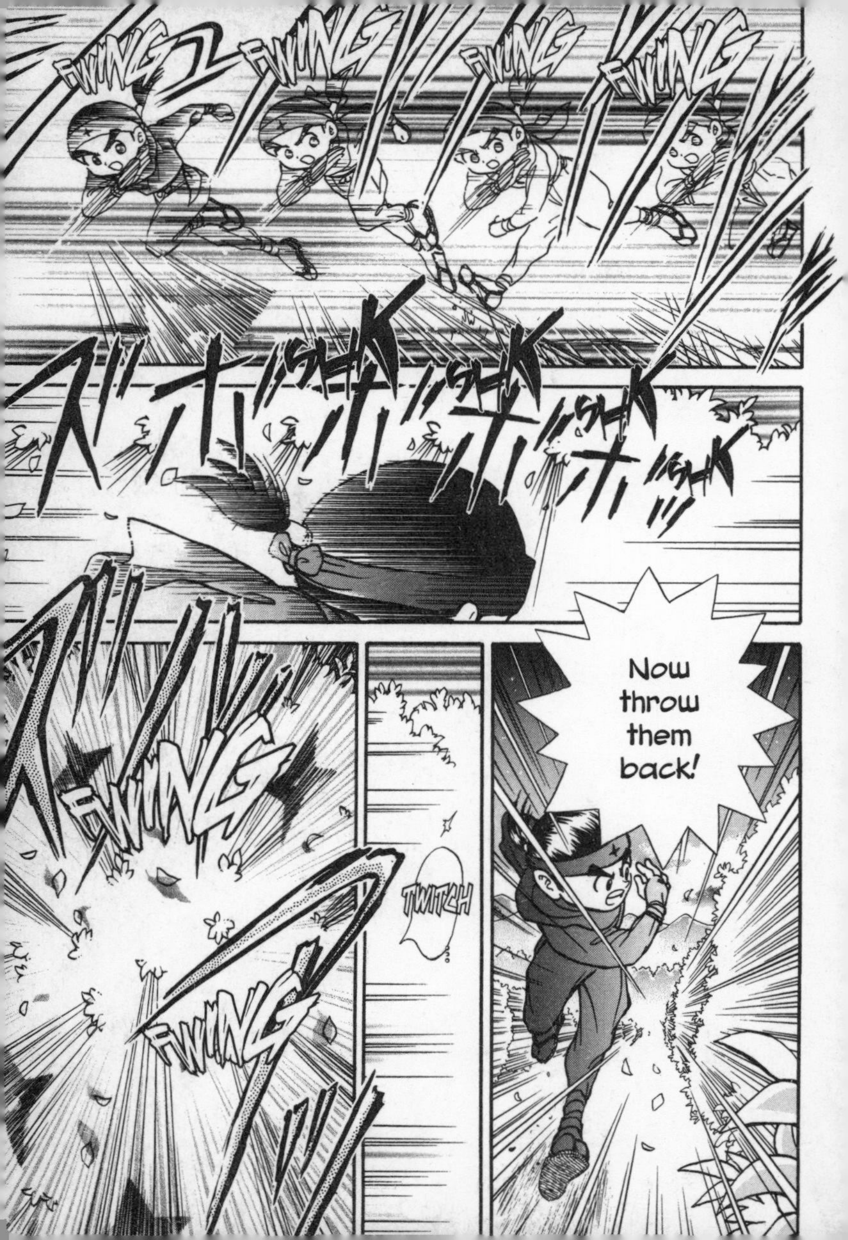
FWING
FWING
FWING
FWING
SHK
SHK
SHK
SHK
SHK
Now throw them back!
TWITCH
FWING
FWING

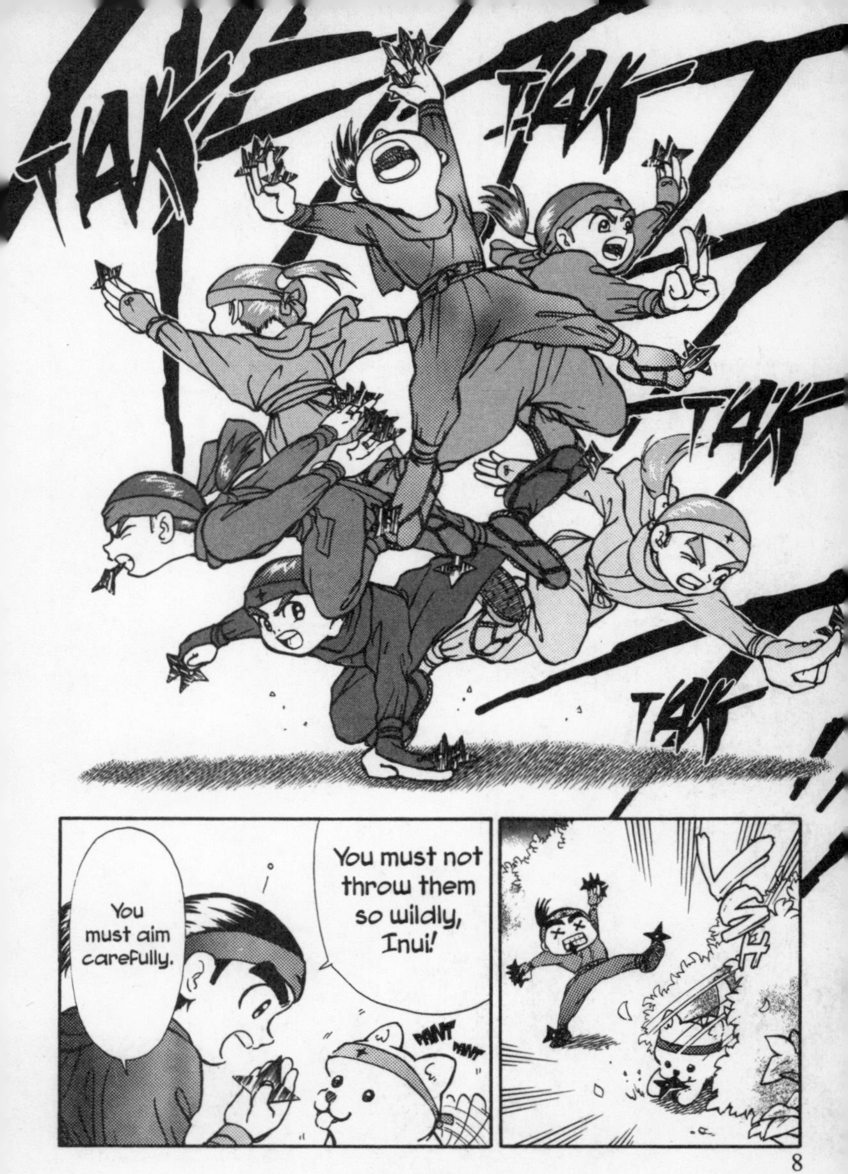
TAK
TAK
TAK
TAK
You must not throw them so wildly, Inui!
You must aim carefully.
PANT
PANT

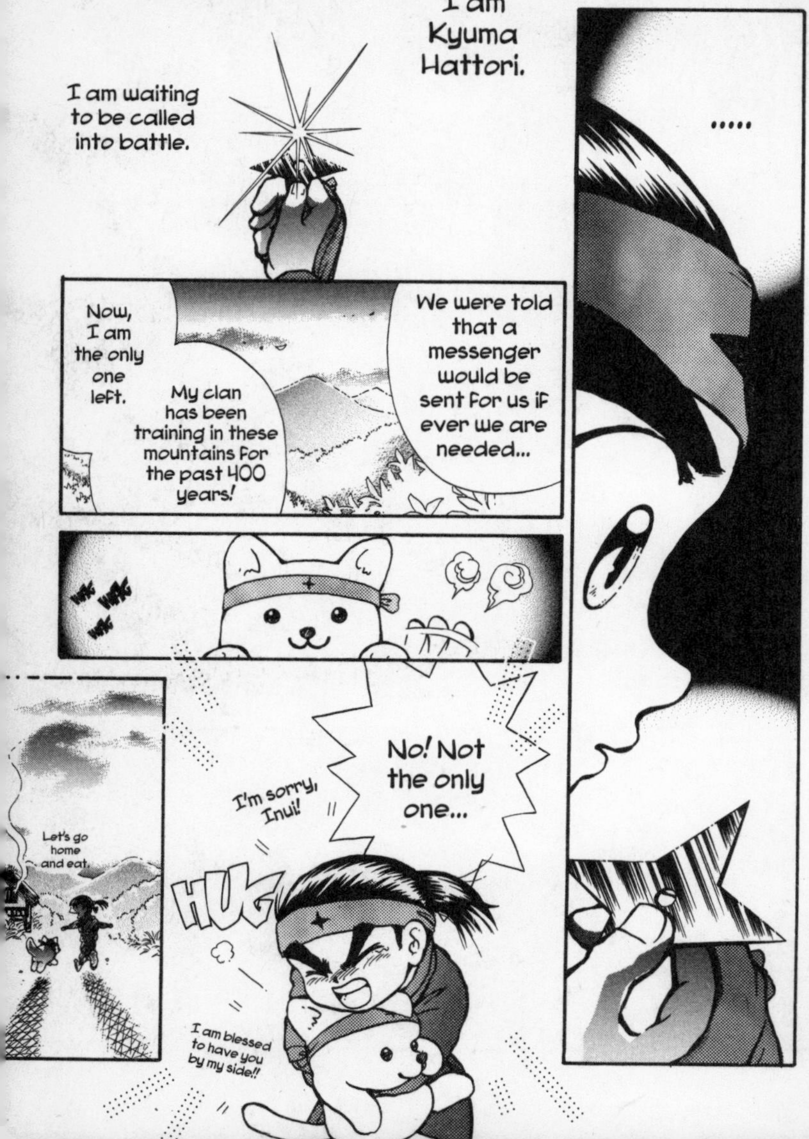
I am Kyuma Hattori.
.....
I am waiting to be called into battle.
We were told that a messenger would be sent for us if ever we are needed...
My clan has been training in these mountains for the past 400 years!
Now, I am the only one left.
No! Not the only one...
I'm sorry, Inui!
HUG
I am blessed to have you by my side!!
Let's go home and eat.

Read this way

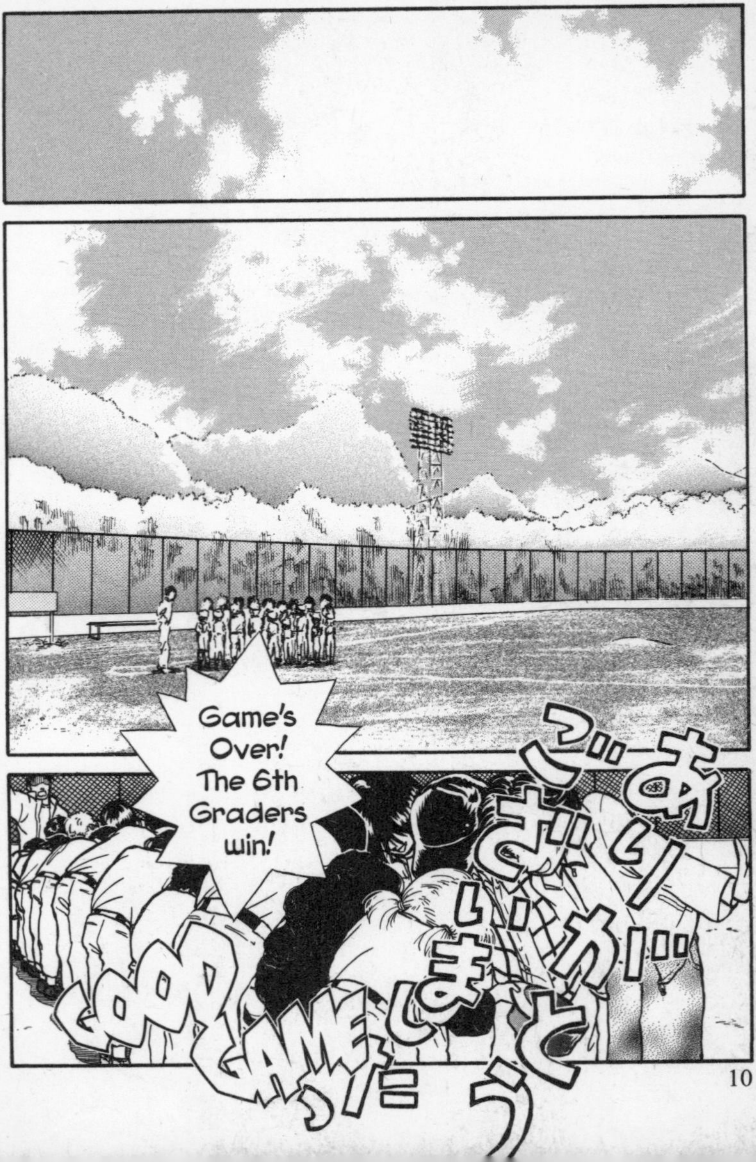
Game's Over! The 6th Graders win!
ありがとうございました
GOOD GAME

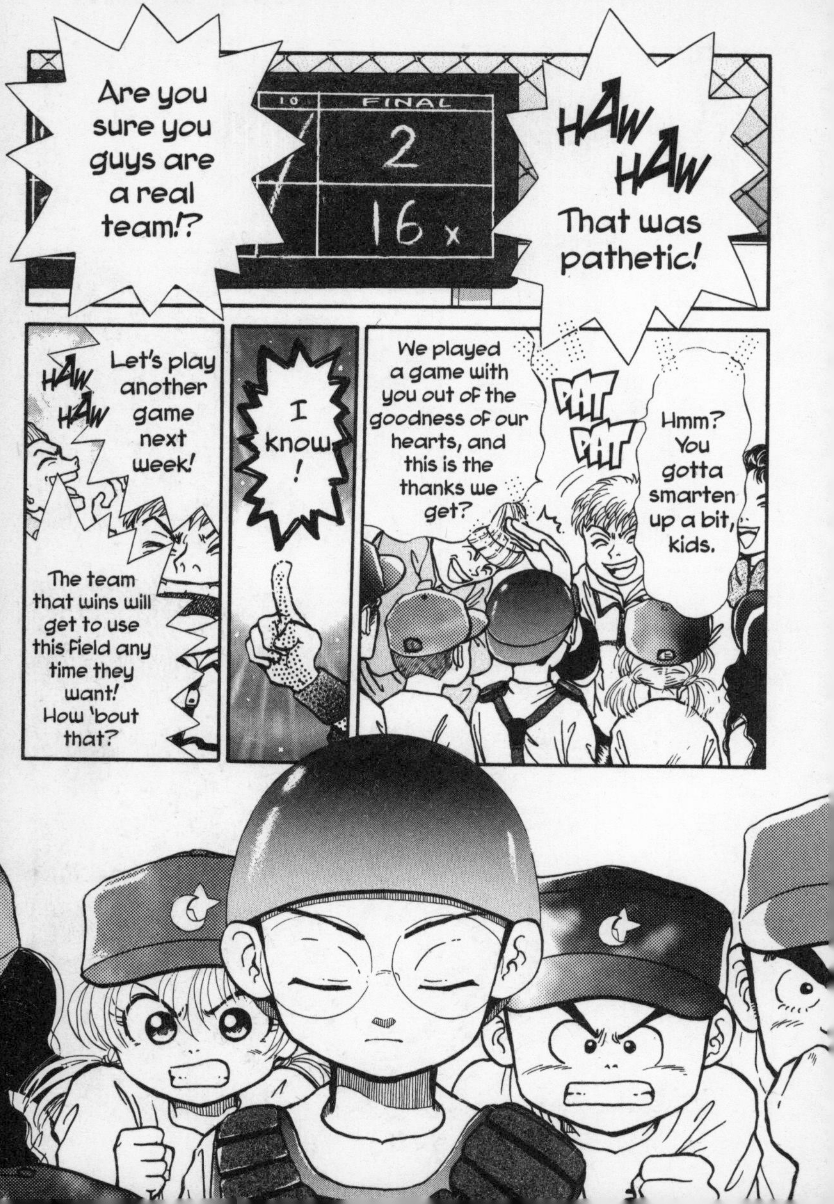
HAW HAW
That was pathetic!
Are you sure you guys are a real team!?
FINAL
2
16 x
We played a game with you out of the goodness of our hearts, and this is the thanks we get?
PAT PAT
Hmm? You gotta smarten up a bit, kids.
I know!
Let's play another game next week!
HAW HAW
The team that wins will get to use this field any time they want! How 'bout that?

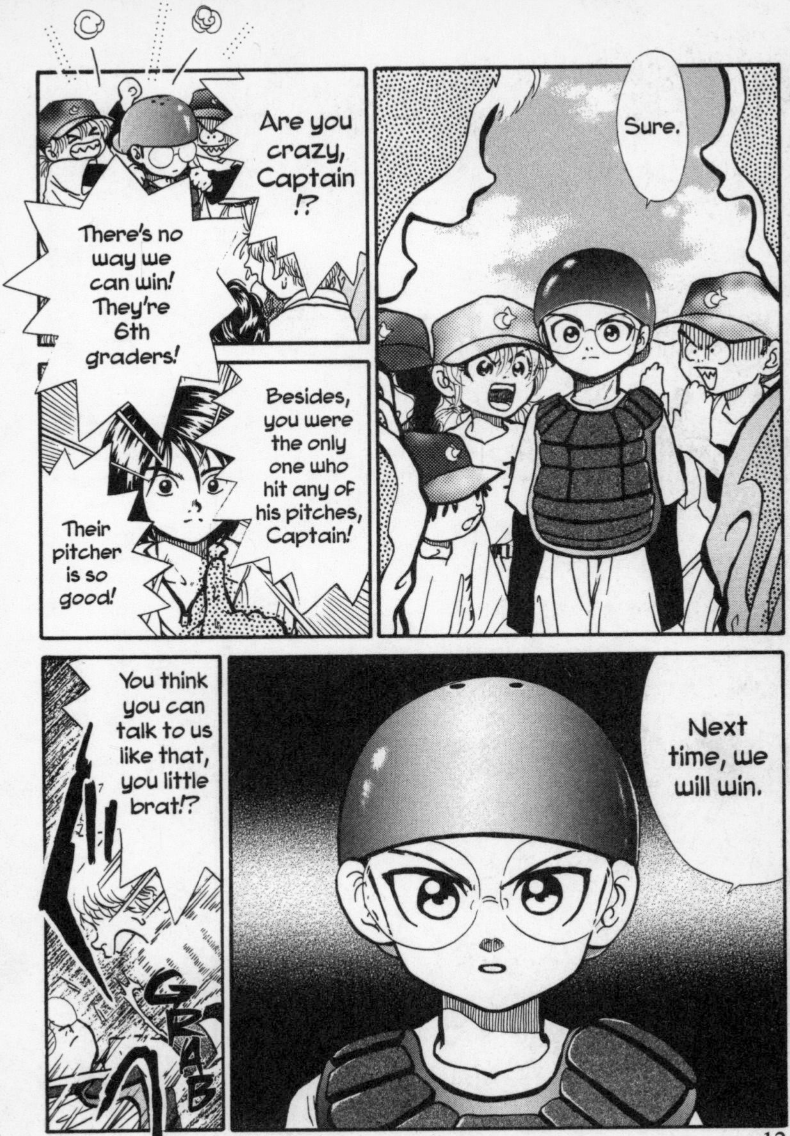
Sure.
Are you crazy, Captain!?
There's no way we can win! They're 6th graders!
Besides, you were the only one who hit any of his pitches, Captain!
Their pitcher is so good!
Next time, we will win.
You think you can talk to us like that, you little brat!?
GRAB

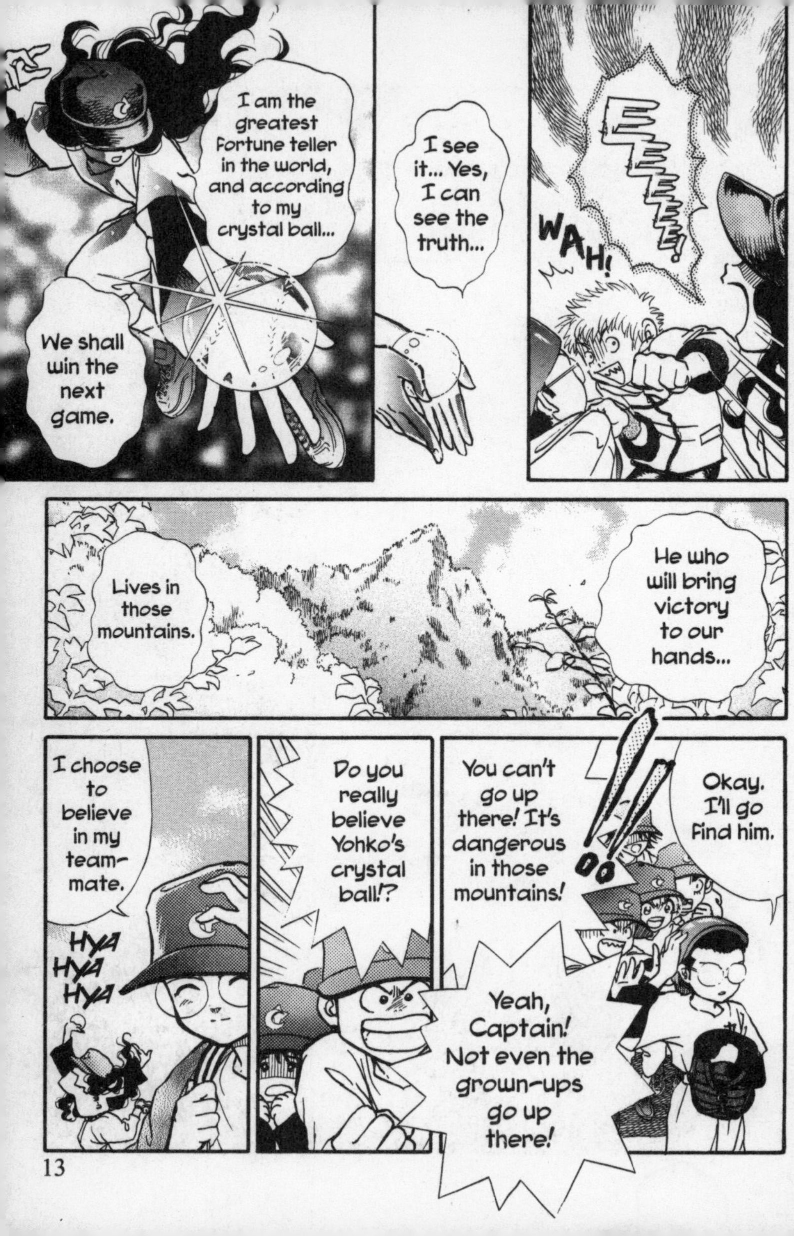
EEEEEE!
WAH!
I see it... Yes, I can see the truth...
I am the greatest fortune teller in the world, and according to my crystal ball...
We shall win the next game.
He who will bring victory to our hands...
Lives in those mountains.
Okay. I'll go find him.
You can't go up there! It's dangerous in those mountains!
Yeah, Captain! Not even the grown-ups go up there!
Do you really believe Yohko's crystal ball!?
I choose to believe in my teammate.
HYA HYA HYA

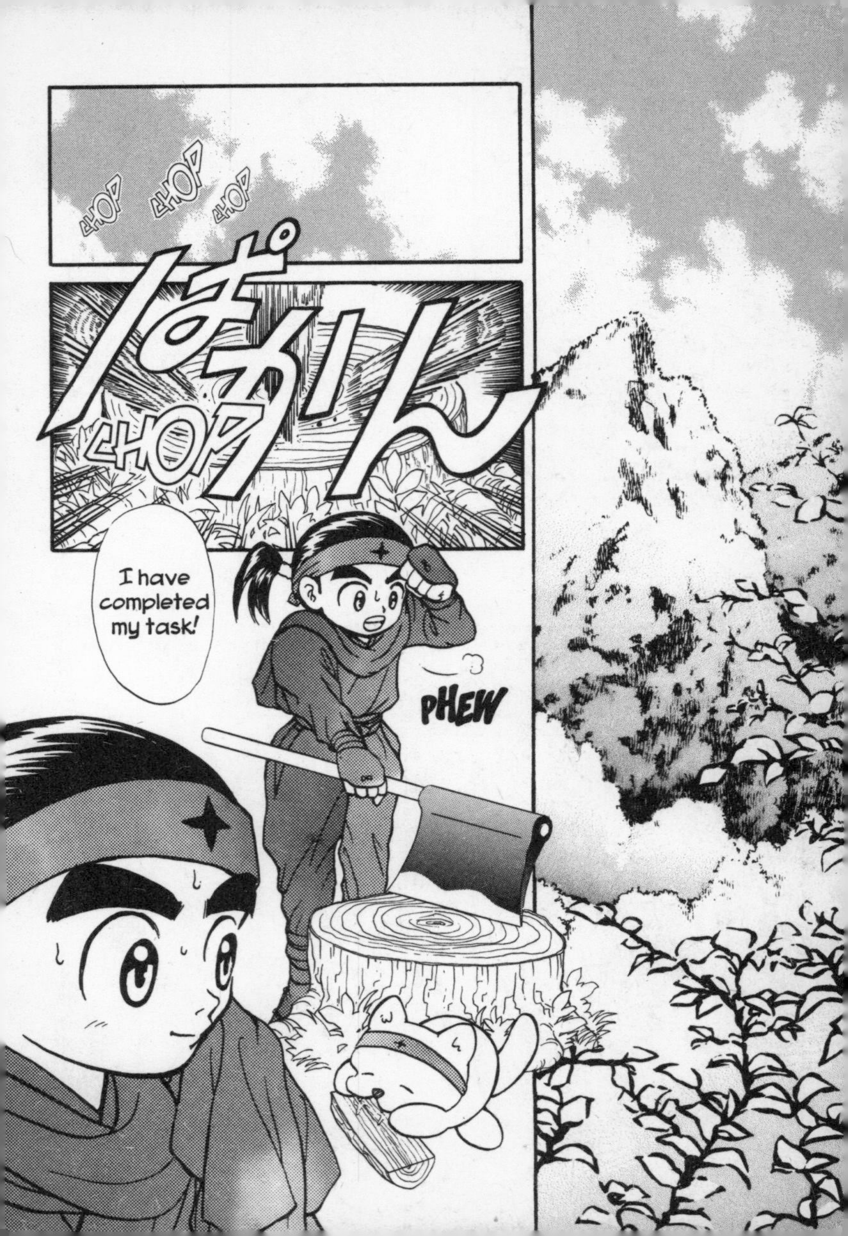
CHOP
CHOP
CHOP
ぱかりん〜
CHOP
I have completed my task!
PHEW

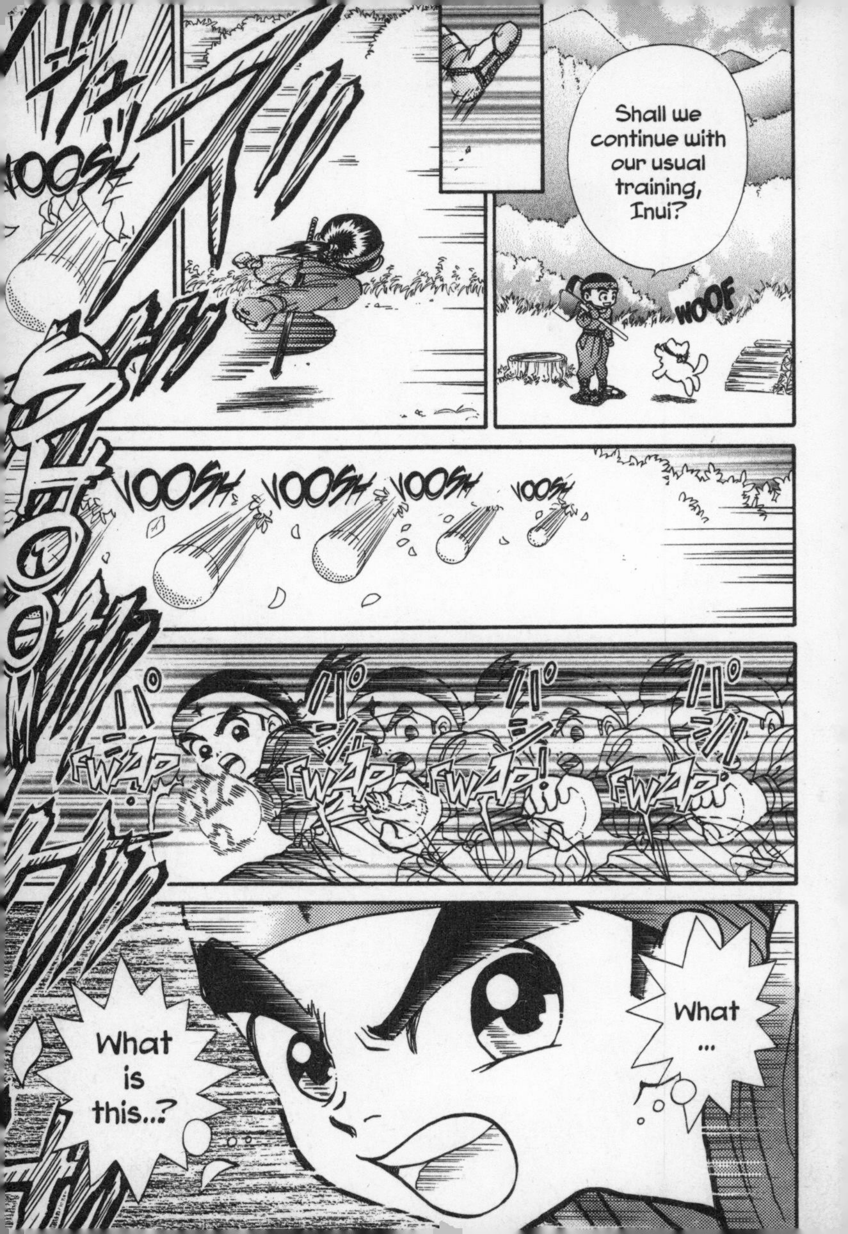
Shall we continue with our usual training, Inui?
WOOF
VOOSH
VOOSH
VOOSH
VOOSH
VOOSH
FWAP!
FWAP!
FWAP!
FWAP!
What ...
What is this..?

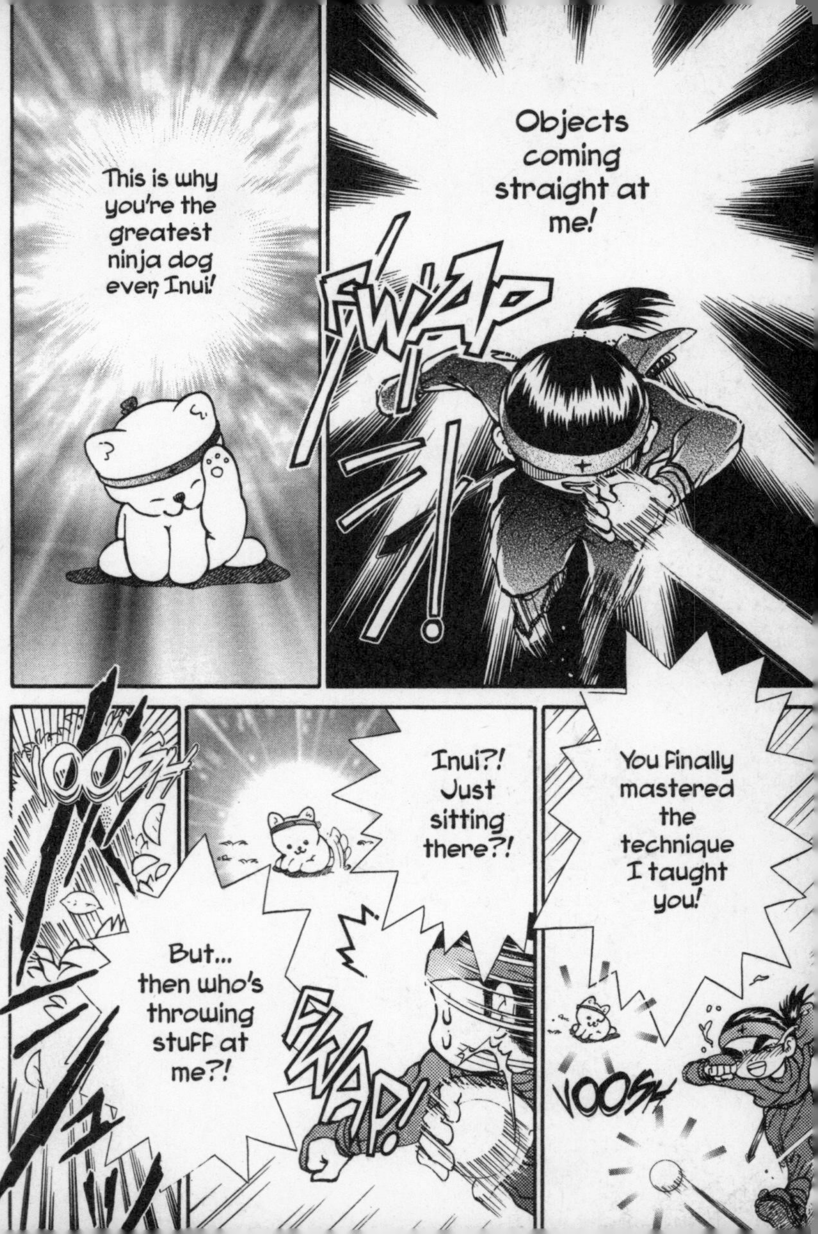
Objects coming straight at me!
FWAP
This is why you're the greatest ninja dog ever, Inui!
You finally mastered the technique I taught you!
VOOSH
Inui?! Just sitting there?!
But... then who's throwing stuff at me?!
FWAP!
VOOSH

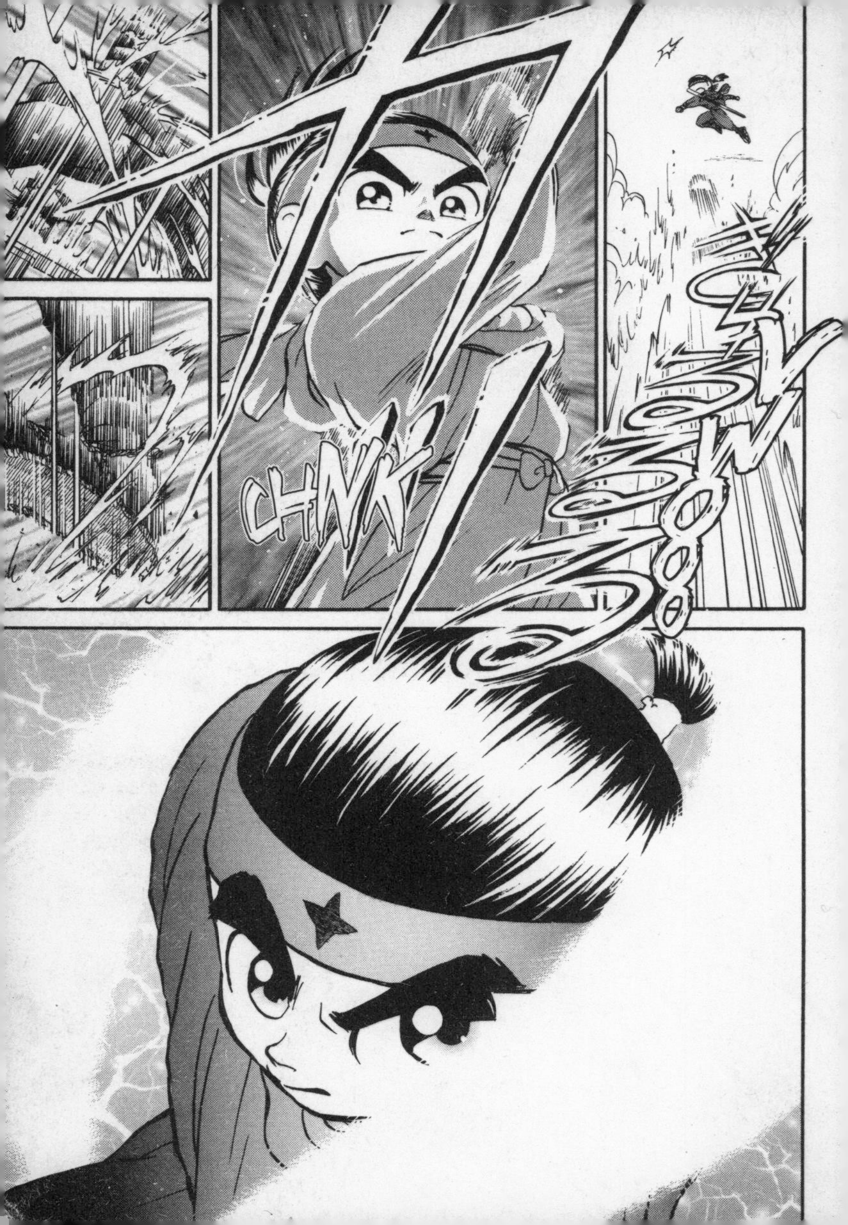
CHINK

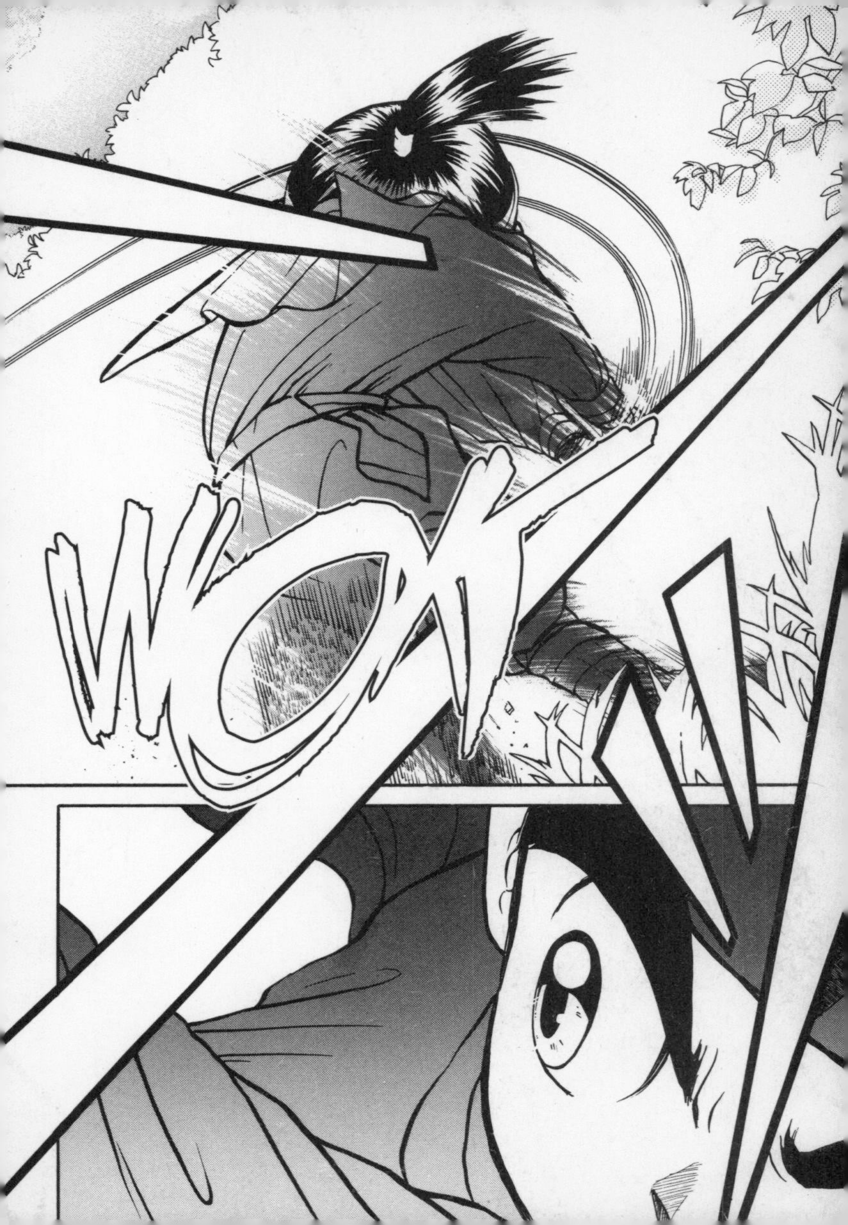

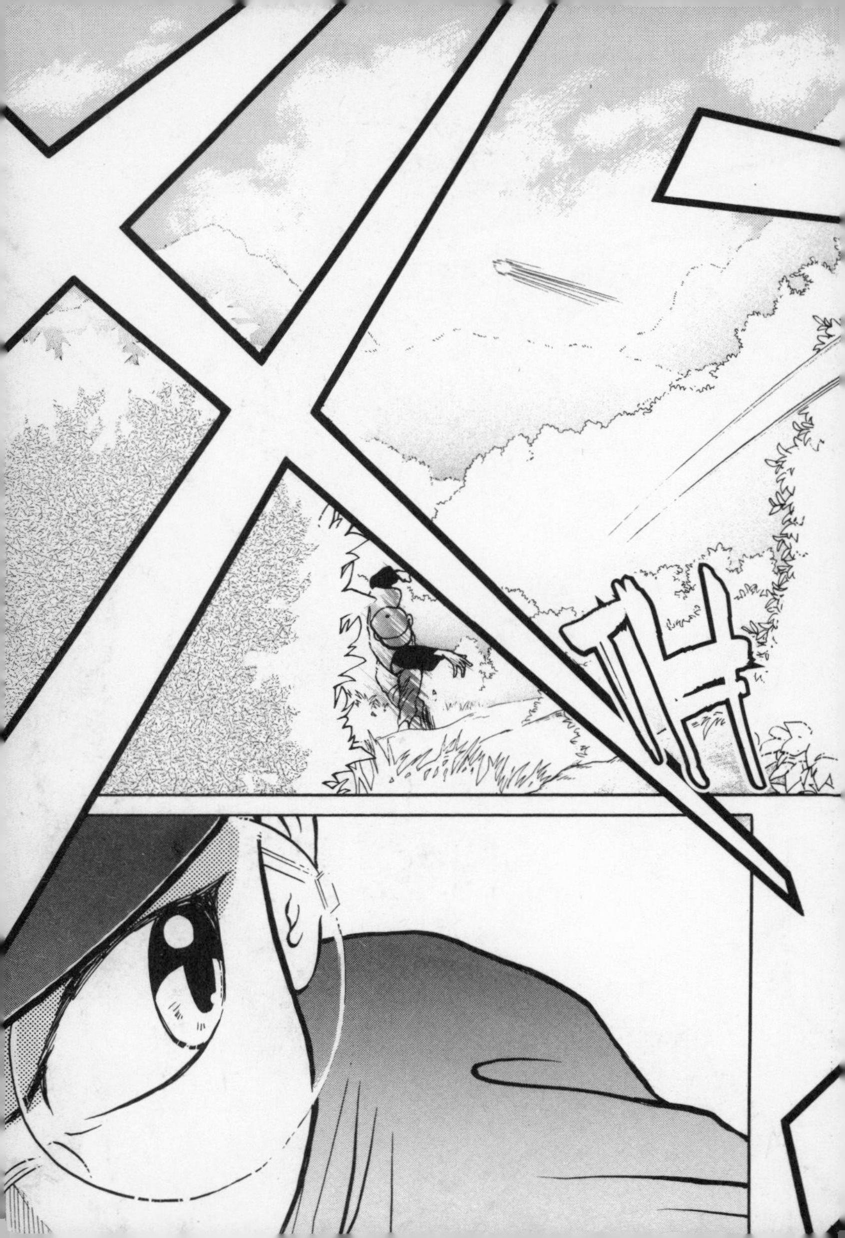

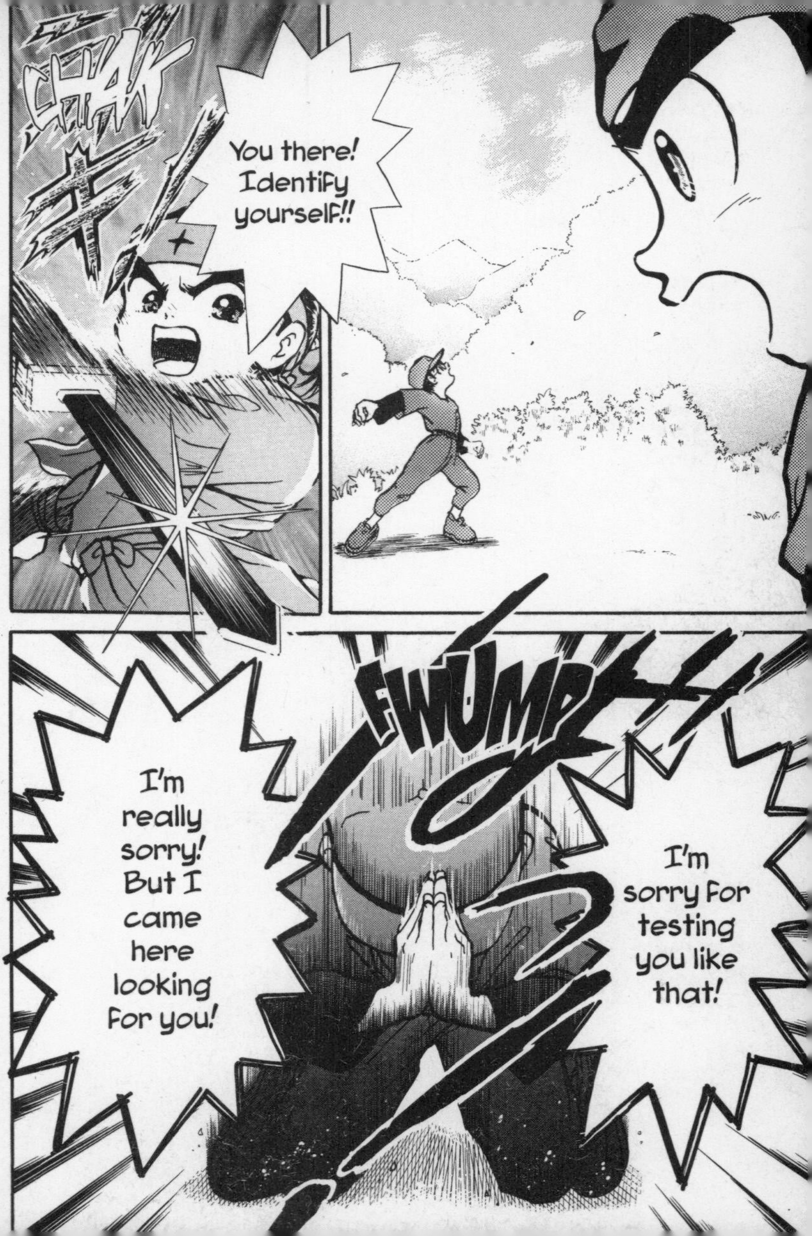
CHAK
You there! Identify yourself!!
FWUMP
I'm sorry for testing you like that!
I'm really sorry! But I came here looking for you!

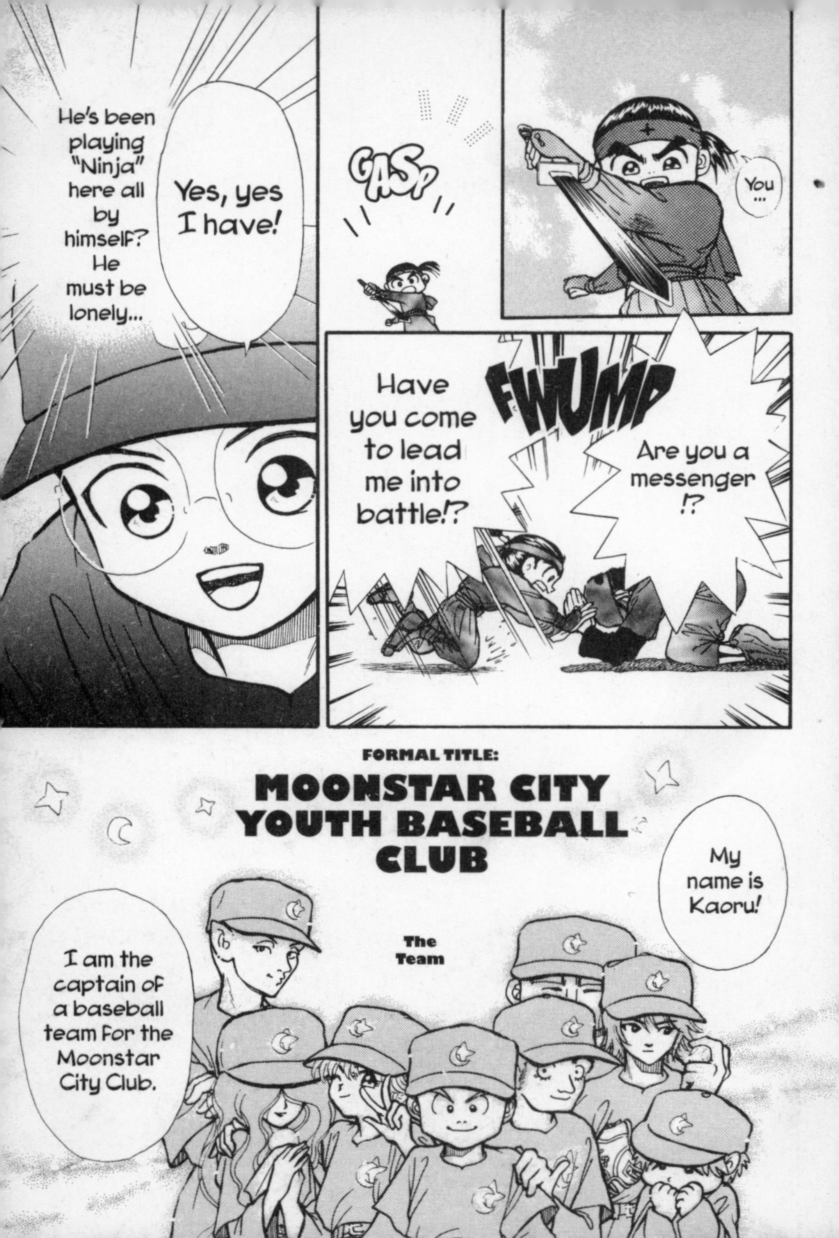
You ...
GASP
FWUMP
Are you a messenger !?
Have you come to lead me into battle!?
Yes, yes I have!
He's been playing "Ninja" here all by himself? He must be lonely...
FORMAL TITLE:
MOONSTAR CITY YOUTH BASEBALL CLUB
My name is Kaoru!
The Team
I am the captain of a baseball team for the Moonstar City Club.

Read this way

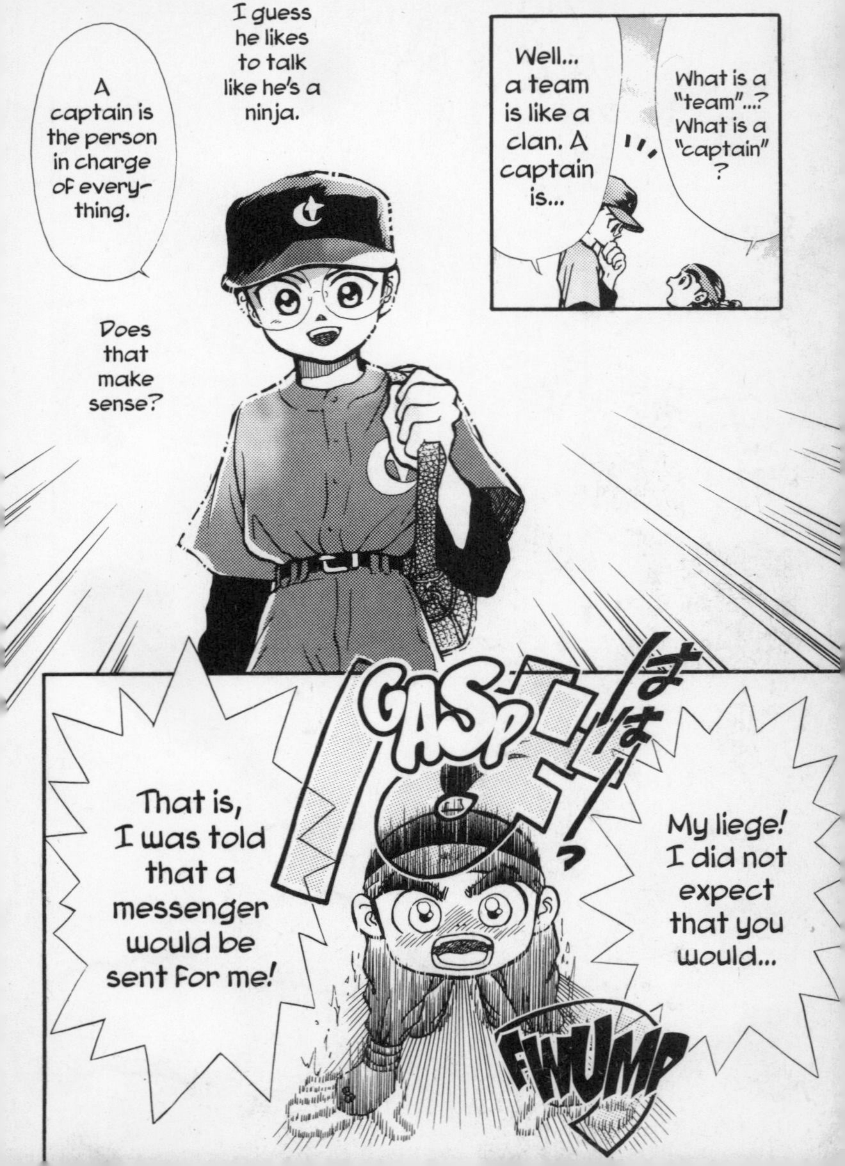
What is a "team"...? What is a "captain"?
Well... a team is like a clan. A captain is...
I guess he likes to talk like he's a ninja.
A captain is the person in charge of every-thing.
Does that make sense?
My liege! I did not expect that you would...
GASP
FWUMP
That is, I was told that a messenger would be sent for me!

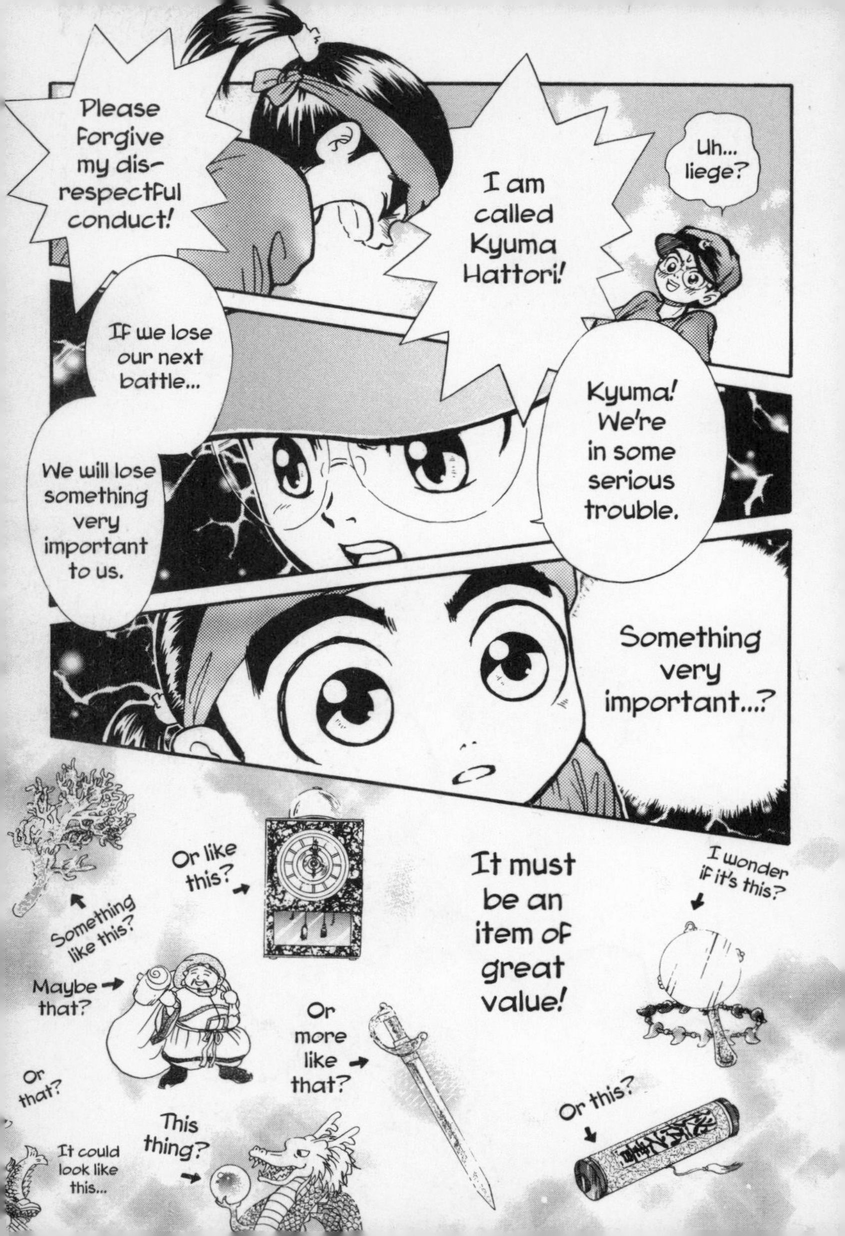

Uh... liege?
I am called Kyuma Hattori!
Please forgive my dis-respectful conduct!
Kyuma! We're in some serious trouble.
If we lose our next battle...
We will lose something very important to us.
Something very important...?
I wonder if it's this?
Or this?
It must be an item of great value!
Or like this?
Or more like that?
Something like this?
Maybe that?
This thing?
Or that?
It could look like this...

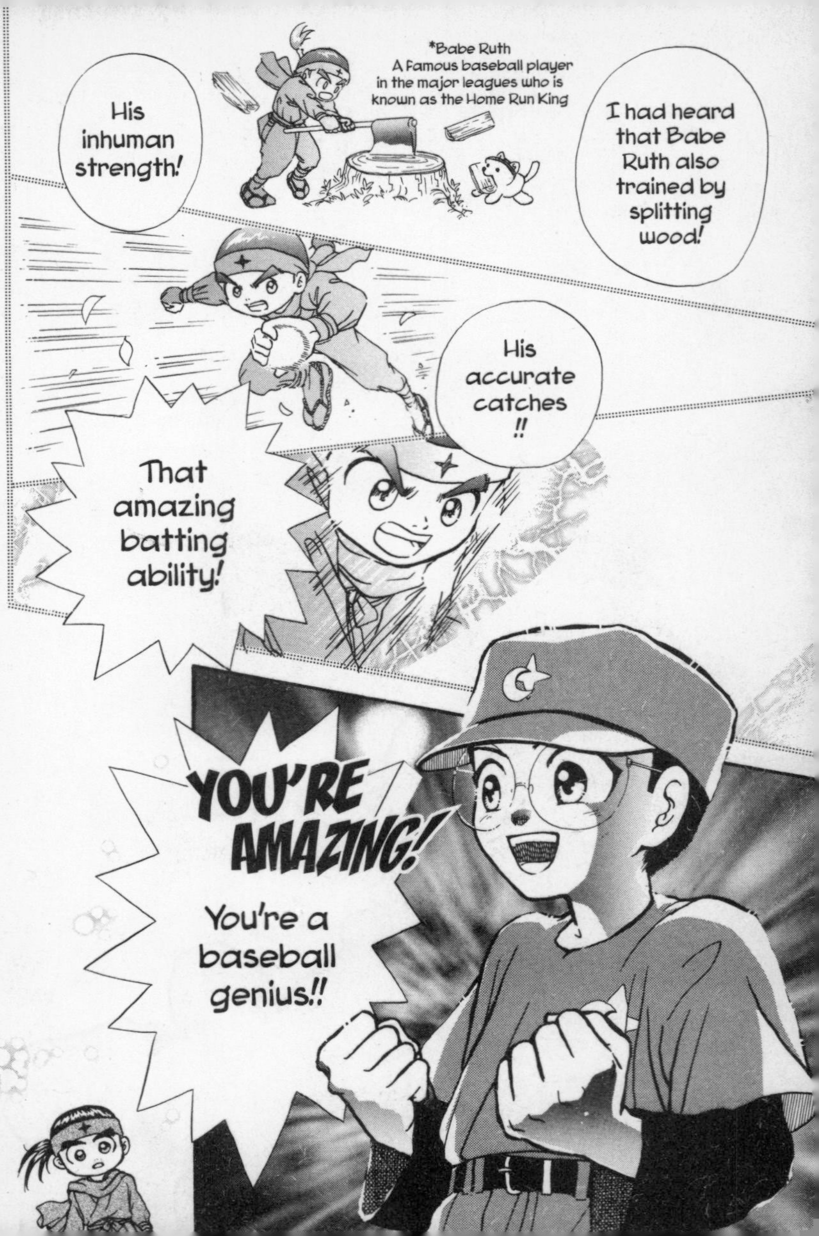
*Babe Ruth A famous baseball player in the major leagues who is known as the Home Run King
I had heard that Babe Ruth also trained by splitting wood!
His inhuman strength!
His accurate catches!!
That amazing batting ability!
YOU'RE AMAZING!
You're a baseball genius!!

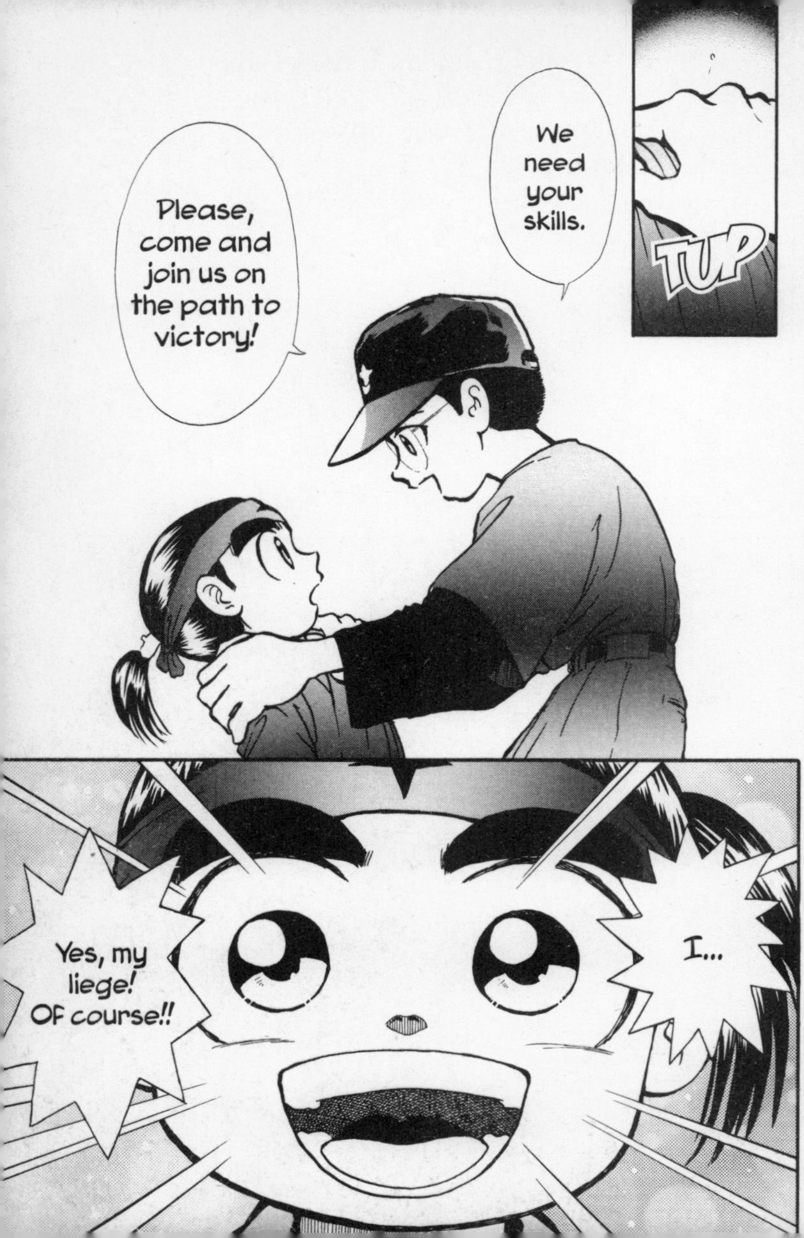
TUP
We need your skills.
Please, come and join us on the path to victory!
I...
Yes, my liege! OF course!!

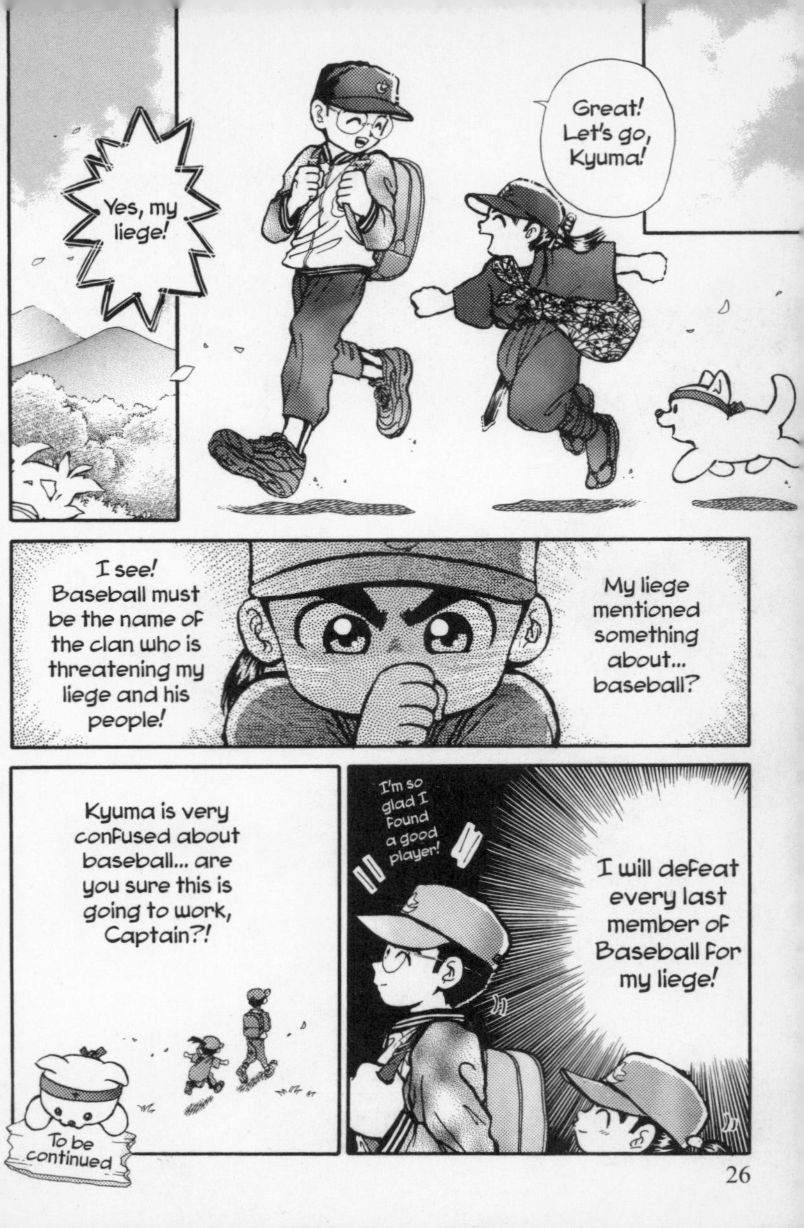

Great! Let's go, Kyuma!
Yes, my liege!
My liege mentioned something about... baseball?
I see! Baseball must be the name of the clan who is threatening my liege and his people!
I'm so glad I found a good player!
I will defeat every last member of Baseball for my liege!
Kyuma is very confused about baseball... are you sure this is going to work, Captain?!
To be continued

Kyuma

A living relative of the famous Hattori Hanzou of Ancient Japan. He grew up hidden away in the mountains training to be a ninja.

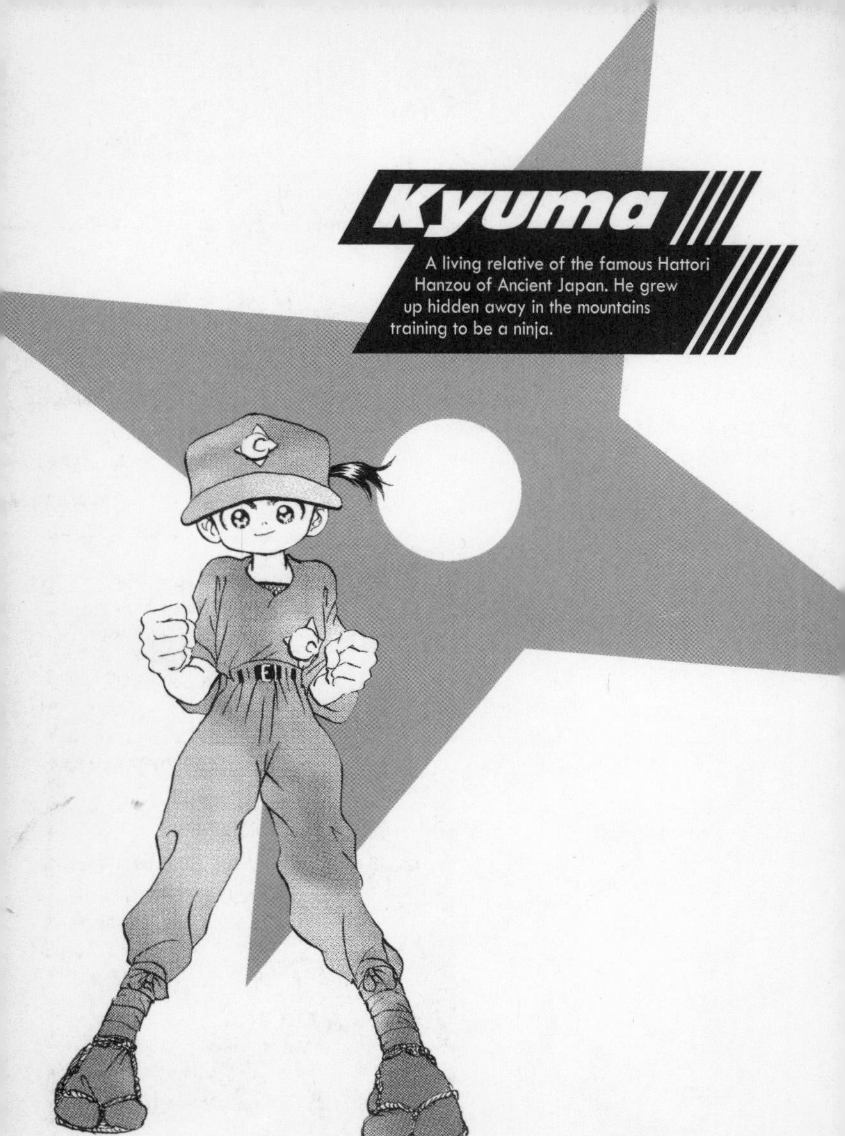

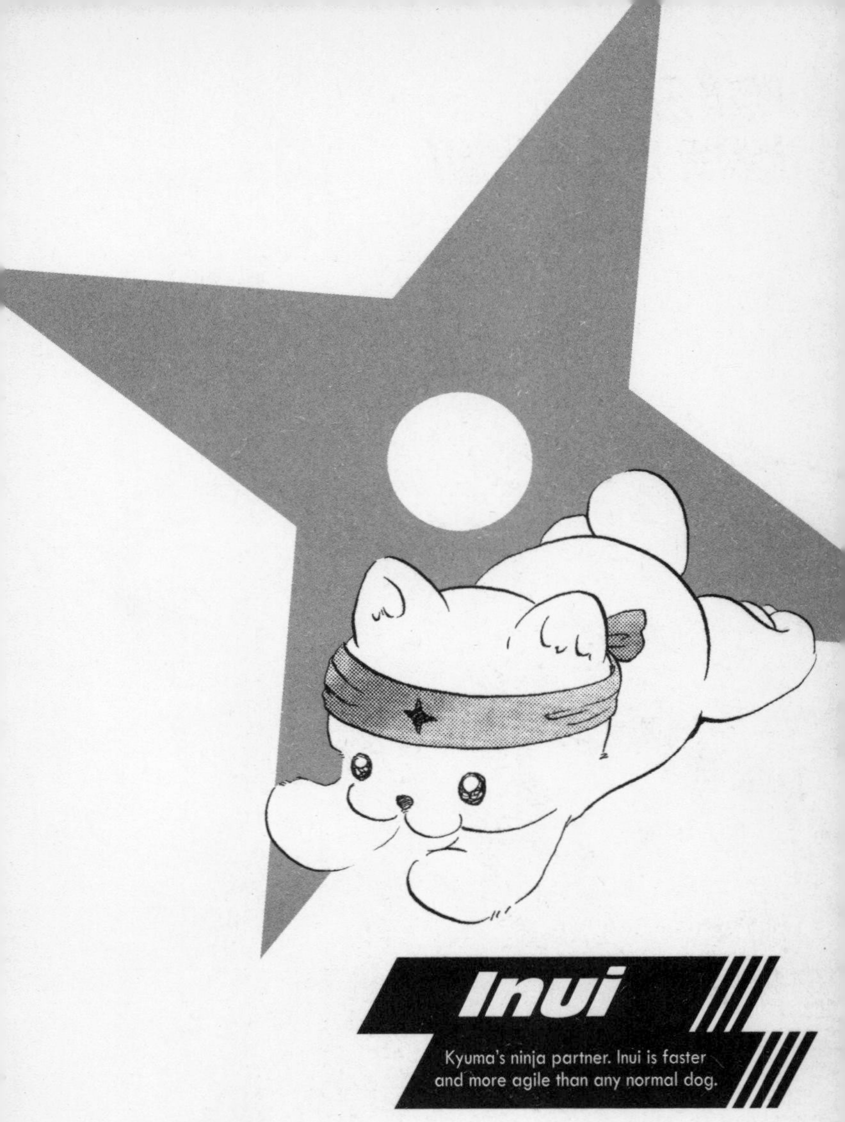

Inui

Kyuma's ninja partner. Inui is faster and more agile than any normal dog.

PITCH 2
KYUMA TRIES BASEBALL

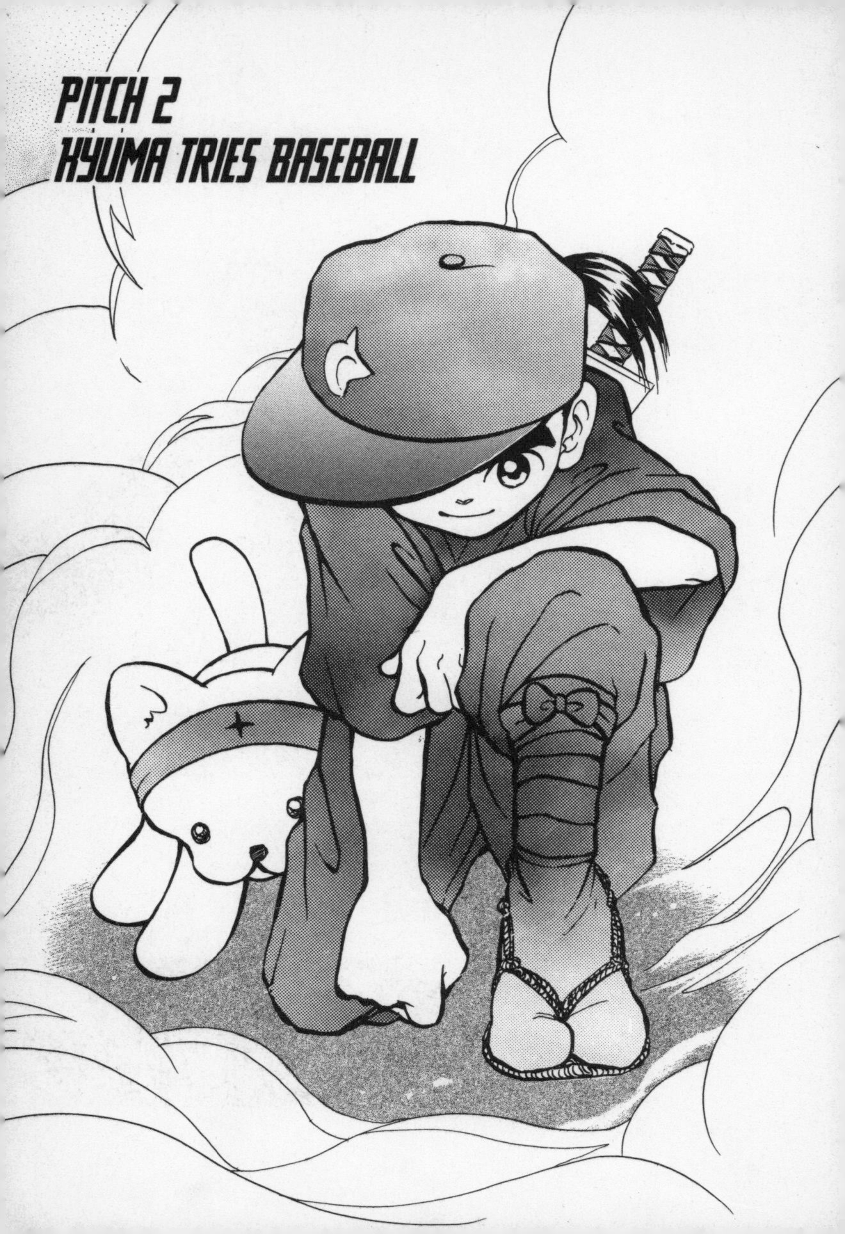

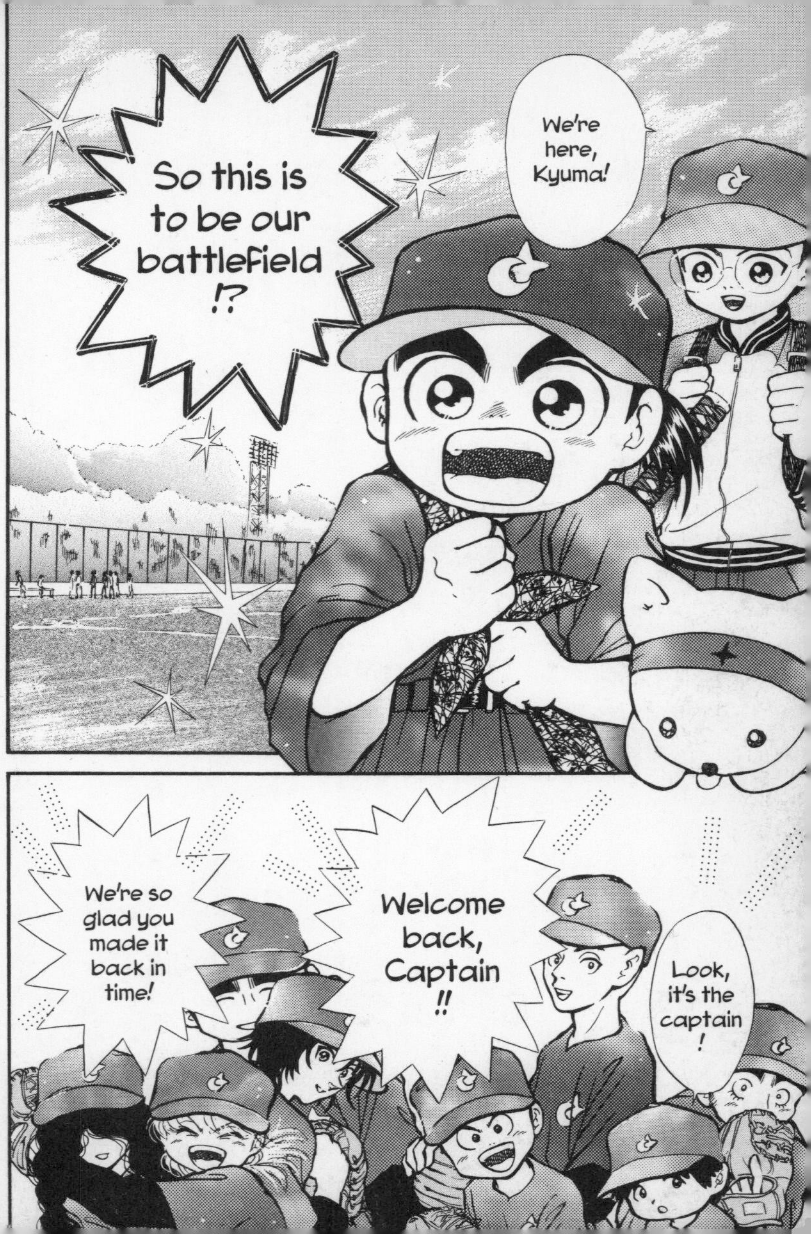
We're here, Kyuma!
So this is to be our battlefield!?
Look, it's the captain!
Welcome back, Captain!!
We're so glad you made it back in time!

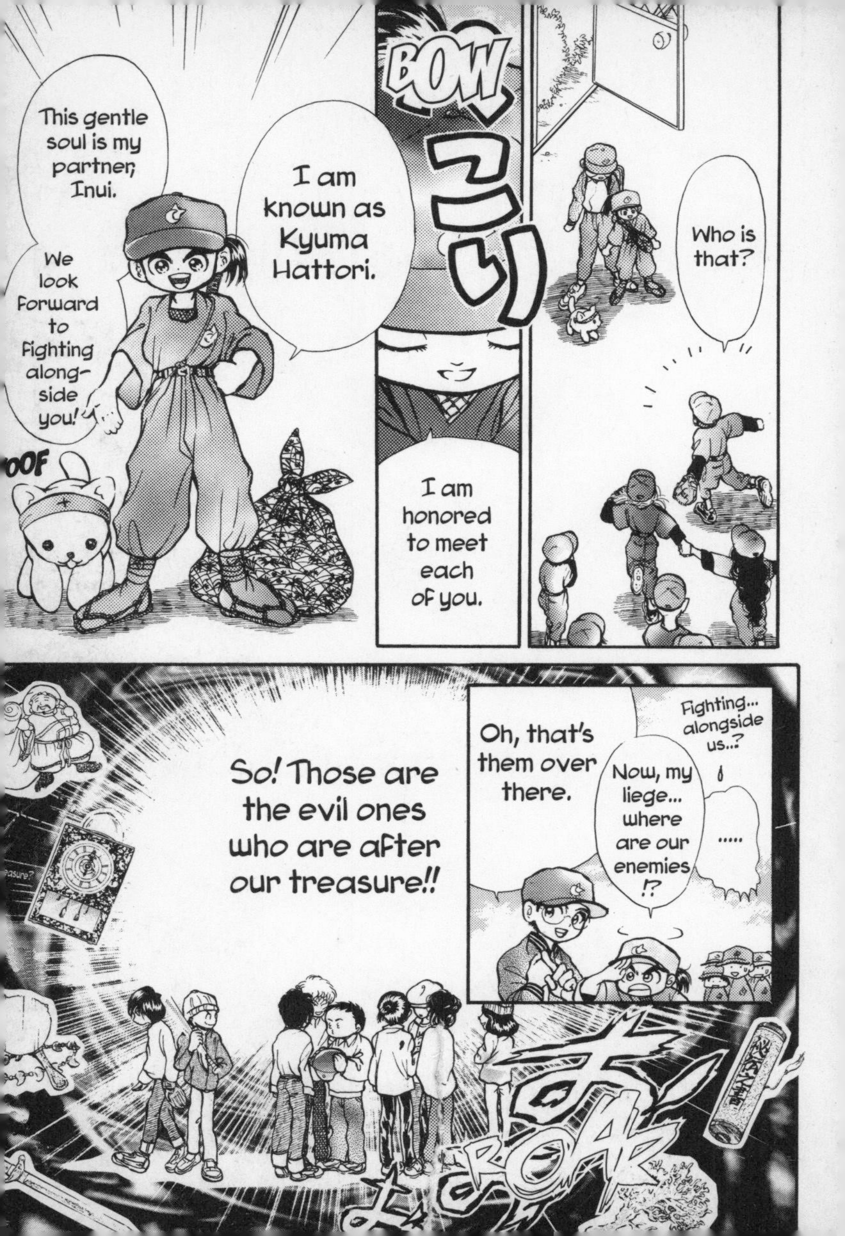
Who is that?
BOW
I am honored to meet each of you.
I am known as Kyuma Hattori.
This gentle soul is my partner, Inui.
We look forward to fighting alongside you!
OOF
Fighting... alongside us..?
.....
Now, my liege... where are our enemies!?
Oh, that's them over there.
So! Those are the evil ones who are after our treasure!!
ROAR

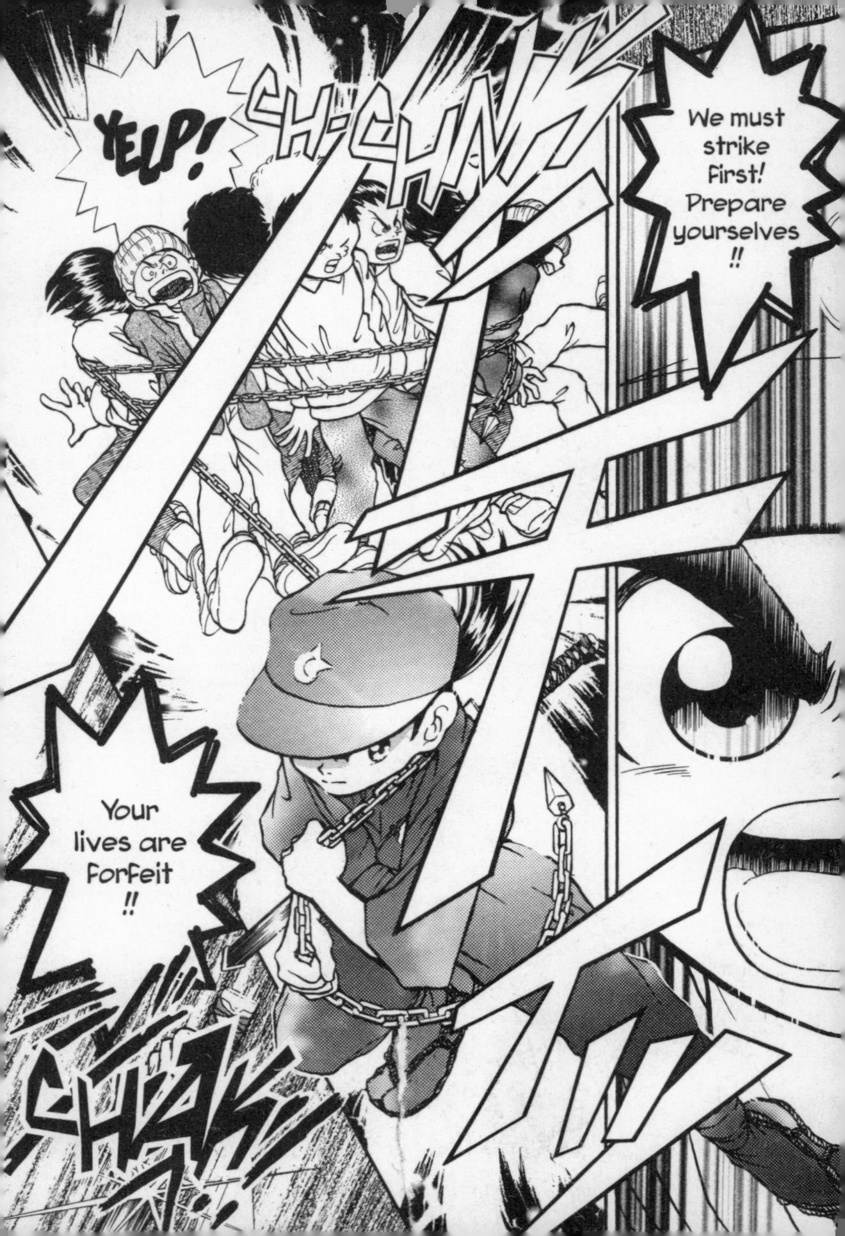
We must strike first! Prepare yourselves!!
CH-CHNK
YELP!
Your lives are forfeit!!

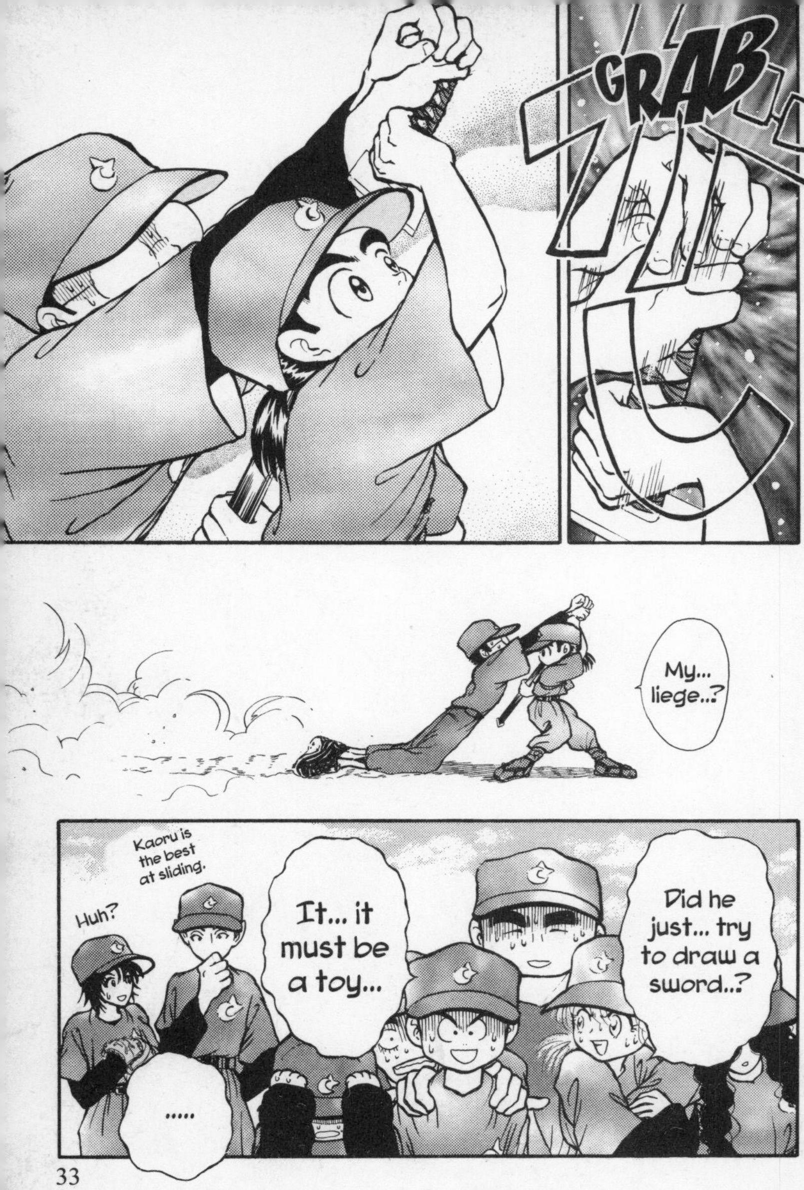
GRAB
My... liege...?
Did he just... try to draw a sword..?
It... it must be a toy...
Kaoru is the best at sliding.
Huh?
.....

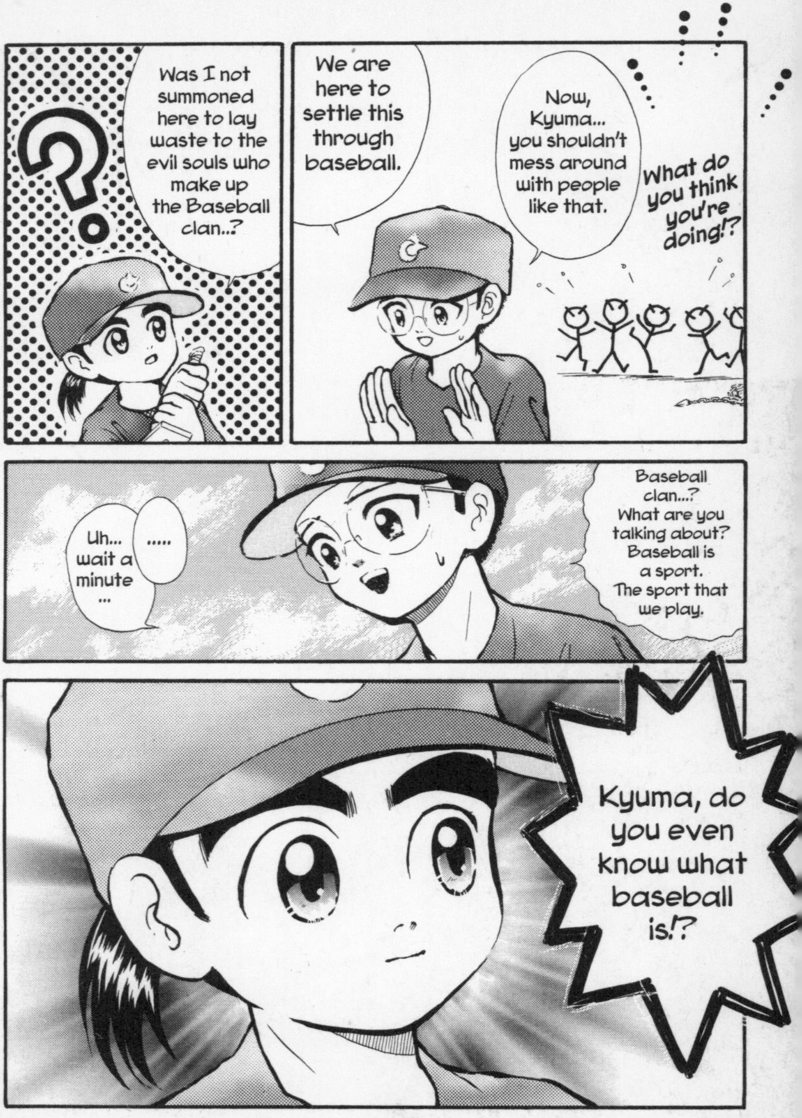
What do you think you're doing!?
Now, Kyuma... you shouldn't mess around with people like that.
We are here to settle this through baseball.
Was I not summoned here to lay waste to the evil souls who make up the Baseball clan...?
Baseball clan...? What are you talking about? Baseball is a sport. The sport that we play.
.....
Uh... wait a minute ...
Kyuma, do you even know what baseball is!?

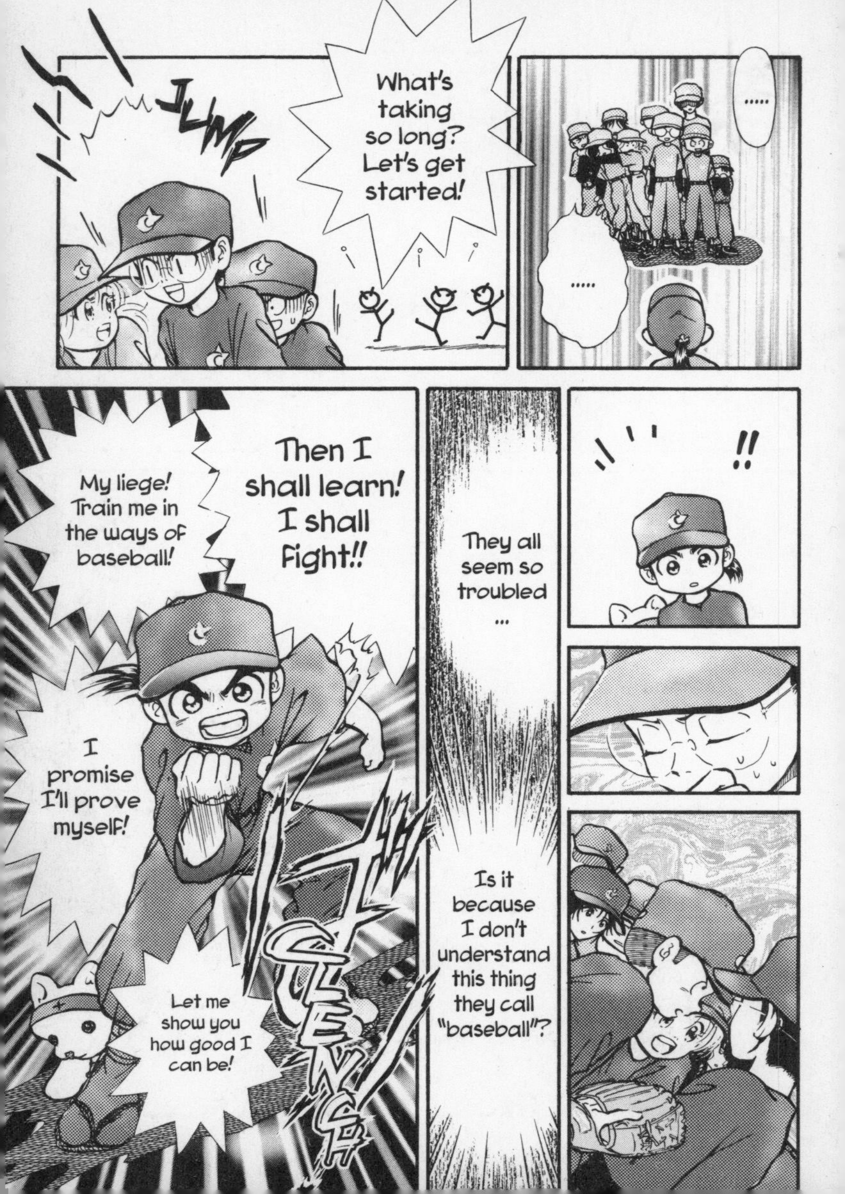
......
......
What's taking so long? Let's get started!
JUMP
!!
They all seem so troubled ...
Is it because I don't understand this thing they call "baseball"?
Then I shall learn! I shall Fight!!
My liege! Train me in the ways of baseball!
I promise I'll prove myself!
Let me show you how good I can be!
CLENCH

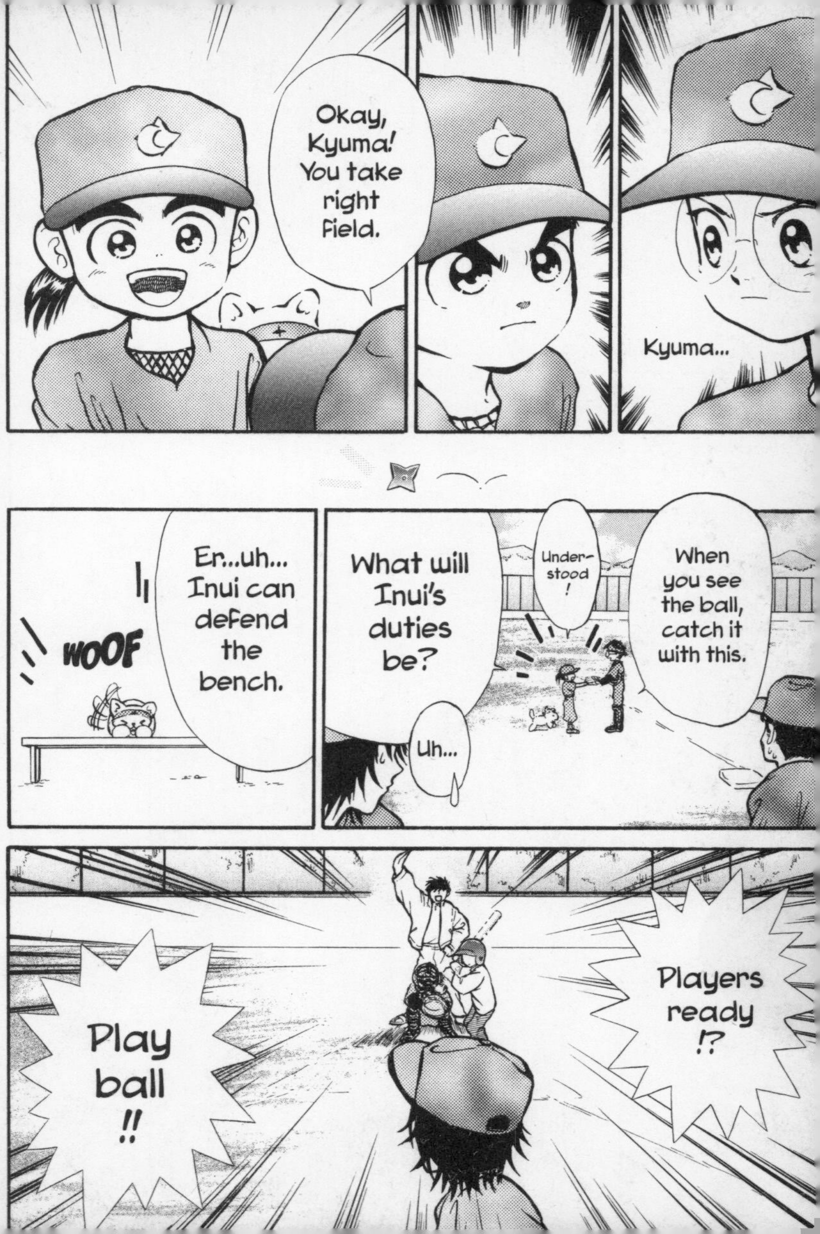
Kyuma...
Okay, Kyuma! You take right field.
When you see the ball, catch it with this.
Understood!
What will Inui's duties be?
Uh...
Er...uh... Inui can defend the bench.
WOOF
Players ready!?
Play ball!!

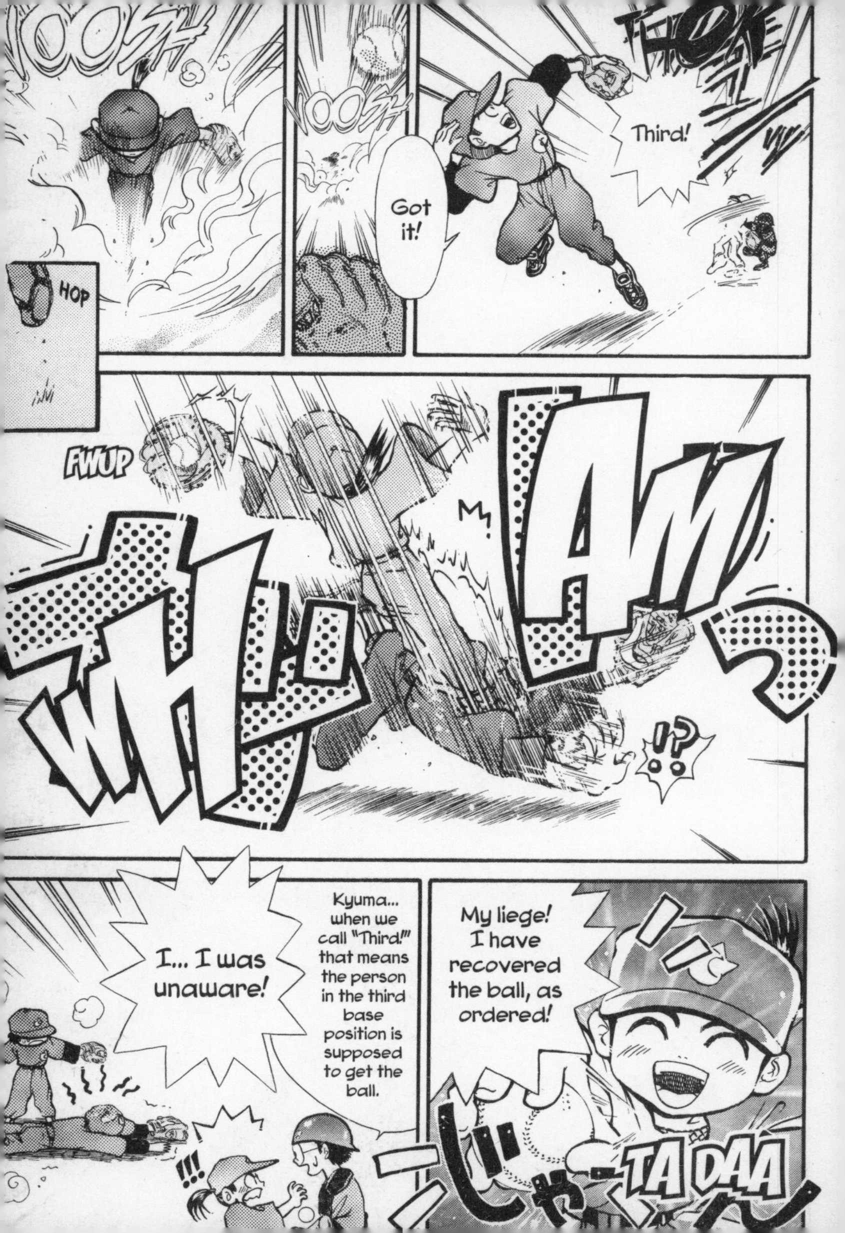
Third!
Got it!
WOOSH
WOOSH
HOP
WHAM
FWUP
!?
My liege! I have recovered the ball, as ordered!
じゃーん
TA DAA
Kyuma... when we call "Third!" that means the person in the third base position is supposed to get the ball.
I... I was unaware!
!!!

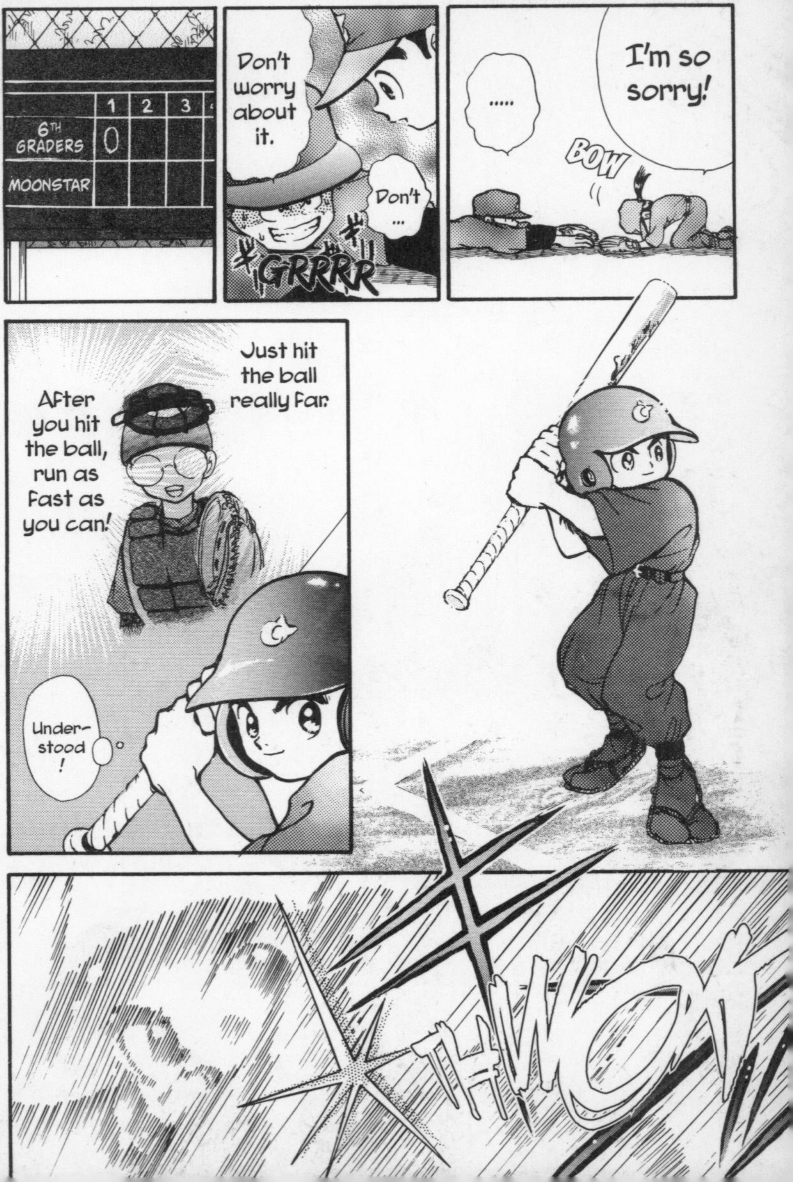
I'm so sorry!
.....
BOW
Don't worry about it.
Don't ...
GRRRR
1 2 3
6TH GRADERS 0
MOONSTAR
Just hit the ball really far.
After you hit the ball, run as fast as you can!
Under-stood!
THWOK

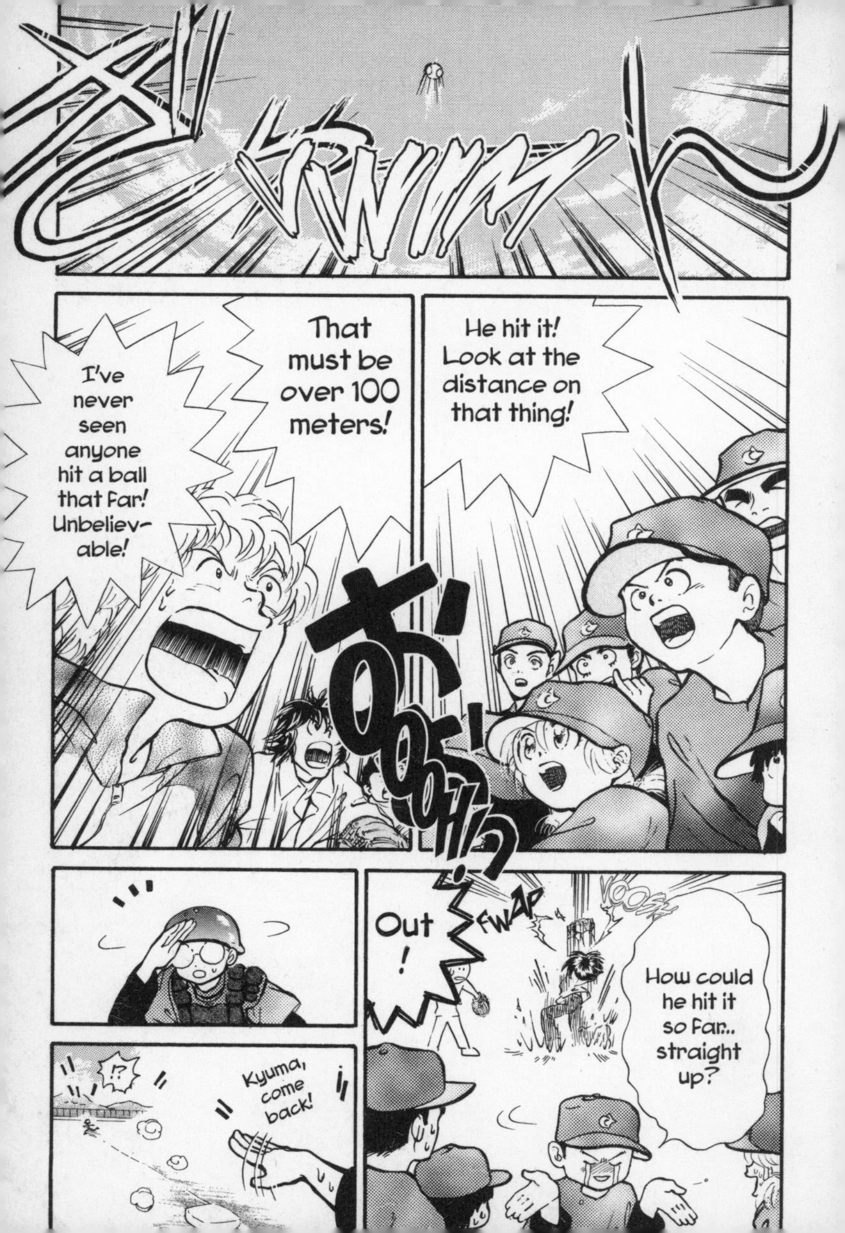
He hit it! Look at the distance on that thing!
That must be over 100 meters!
I've never seen anyone hit a ball that far! Unbelievable!
Out!
FWAP
VOOSH
How could he hit it so far... straight up?
!?
Kyuma, come back!

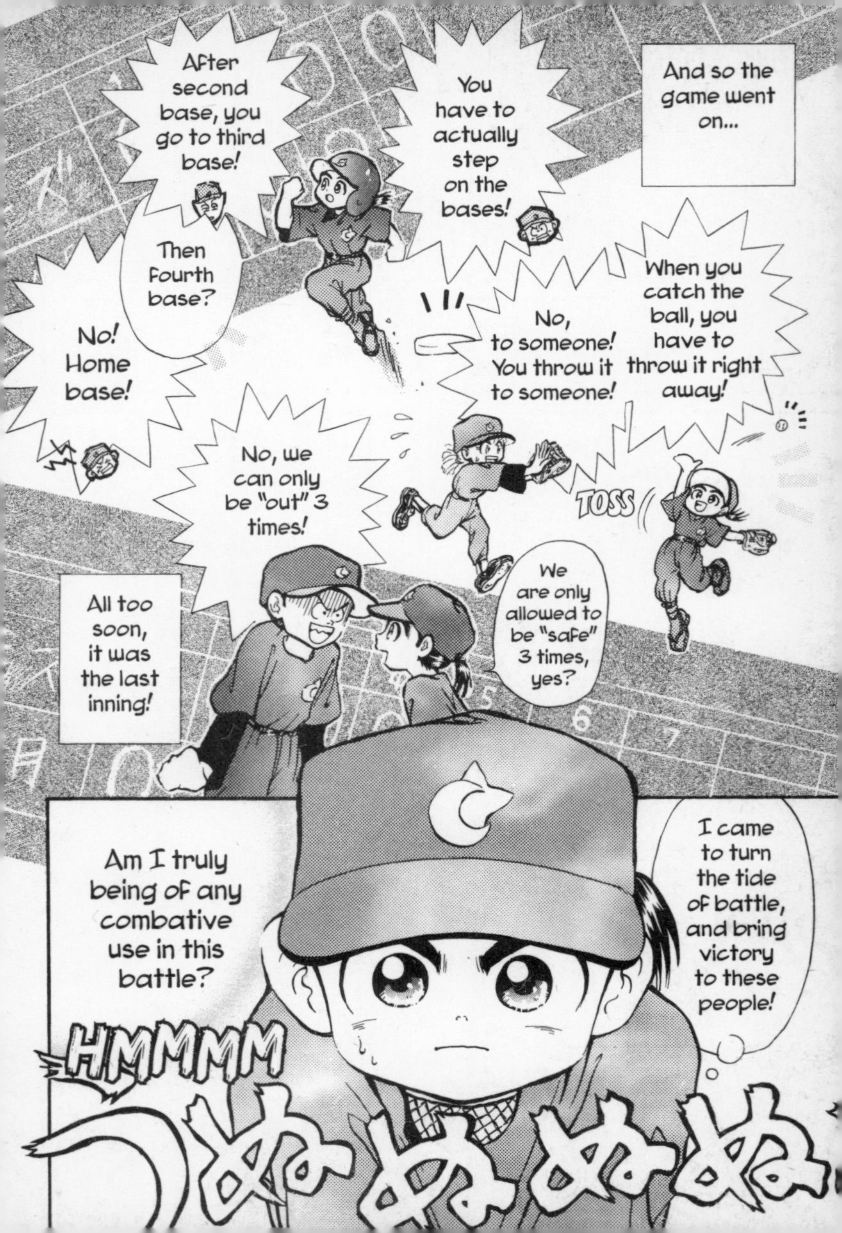
And so the game went on...
You have to actually step on the bases!
After second base, you go to third base!
When you catch the ball, you have to throw it right away!
No, to someone! You throw it to someone!
Then fourth base?
No! Home base!
TOSS
We are only allowed to be "safe" 3 times, yes?
No, we can only be "out" 3 times!
All too soon, it was the last inning!
I came to turn the tide of battle, and bring victory to these people!
Am I truly being of any combative use in this battle?
HMMMM
ぬぬぬぬ

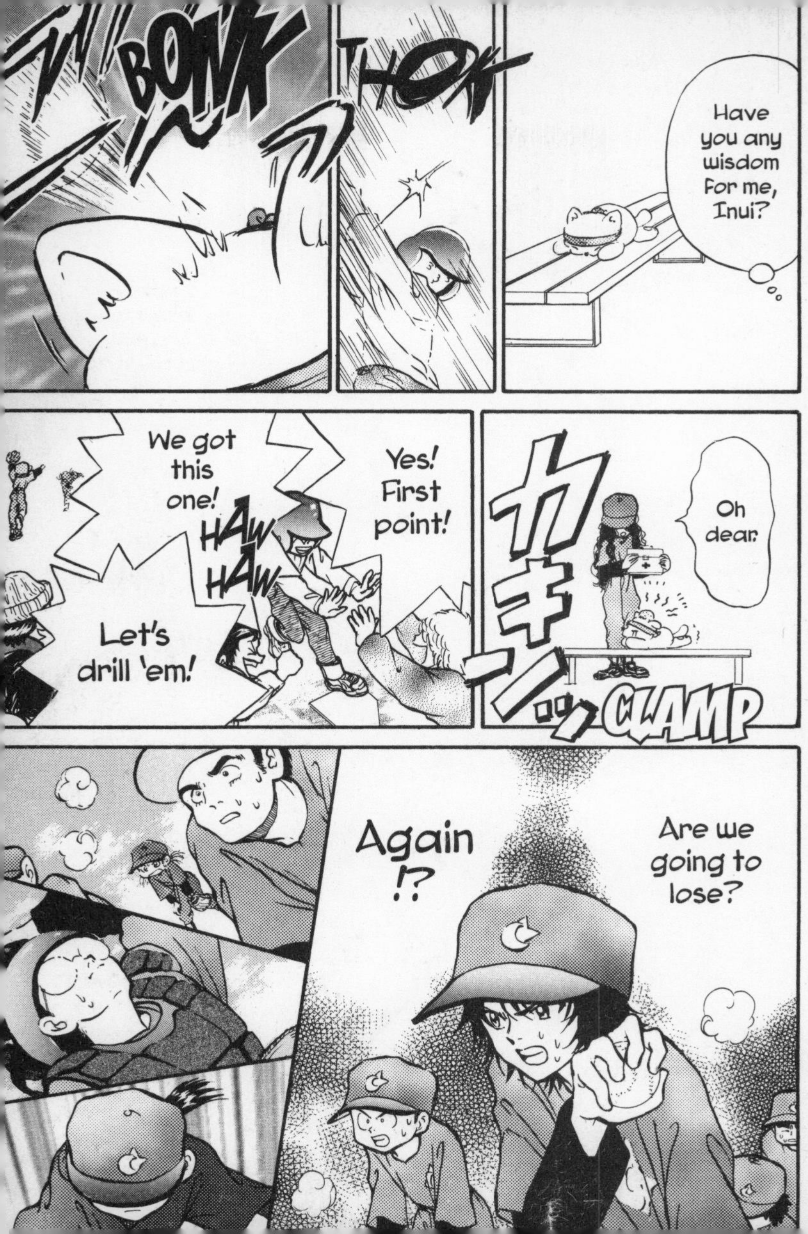
Have you any wisdom for me, Inui?
THOK
BONK
Oh dear.
カキーン
CLAMP
Yes! First point!
HAW HAW
We got this one!
Let's drill 'em!
Are we going to lose?
Again !?

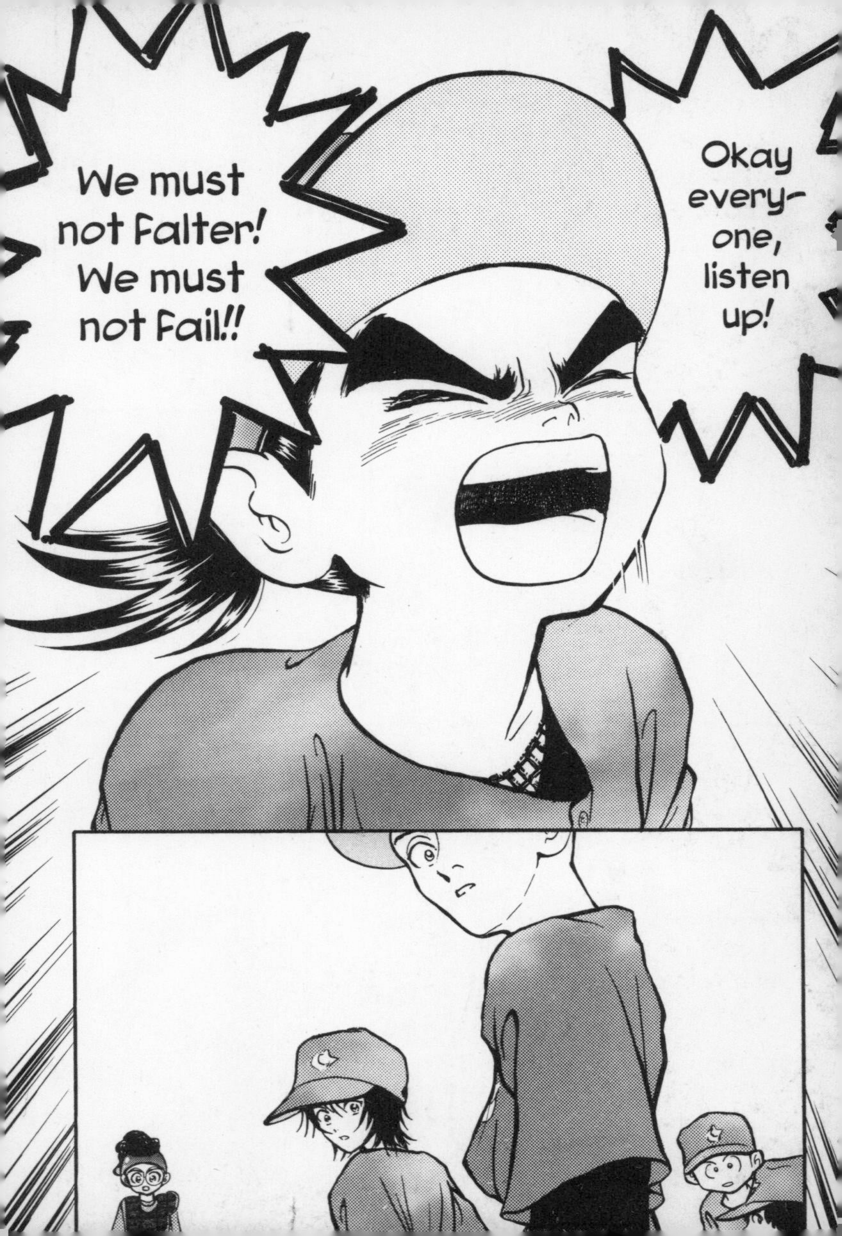
Okay everyone, listen up!
We must not falter! We must not fail!!

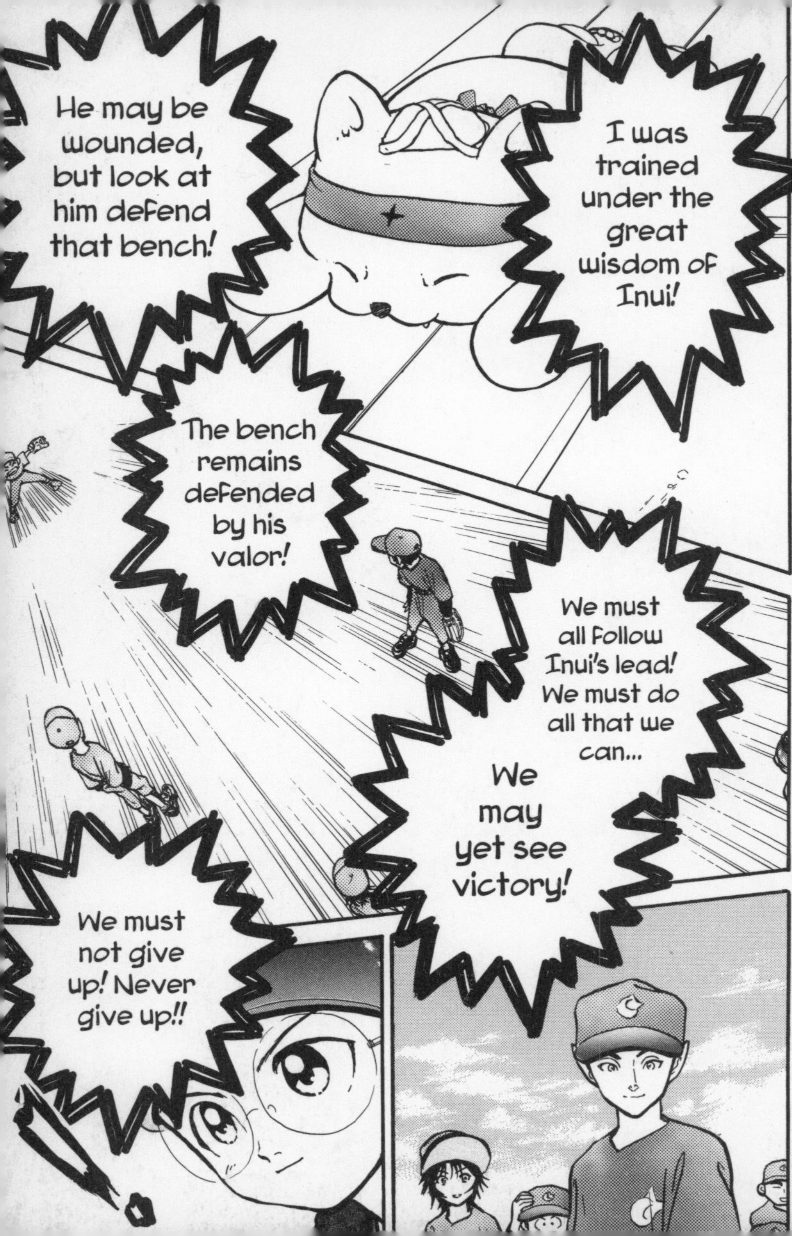
I was trained under the great wisdom of Inui!
He may be wounded, but look at him defend that bench!
The bench remains defended by his valor!
We must all follow Inui's lead! We must do all that we can...
We may yet see victory!
We must not give up! Never give up!!

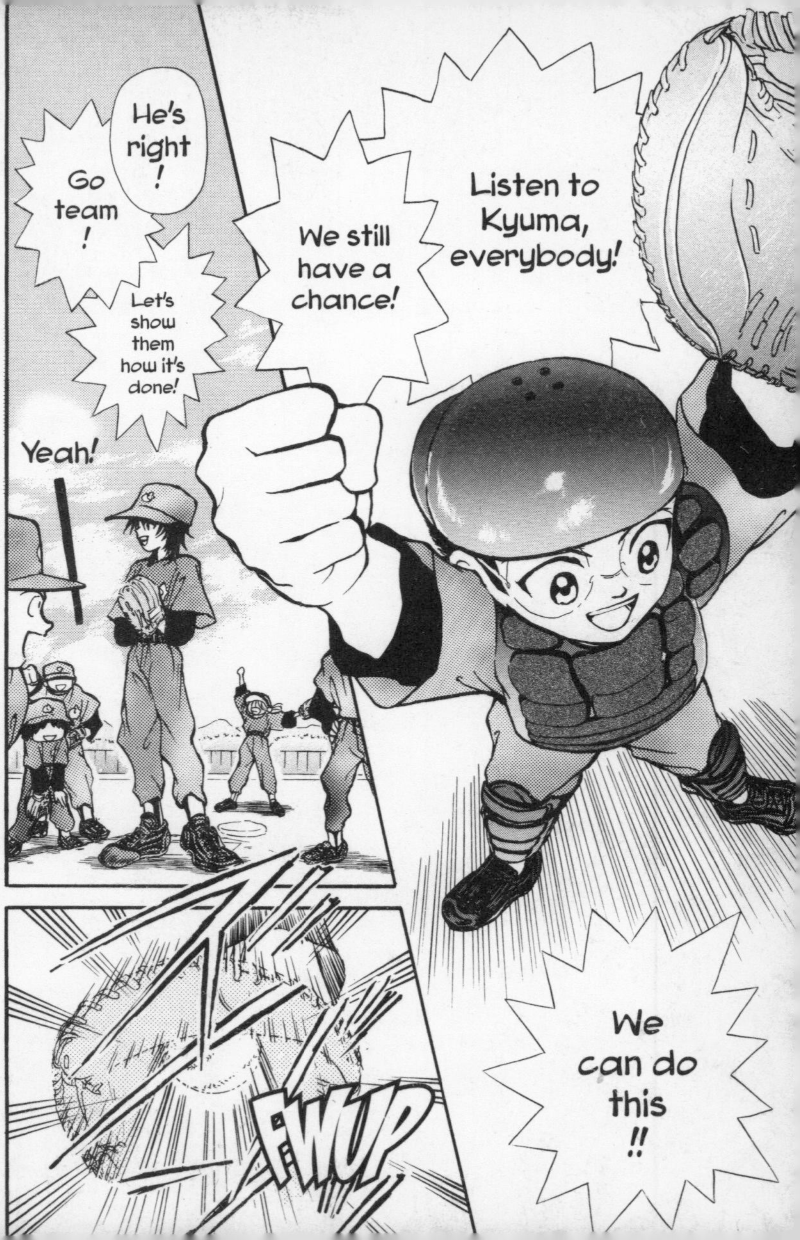
Listen to Kyuma, everybody!
We still have a chance!
We can do this !!
He's right !
Go team !
Let's show them how it's done!
Yeah!
FWUP

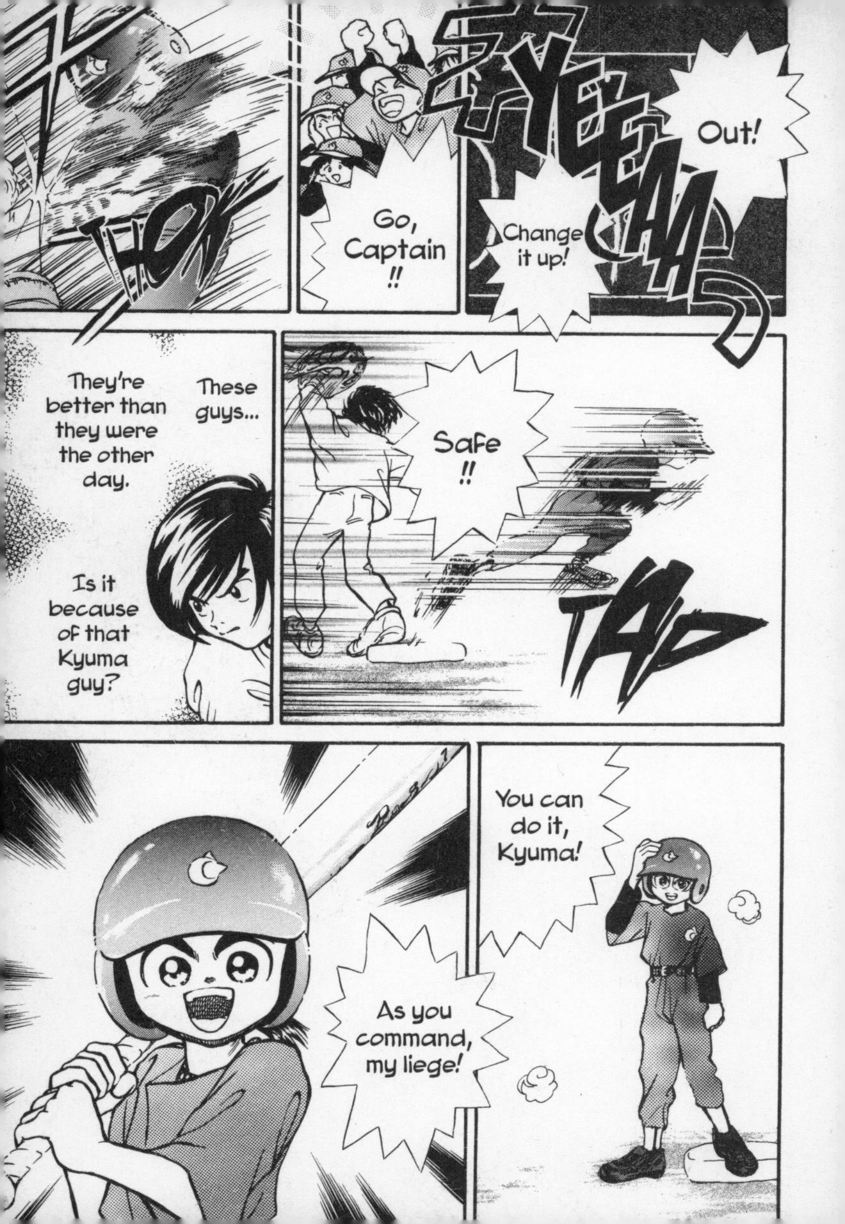
YEEEAAA
Out!
Change it up!
Go, Captain !!
THOK
Safe !!
TAP
These guys...
They're better than they were the other day.
Is it because of that Kyuma guy?
You can do it, Kyuma!
As you command, my liege!

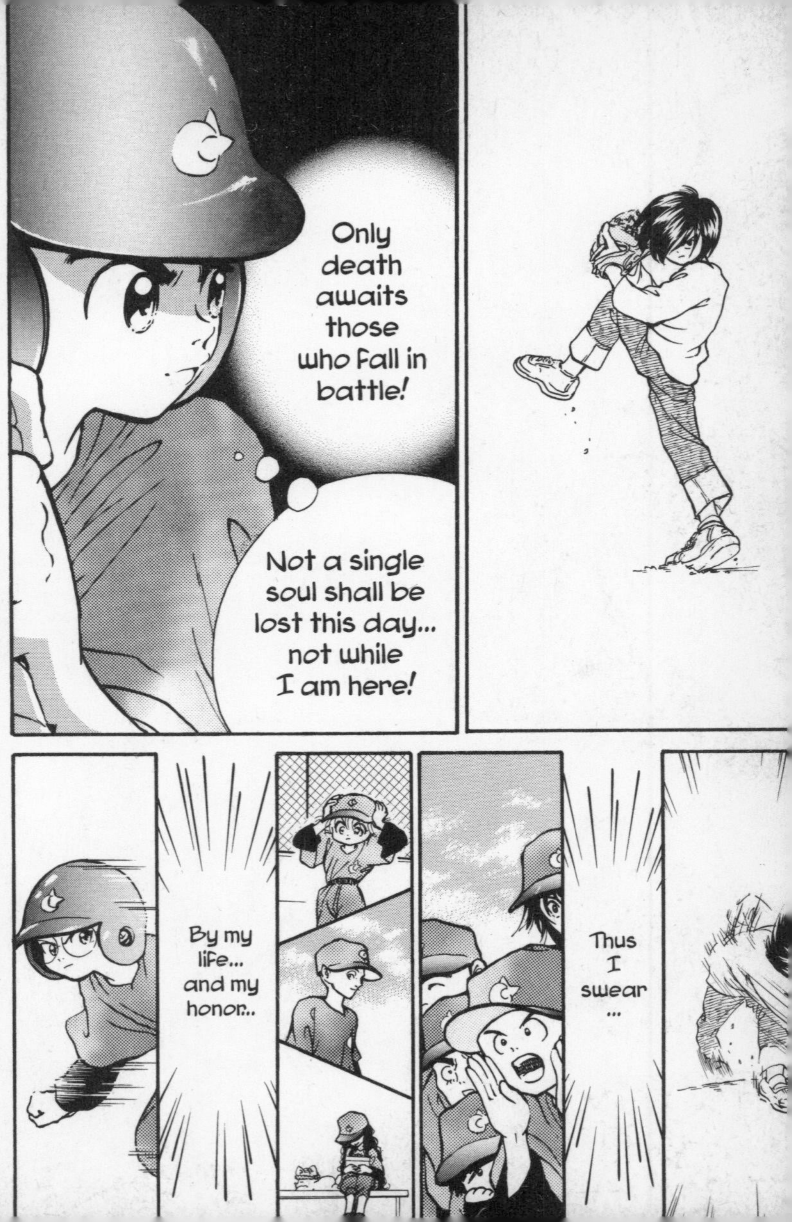
Only death awaits those who fall in battle!
Not a single soul shall be lost this day... not while I am here!
Thus I swear ...
By my life... and my honor...

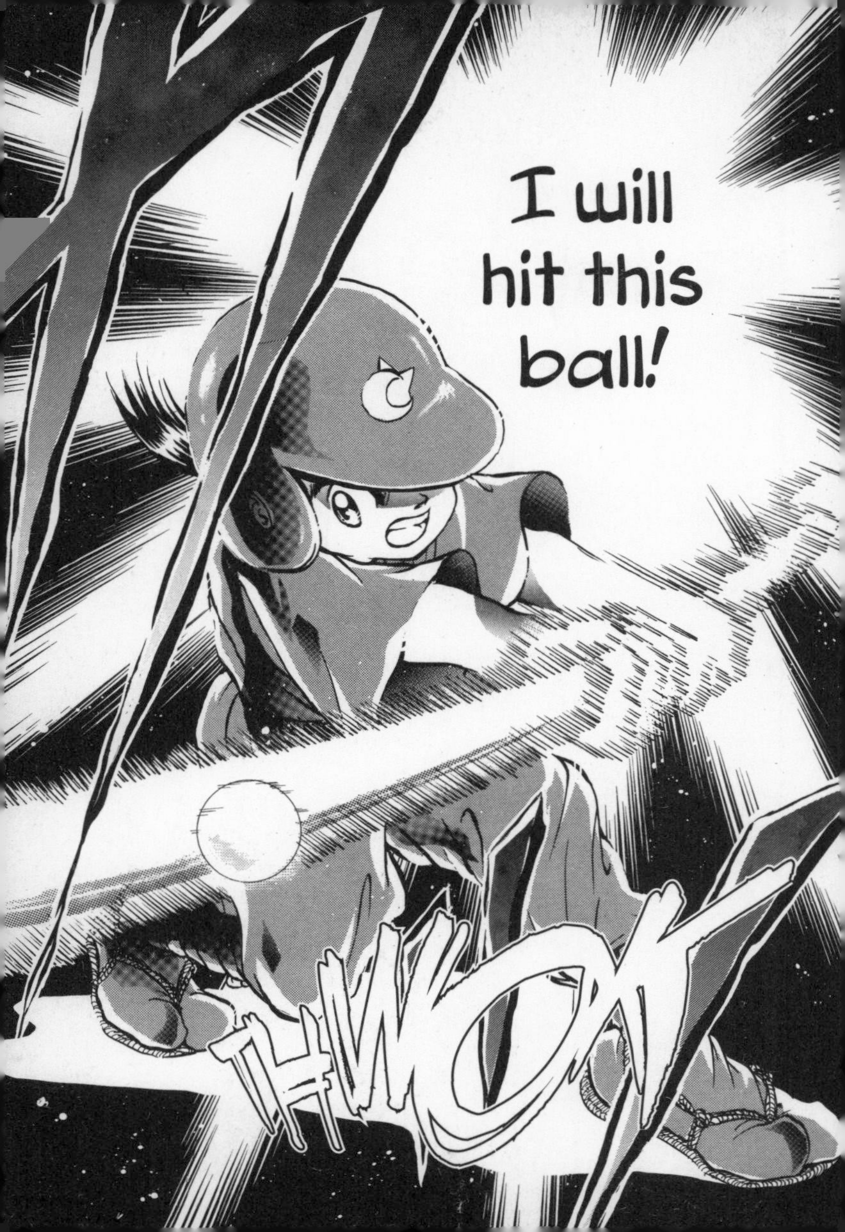
I will hit this ball!
THWOCK

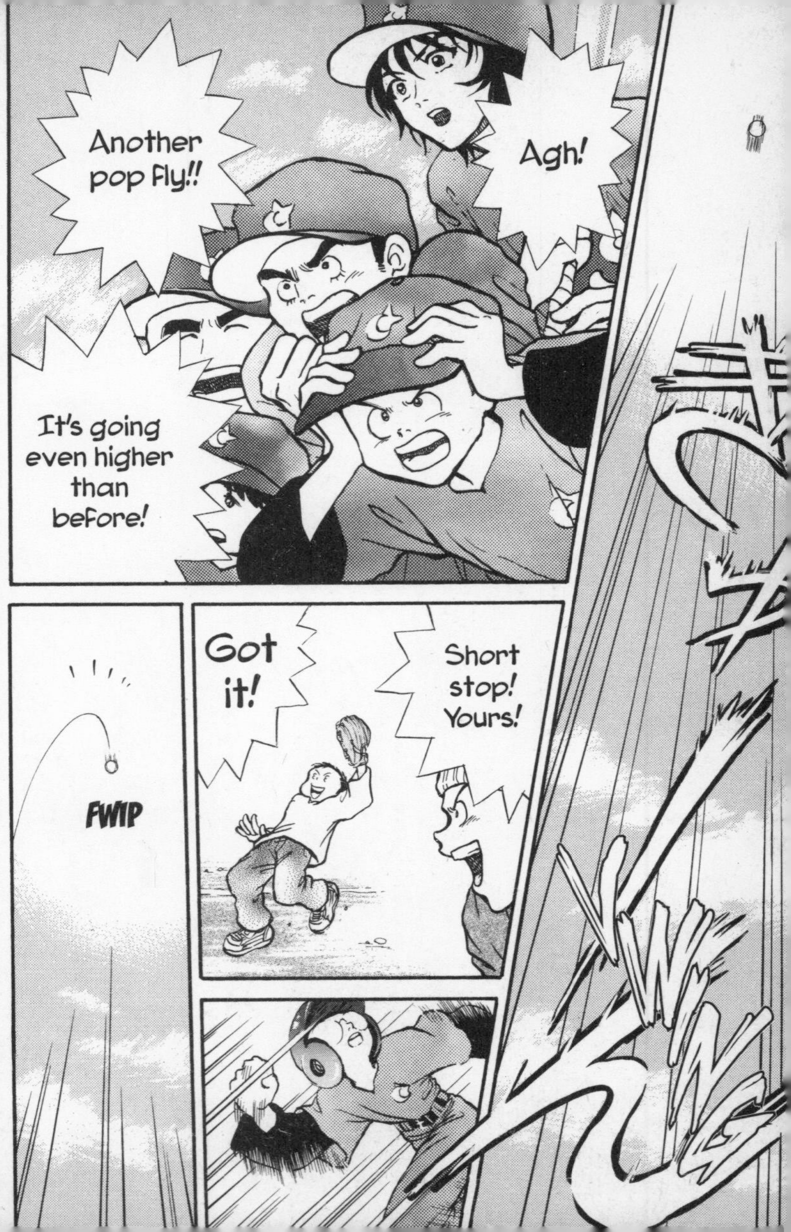
Agh!
Another pop fly!!
It's going even higher than before!
Short stop! Yours!
Got it!
FWIP

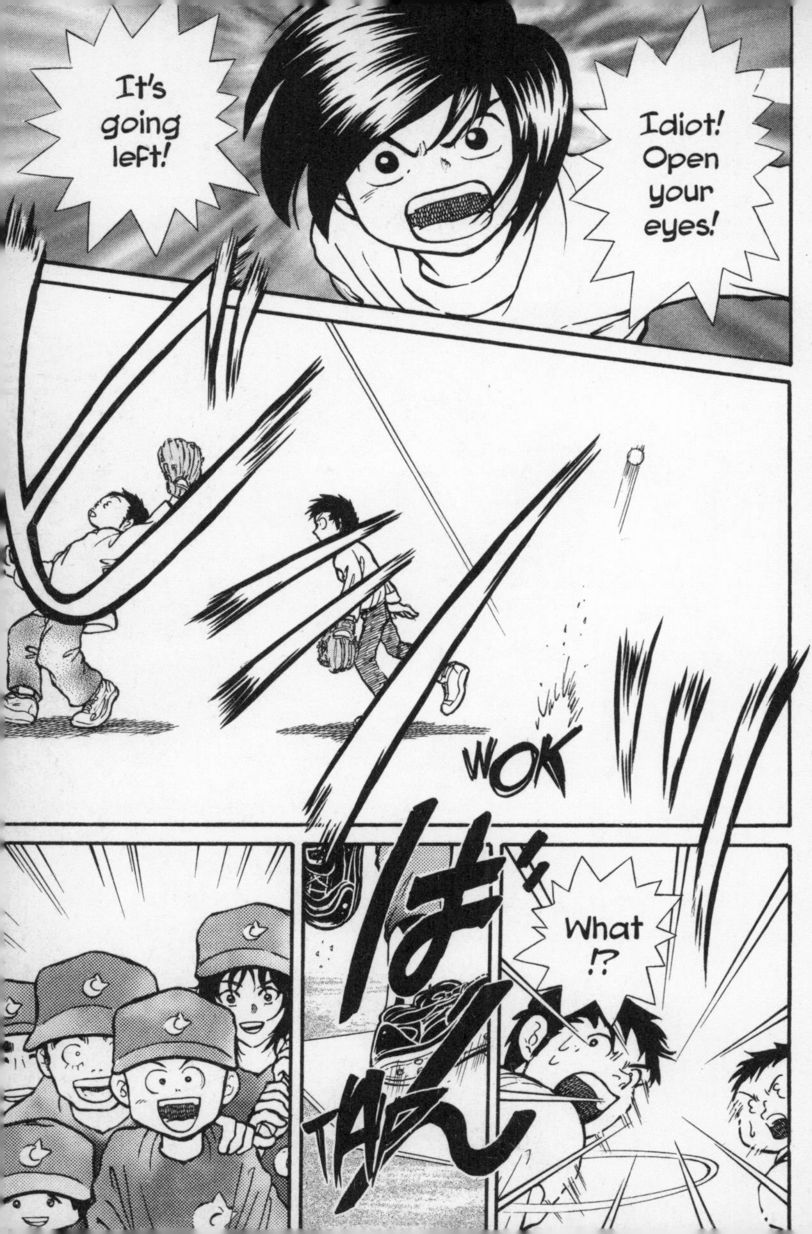
Idiot! Open your eyes!
It's going left!
WOK
What !?

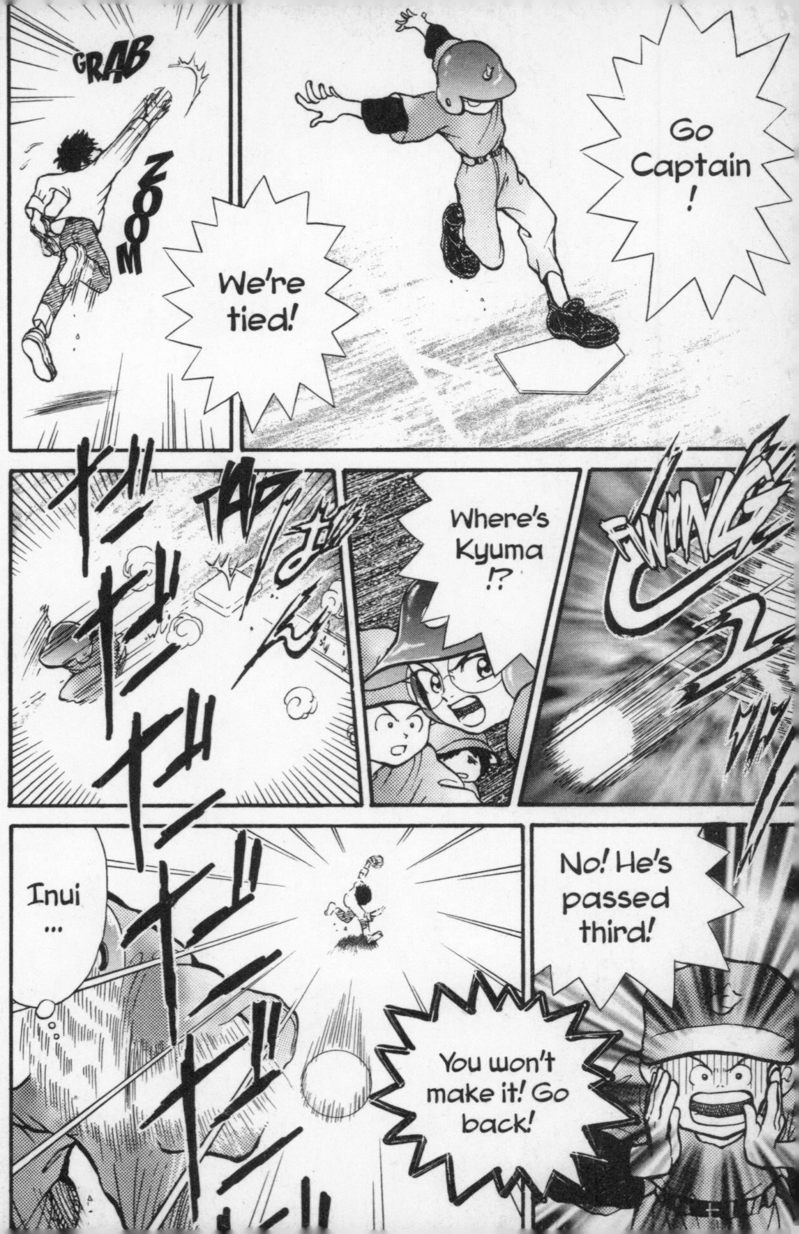
Go Captain!
We're tied!
GRAB
ZOOM
FWING
Where's Kyuma!?
TAP
No! He's passed third!
You won't make it! Go back!
Inui ...

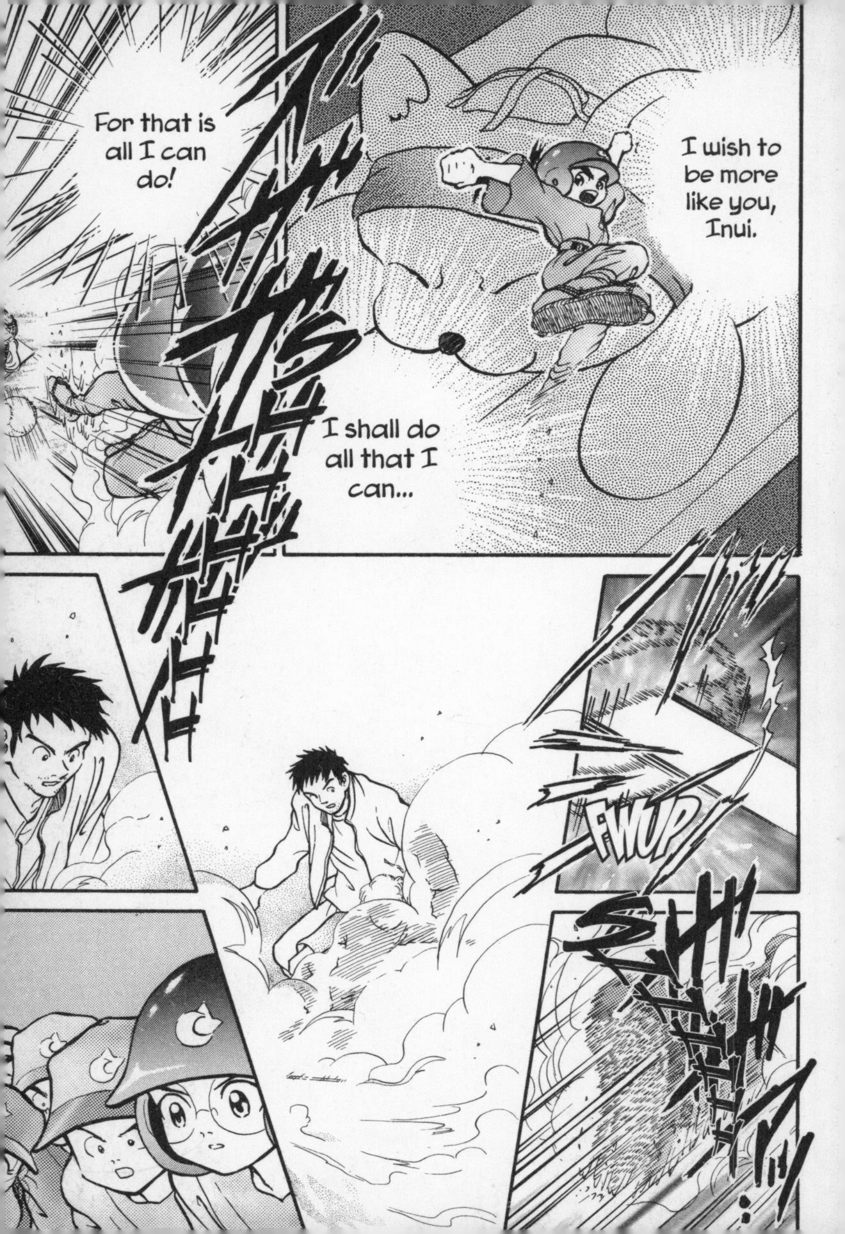
I wish to be more like you, Inui.
I shall do all that I can...
For that is all I can do!
FWUP

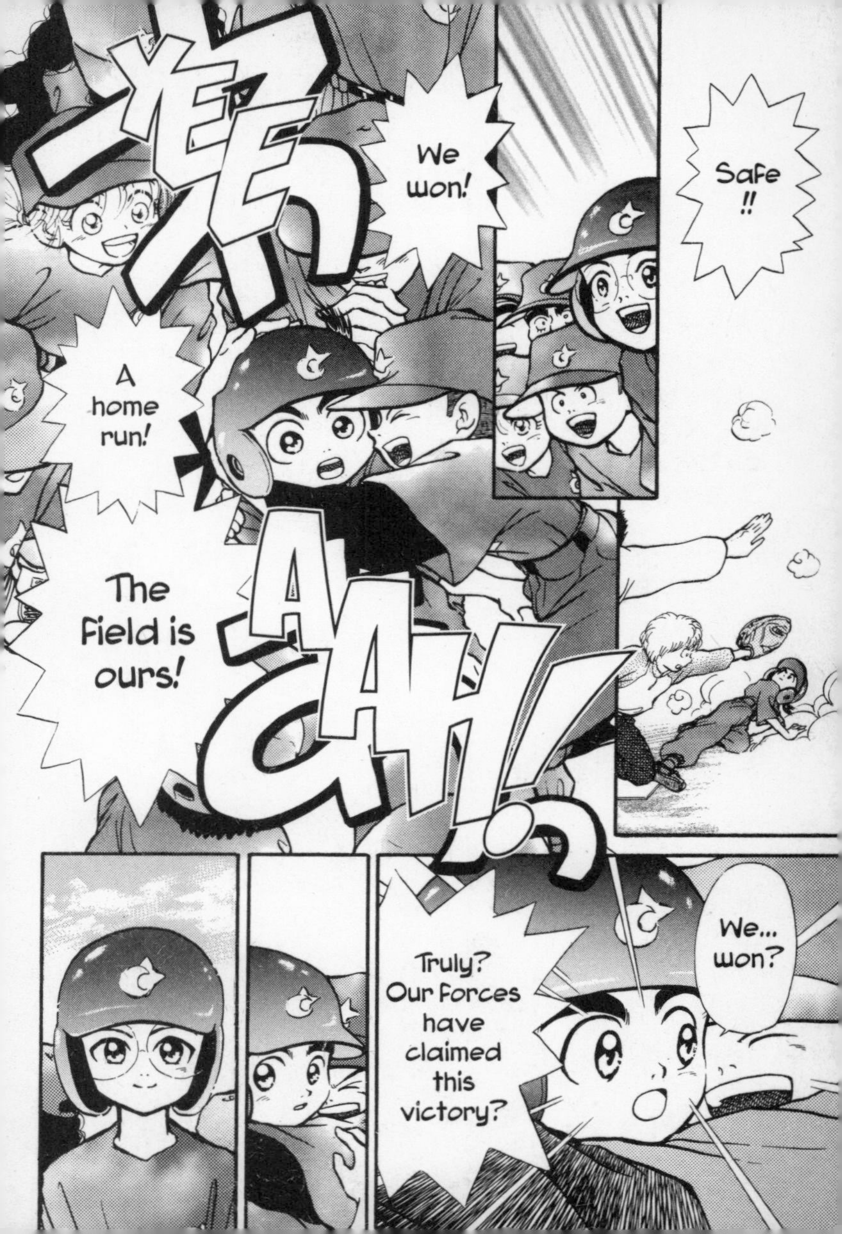
Safe!!
We won!
YEES
A home run!
The field is ours!
AAH!?
We... won?
Truly? Our forces have claimed this victory?

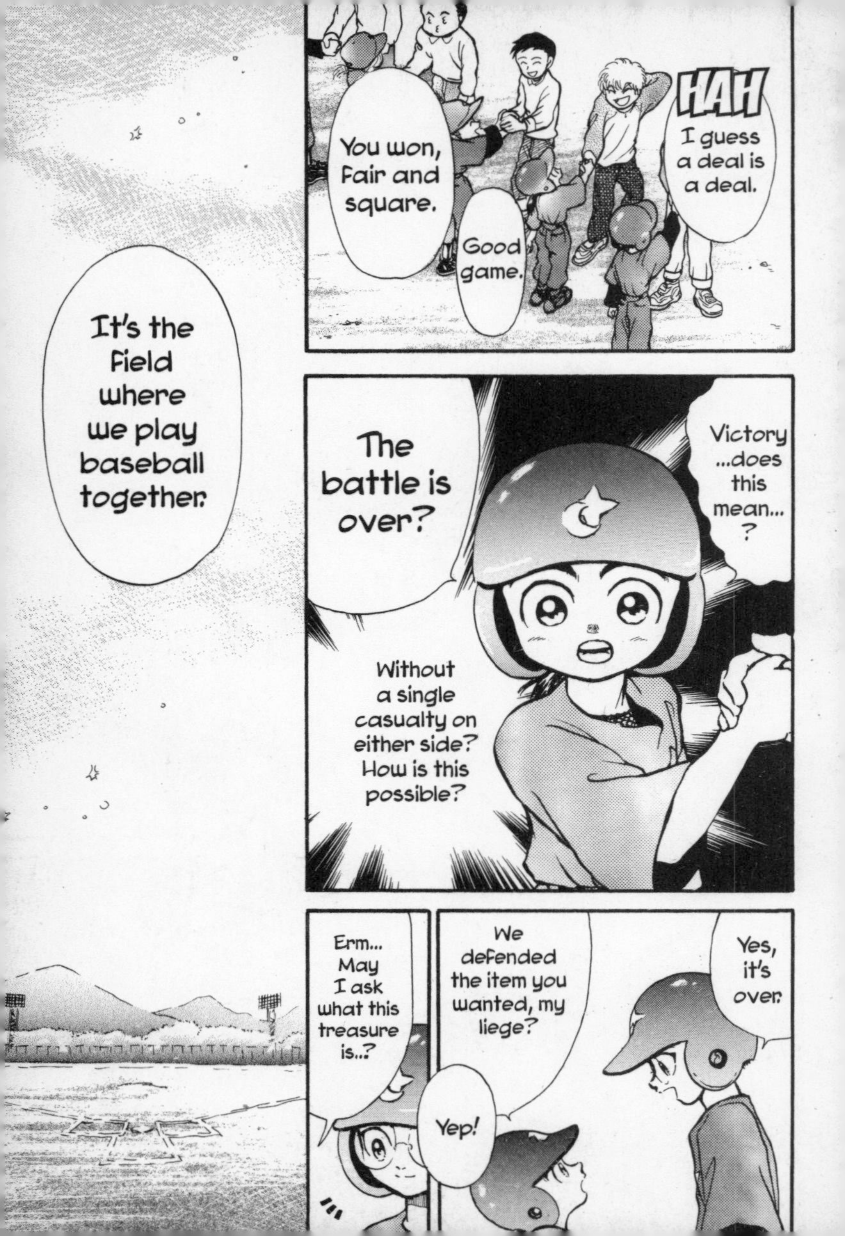
HAH
I guess a deal is a deal.
You won, fair and square.
Good game.
Victory ...does this mean...?
The battle is over?
Without a single casualty on either side? How is this possible?
Yes, it's over.
We defended the item you wanted, my liege?
Yep!
Erm... May I ask what this treasure is..?
It's the field where we play baseball together.

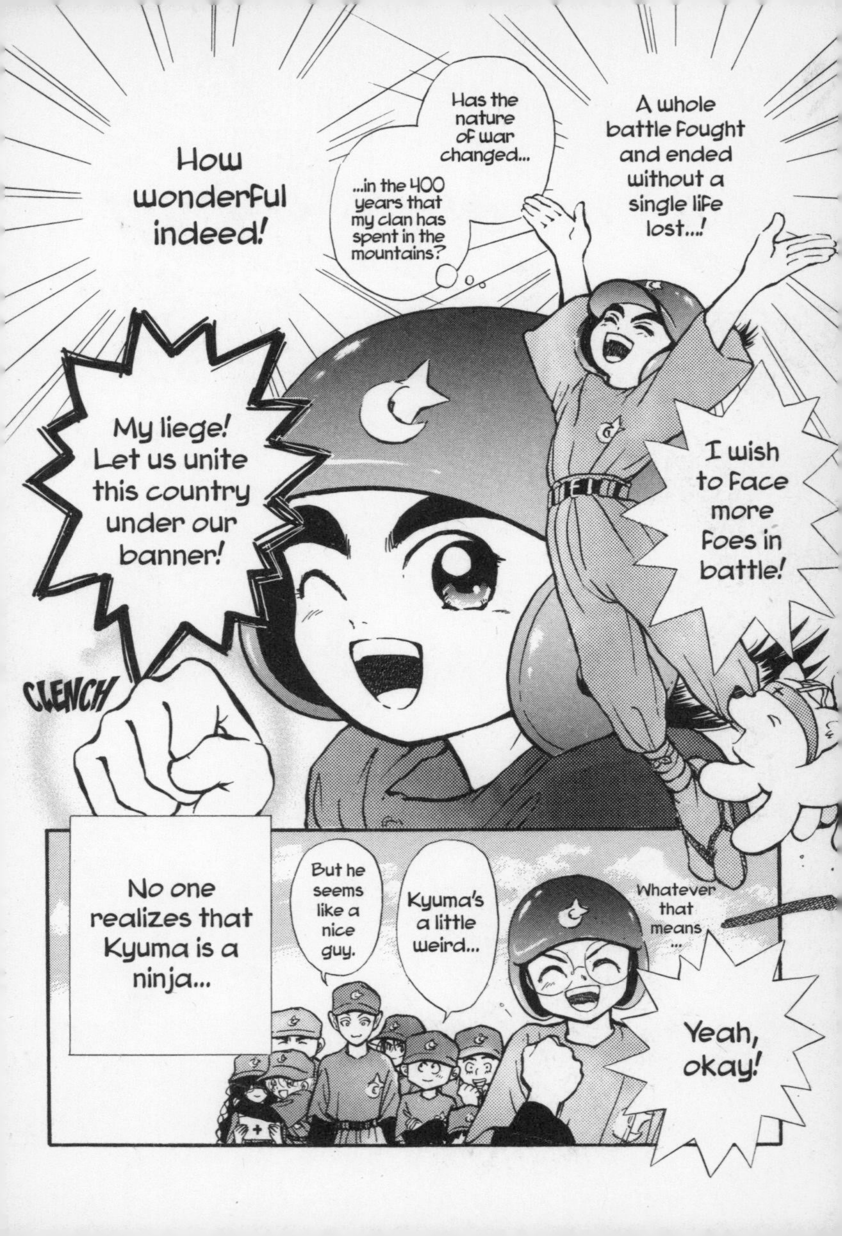
A whole battle fought and ended without a single life lost...!
Has the nature of war changed...
...in the 400 years that my clan has spent in the mountains?
How wonderful indeed!
I wish to face more foes in battle!
My liege! Let us unite this country under our banner!
CLENCH
Whatever that means...
Yeah, okay!
Kyuma's a little weird...
But he seems like a nice guy.
No one realizes that Kyuma is a ninja...

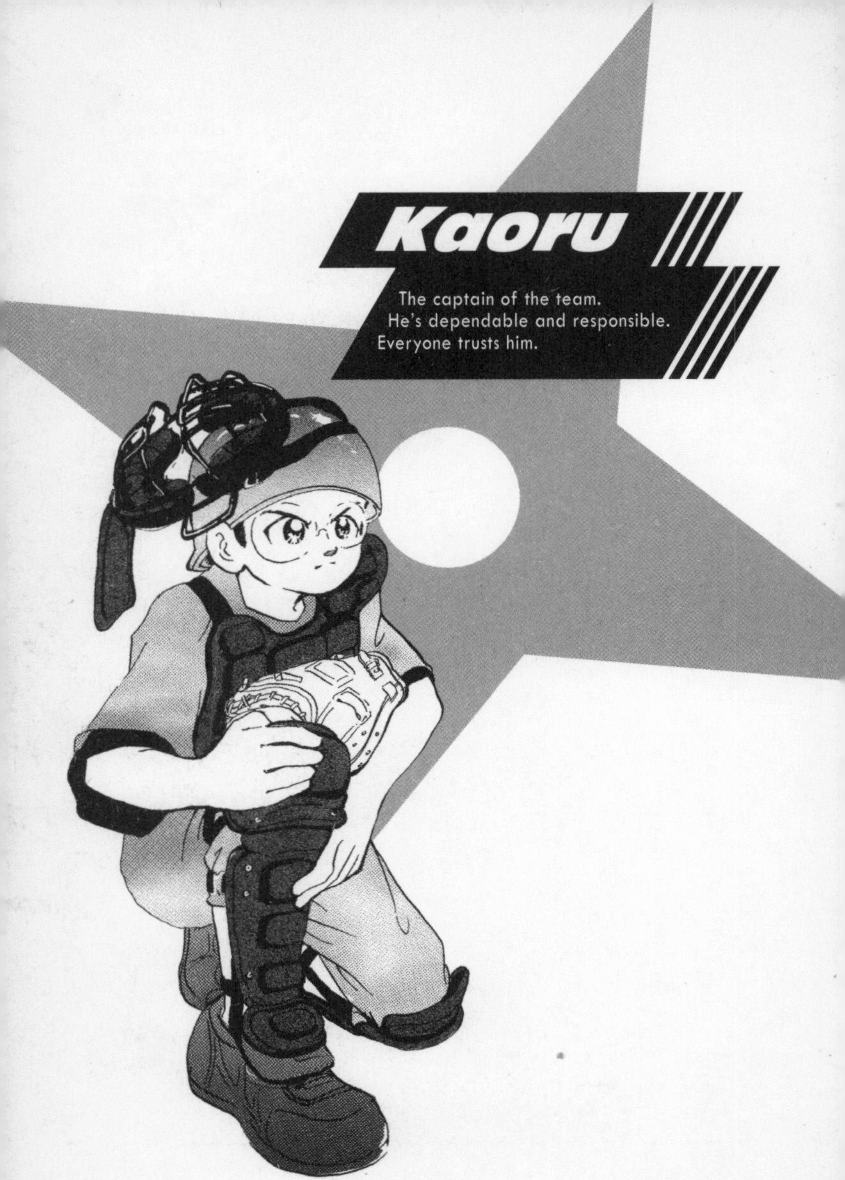
Kaoru
The captain of the team.
He's dependable and responsible.
Everyone trusts him.

Michi

The cool and collected second in command. He looks older, but he's an elementary student just like the others.

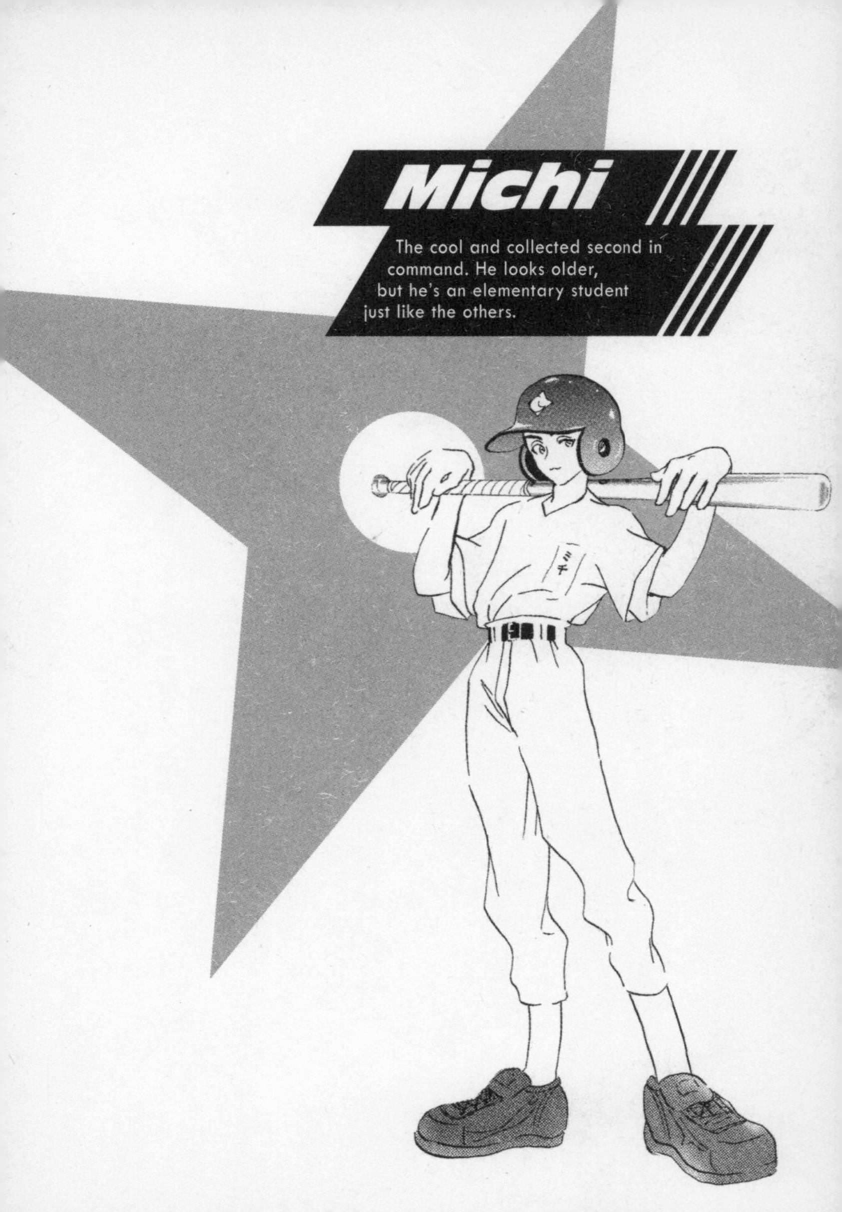

PITCH 3
LUO'S PITCHER'S MOUND

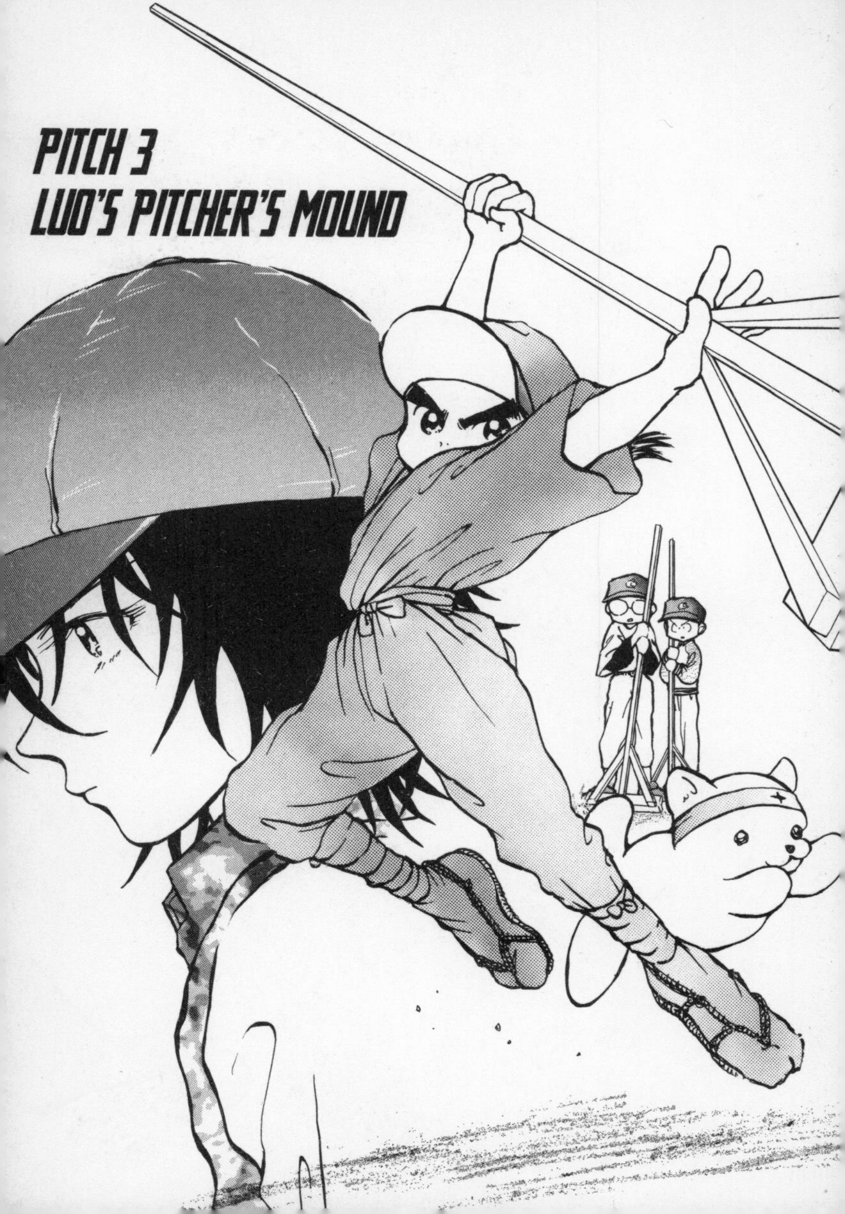

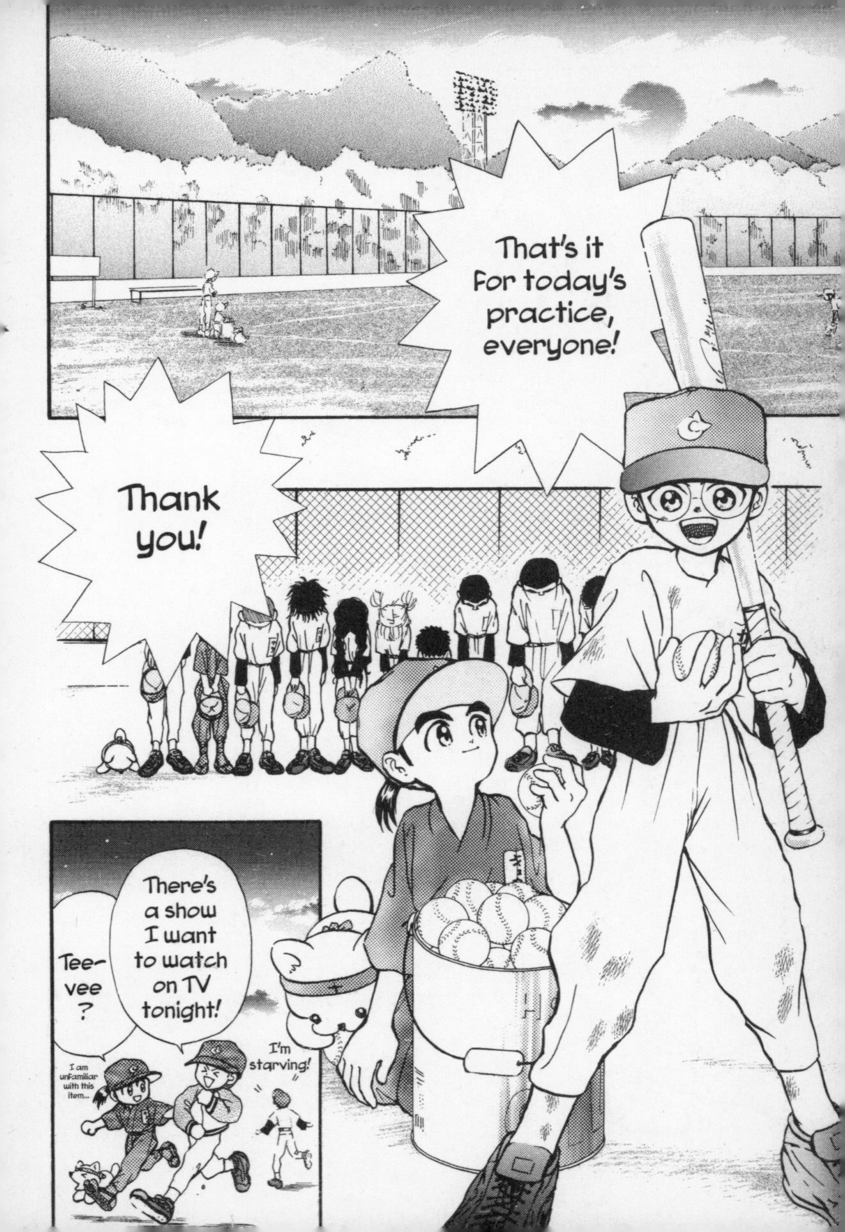
That's it for today's practice, everyone!
Thank you!
There's a show I want to watch on TV tonight!
Tee-vee?
I'm starving!
I am unfamiliar with this item...

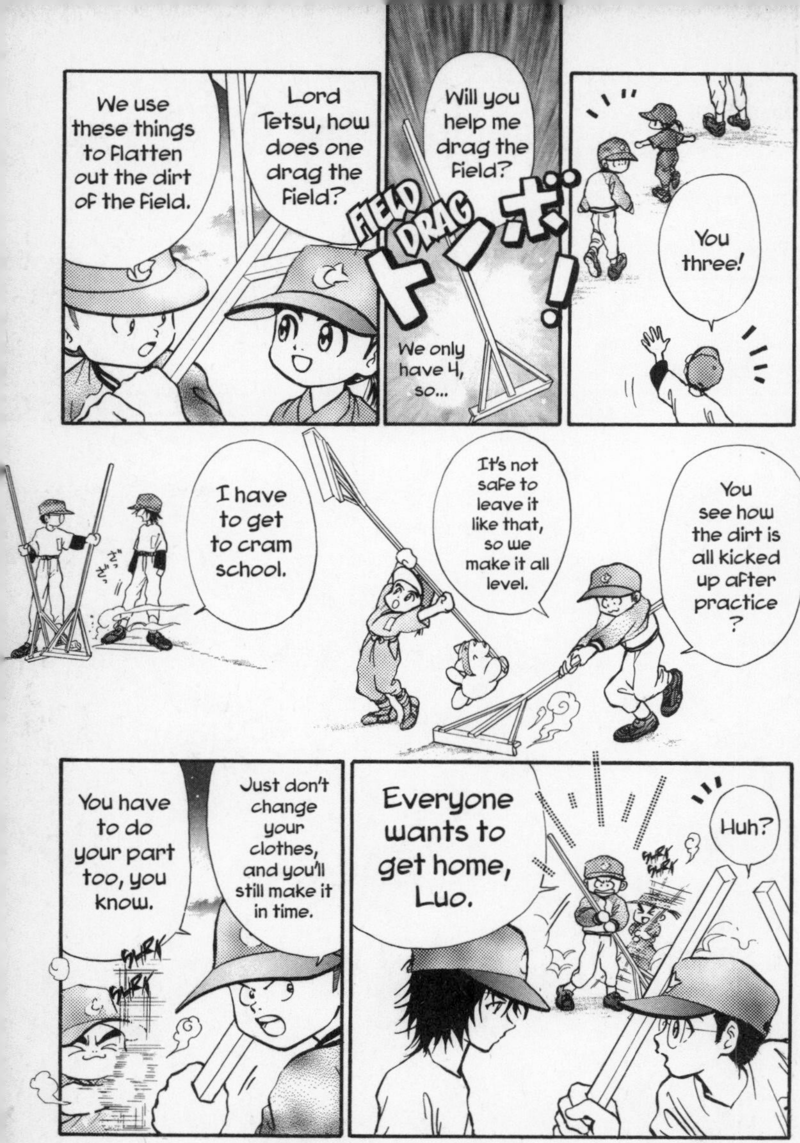
You three!
Will you help me drag the field?
FIELD DRAG
We only have 4, so...
Lord Tetsu, how does one drag the field?
We use these things to flatten out the dirt of the field.
You see how the dirt is all kicked up after practice?
It's not safe to leave it like that, so we make it all level.
I have to get to cram school.
Huh?
SHRK SHRK
Everyone wants to get home, Luo.
Just don't change your clothes, and you'll still make it in time.
You have to do your part too, you know.
SHRK SHRK

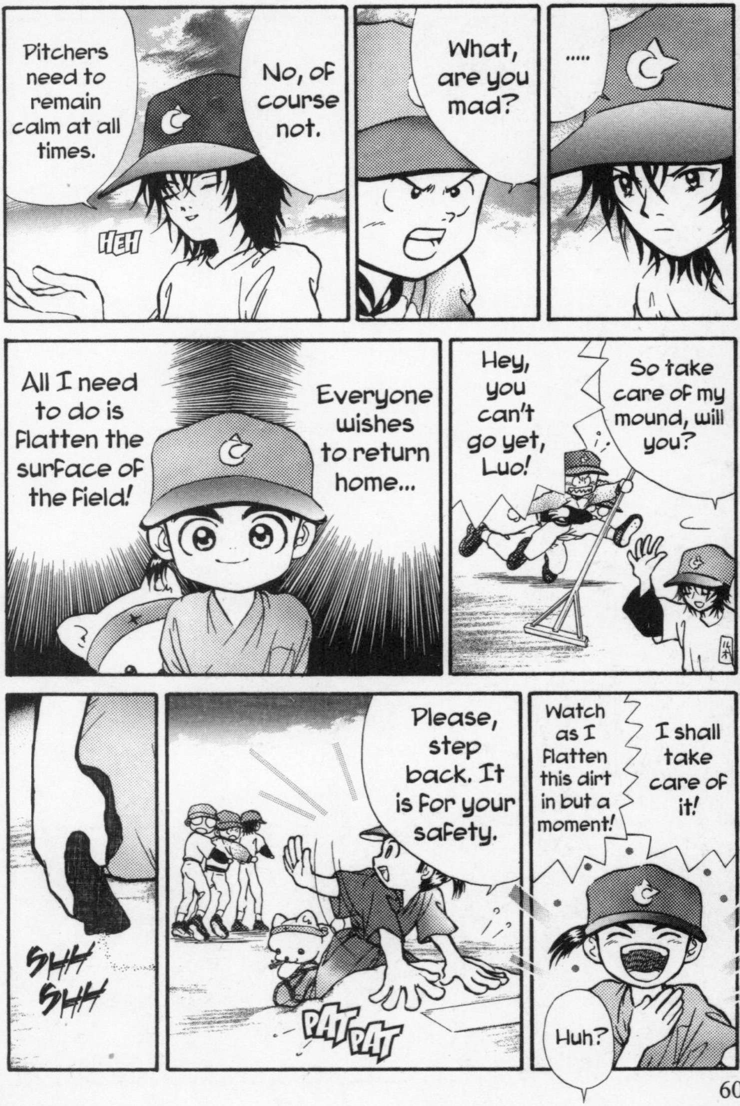
.....
What, are you mad?
No, of course not.
Pitchers need to remain calm at all times.
HEH
So take care of my mound, will you?
Hey, you can't go yet, Luo!
Everyone wishes to return home...
All I need to do is flatten the surface of the field!
I shall take care of it!
Watch as I flatten this dirt in but a moment!
Huh?
Please, step back. It is for your safety.
PAT PAT
SHH SHH

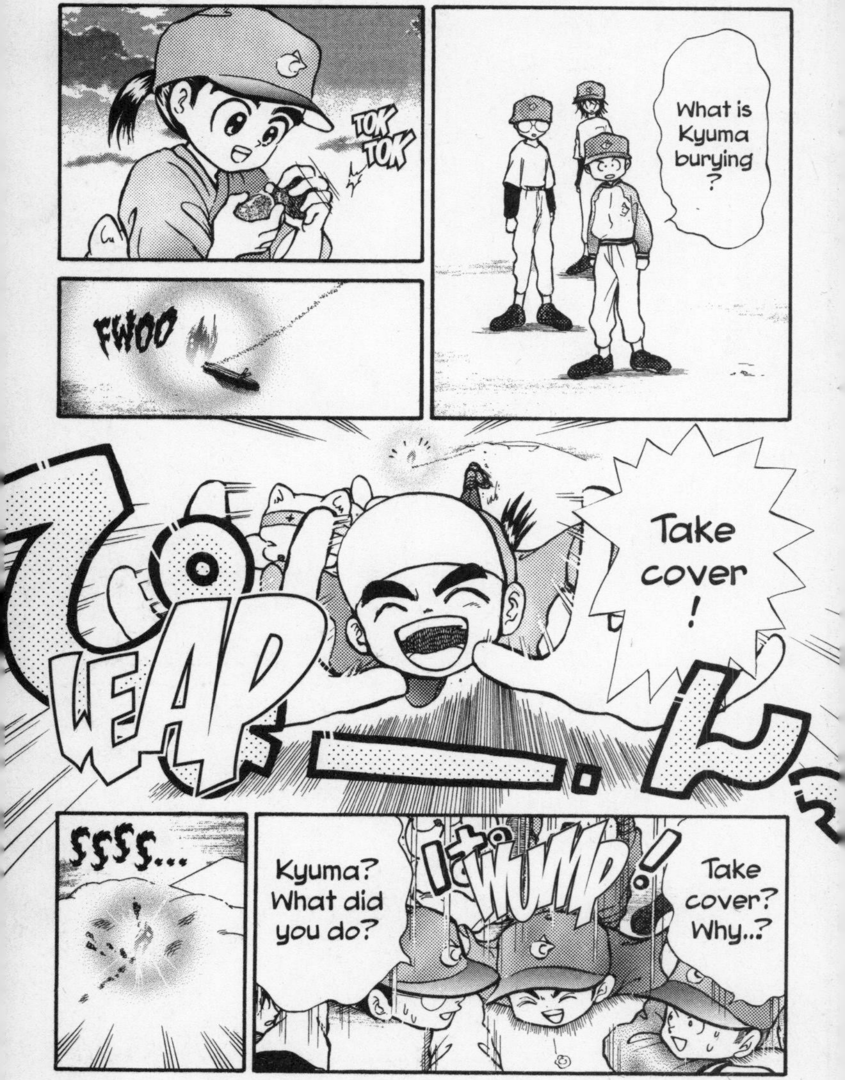
What is Kyuma burying?
TOK TOK
FWOO
Take cover!
LEAP
Take cover? Why..?
WUMP!
Kyuma? What did you do?
SSSS...

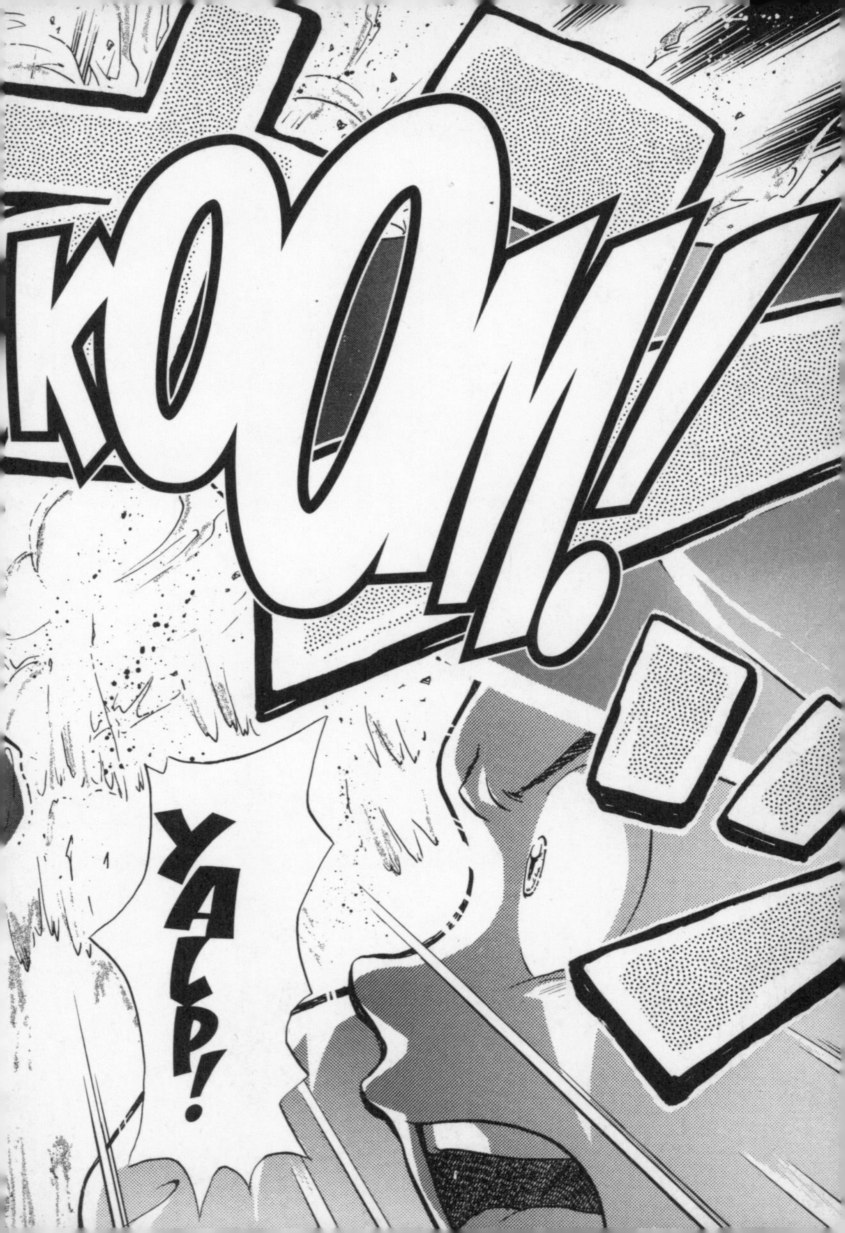
KOOM!
YALP!

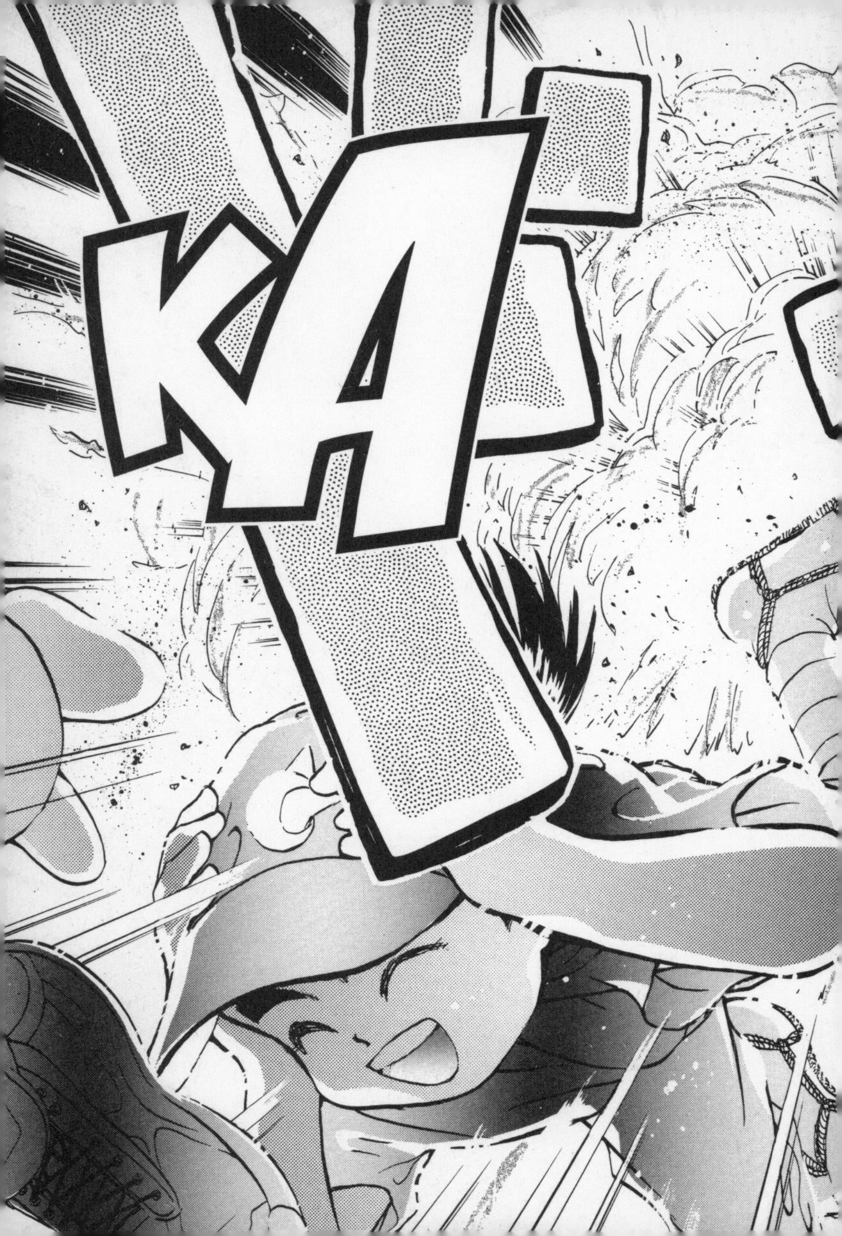
KA

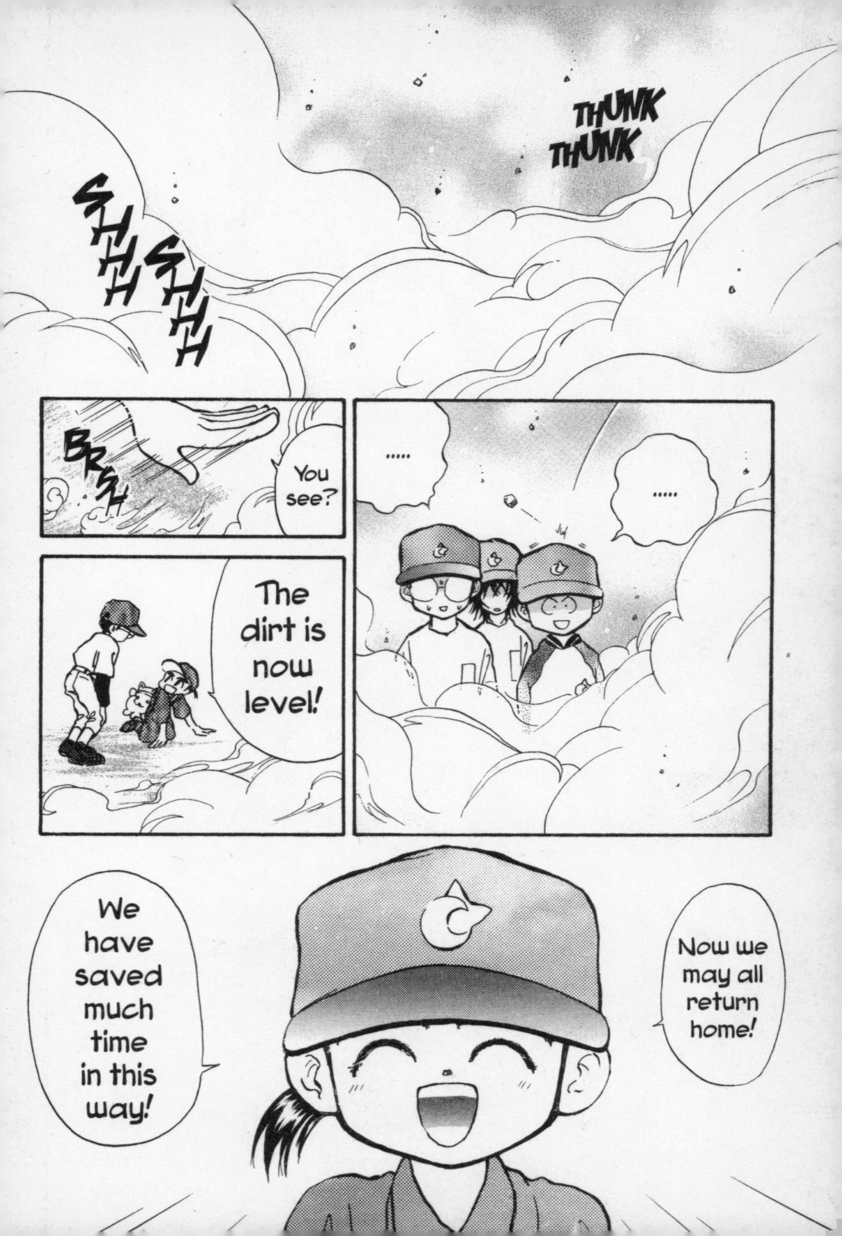
THUNK THUNK
SHHHH SHHHH
.....
.....
BRSH
You see?
The dirt is now level!
Now we may all return home!
We have saved much time in this way!

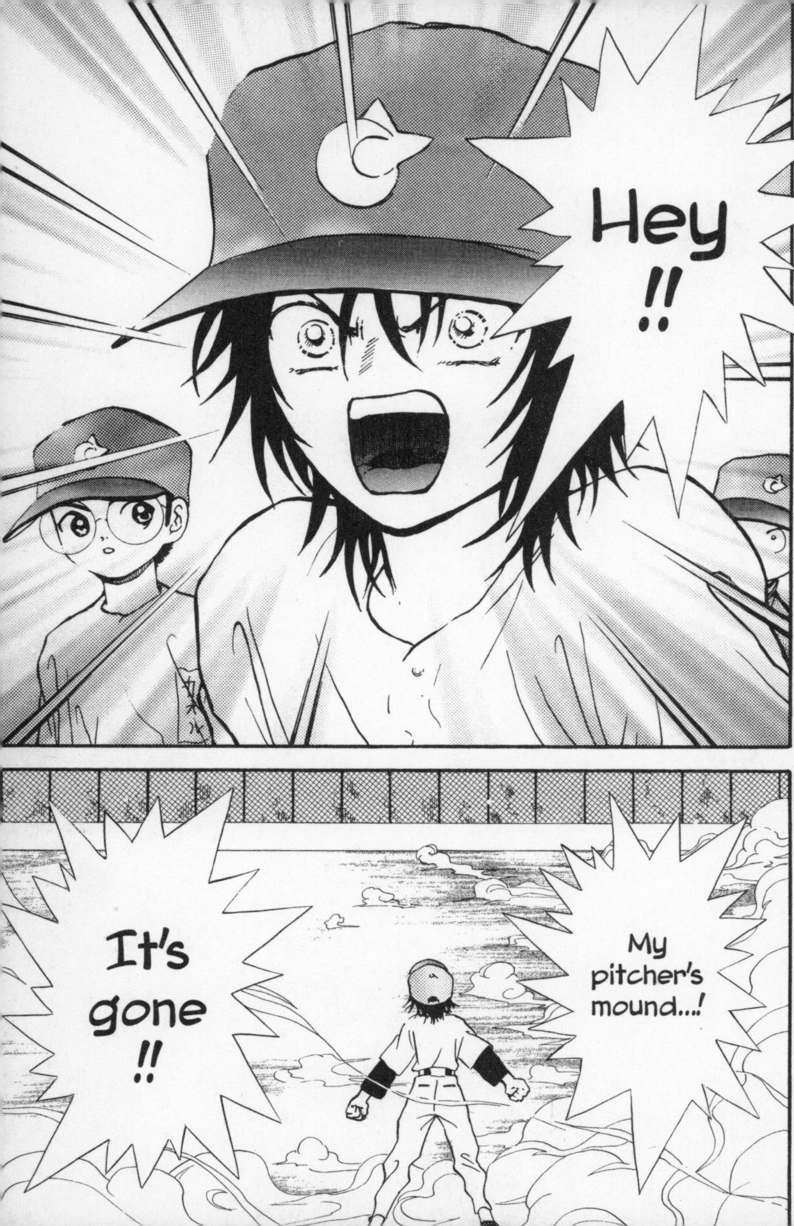
Hey!!
My pitcher's mound...!
It's gone!!

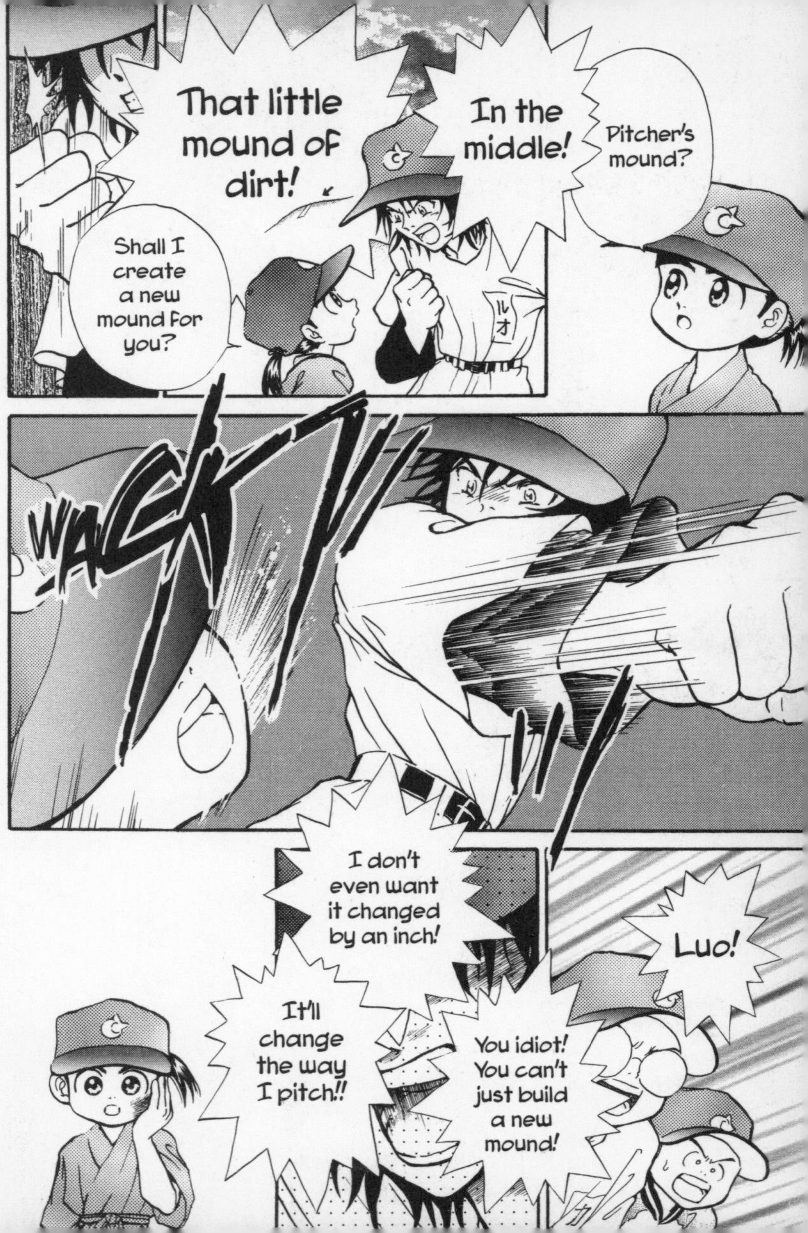
Pitcher's mound?
In the middle!
That little mound of dirt!
Shall I create a new mound for you?
ルオ
WACK
Luo!
You idiot! You can't just build a new mound!
I don't even want it changed by an inch!
It'll change the way I pitch!!

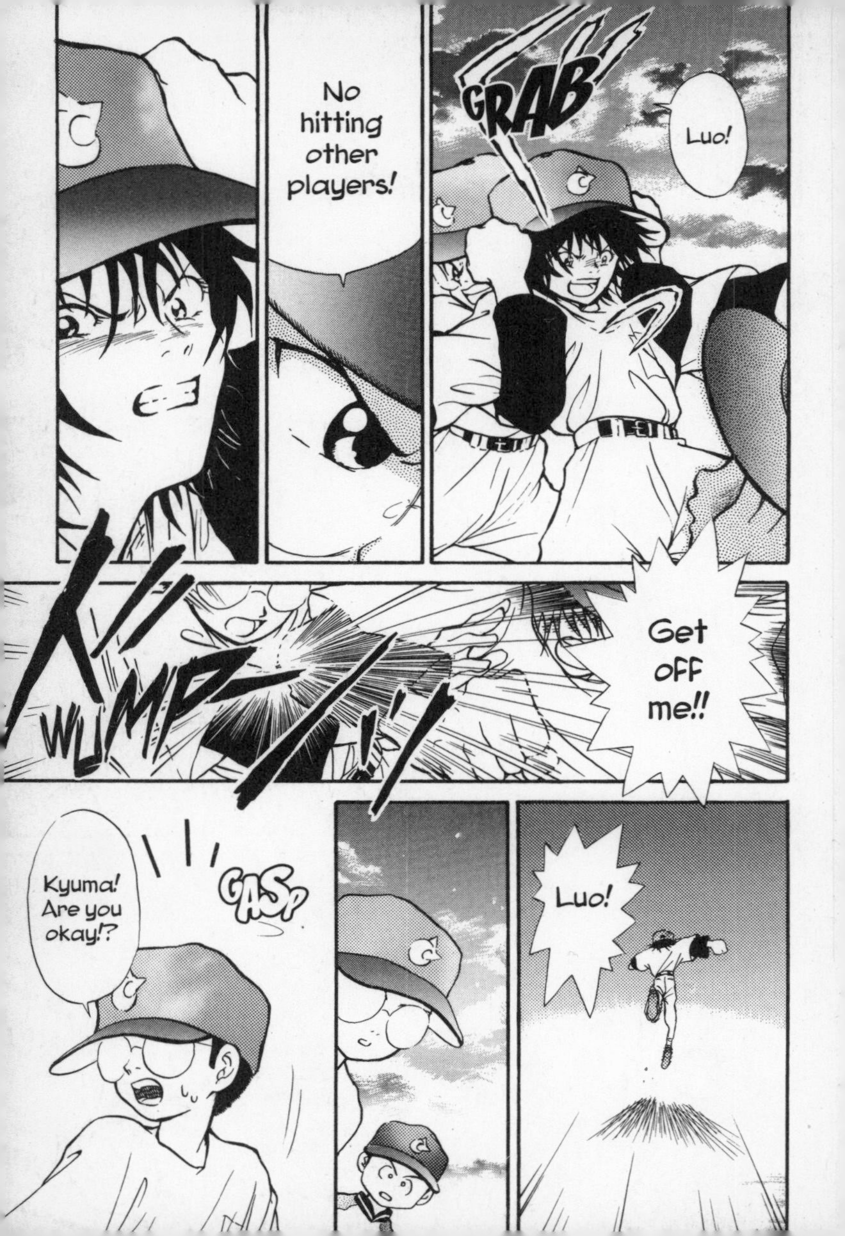
GRAB
Luo!
No hitting other players!
Get off me!!
K-WUMP!!
Luo!
GASP
Kyuma! Are you okay!?

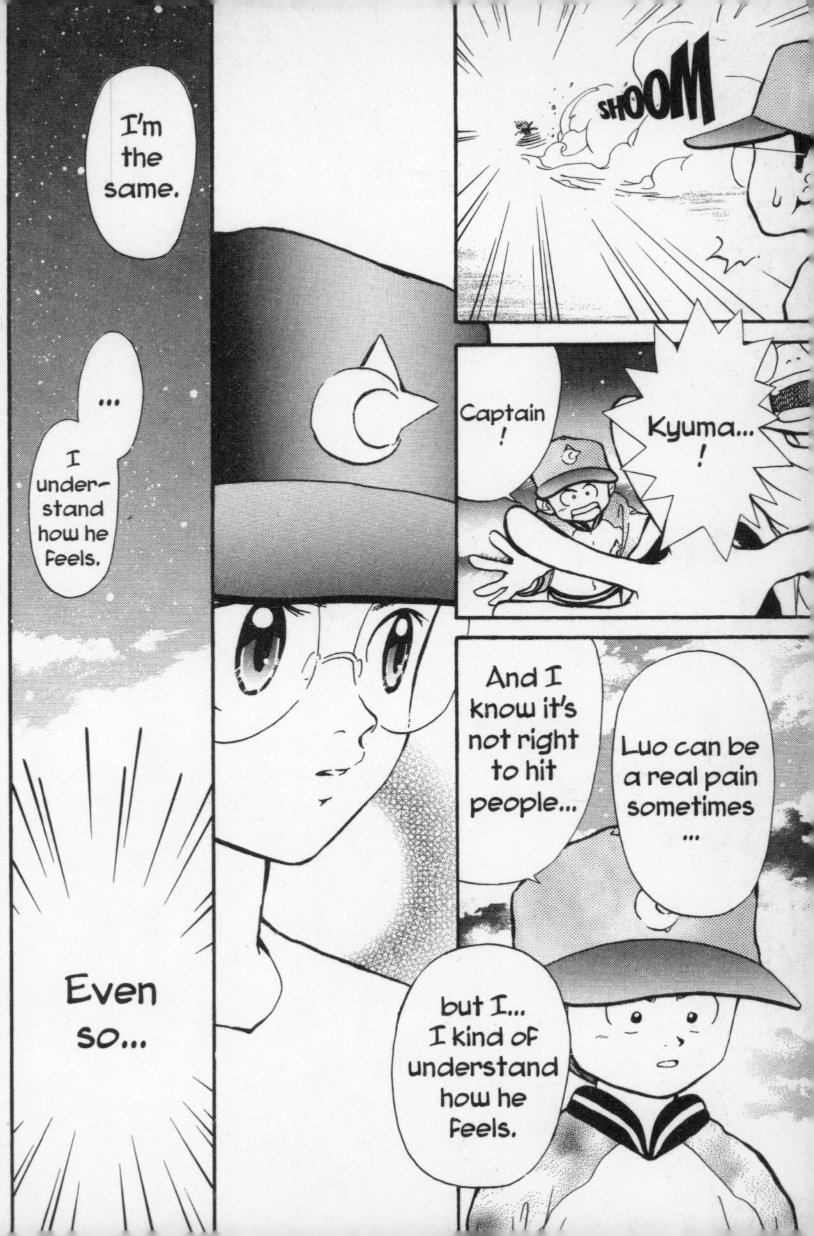
SHOOM
Kyuma... !
Captain !
Luo can be a real pain sometimes ...
And I know it's not right to hit people...
but I... I kind of understand how he feels.
I'm the same.
...
I understand how he feels.
Even so...

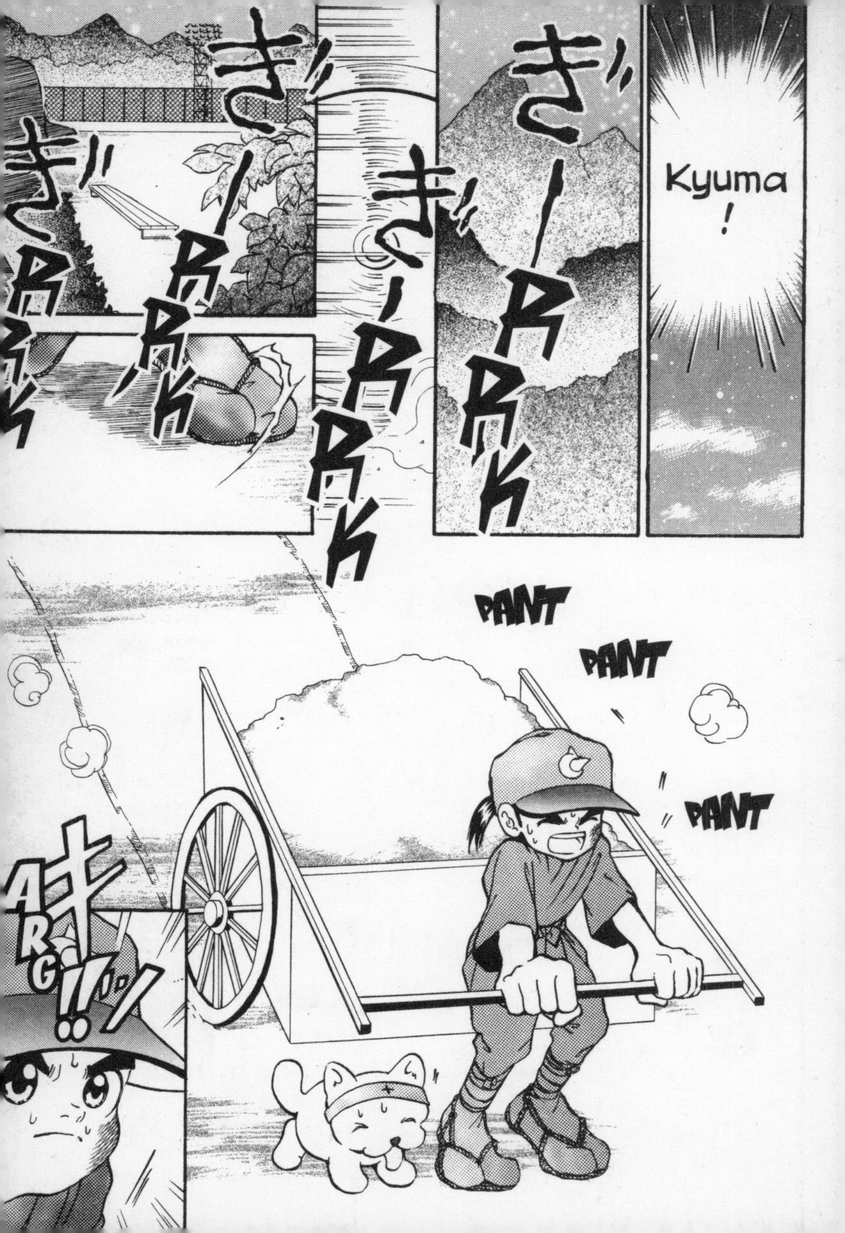

Kyuma!
ぎーRRK
ぎーRRK
ぎーRRK
ぎーRRK
PANT
PANT
PANT
ARG!!

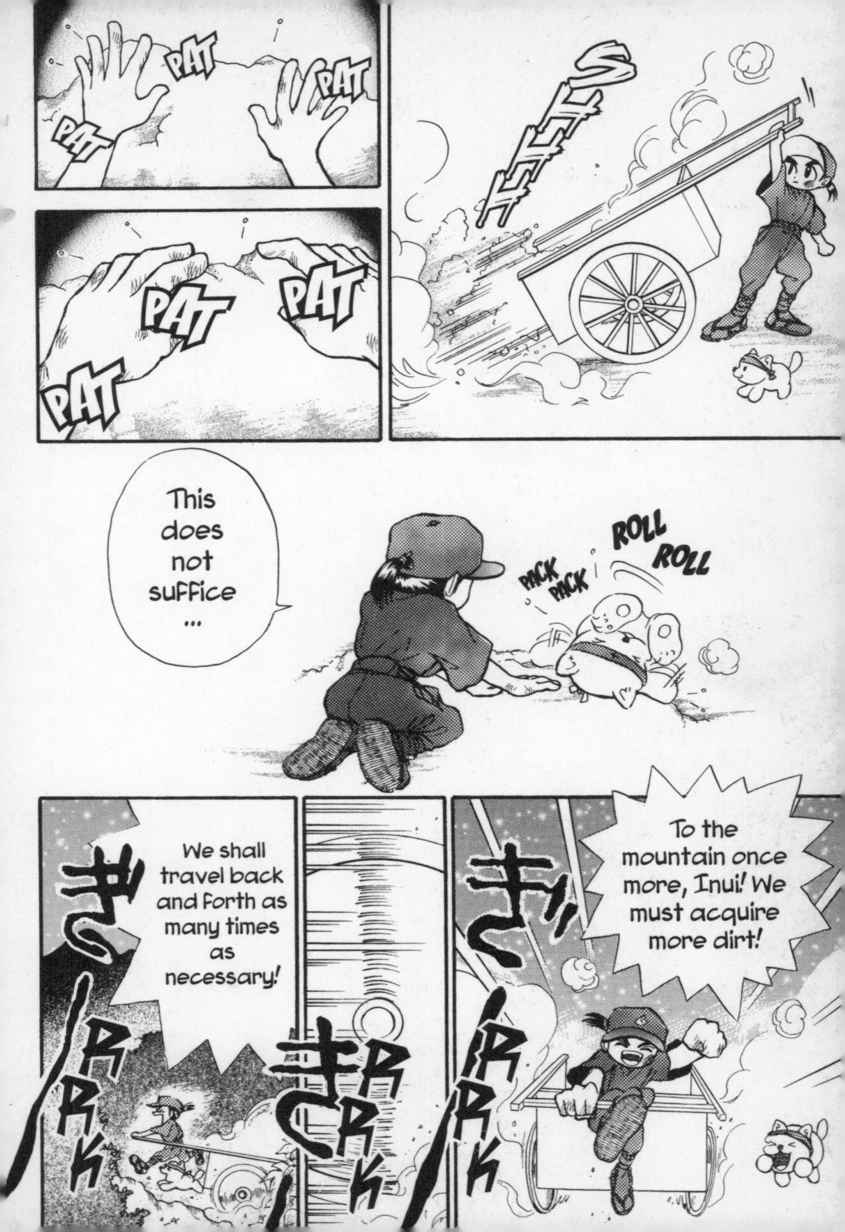
PAT
PAT
PAT
PAT
PAT
PAT
ROLL
ROLL
PACK
PACK
This does not suffice ...
To the mountain once more, Inui! We must acquire more dirt!
RRK
RRK
RRK
We shall travel back and forth as many times as necessary!

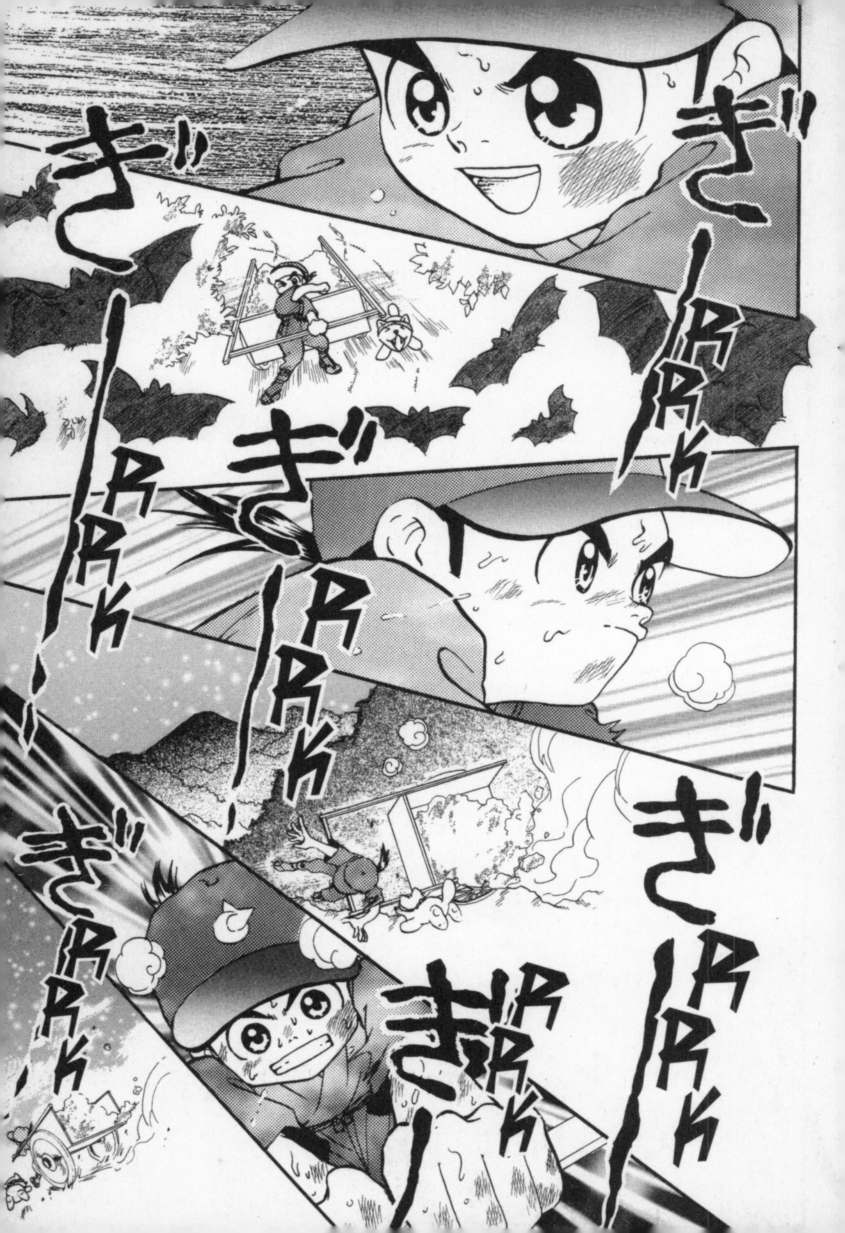

ぎーRRk
ぎーRRk
きーRRk
ぎーRRk
ぎーRRk
ぎRRk

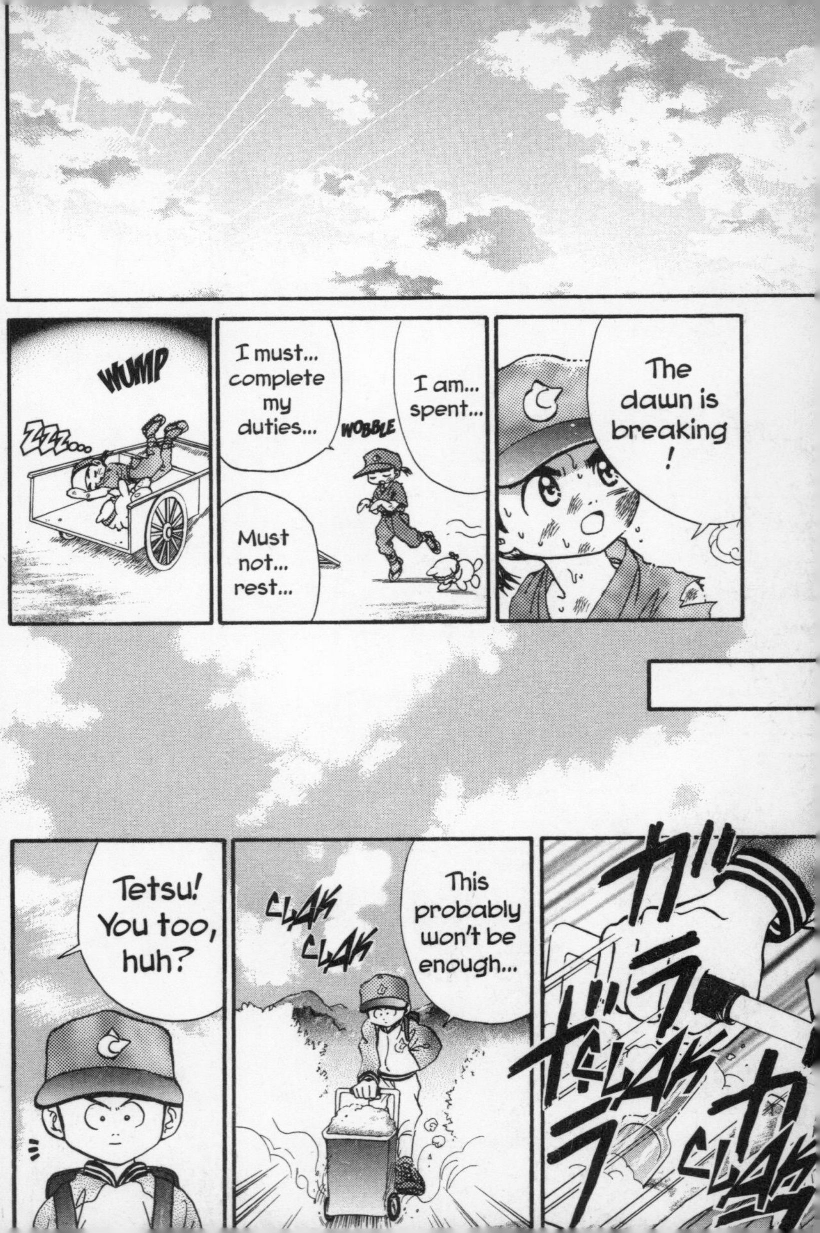
The dawn is breaking!
I am... spent...
I must... complete my duties...
WOBBLE
Must not... rest...
WUMP
ZZZ...
CLAK
CLAK
This probably won't be enough...
CLAK
CLAK
Tetsu! You too, huh?

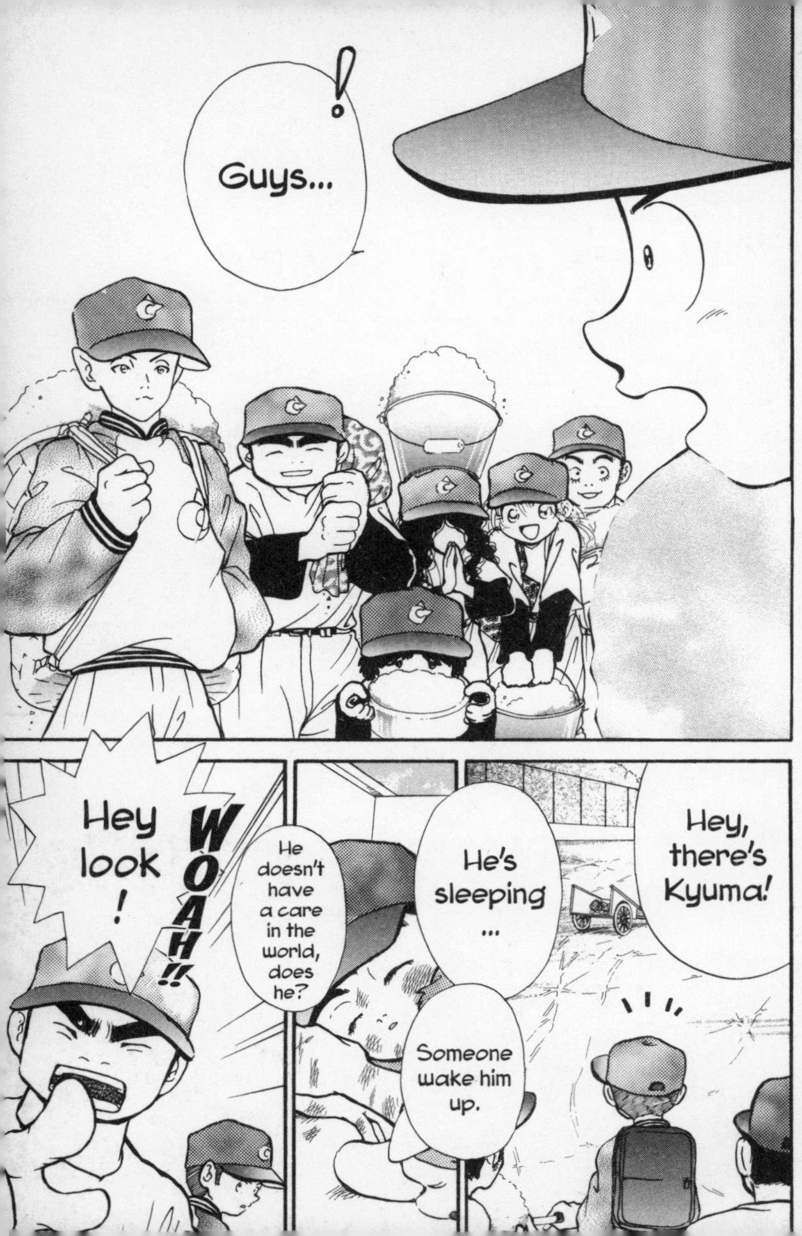
!
Guys...
Hey, there's Kyuma!
He's sleeping ...
Someone wake him up.
He doesn't have a care in the world, does he?
WOAH!!
Hey look !

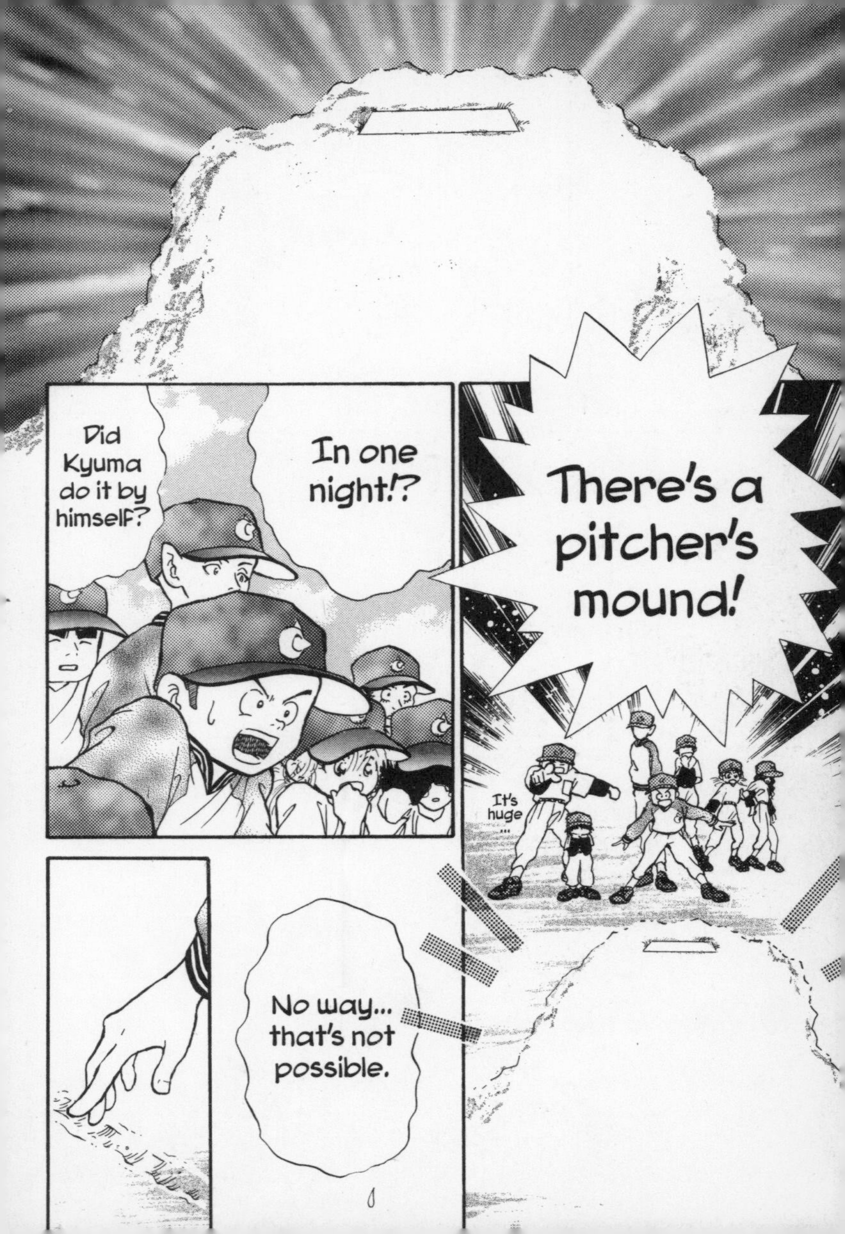
There's a pitcher's mound!
It's huge...
In one night!?
Did Kyuma do it by himself?
No way... that's not possible.

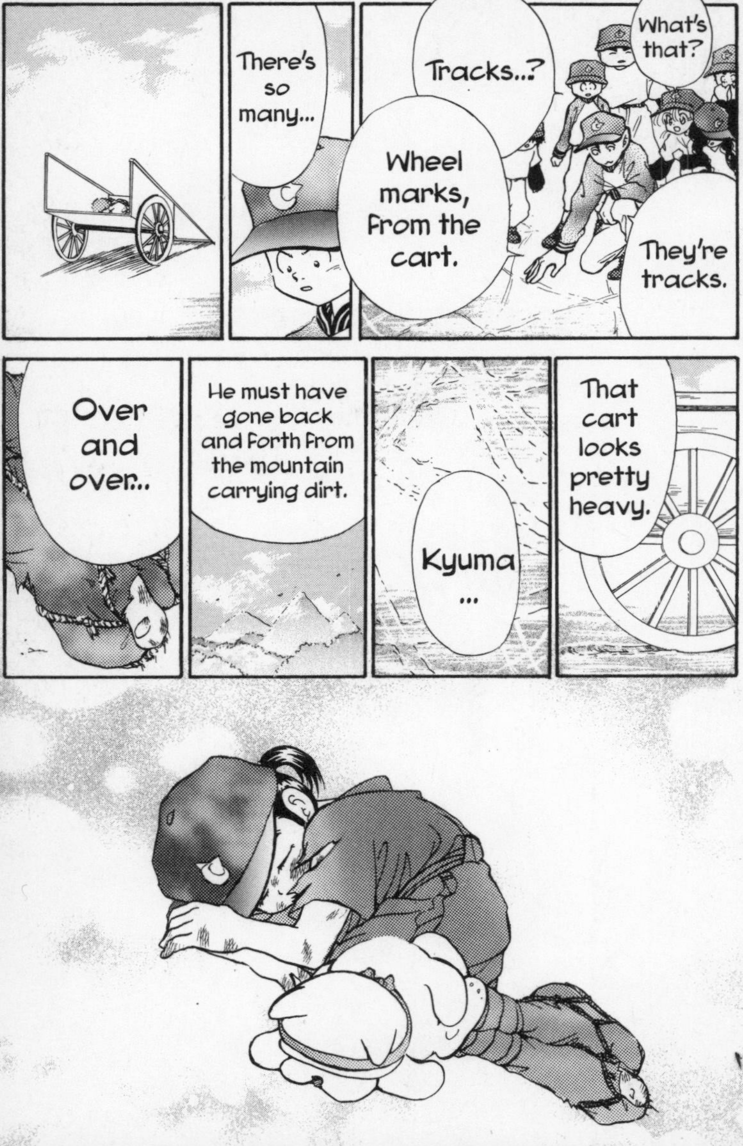
What's that?
Tracks...?
They're tracks.
Wheel marks, from the cart.
There's so many...
That cart looks pretty heavy.
Kyuma ...
He must have gone back and forth from the mountain carrying dirt.
Over and over...

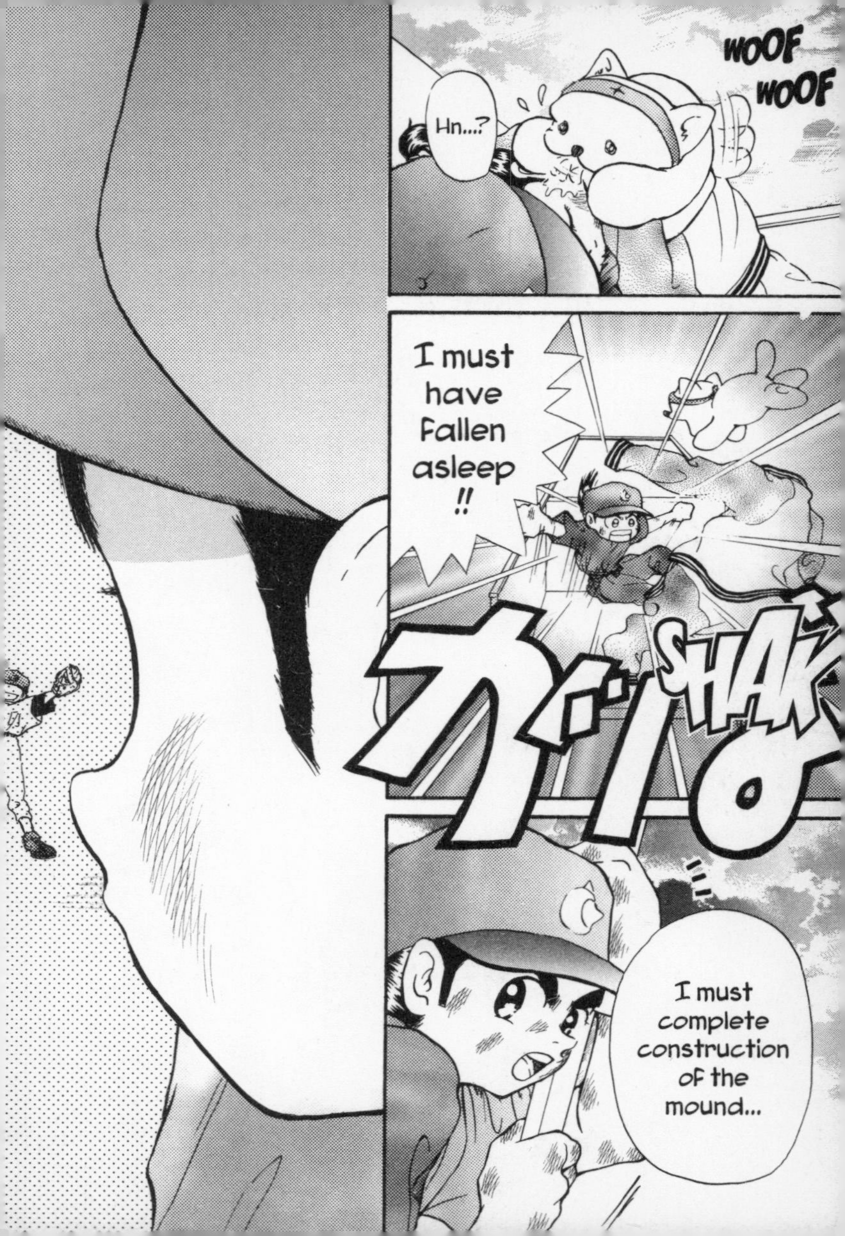
WOOF
WOOF
Hn...?
I must have fallen asleep!!
SHAK
I must complete construction of the mound...

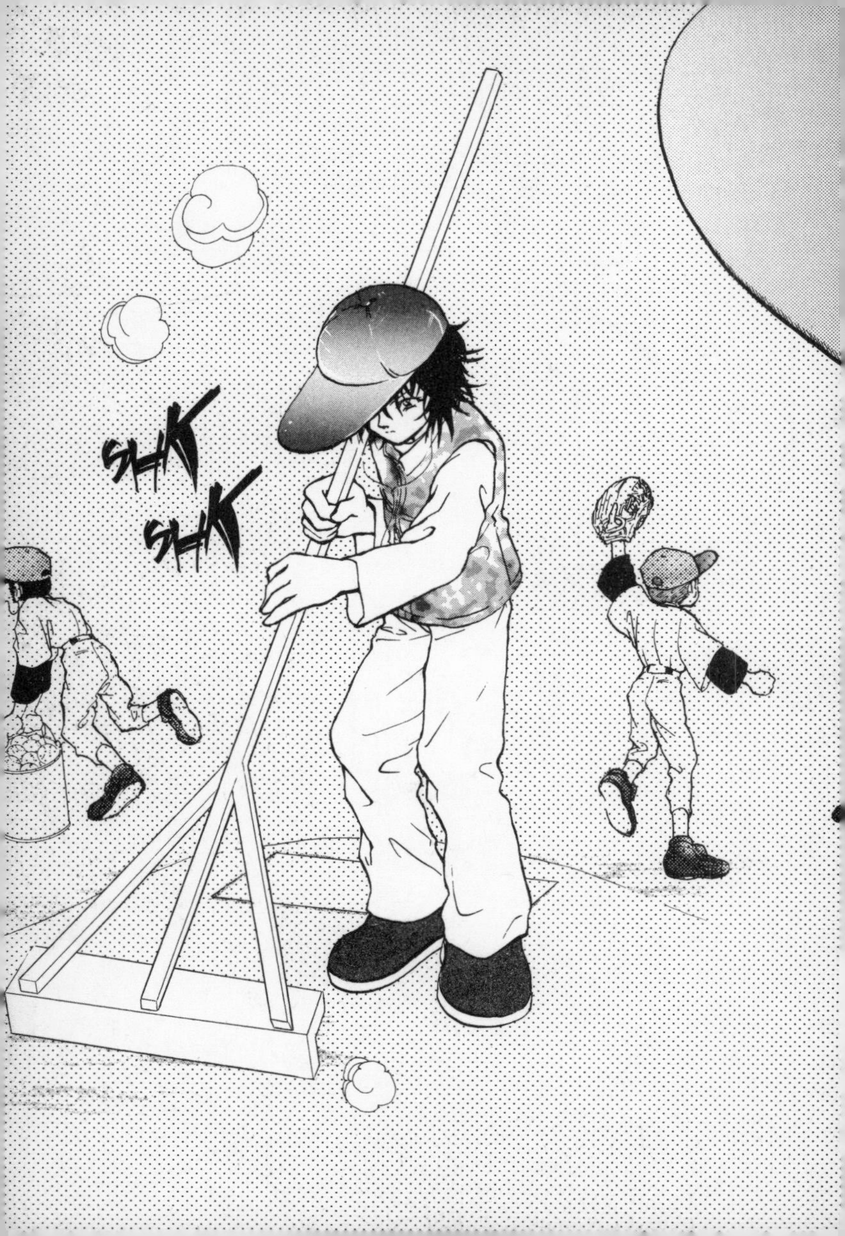
SHK
SHK

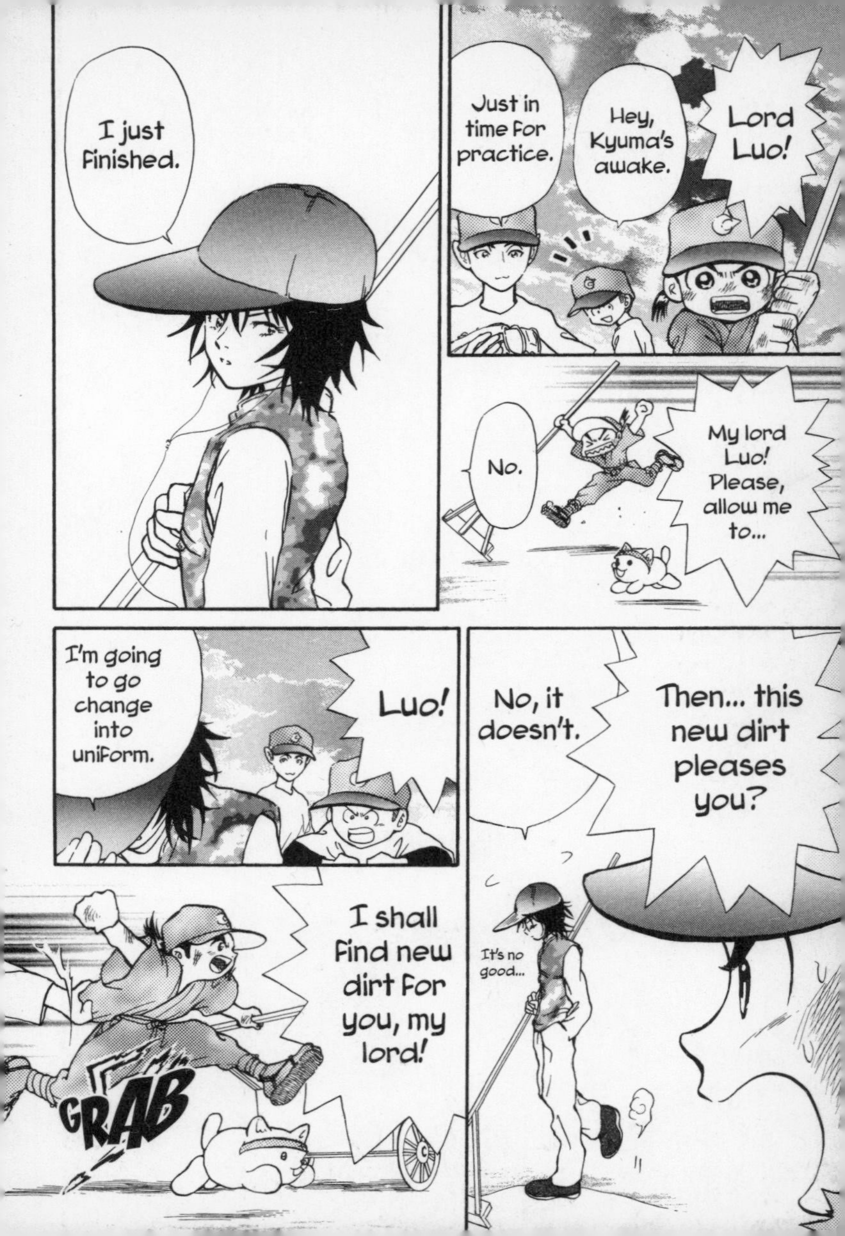

Lord Luo!
Hey, Kyuma's awake.
Just in time for practice.
My lord Luo! Please, allow me to...
No.
I just finished.
Then... this new dirt pleases you?
No, it doesn't.
It's no good...
Luo!
I'm going to go change into uniform.
I shall find new dirt for you, my lord!
GRAB

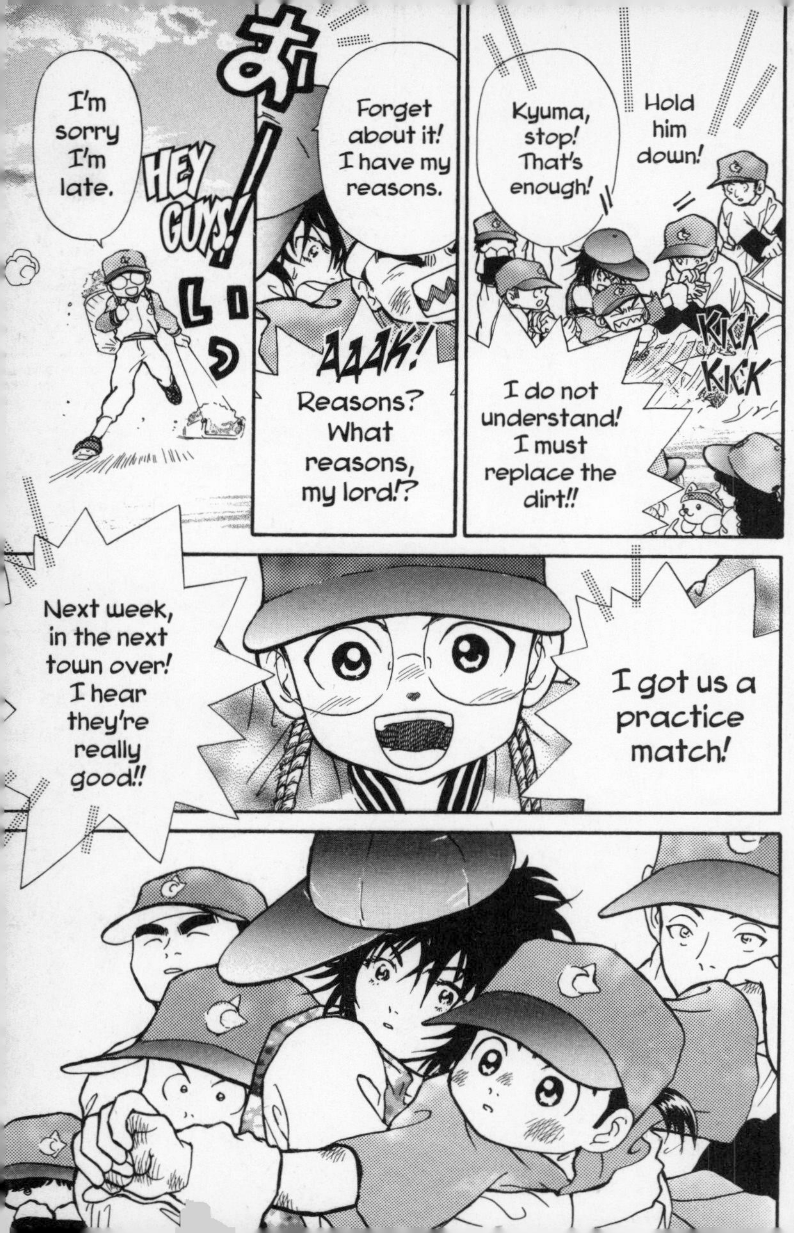

Hold him down!
Kyuma, stop! That's enough!
KICK KICK
I do not understand! I must replace the dirt!!
Forget about it! I have my reasons.
AAAK!
Reasons? What reasons, my lord!?
おーいっ
HEY GUYS!
I'm sorry I'm late.
I got us a practice match!
Next week, in the next town over! I hear they're really good!!

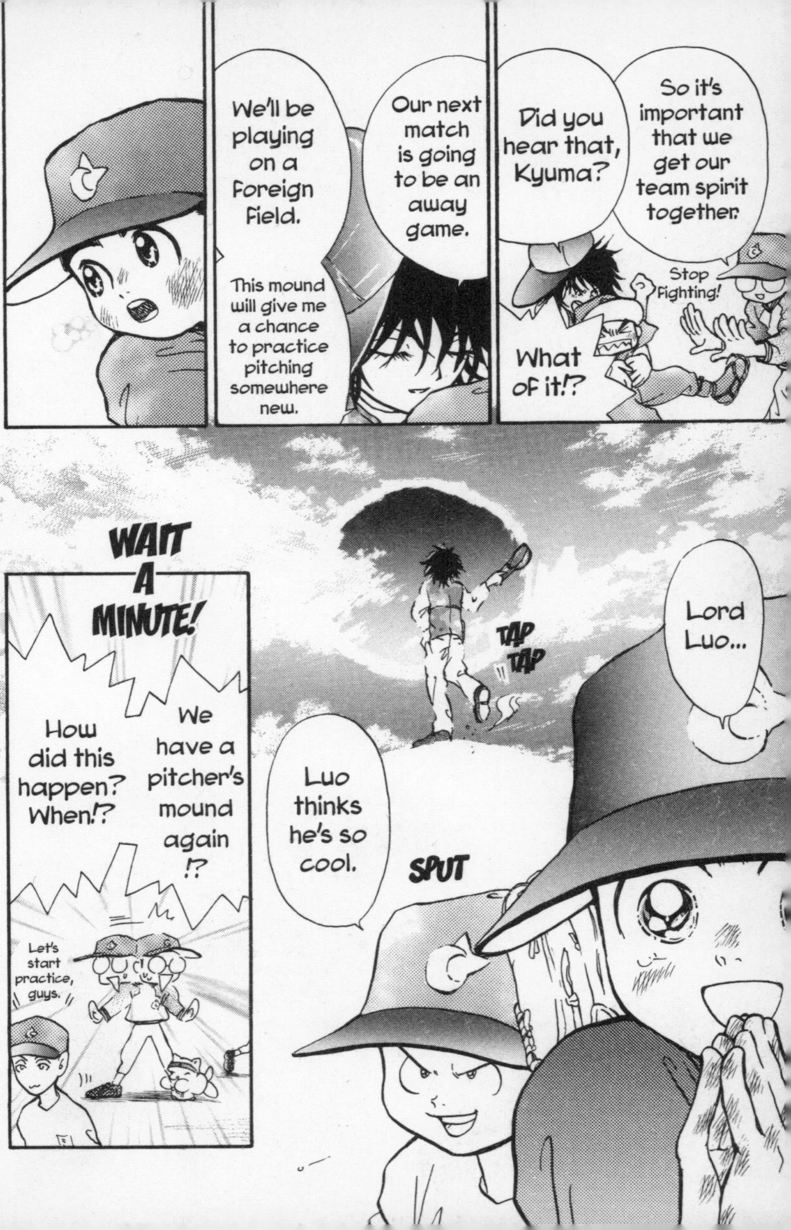
So it's important that we get our team spirit together.
Did you hear that, Kyuma?
Stop Fighting!
What of it!?
Our next match is going to be an away game.
This mound will give me a chance to practice pitching somewhere new.
We'll be playing on a foreign field.
Lord Luo...
TAP TAP
Luo thinks he's so cool.
SPUT
WAIT A MINUTE!
We have a pitcher's mound again!?
How did this happen? When!?
Let's start practice, guys.

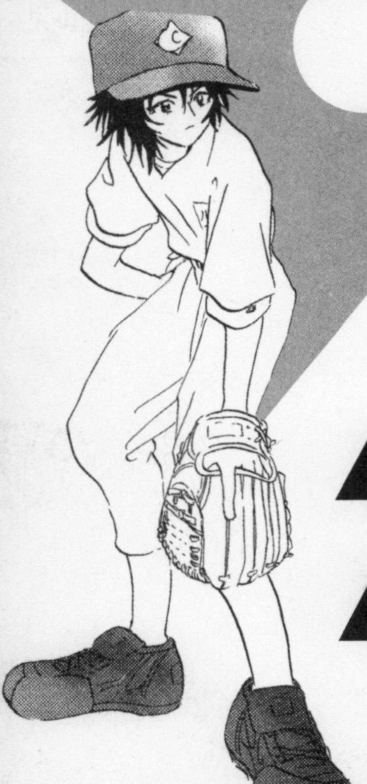

LUO

The team's pitcher. He gets depressed if someone hits one of his pitches. He's the most trendy member of the team.

Tetsu

Full of energy, Tetsu keeps everyone's mood up. He is quick to make new friends.

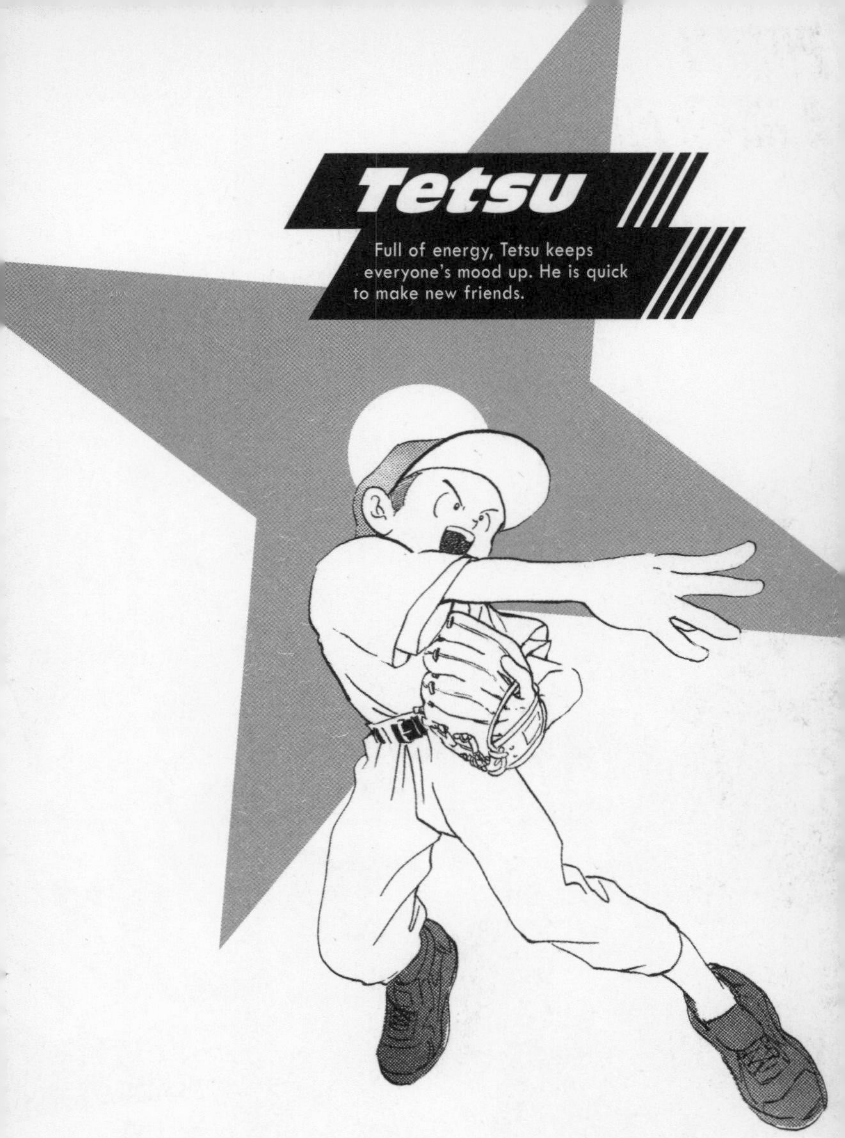

PITCH 4
A TOUGH RIVAL!

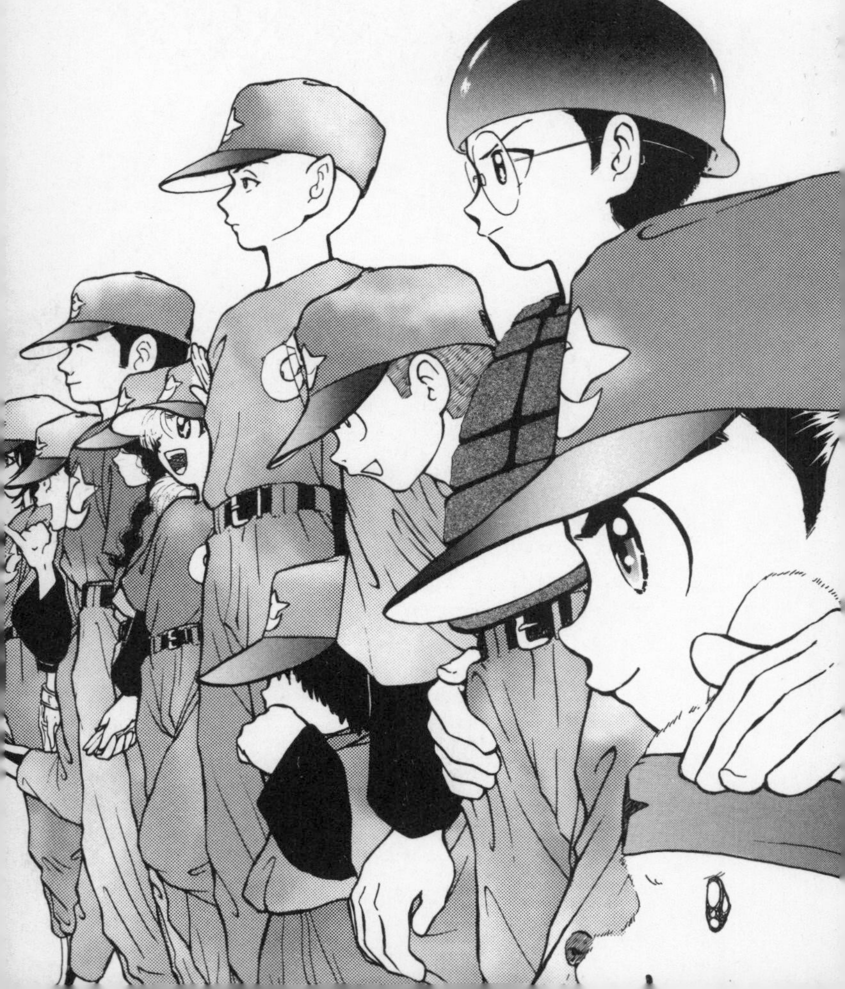

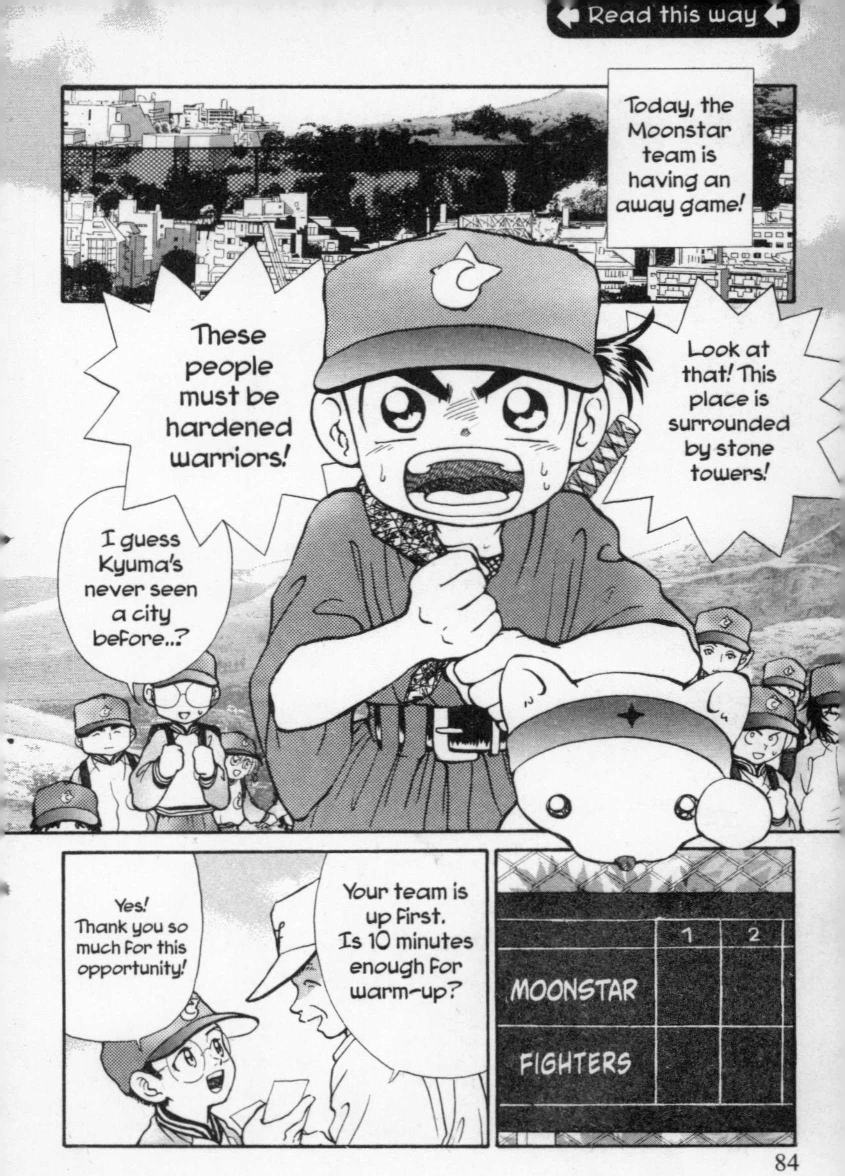
Today, the Moonstar team is having an away game!
Look at that! This place is surrounded by stone towers!
These people must be hardened warriors!
I guess Kyuma's never seen a city before..?
1
2
MOONSTAR
FIGHTERS
Your team is up first. Is 10 minutes enough for warm-up?
Yes! Thank you so much for this opportunity!

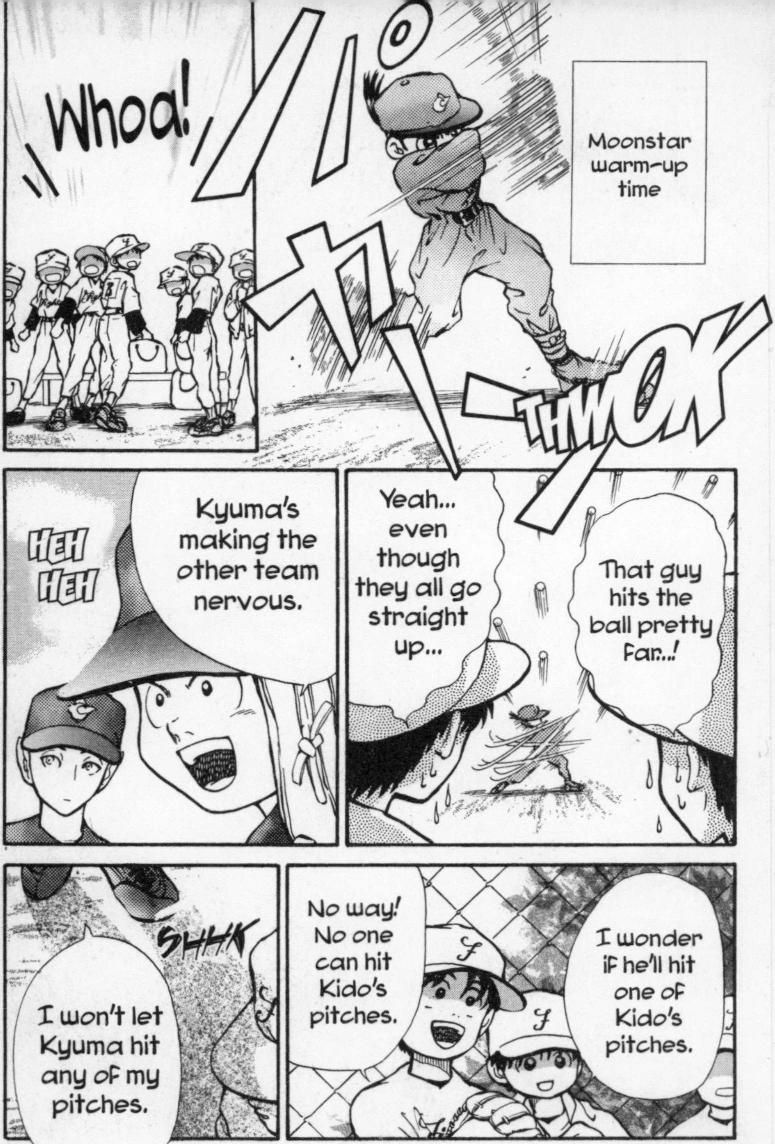
Moonstar warm-up time
THWOCK
Whoa!
That guy hits the ball pretty far...!
Yeah... even though they all go straight up...
Kyuma's making the other team nervous.
HEH HEH
I wonder if he'll hit one of Kido's pitches.
No way! No one can hit Kido's pitches.
SHHK
I won't let Kyuma hit any of my pitches.

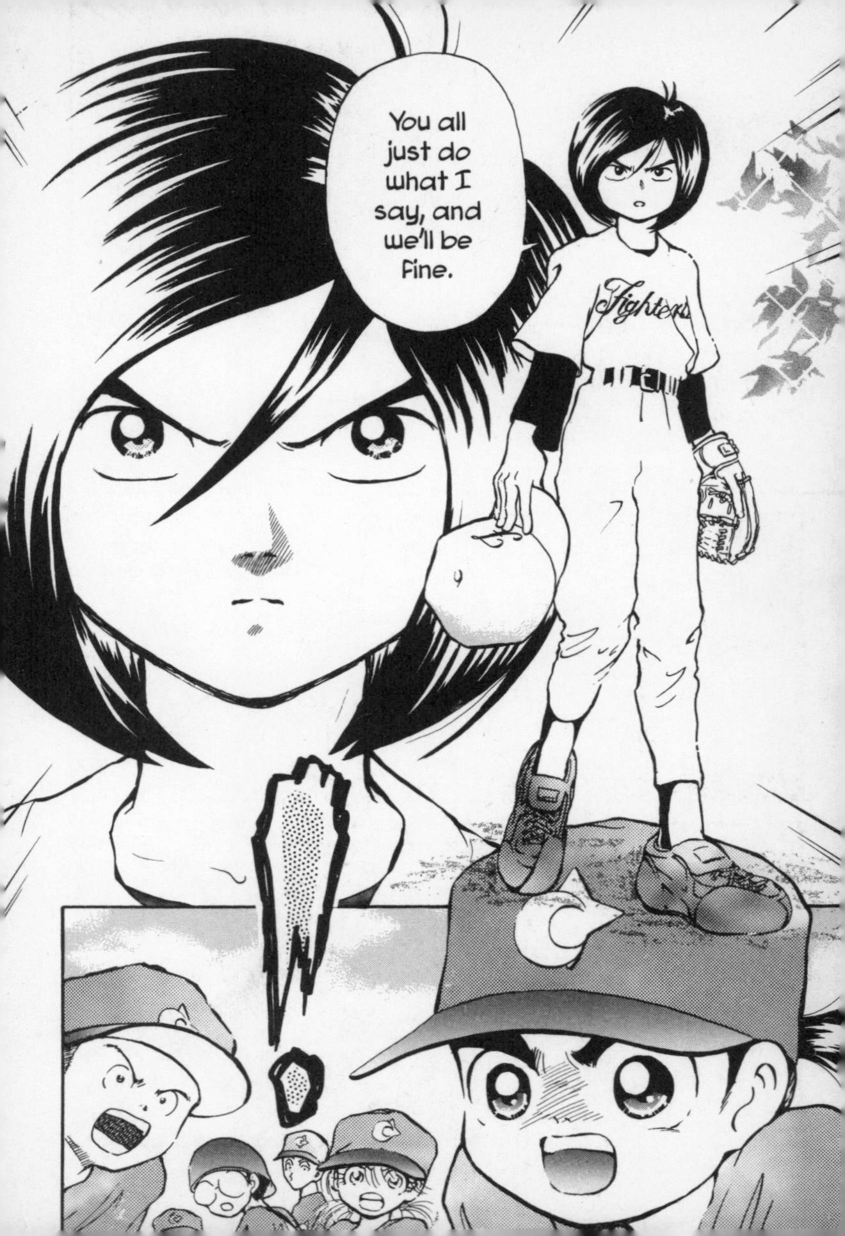
You all just do what I say, and we'll be fine.

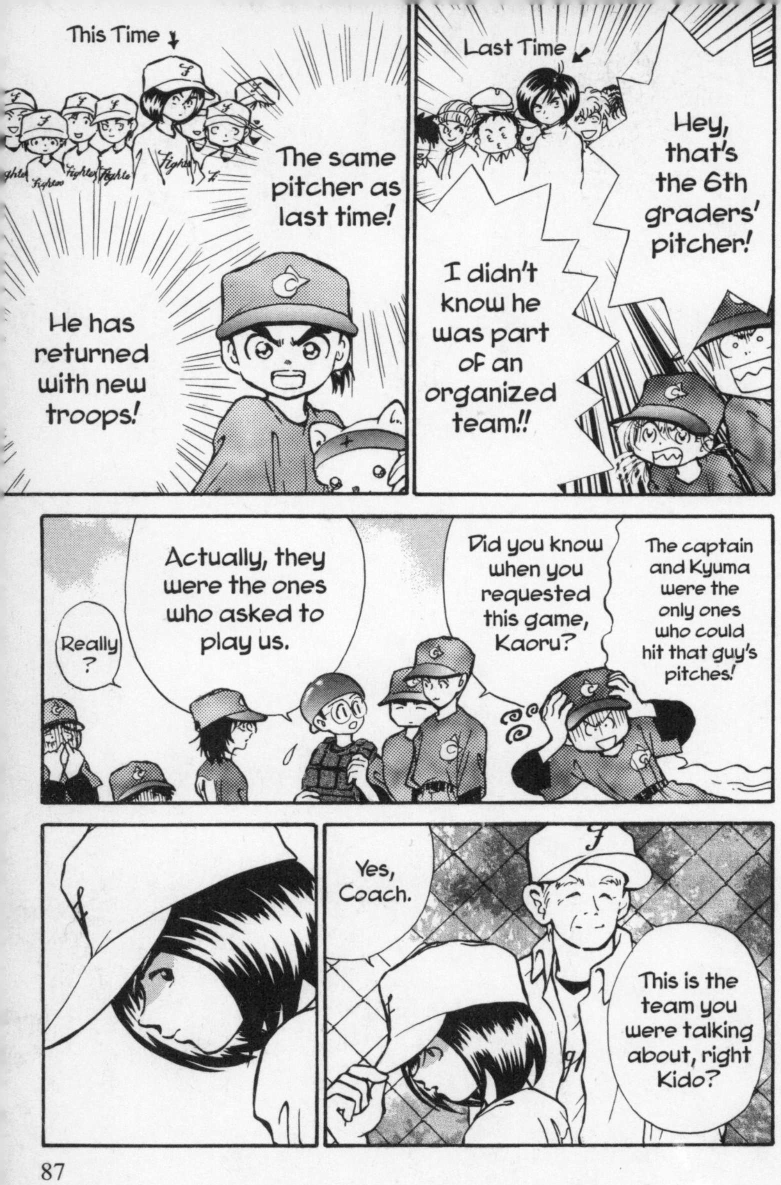

Last Time
Hey, that's the 6th graders' pitcher!
I didn't know he was part of an organized team!!
This Time
The same pitcher as last time!
He has returned with new troops!
The captain and Kyuma were the only ones who could hit that guy's pitches!
Did you know when you requested this game, Kaoru?
Actually, they were the ones who asked to play us.
Really?
This is the team you were talking about, right Kido?
Yes, Coach.

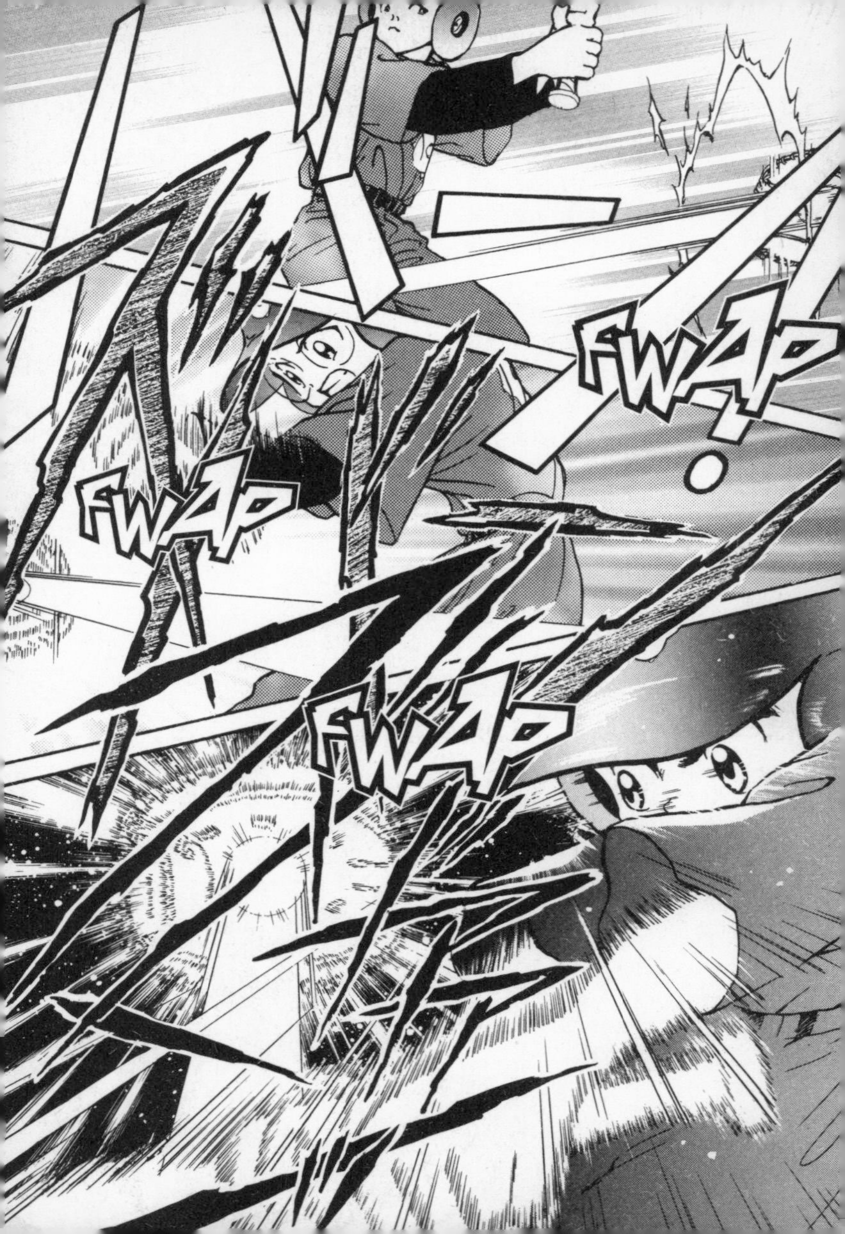
FWAP
FWAP
FWAP

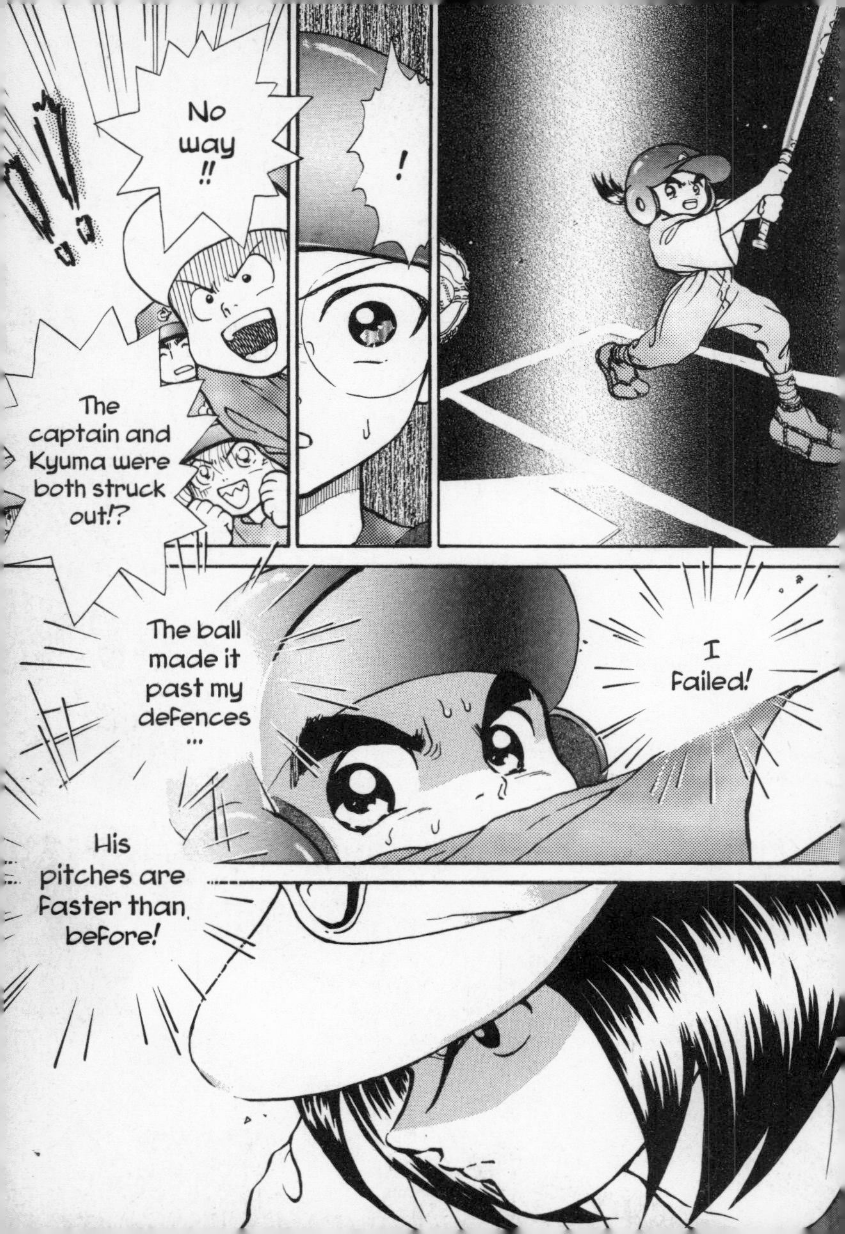
!
No way !!
The captain and Kyuma were both struck out!?
I Failed!
The ball made it past my defences ...
His pitches are faster than before!

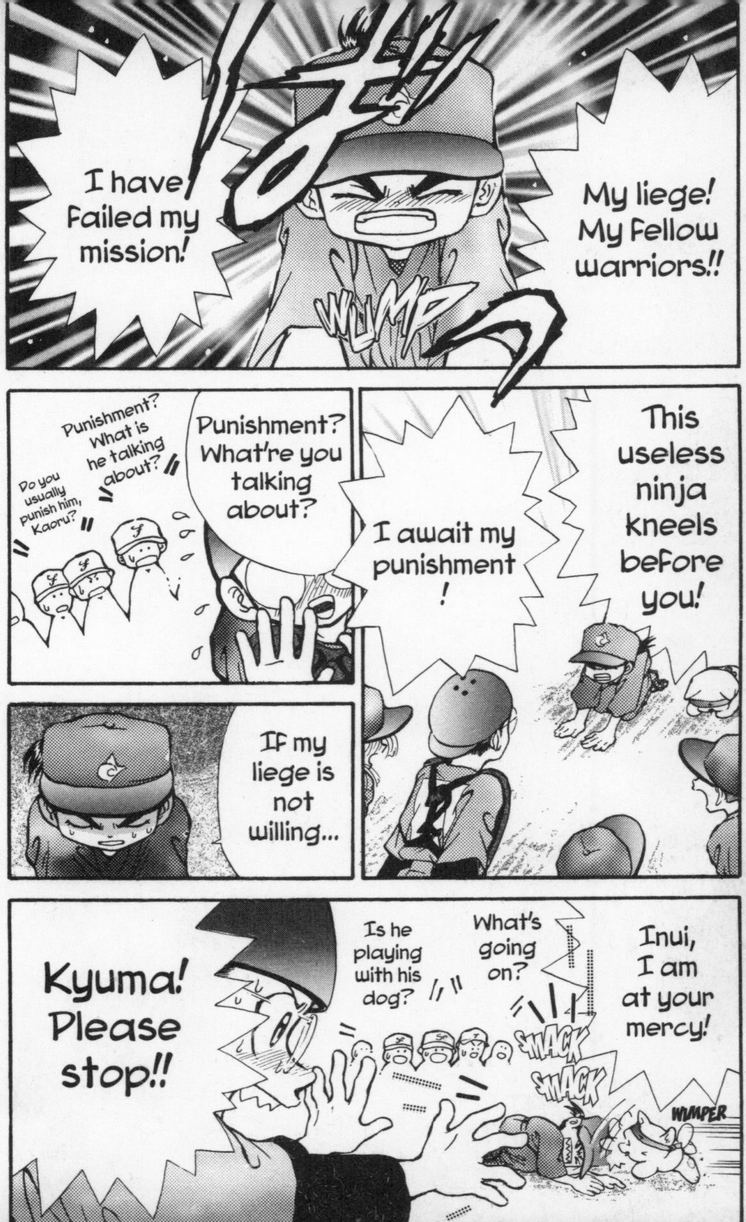
My liege! My fellow warriors!!
I have failed my mission!
WUMP
This useless ninja kneels before you!
I await my punishment!
Punishment? What're you talking about?
Punishment? What is he talking about?
Do you usually punish him, Kaoru?
If my liege is not willing...
Inui, I am at your mercy!
SMACK
SMACK
WIMPER
What's going on?
Is he playing with his dog?
Kyuma! Please stop!!

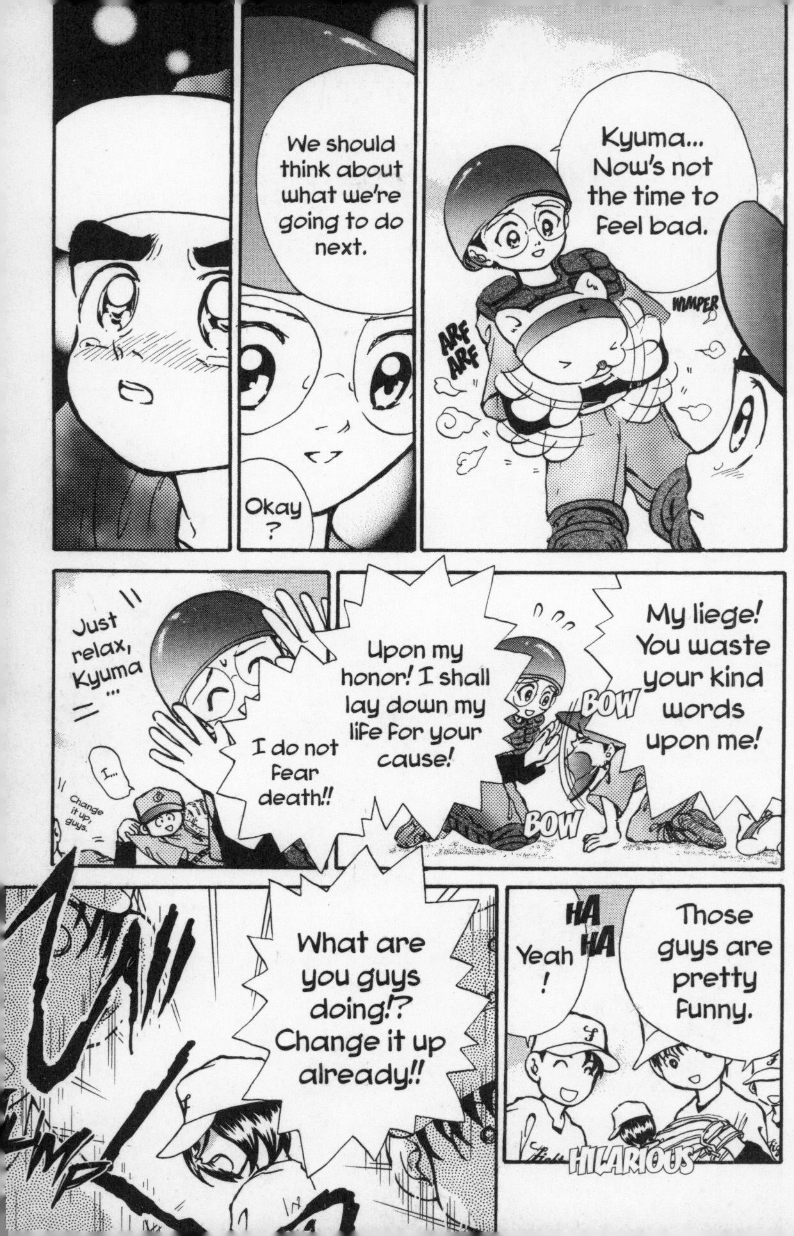
Kyuma... Now's not the time to feel bad.
WIMPER
ARF ARF
We should think about what we're going to do next.
Okay?
My liege! You waste your kind words upon me!
BOW
BOW
Upon my honor! I shall lay down my life for your cause!
Just relax, Kyuma...
I do not fear death!!
I...
Change it up, guys.
Those guys are pretty funny.
HA HA
Yeah!
HILARIOUS
What are you guys doing!? Change it up already!!

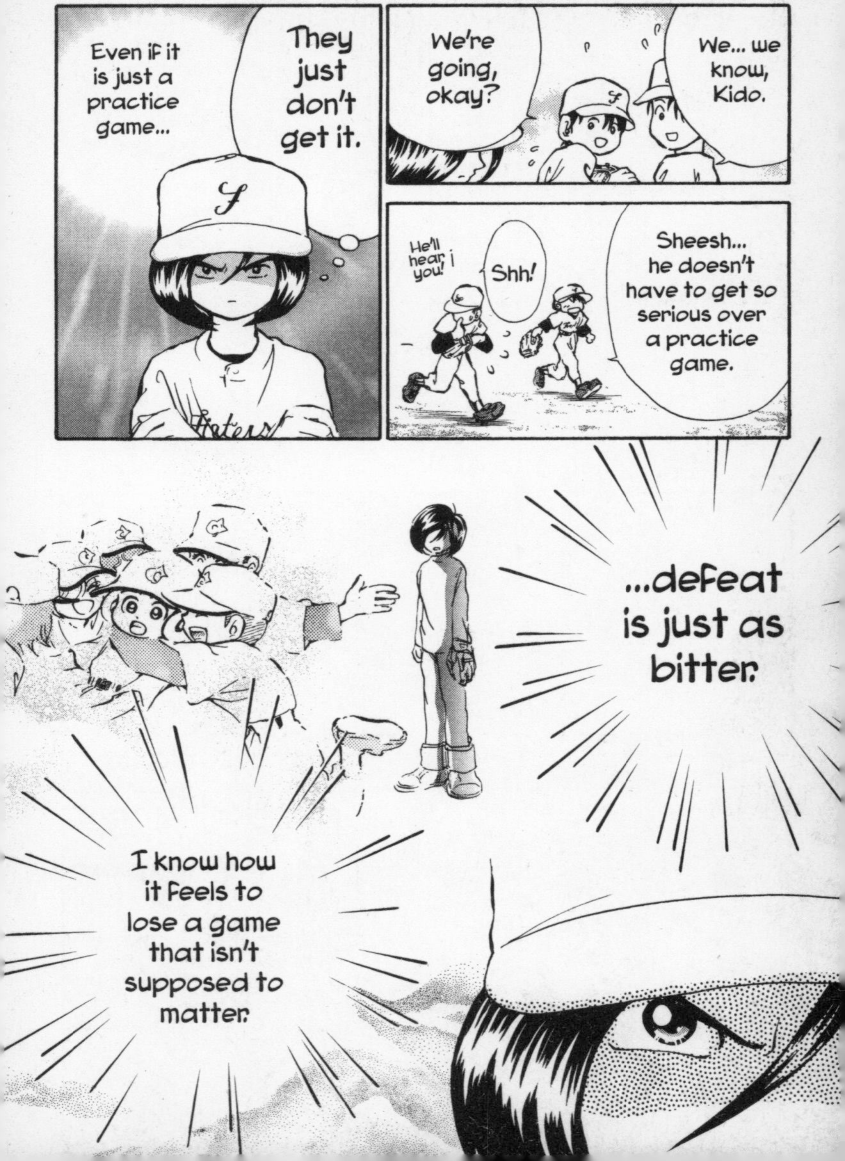
We... we know, Kido.
We're going, okay?
Sheesh... he doesn't have to get so serious over a practice game.
Shh!
He'll hear you!
They just don't get it.
Even if it is just a practice game...
...defeat is just as bitter.
I know how it feels to lose a game that isn't supposed to matter.

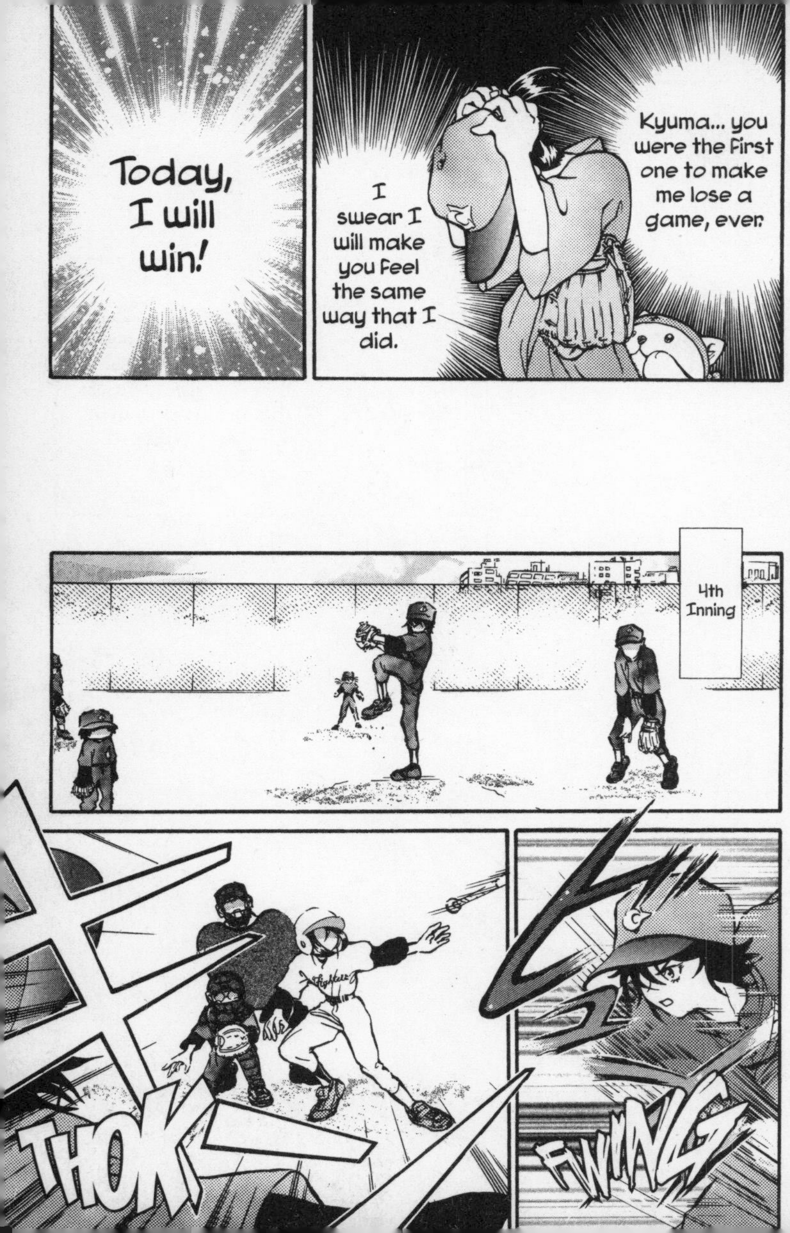
Kyuma... you were the first one to make me lose a game, ever.
I swear I will make you feel the same way that I did.
Today, I will win!
4th Inning
FWING
THOK

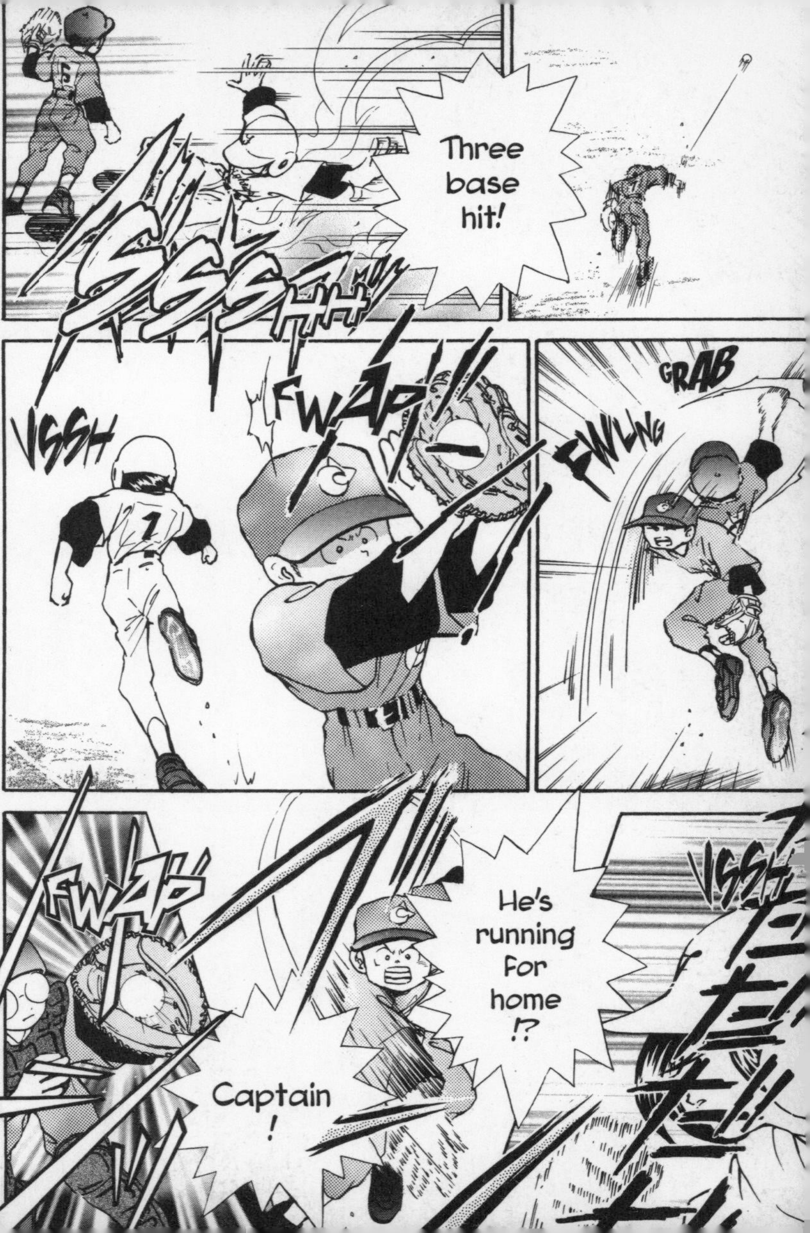
Three base hit!
SSSHHH
GRAB
FWUNG
FWAP
VSSH
VSSH
He's running for home !?
FWAP
Captain !

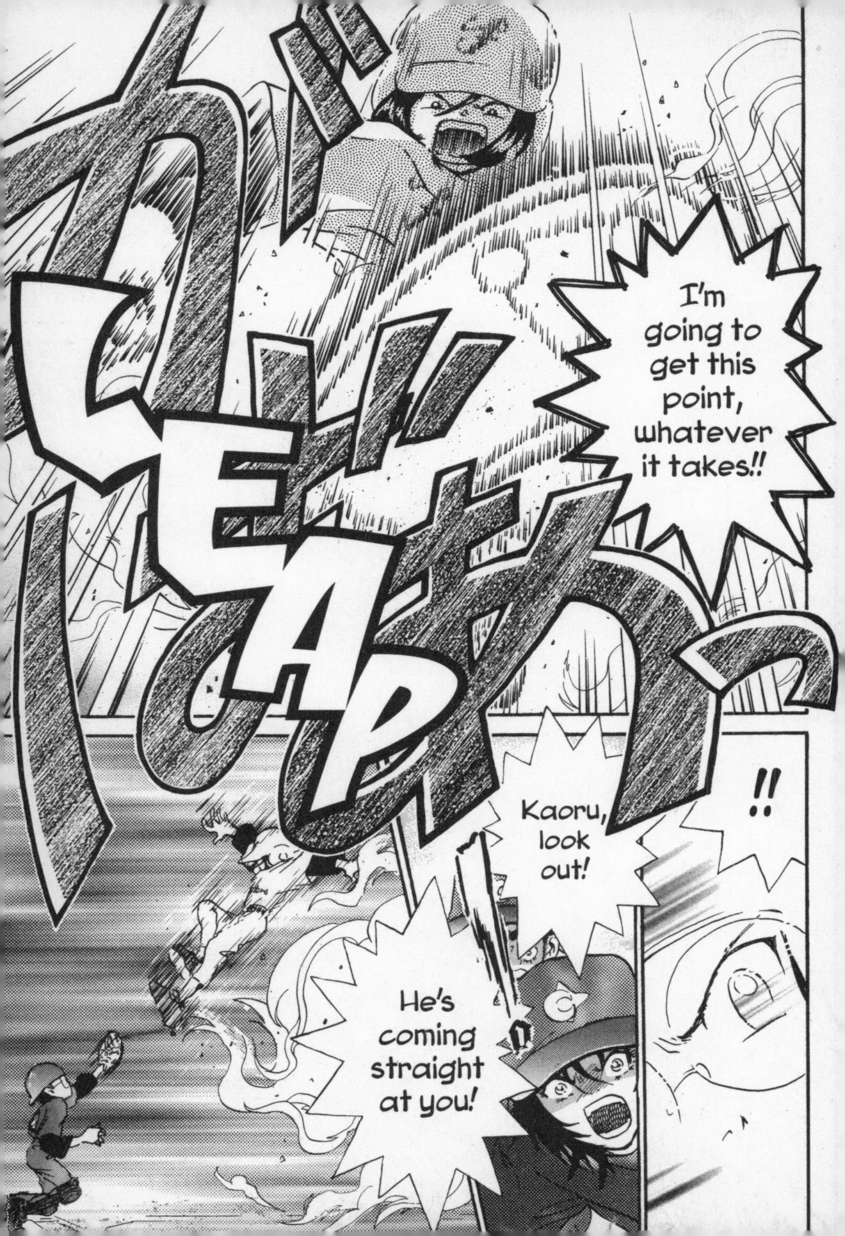
I'm going to get this point, whatever it takes!!
LEAP
!!
Kaoru, look out!
He's coming straight at you!

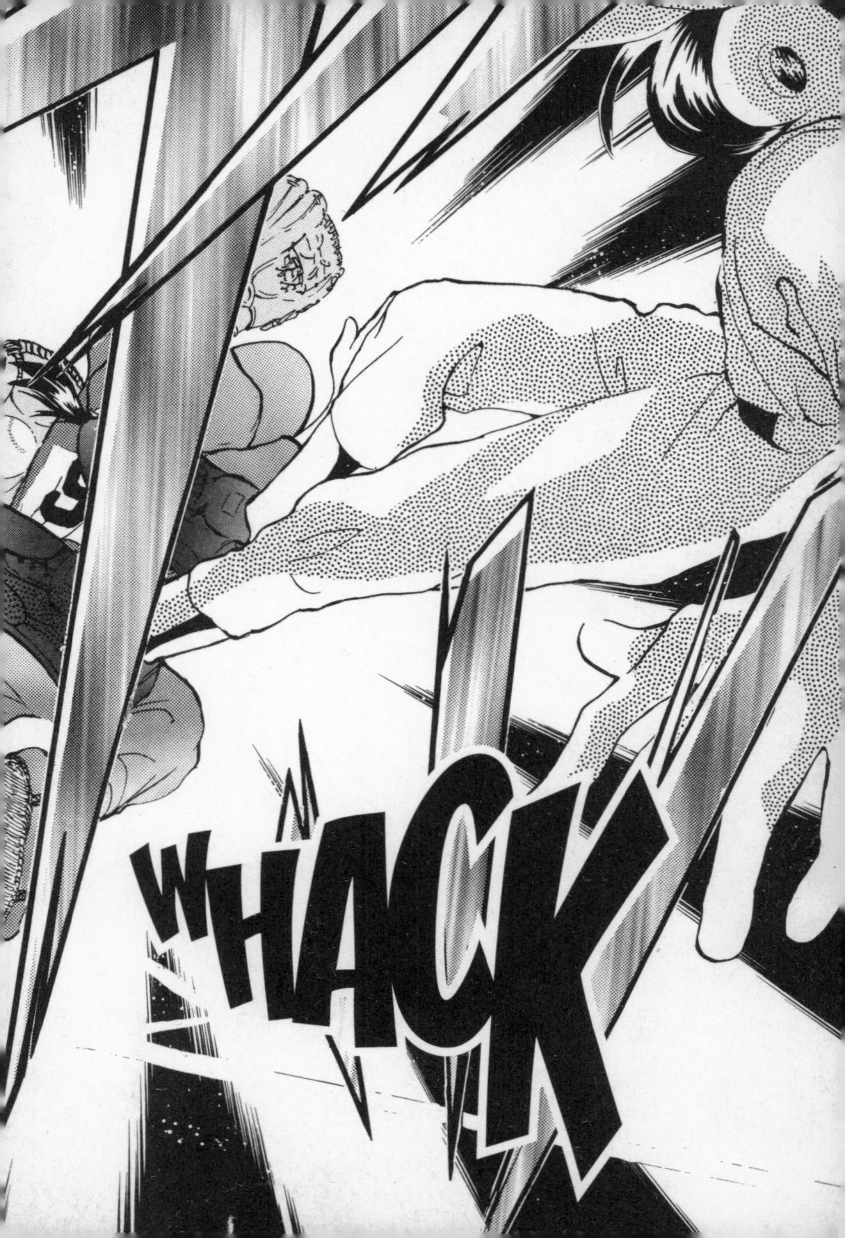
WHACK

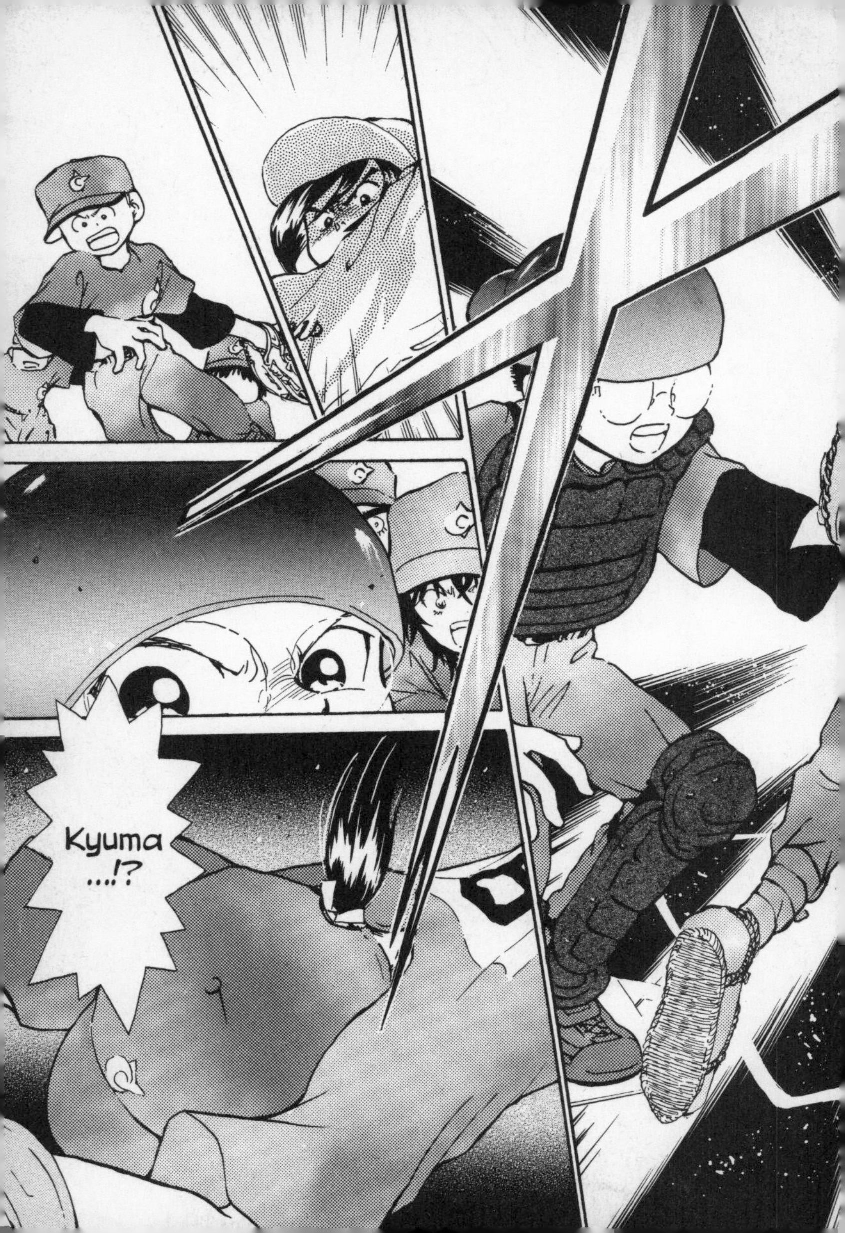
Kyuma ...!?

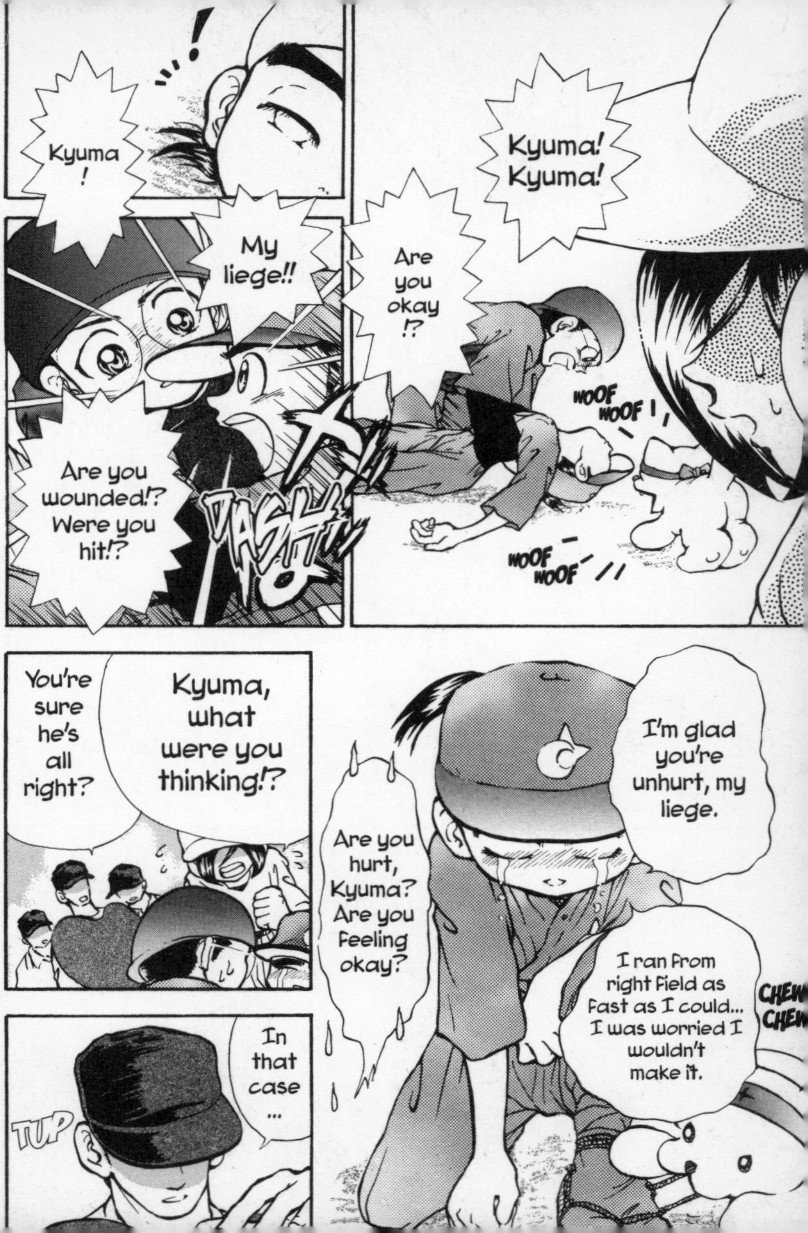
Kyuma! Kyuma!
Are you okay!?
WOOF WOOF
WOOF WOOF
Kyuma!
My liege!!
Are you wounded!? Were you hit!?
DASH
I'm glad you're unhurt, my liege.
Are you hurt, Kyuma? Are you feeling okay?
I ran from right field as fast as I could... I was worried I wouldn't make it.
Kyuma, what were you thinking!?
You're sure he's all right?
In that case ...
TUP

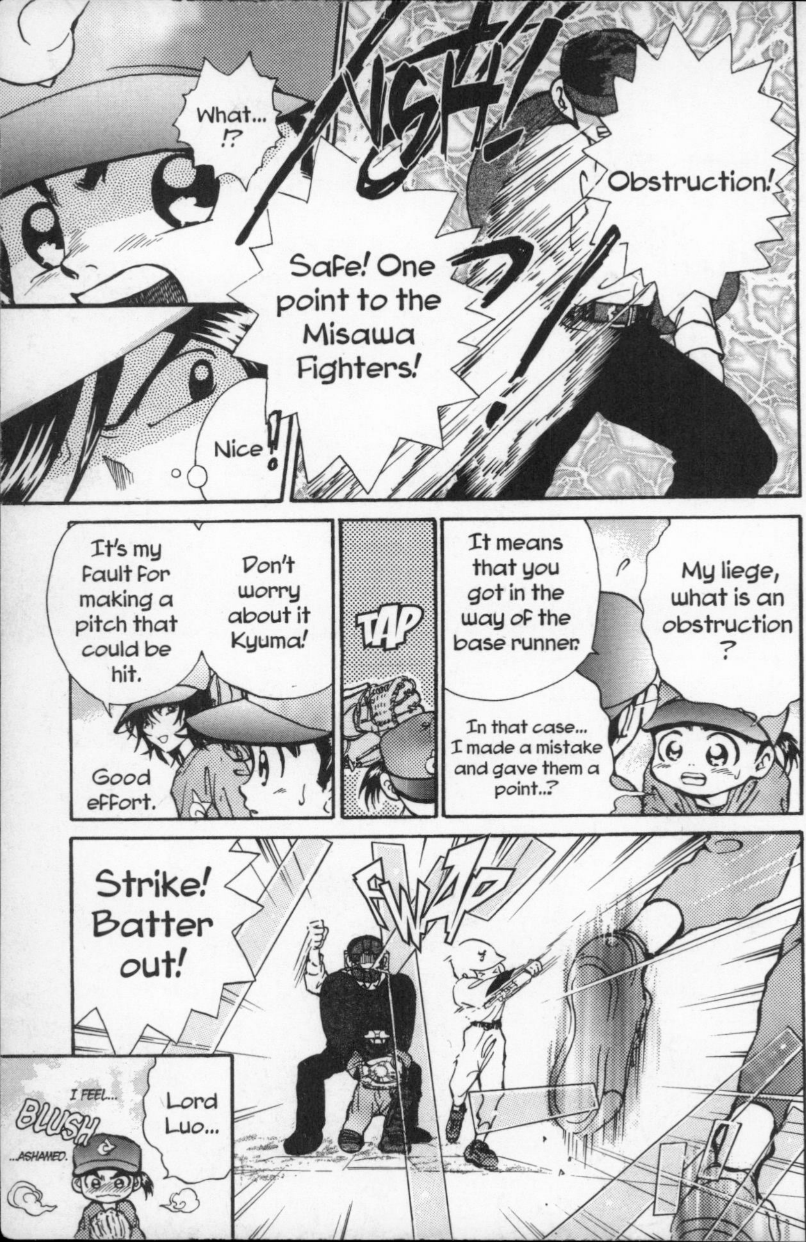
Obstruction!
Safe! One point to the Misawa Fighters!
What... !?
Nice!
My liege, what is an obstruction?
It means that you got in the way of the base runner.
In that case... I made a mistake and gave them a point..?
TAP
Don't worry about it Kyuma!
It's my fault for making a pitch that could be hit.
Good effort.
Strike! Batter out!
Lord Luo...
I FEEL...
BLUSH
...ASHAMED.

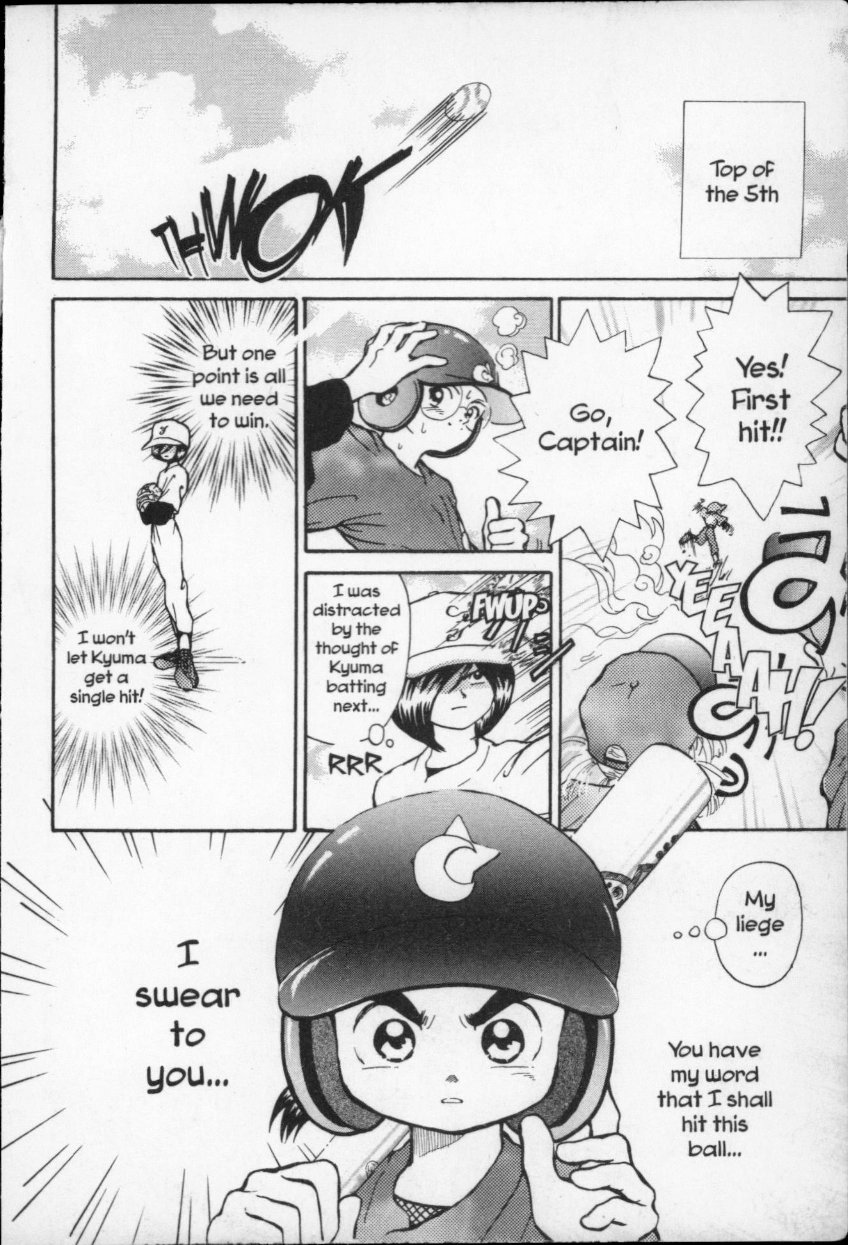
Top of the 5th
THWOK
Yes! First hit!!
YEEEAAAH!
Go, Captain!
FWUP
I was distracted by the thought of Kyuma batting next...
RRR
But one point is all we need to win.
I won't let Kyuma get a single hit!
My liege...
You have my word that I shall hit this ball...
I swear to you...

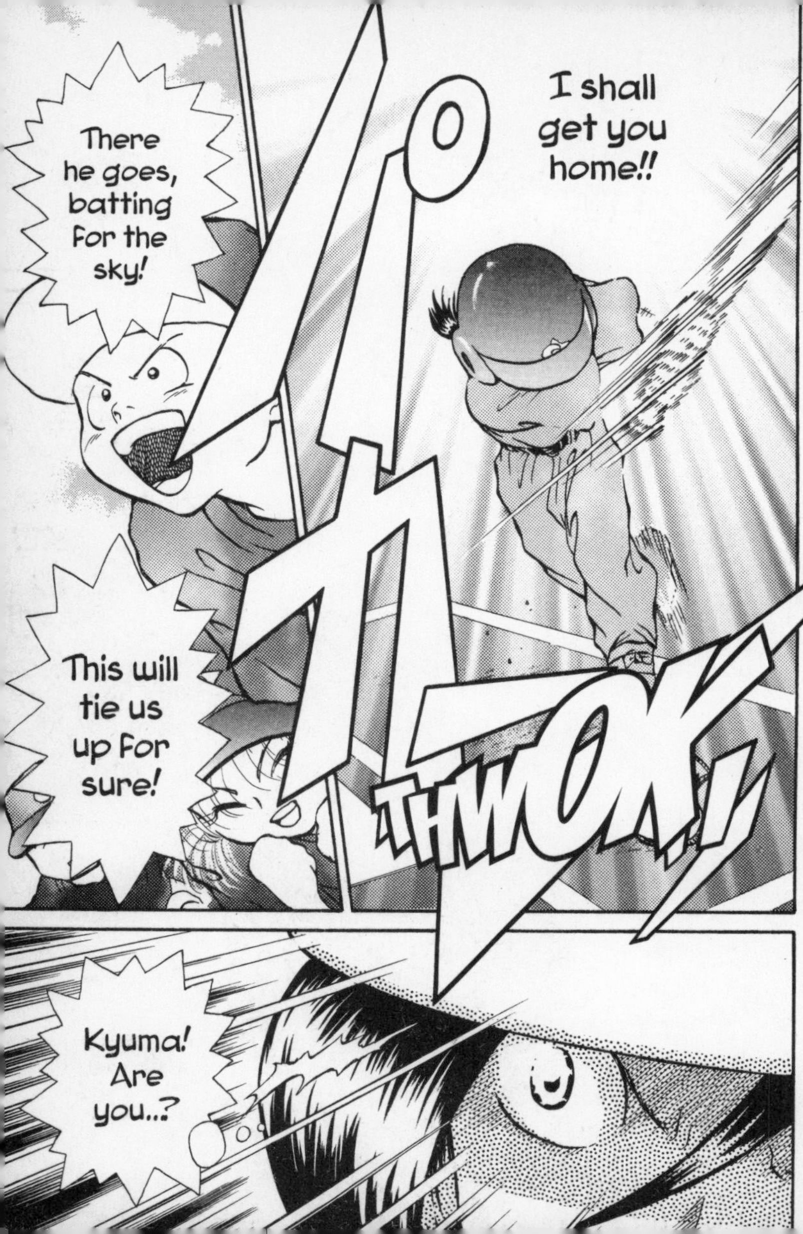
I shall get you home!!
There he goes, batting for the sky!
This will tie us up for sure!
THWOK!
Kyuma! Are you..?

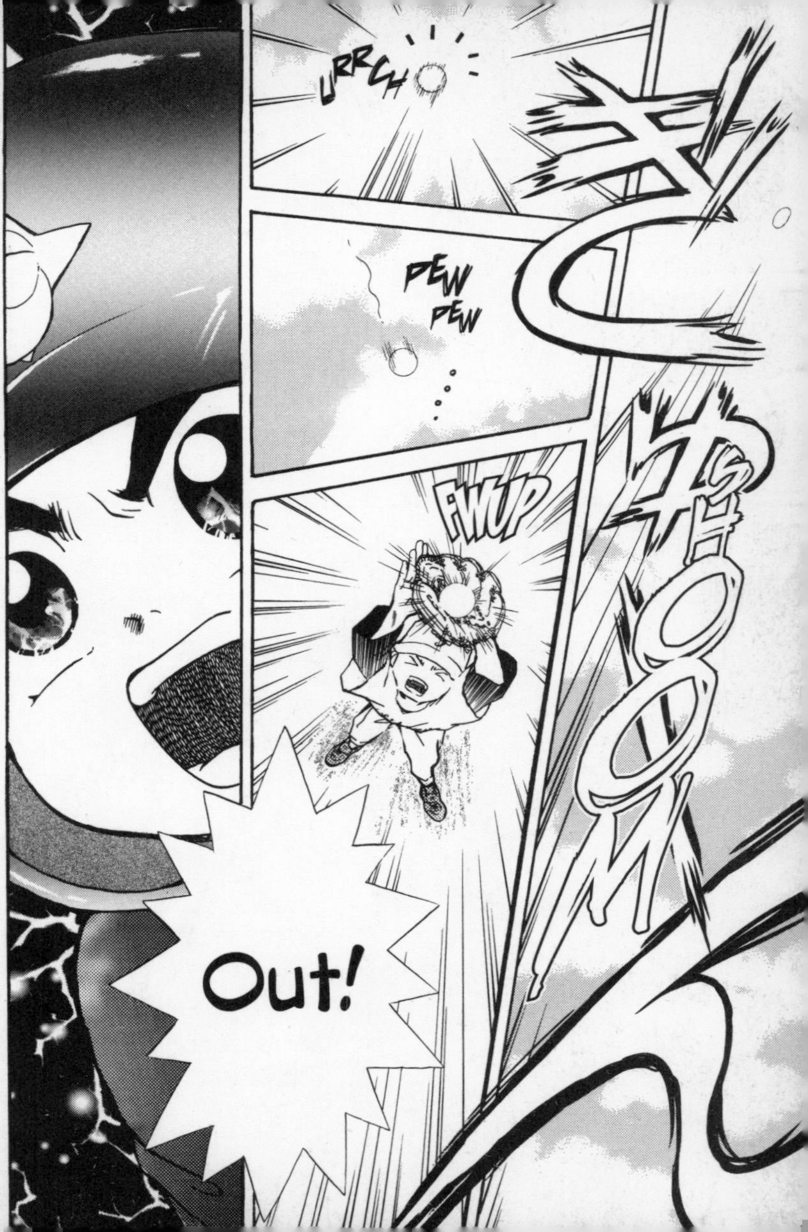
URRCH
PEW PEW
FWUP
Out!

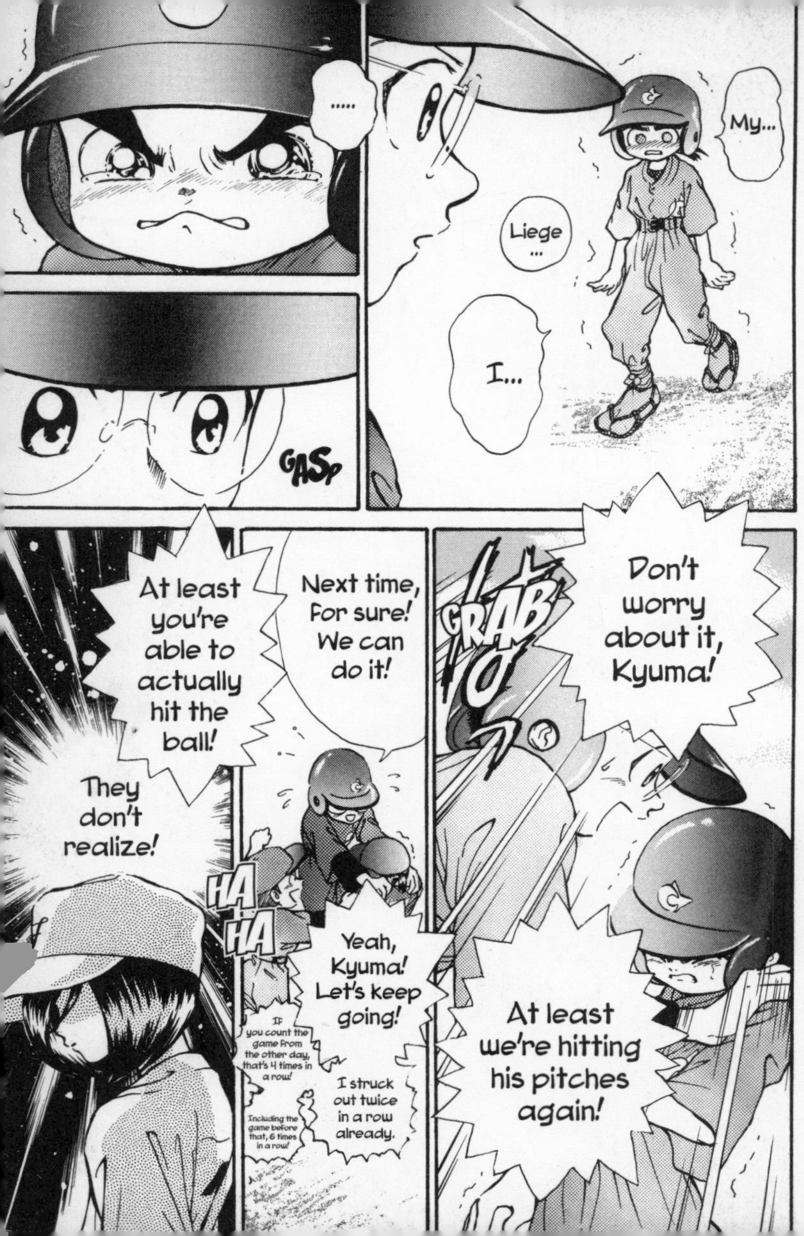
My...
Liege ...
I...
.....
GASP
Don't worry about it, Kyuma!
GRAB
At least we're hitting his pitches again!
Next time, for sure! We can do it!
HA HA
Yeah, Kyuma! Let's keep going!
I struck out twice in a row already.
If you count the game from the other day, that's 4 times in a row!
Including the game before that, 6 times in a row!
At least you're able to actually hit the ball!
They don't realize!

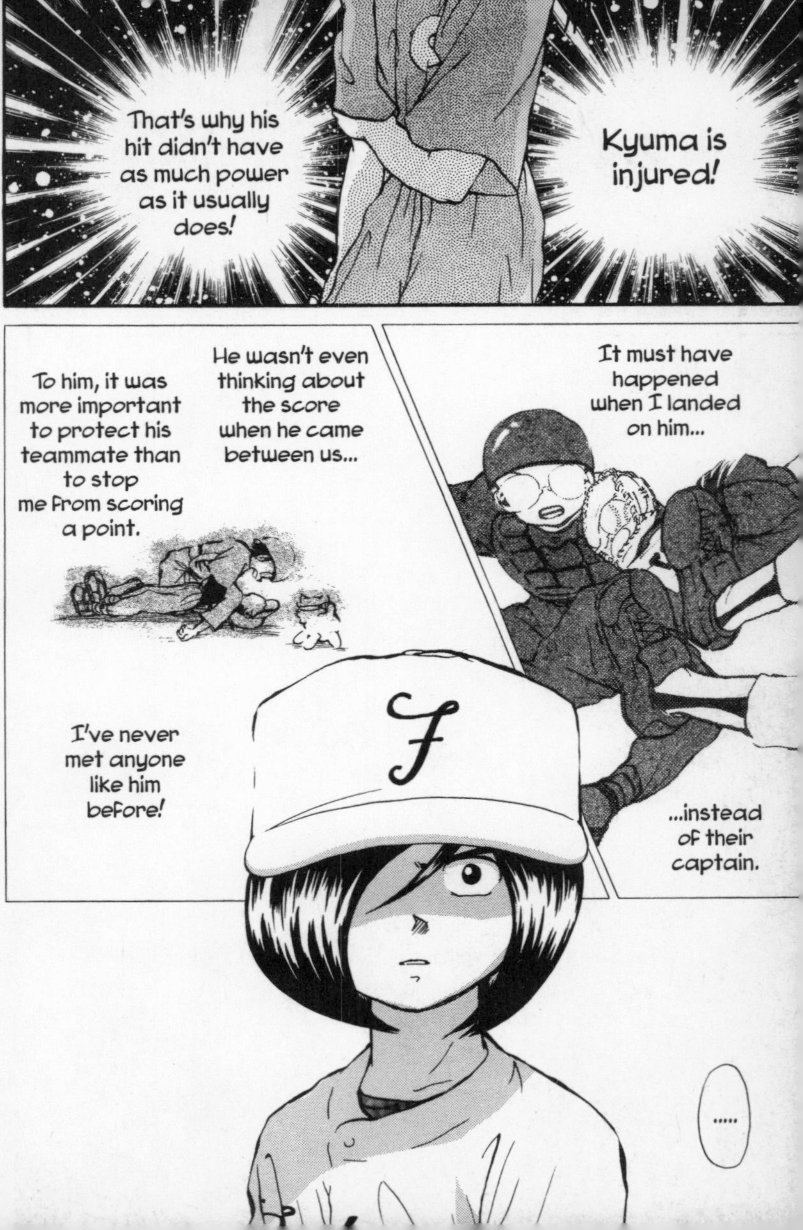
Kyuma is injured!
That's why his hit didn't have as much power as it usually does!
It must have happened when I landed on him...
...instead of their captain.
He wasn't even thinking about the score when he came between us...
To him, it was more important to protect his teammate than to stop me from scoring a point.
I've never met anyone like him before!
.....

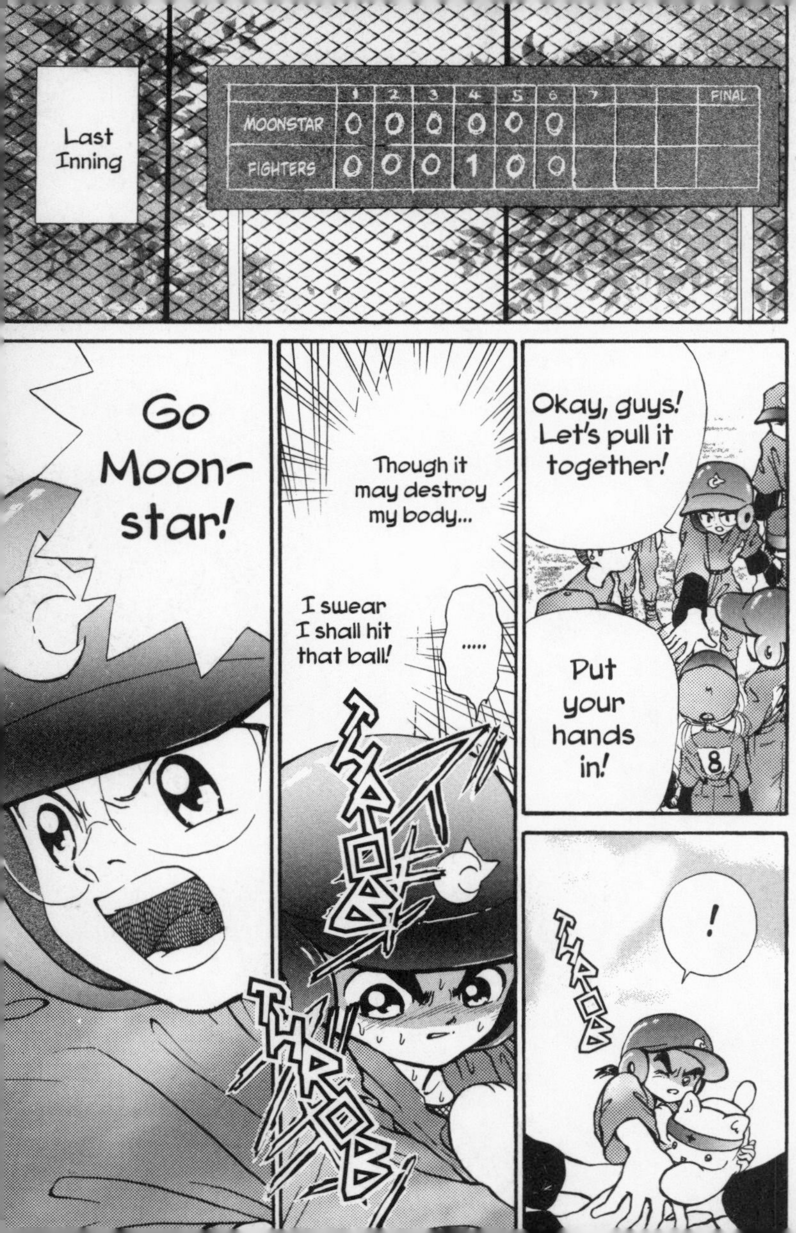
Last Inning
1 2 3 4 5 6 7 FINAL
MOONSTAR 0 0 0 0 0 0
FIGHTERS 0 0 0 1 0 0
Okay, guys! Let's pull it together!
Put your hands in!
!
THROB
Though it may destroy my body...
I swear I shall hit that ball!
.....
THROB
THROB
THROB
Go Moon-star!

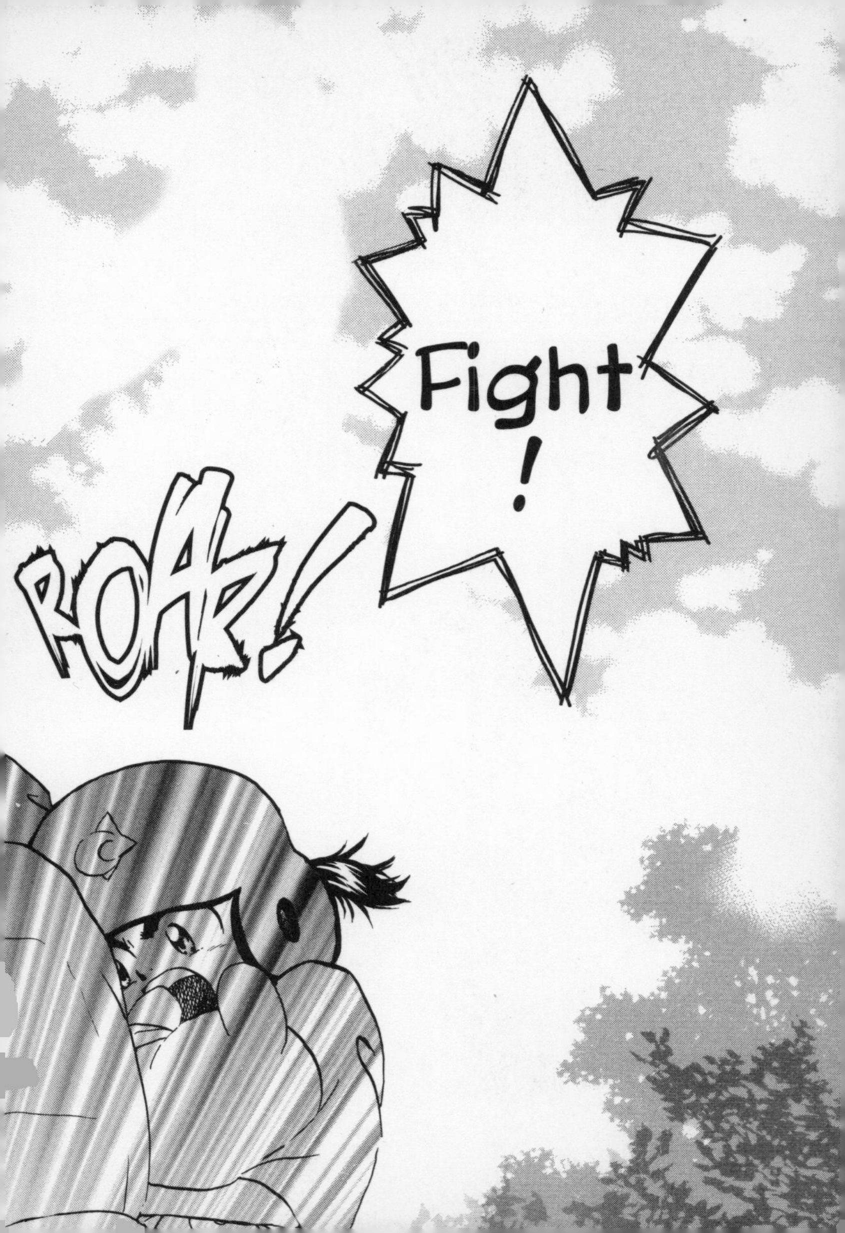

Fight!
ROAR!

Kunosuke

Kunosuke is very flexible, and will sometimes move in strange ways. He is very picky about staying clean all the time.

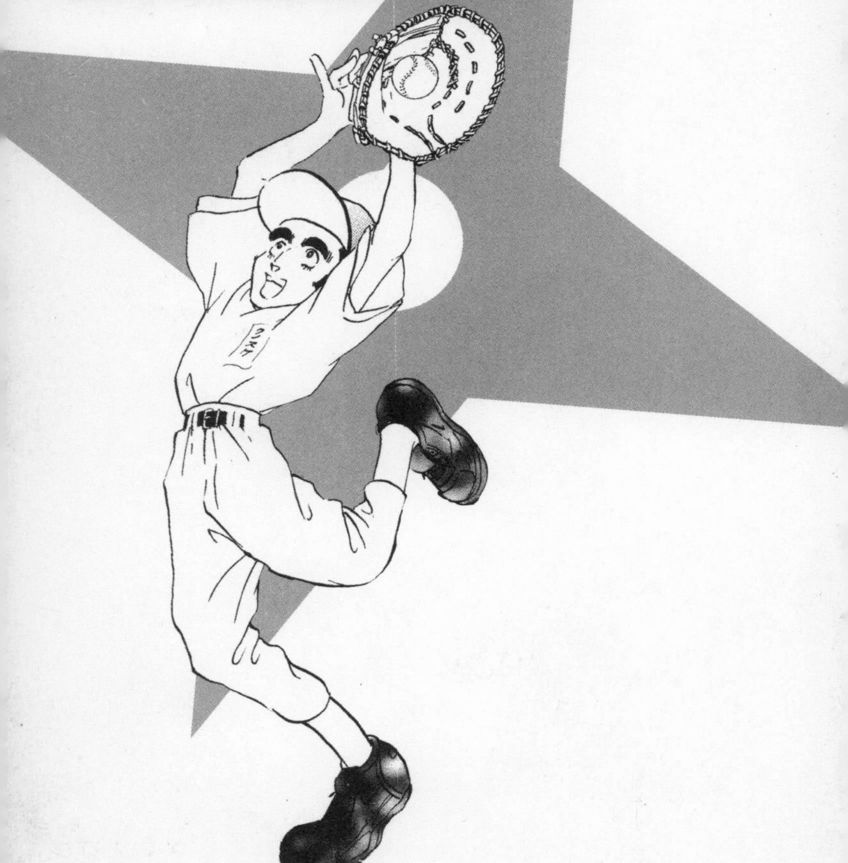

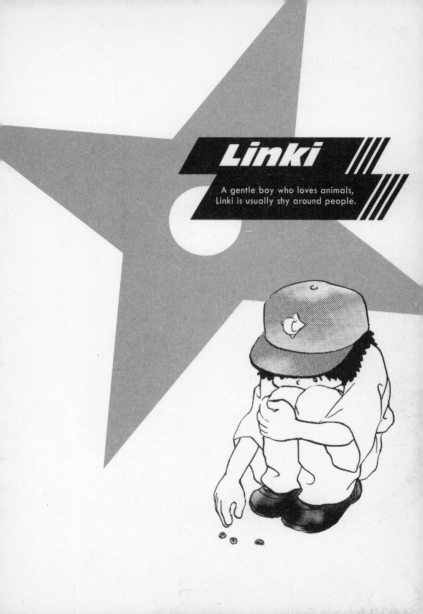

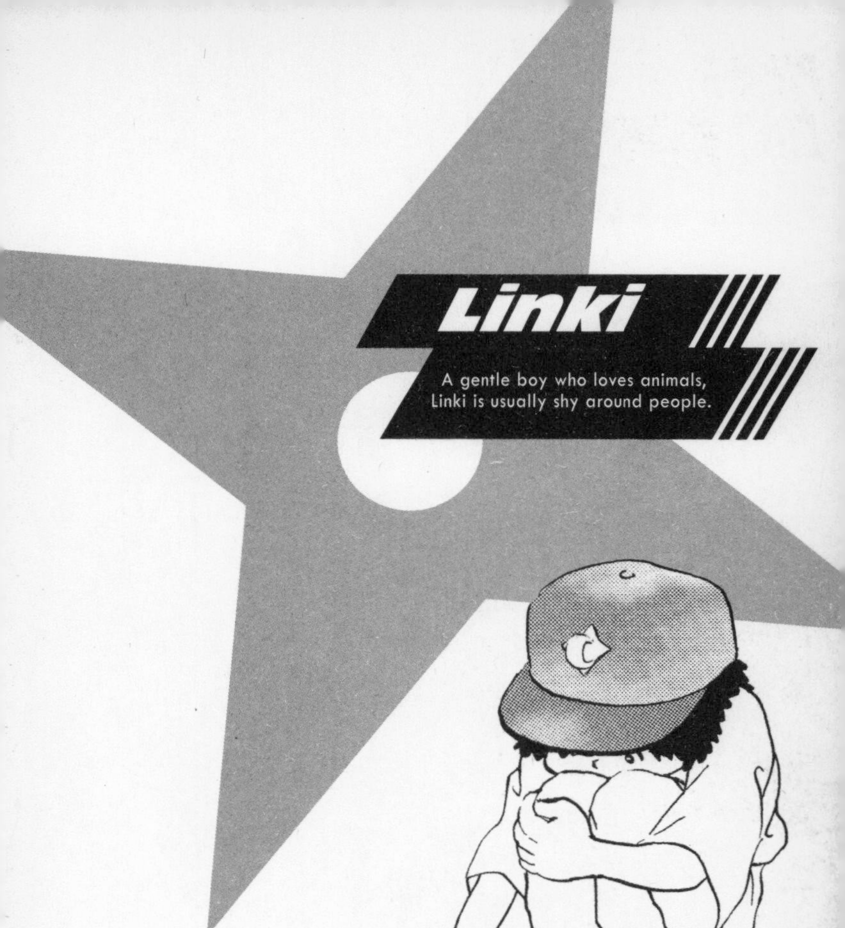
Linki
A gentle boy who loves animals,
Linki is usually shy around people.

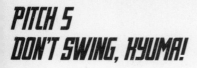

PITCH 5
DON'T SWING, KYUMA!

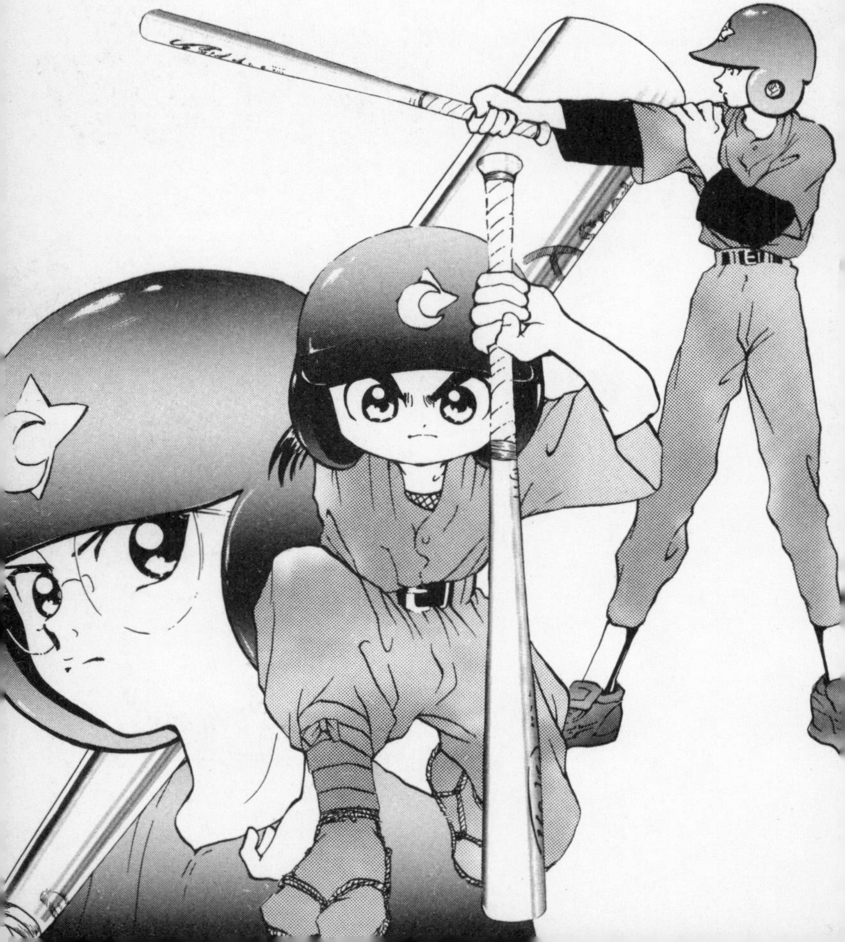

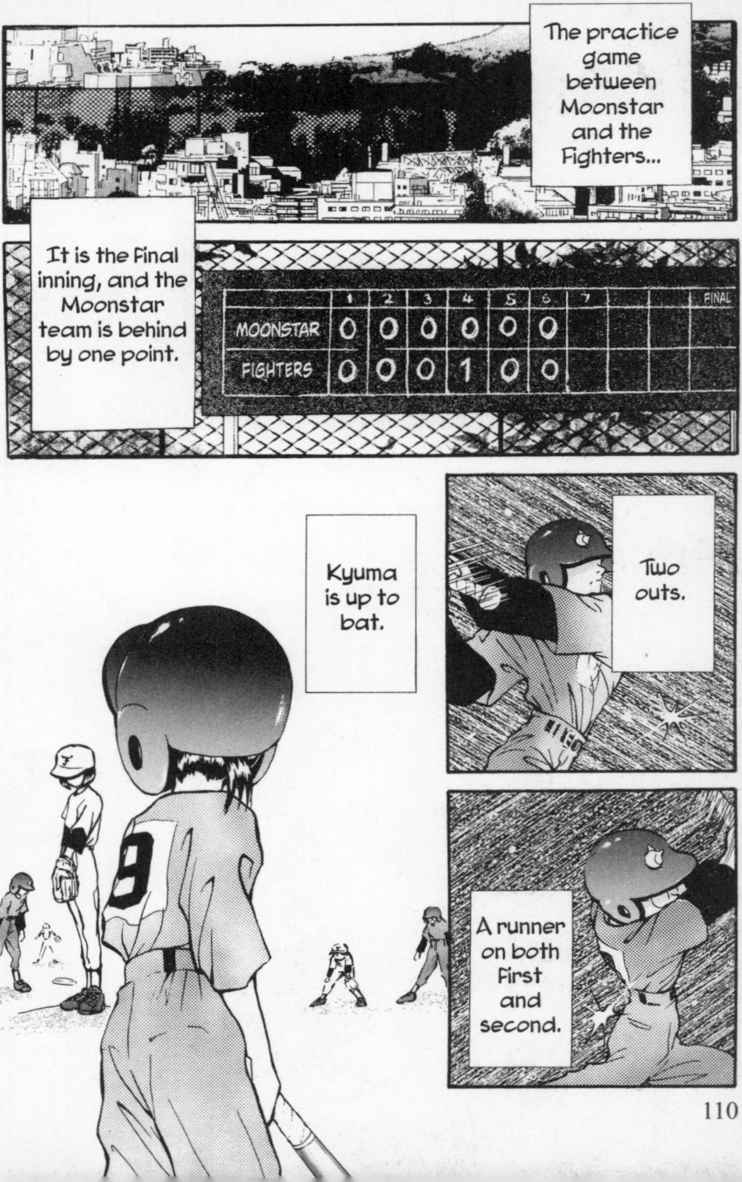
The practice game between Moonstar and the Fighters...
It is the final inning, and the Moonstar team is behind by one point.
1 2 3 4 5 6 7 FINAL
MOONSTAR 0 0 0 0 0 0
FIGHTERS 0 0 0 1 0 0
Two outs.
A runner on both first and second.
Kyuma is up to bat.

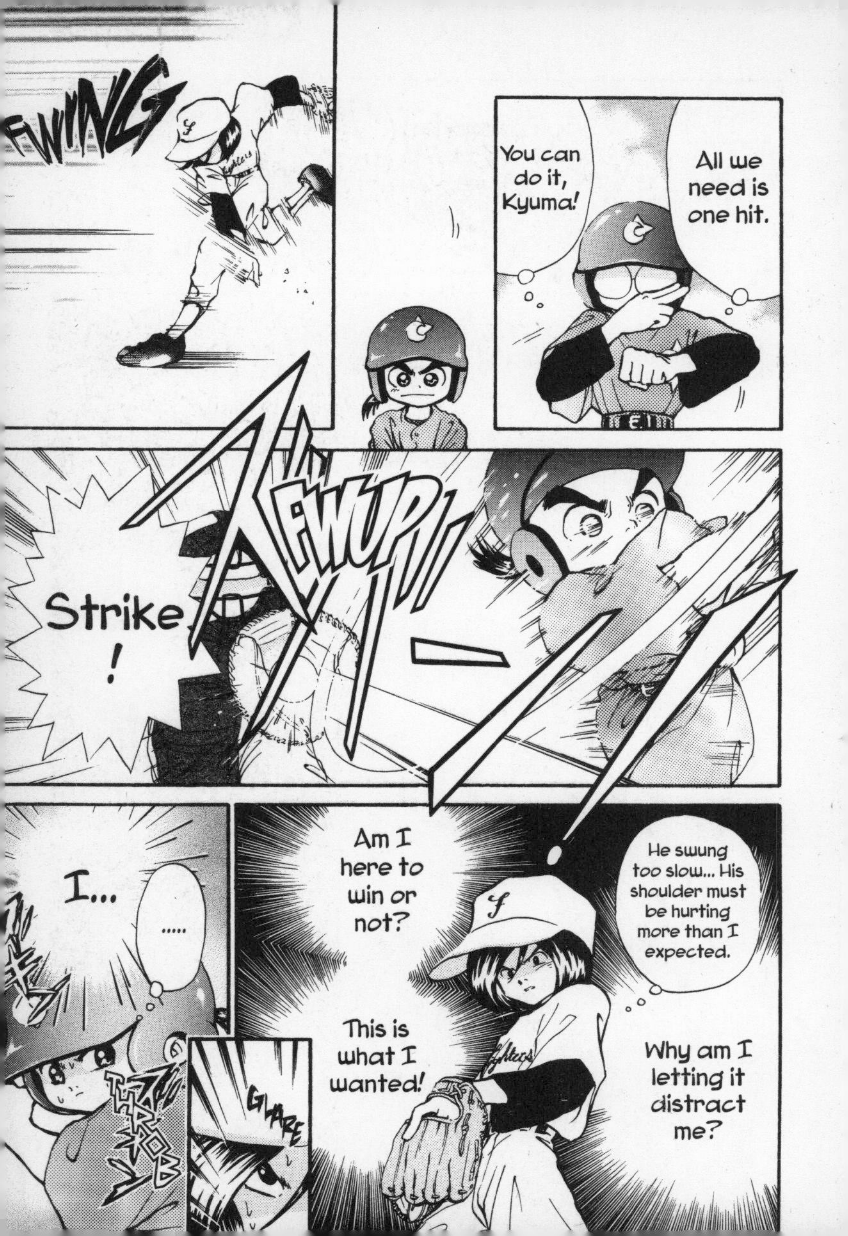
All we need is one hit.
You can do it, Kyuma!
FWING
KFWUP
Strike!
He swung too slow... His shoulder must be hurting more than I expected.
Am I here to win or not?
Why am I letting it distract me?
This is what I wanted!
I...
.....
THROB
GLARE

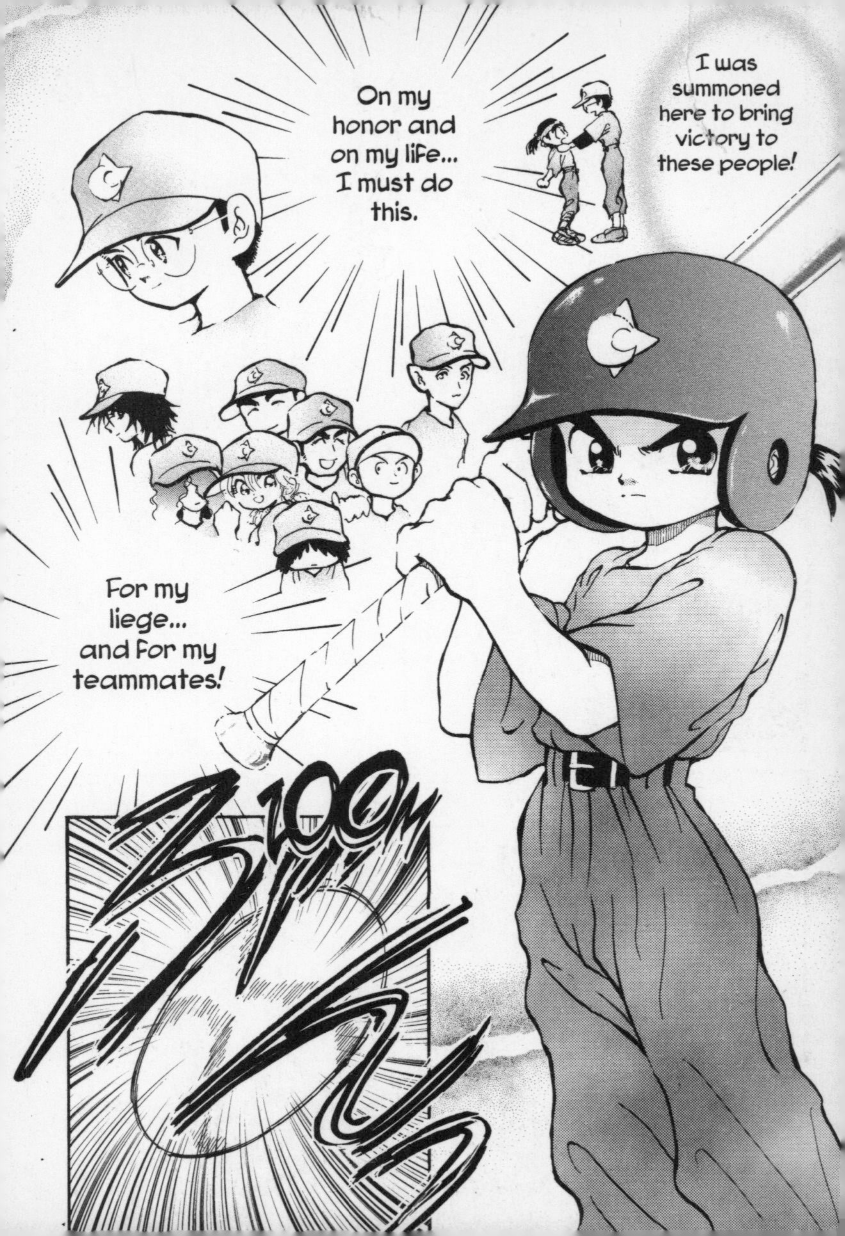
I was summoned here to bring victory to these people!
On my honor and on my life... I must do this.
For my liege... and for my teammates!

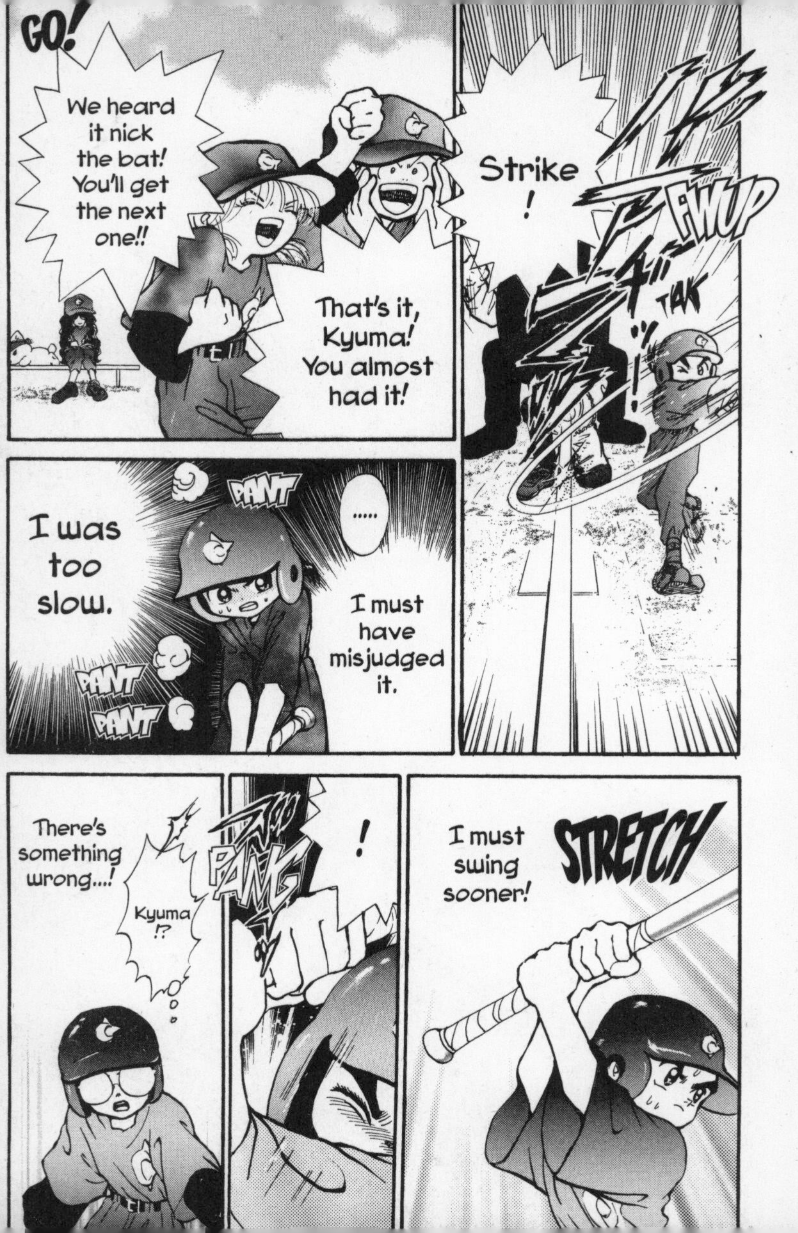
Strike!
FWUP
TAK
GO!
We heard it nick the bat! You'll get the next one!!
That's it, Kyuma! You almost had it!
.....
PANT
I was too slow.
I must have misjudged it.
PANT
PANT
STRETCH
I must swing sooner!
!
PANG
There's something wrong....!
Kyuma!?

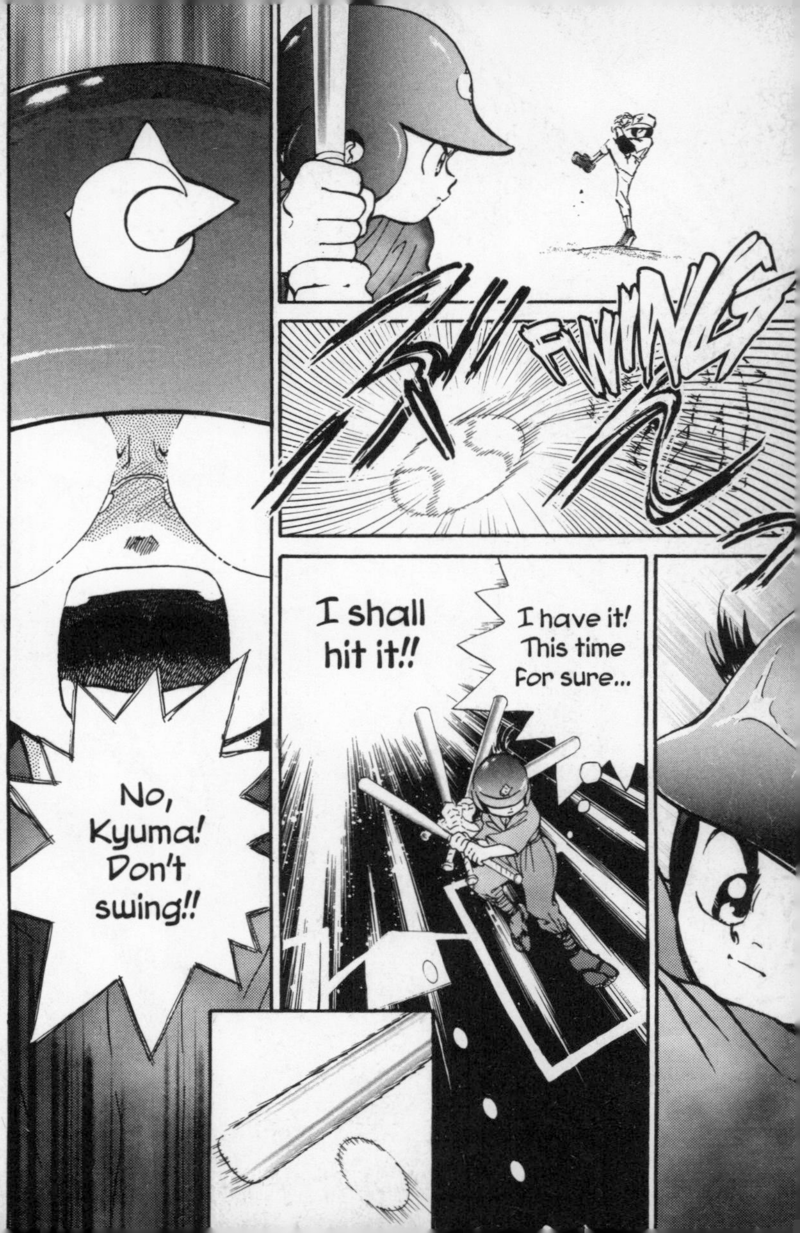
FWING
I have it! This time for sure...
I shall hit it!!
No, Kyuma! Don't swing!!

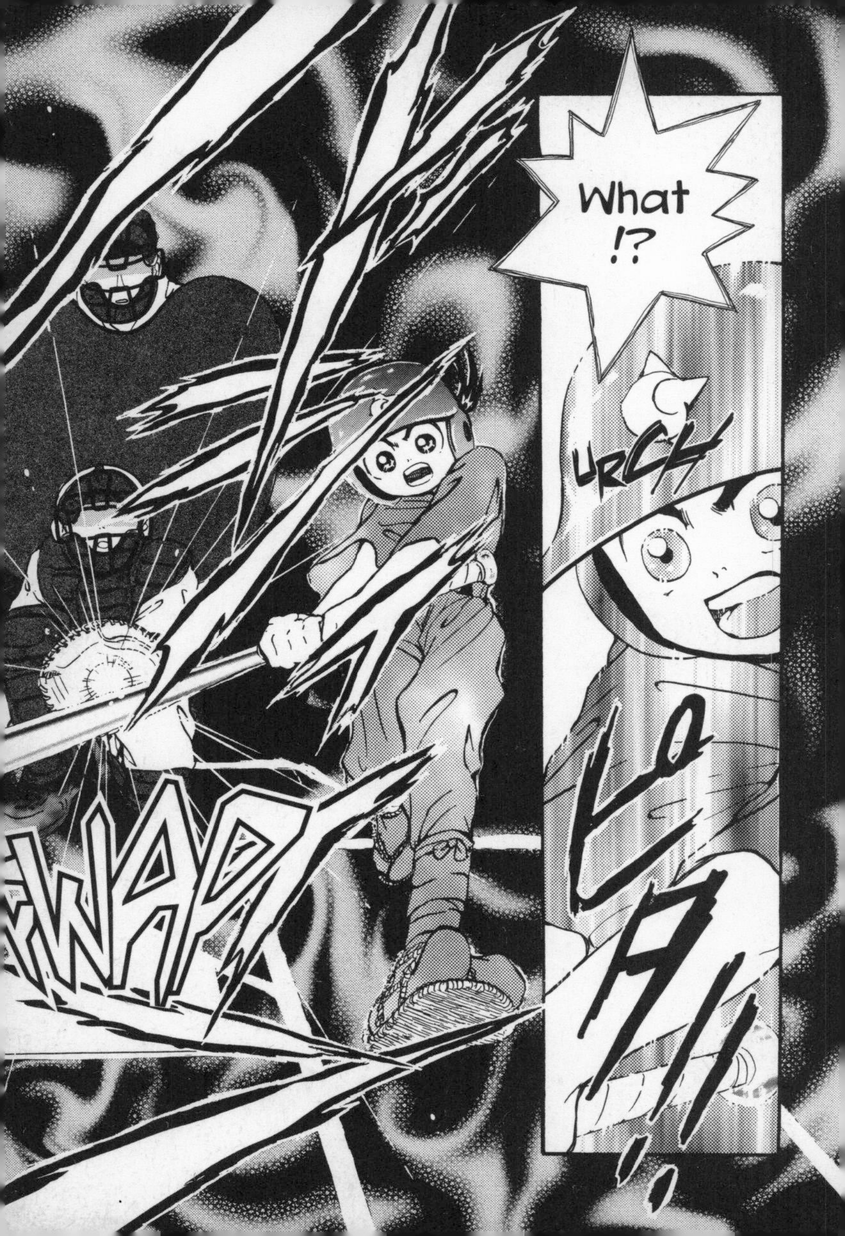
What !?
URCH

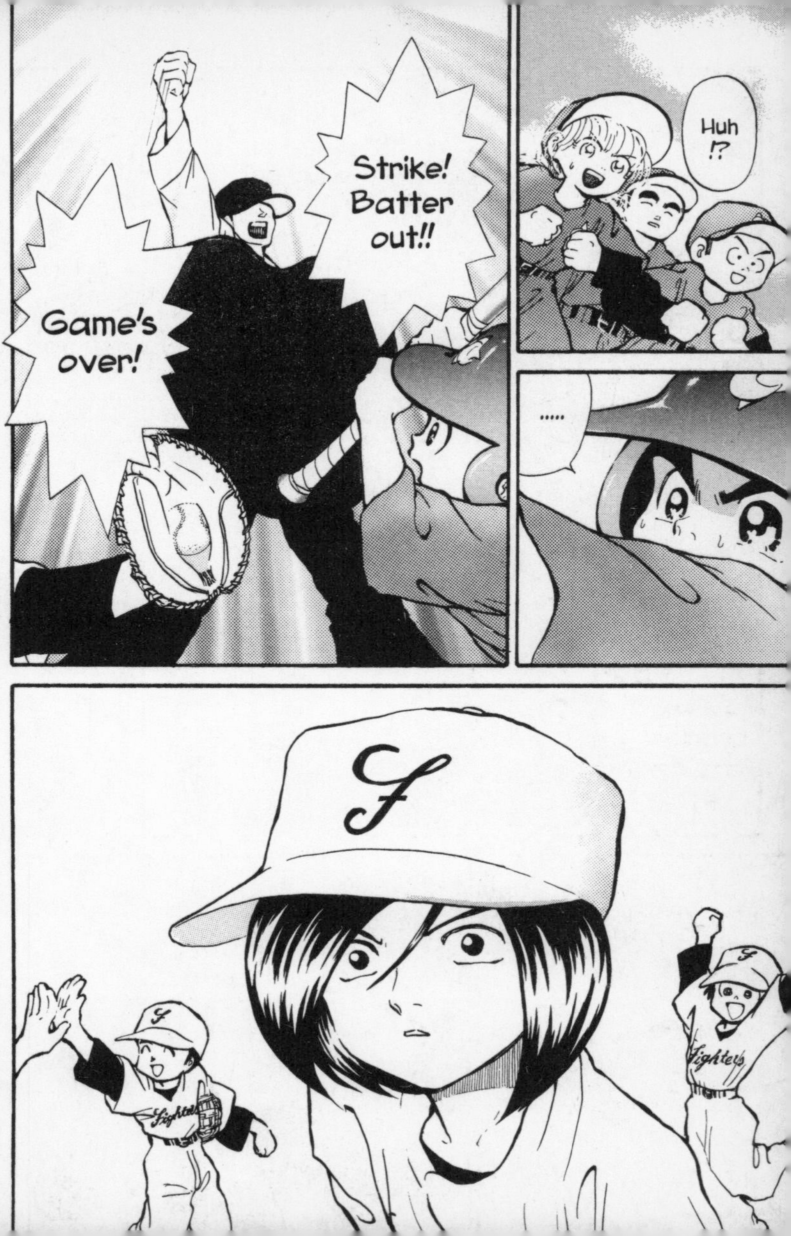
Huh !?
.....
Strike! Batter out!!
Game's over!

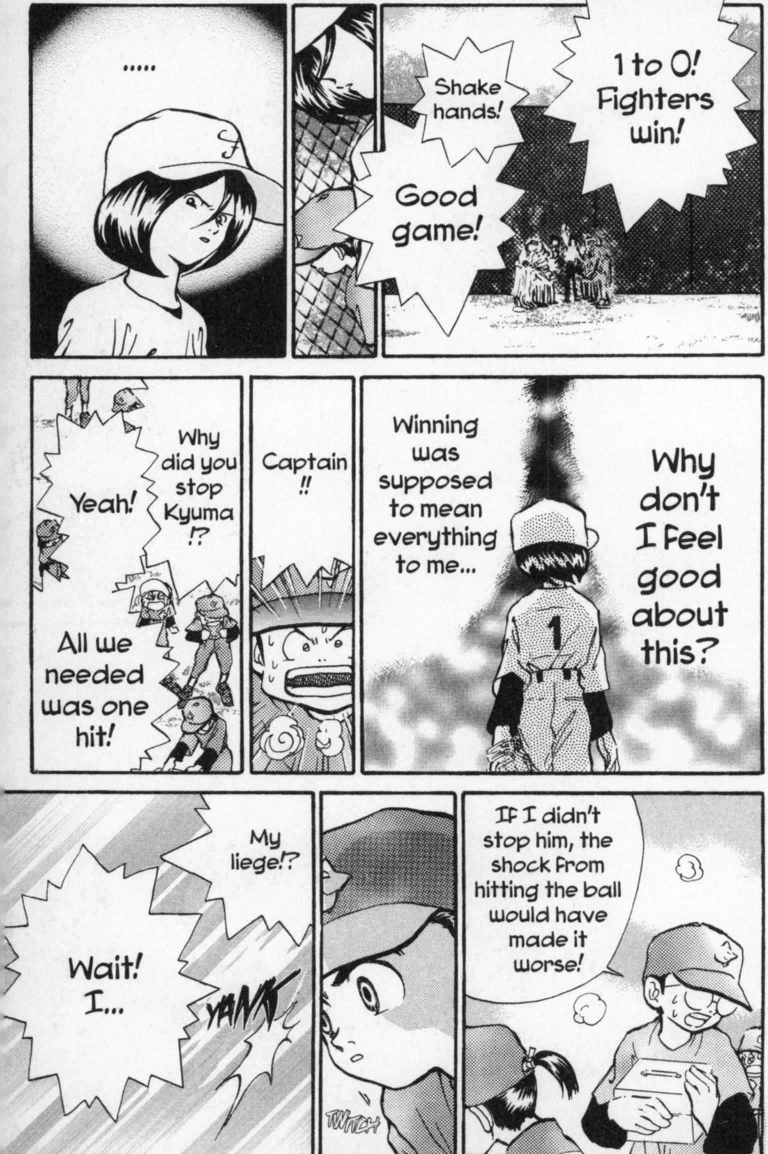
1 to 0! Fighters win!
Shake hands!
Good game!
.....
Why don't I feel good about this?
Winning was supposed to mean everything to me...
Captain!!
Why did you stop Kyuma!?
Yeah!
All we needed was one hit!
If I didn't stop him, the shock from hitting the ball would have made it worse!
TWITCH
My liege!?
YANK
Wait! I...

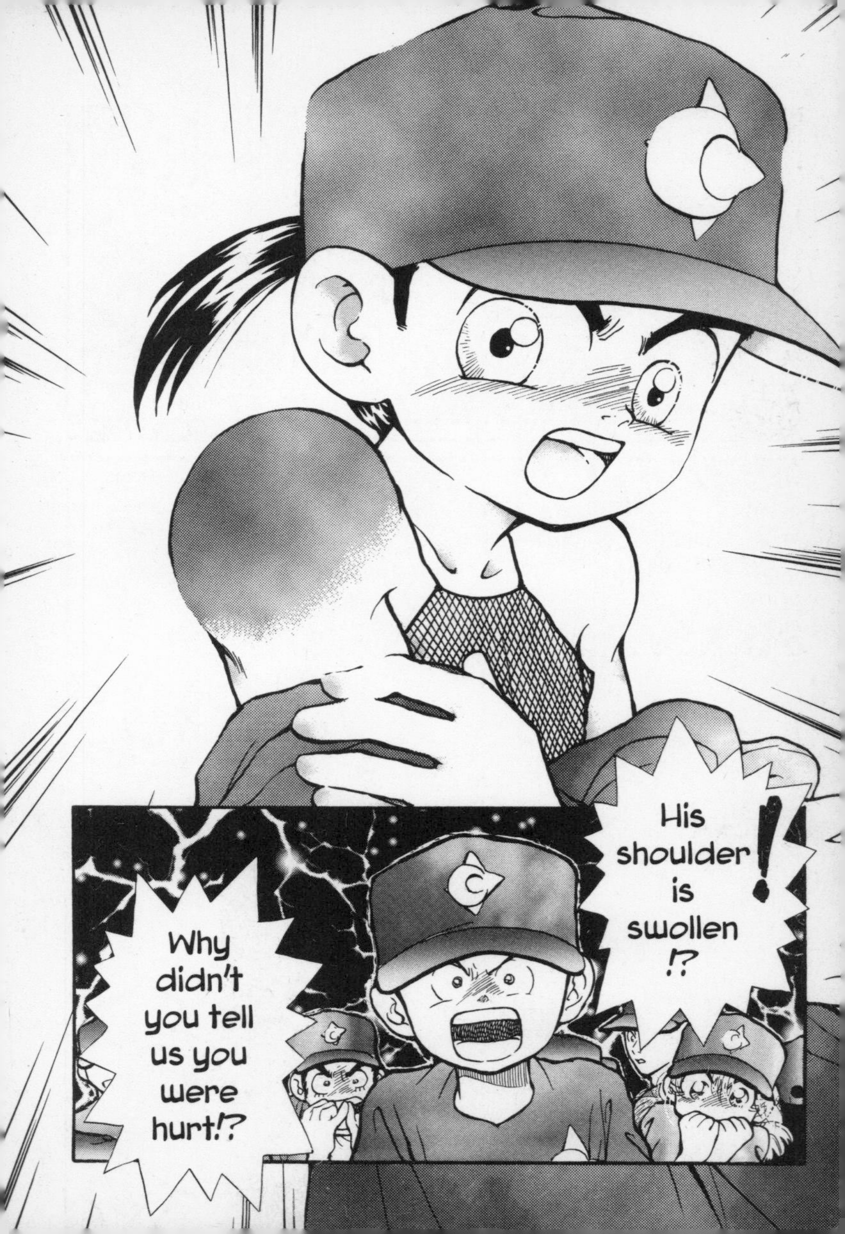
His shoulder is swollen!?
Why didn't you tell us you were hurt!?

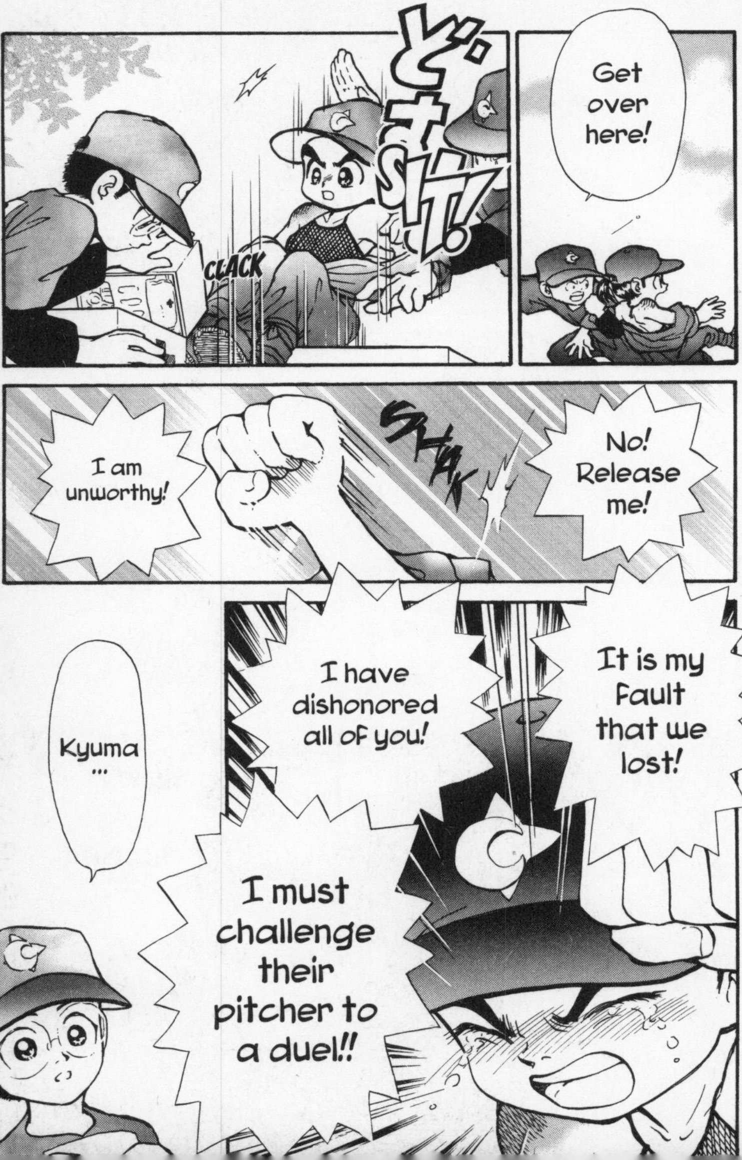
Get over here!
どすッ
SIT!
CLACK
No! Release me!
I am unworthy!
It is my fault that we lost!
I have dishonored all of you!
Kyuma ...
I must challenge their pitcher to a duel!!

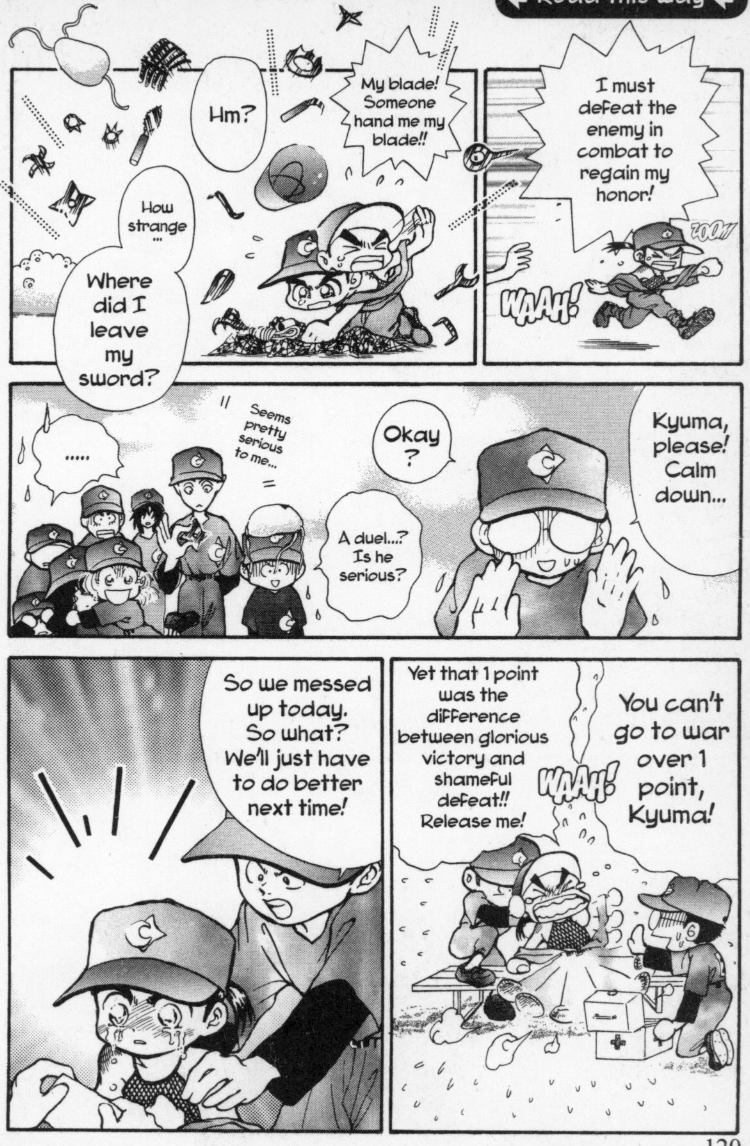
I must defeat the enemy in combat to regain my honor!
ZOOM
WAAH!
My blade! Someone hand me my blade!!
Hm?
How strange ...
Where did I leave my sword?
Kyuma, please! Calm down...
Okay?
A duel...? Is he serious?
Seems pretty serious to me...
.....
You can't go to war over 1 point, Kyuma!
Yet that 1 point was the difference between glorious victory and shameful defeat!! Release me!
WAAH!
So we messed up today. So what? We'll just have to do better next time!

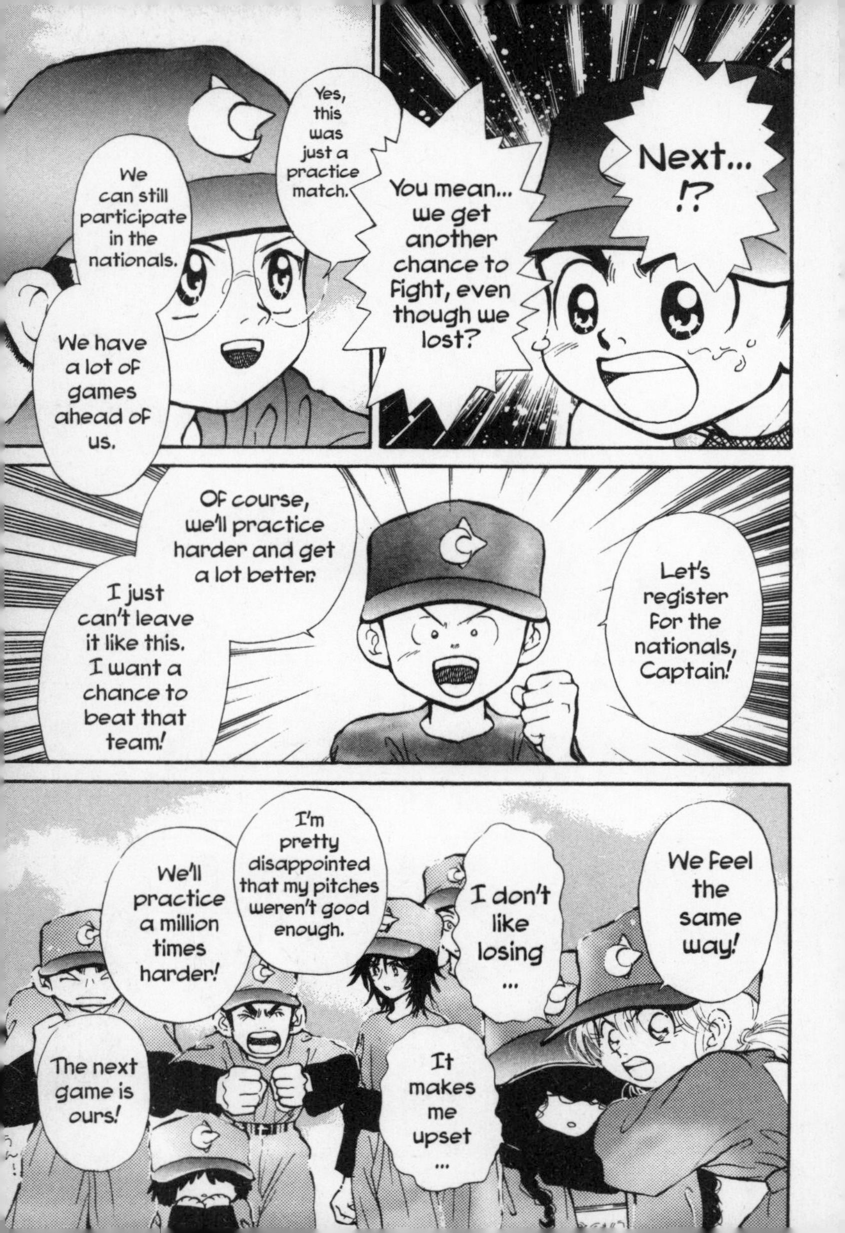
Next... !?
You mean... we get another chance to fight, even though we lost?
Yes, this was just a practice match.
We can still participate in the nationals.
We have a lot of games ahead of us.
Let's register for the nationals, Captain!
Of course, we'll practice harder and get a lot better.
I just can't leave it like this. I want a chance to beat that team!
We feel the same way!
I don't like losing ...
It makes me upset ...
I'm pretty disappointed that my pitches weren't good enough.
We'll practice a million times harder!
The next game is ours!

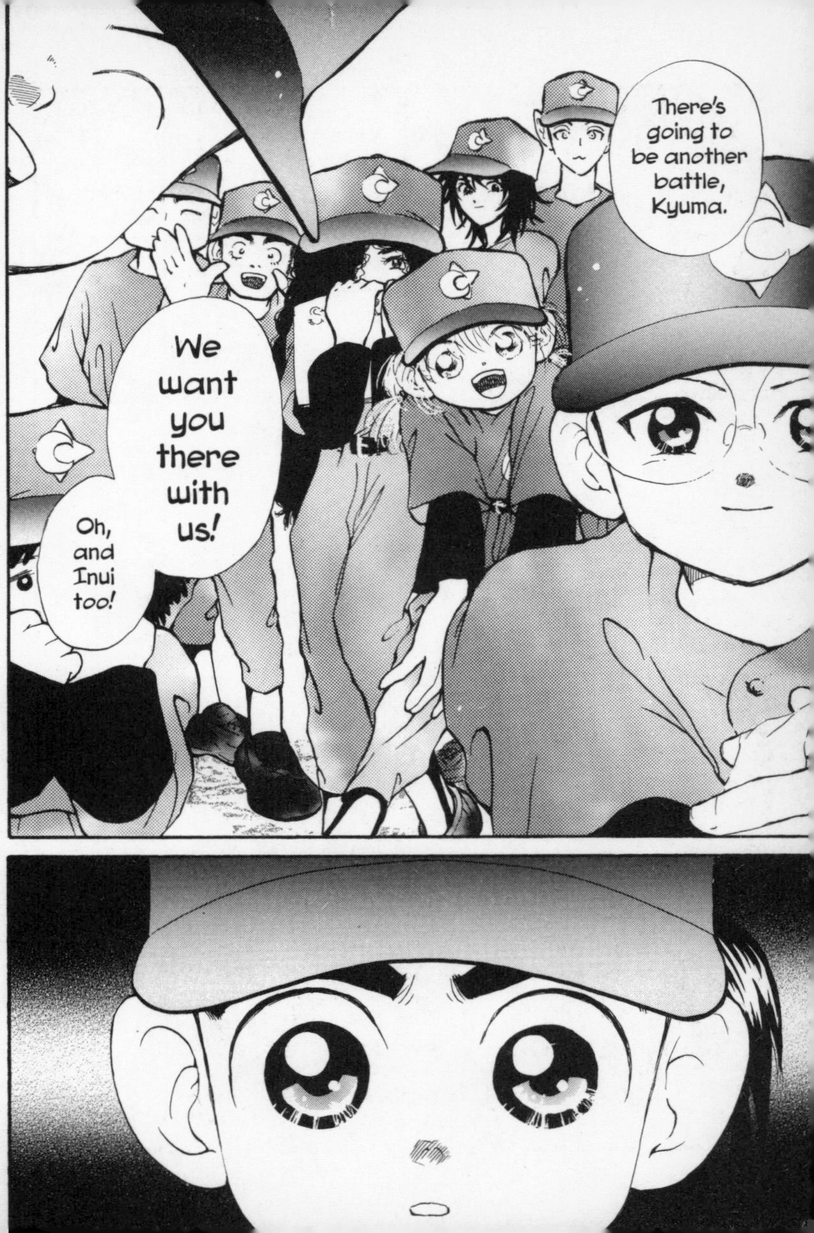
There's going to be another battle, Kyuma.
We want you there with us!
Oh, and Inui too!

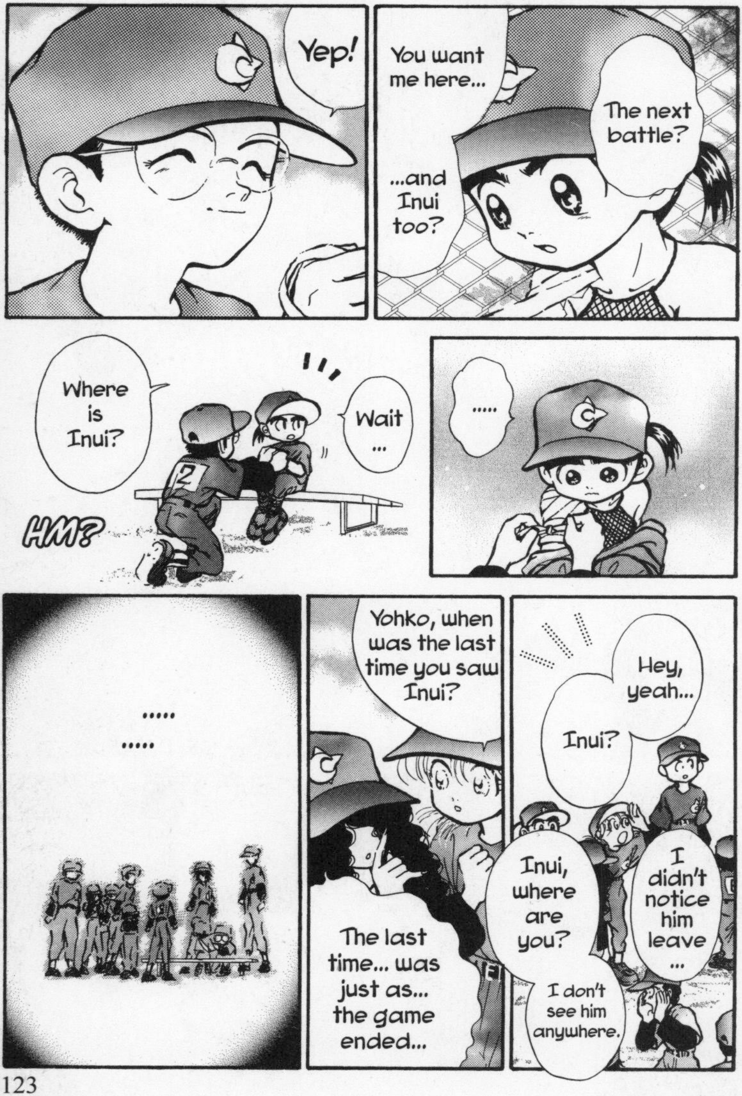
The next battle?
You want me here...
...and Inui too?
Yep!
.....
Wait ...
Where is Inui?
HM?
Hey, yeah...
Inui?
I didn't notice him leave ...
Inui, where are you?
I don't see him anywhere.
Yohko, when was the last time you saw Inui?
The last time... was just as... the game ended...
.....
.....

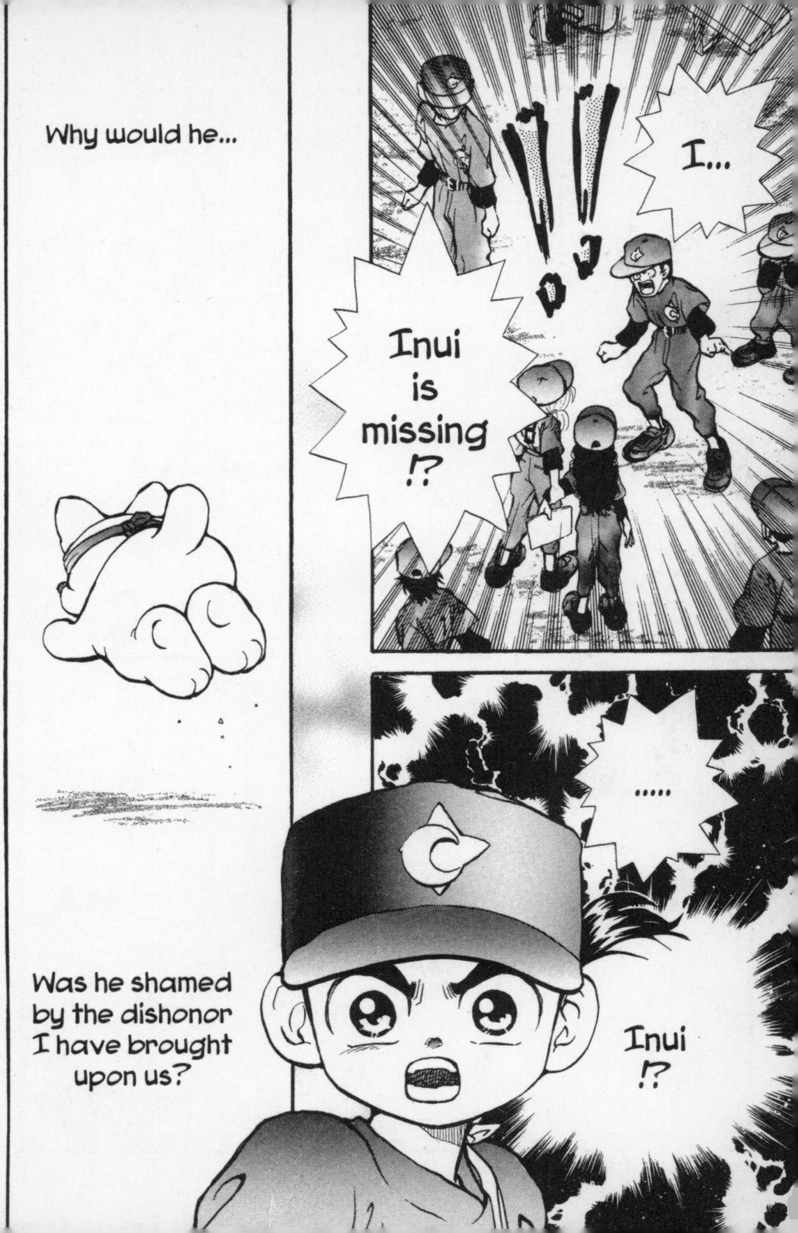
I...
Inui is missing !?
.....
Inui !?
Why would he...
Was he shamed by the dishonor I have brought upon us?

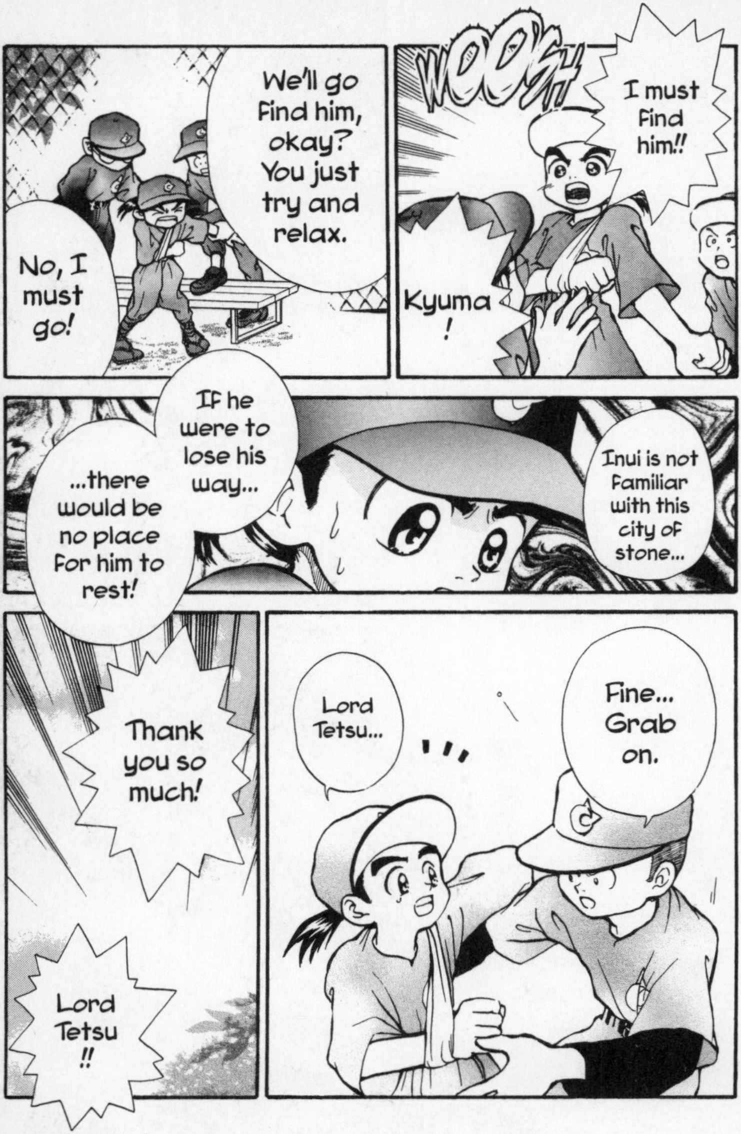
I must find him!!
WOOSH
Kyuma!
We'll go find him, okay? You just try and relax.
No, I must go!
Inui is not familiar with this city of stone...
If he were to lose his way...
...there would be no place for him to rest!
Fine... Grab on.
Lord Tetsu...
Thank you so much!
Lord Tetsu!!

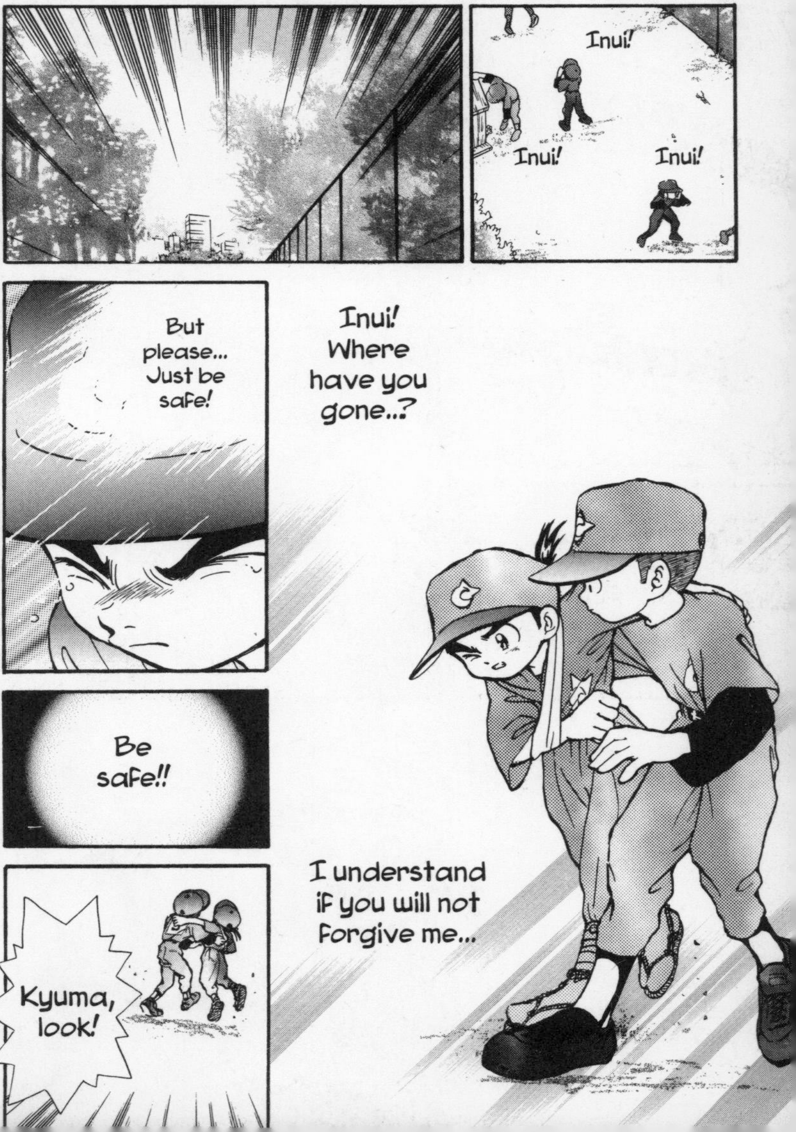
Inui!
Inui!
Inui!
Inui! Where have you gone..?
I understand if you will not forgive me...
But please... Just be safe!
Be safe!!
Kyuma, look!

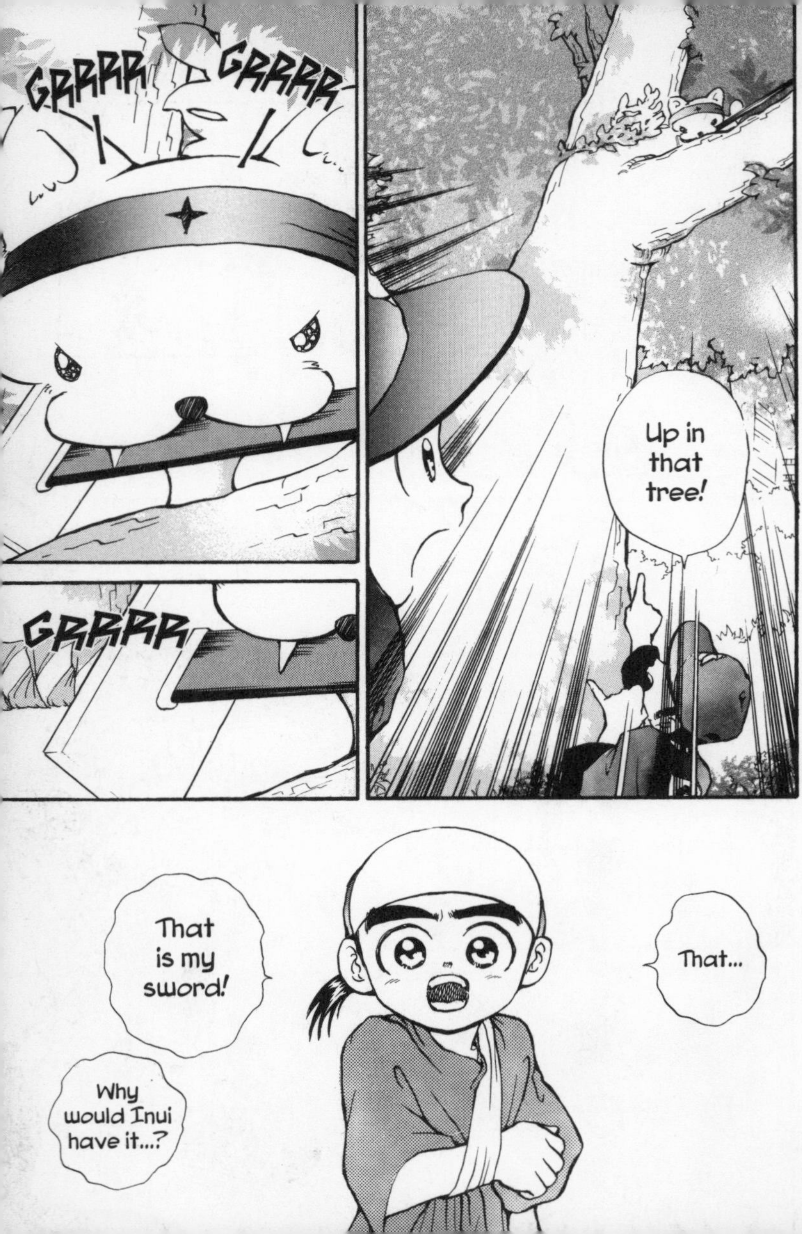
Up in that tree!
GRRRR GRRRR
GRRRR
That...
That is my sword!
Why would Inui have it...?

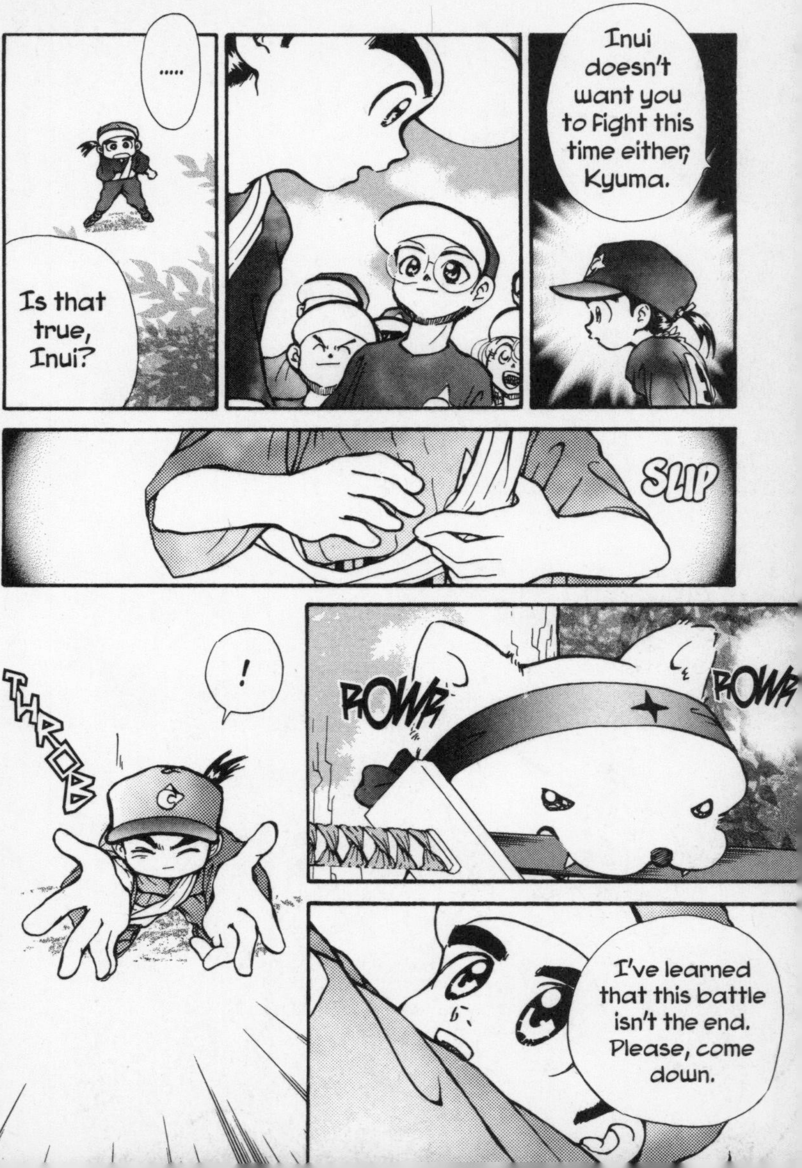
Inui doesn't want you to fight this time either, Kyuma.
.....
Is that true, Inui?
SLIP
ROWR
ROWR
I've learned that this battle isn't the end. Please, come down.
!
THROB

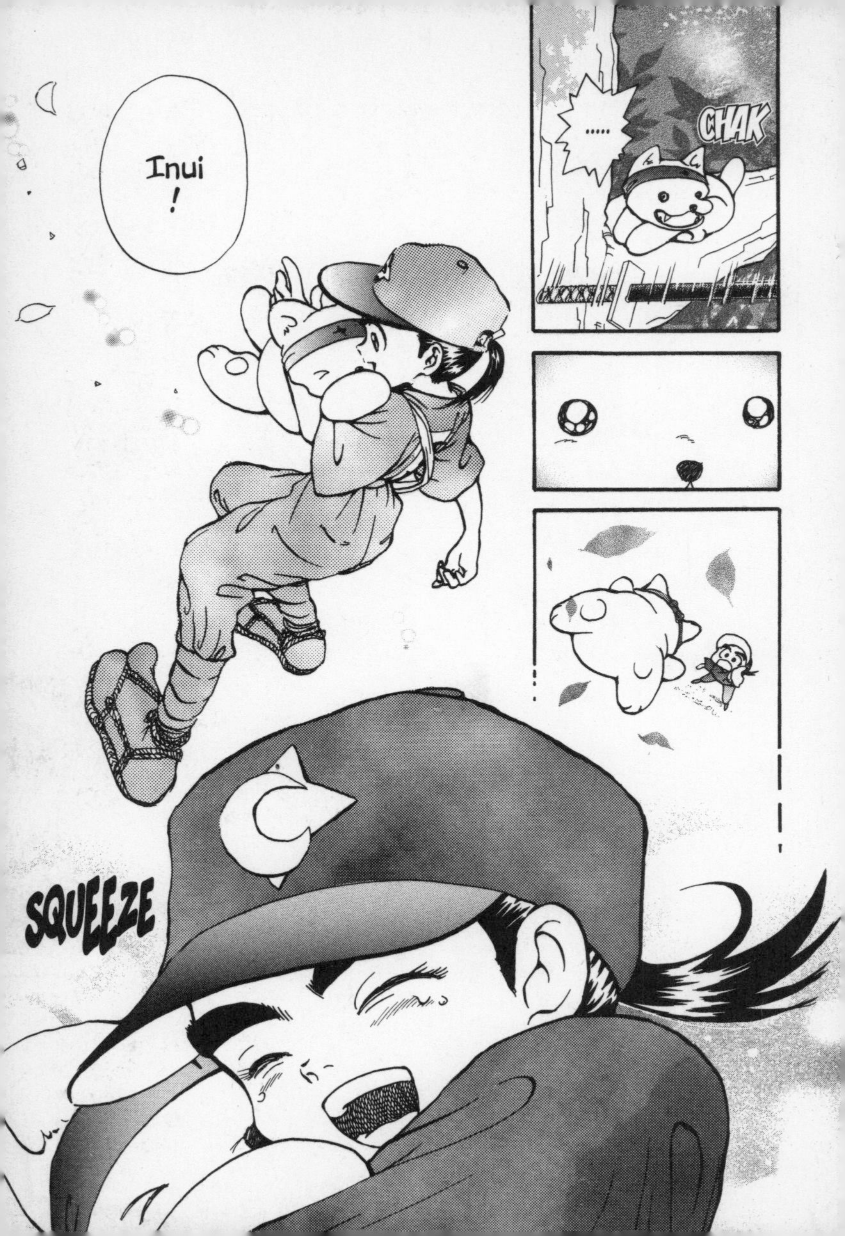

......
CHAK
Inui !
SQUEEZE

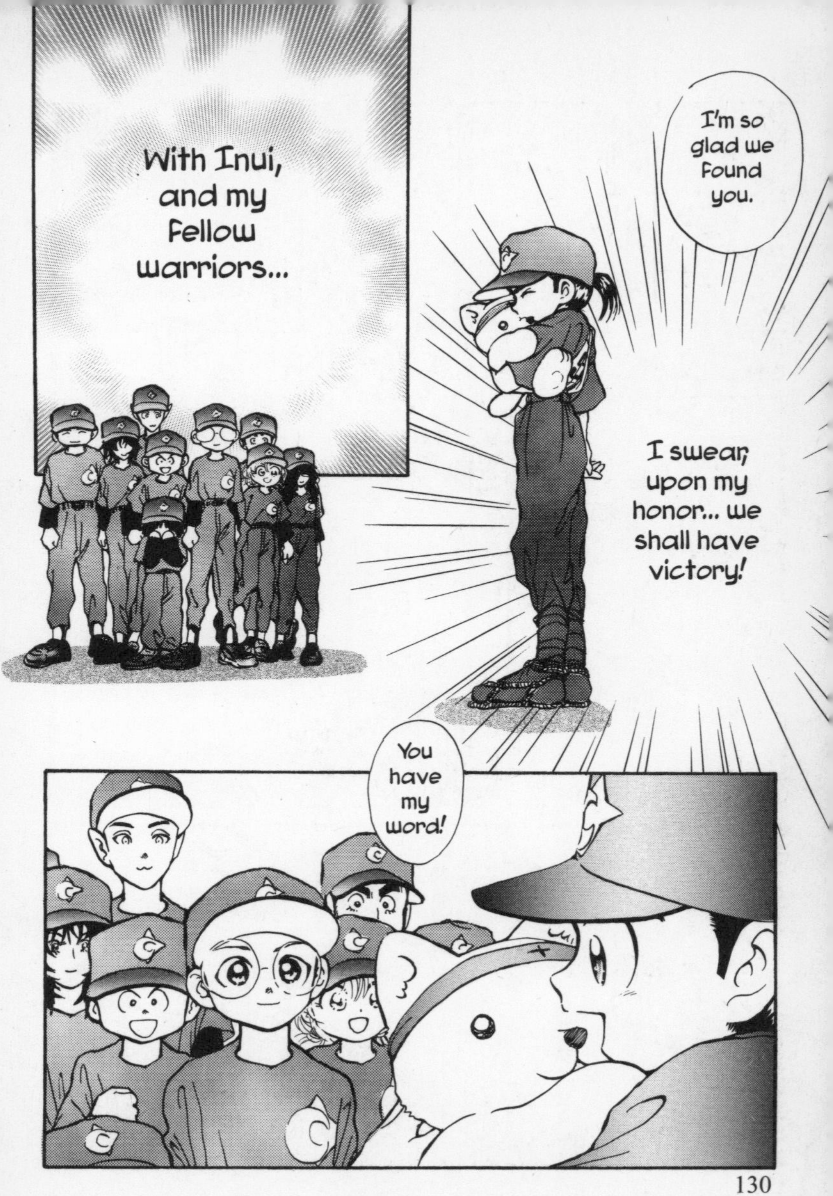
I'm so glad we found you.
I swear, upon my honor... we shall have victory!
With Inui, and my fellow warriors...
You have my word!

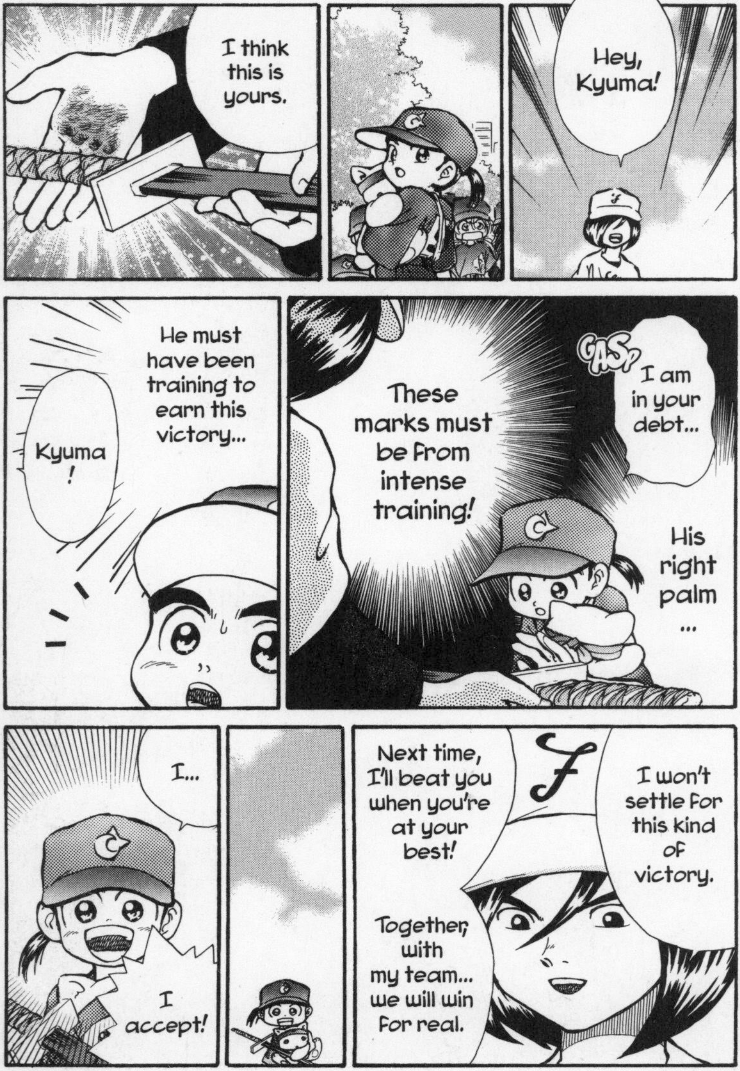
Hey, Kyuma!
I think this is yours.
GASP
I am in your debt...
His right palm ...
These marks must be from intense training!
He must have been training to earn this victory...
Kyuma!
I won't settle for this kind of victory.
Next time, I'll beat you when you're at your best!
Together, with my team... we will win for real.
I...
I accept!

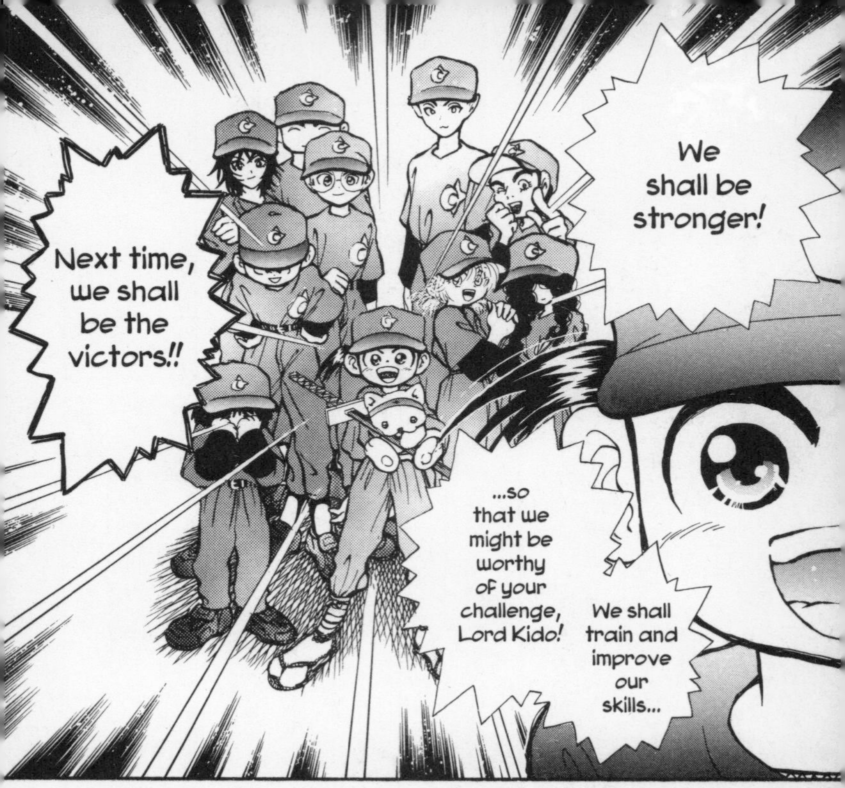
We shall be stronger!
We shall train and improve our skills...
...so that we might be worthy of your challenge, Lord Kido!
Next time, we shall be the victors!!

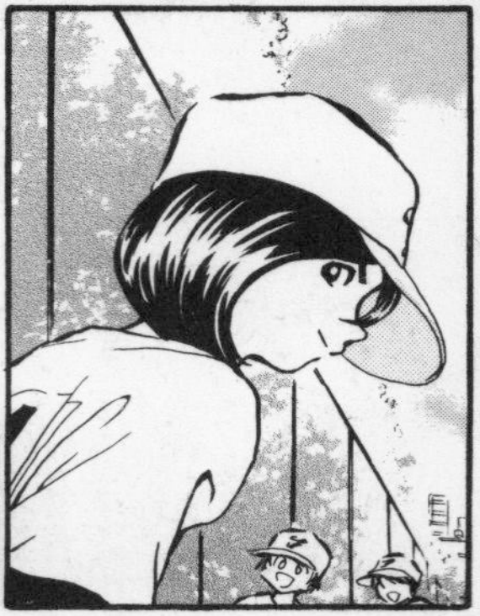

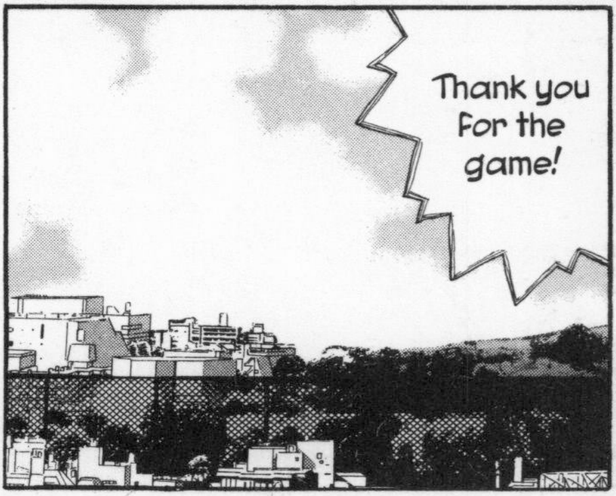
Thank you for the game!

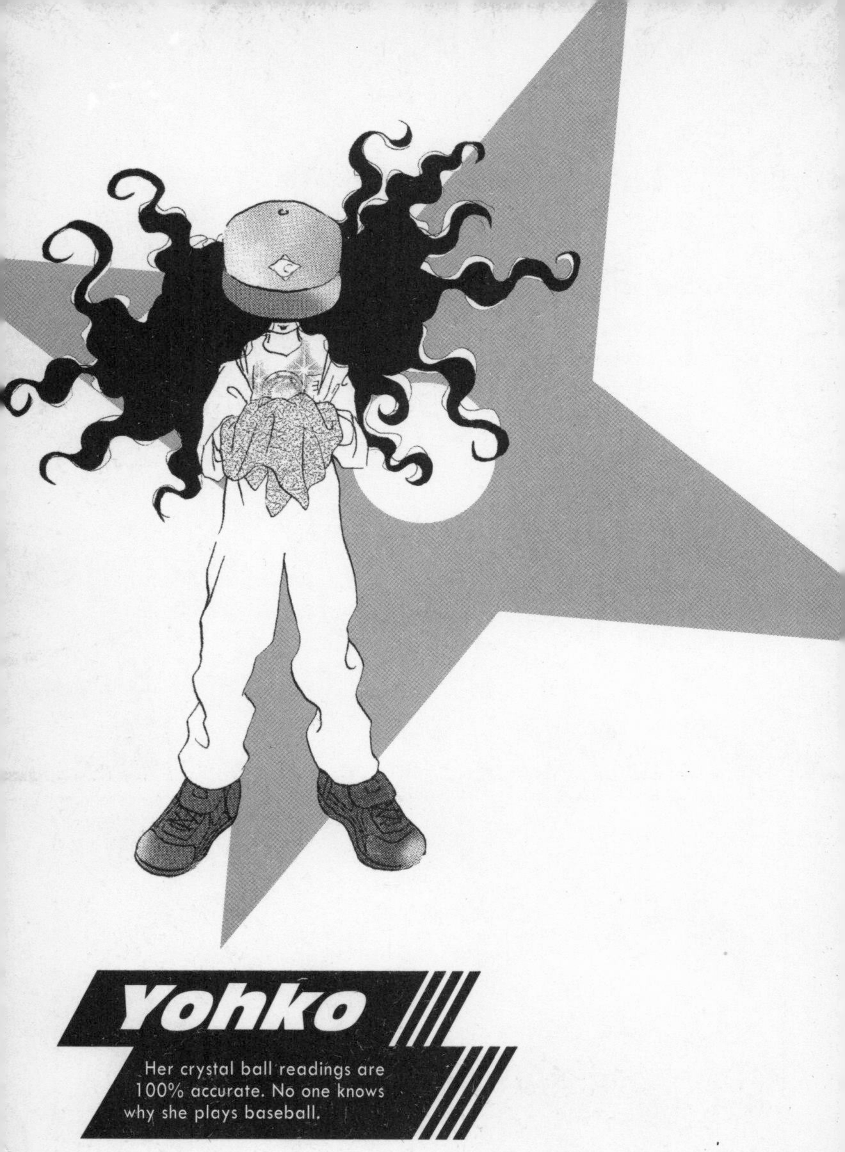

Yohko

Her crystal ball readings are 100% accurate. No one knows why she plays baseball.

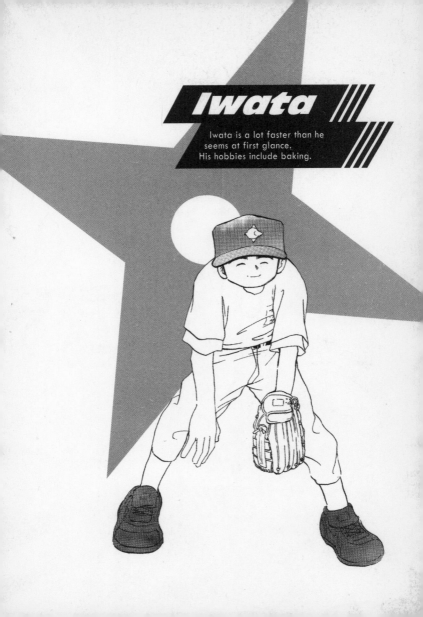

Iwata

Iwata is a lot faster than he
seems at first glance.
His hobbies include baking.

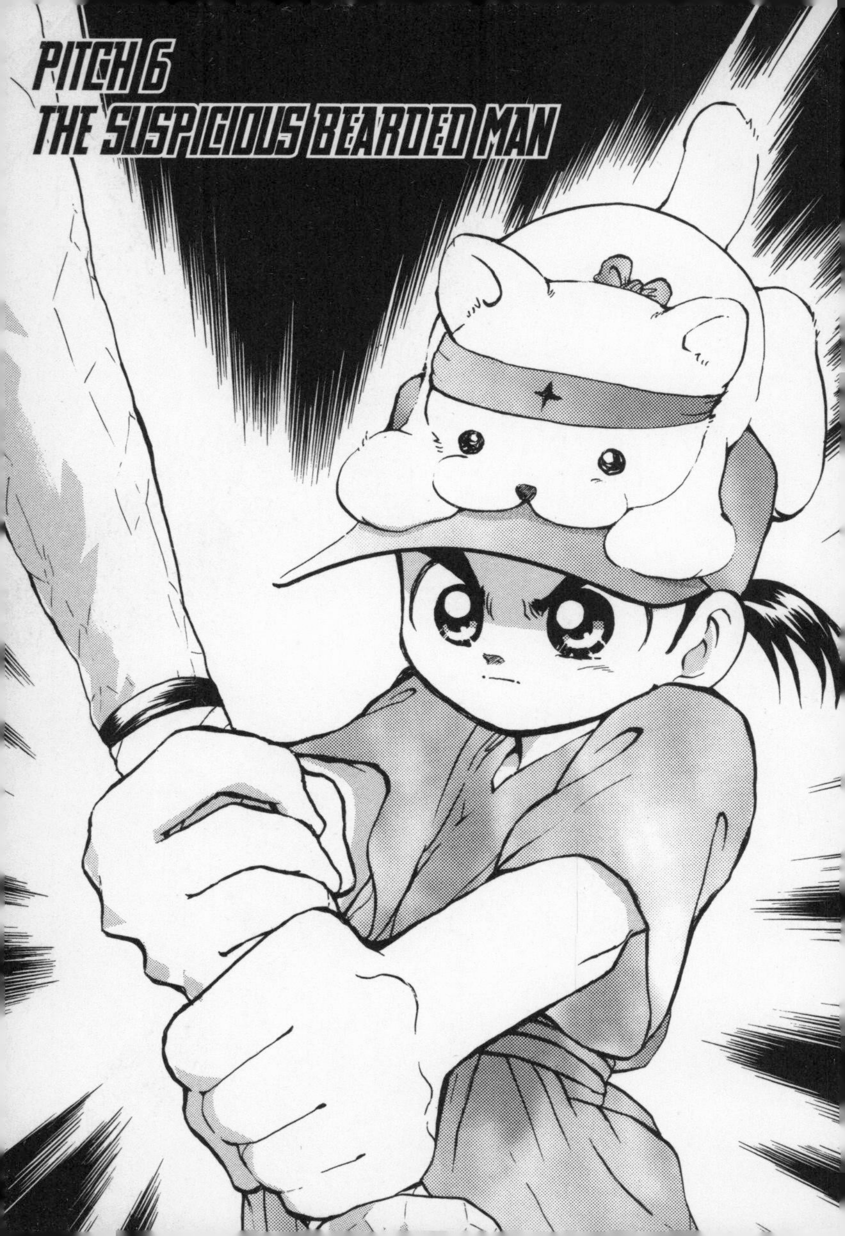
PITCH 6
THE SUSPICIOUS BEARDED MAN

Read this way

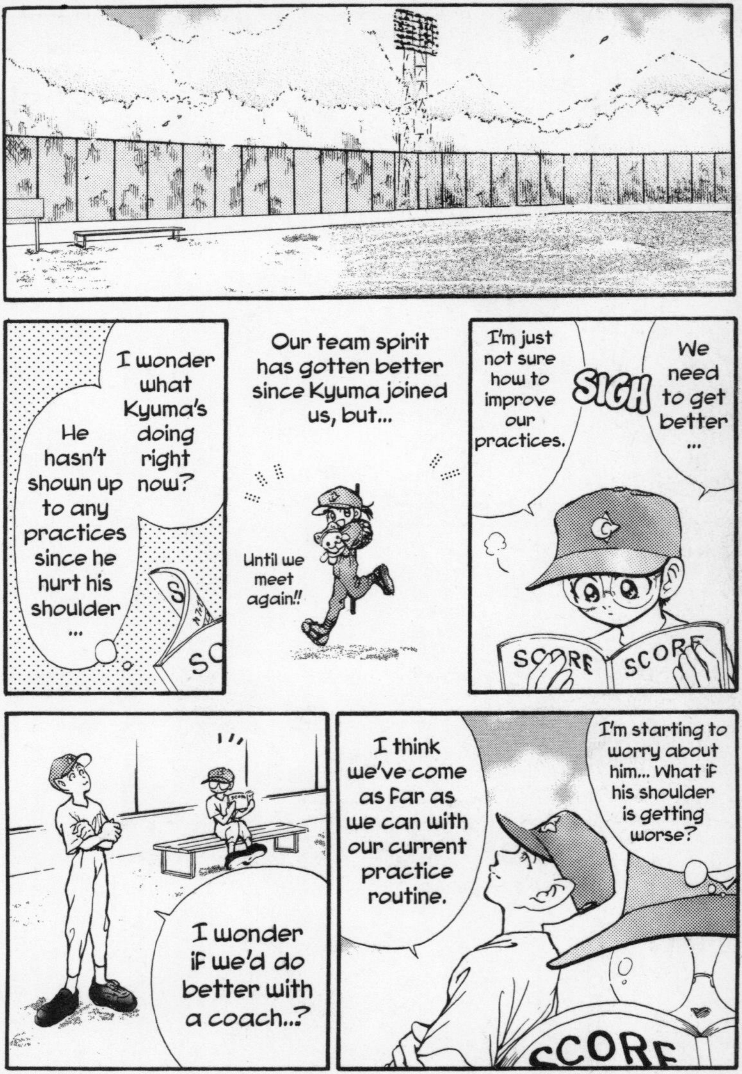

We need to get better...
SIGH
I'm just not sure how to improve our practices.
SCORE SCORE
Our team spirit has gotten better since Kyuma joined us, but...
Until we meet again!!
I wonder what Kyuma's doing right now?
He hasn't shown up to any practices since he hurt his shoulder...
I'm starting to worry about him... What if his shoulder is getting worse?
I think we've come as far as we can with our current practice routine.
SCORE
I wonder if we'd do better with a coach..?

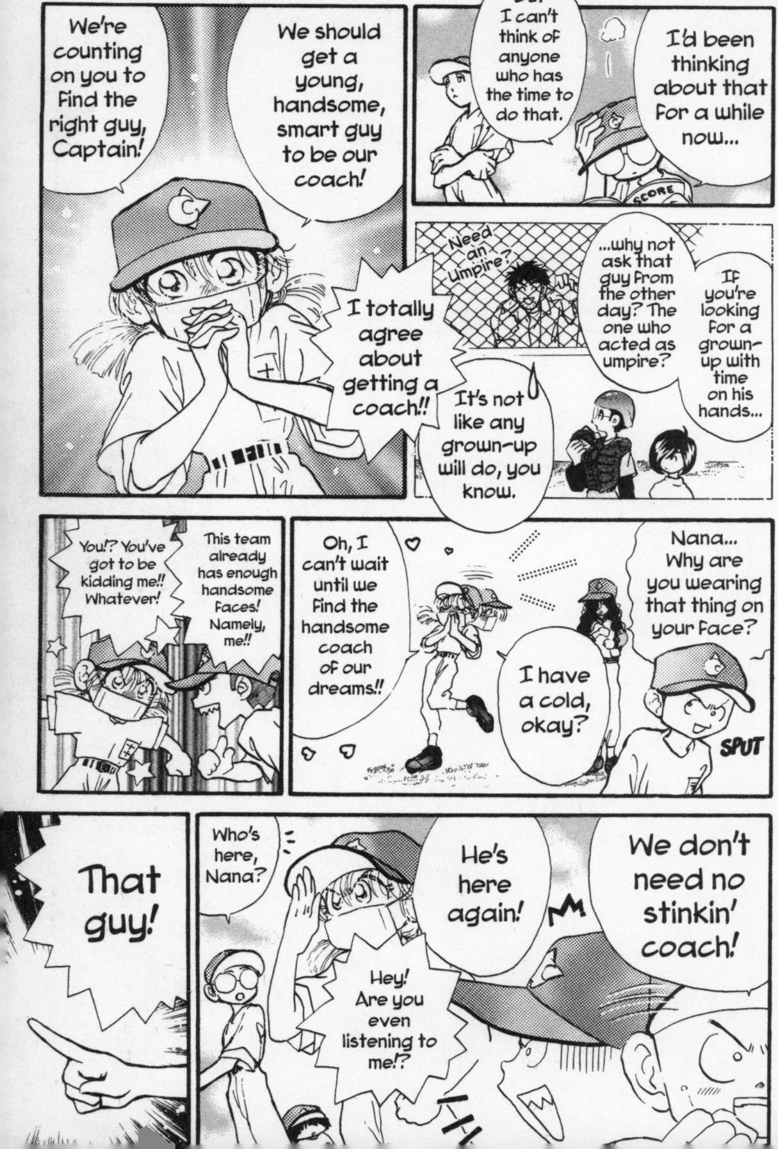
I'd been thinking about that for a while now...
But I can't think of anyone who has the time to do that.
If you're looking for a grown-up with time on his hands...
...why not ask that guy from the other day? The one who acted as umpire?
Need an Umpire?
It's not like any grown-up will do, you know.
We should get a young, handsome, smart guy to be our coach!
We're counting on you to find the right guy, Captain!
I totally agree about getting a coach!!
Nana... Why are you wearing that thing on your face?
SPUT
I have a cold, okay?
Oh, I can't wait until we find the handsome coach of our dreams!!
This team already has enough handsome faces! Namely, me!!
You!? You've got to be kidding me!! Whatever!
We don't need no stinkin' coach!
He's here again!
Who's here, Nana?
Hey! Are you even listening to me!?
That guy!

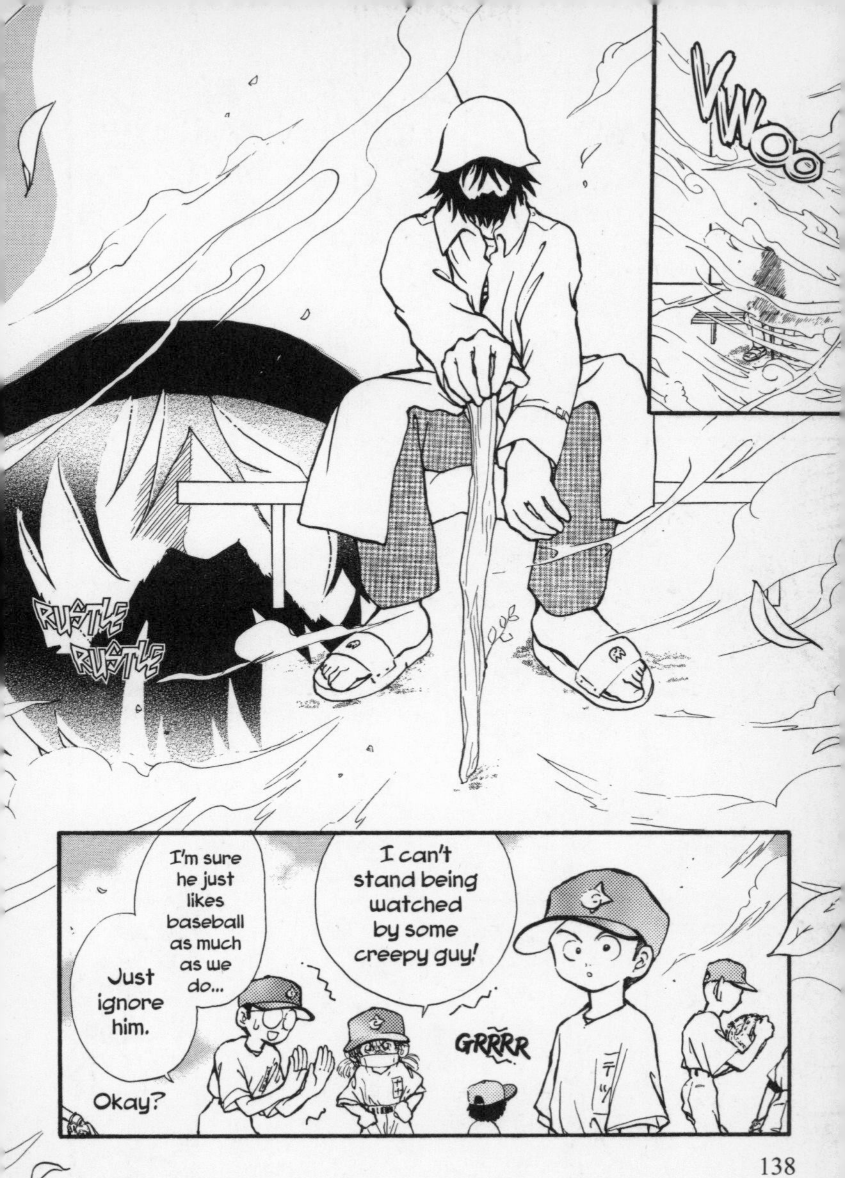
VWOO
RUSTLE RUSTLE
I can't stand being watched by some creepy guy!
GRRRR
I'm sure he just likes baseball as much as we do...
Just ignore him.
Okay?

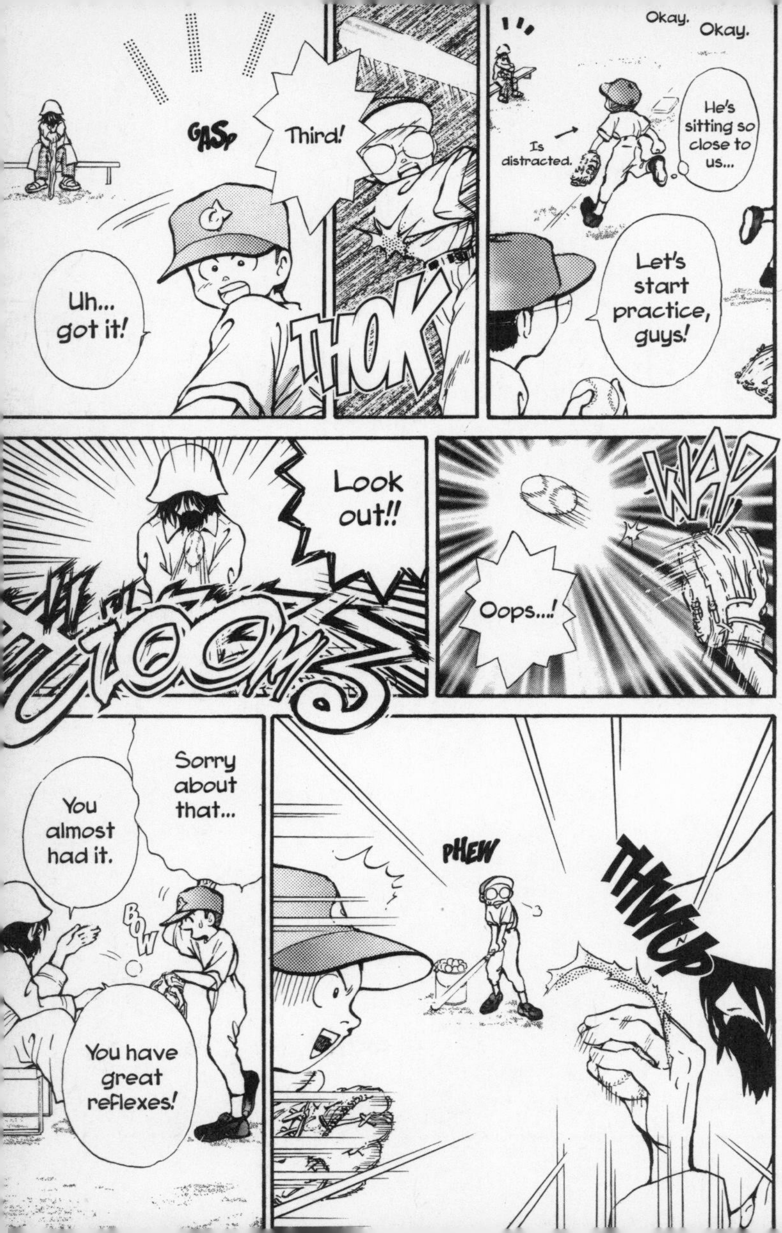
Okay.
Okay.
He's sitting so close to us...
Is distracted.
Let's start practice, guys!
THOK
Third!
GASP
Uh... got it!
WAP
Oops...!
Look out!!
ZOOM
PHEW
THWUP
Sorry about that...
You almost had it.
BOW
You have great reflexes!

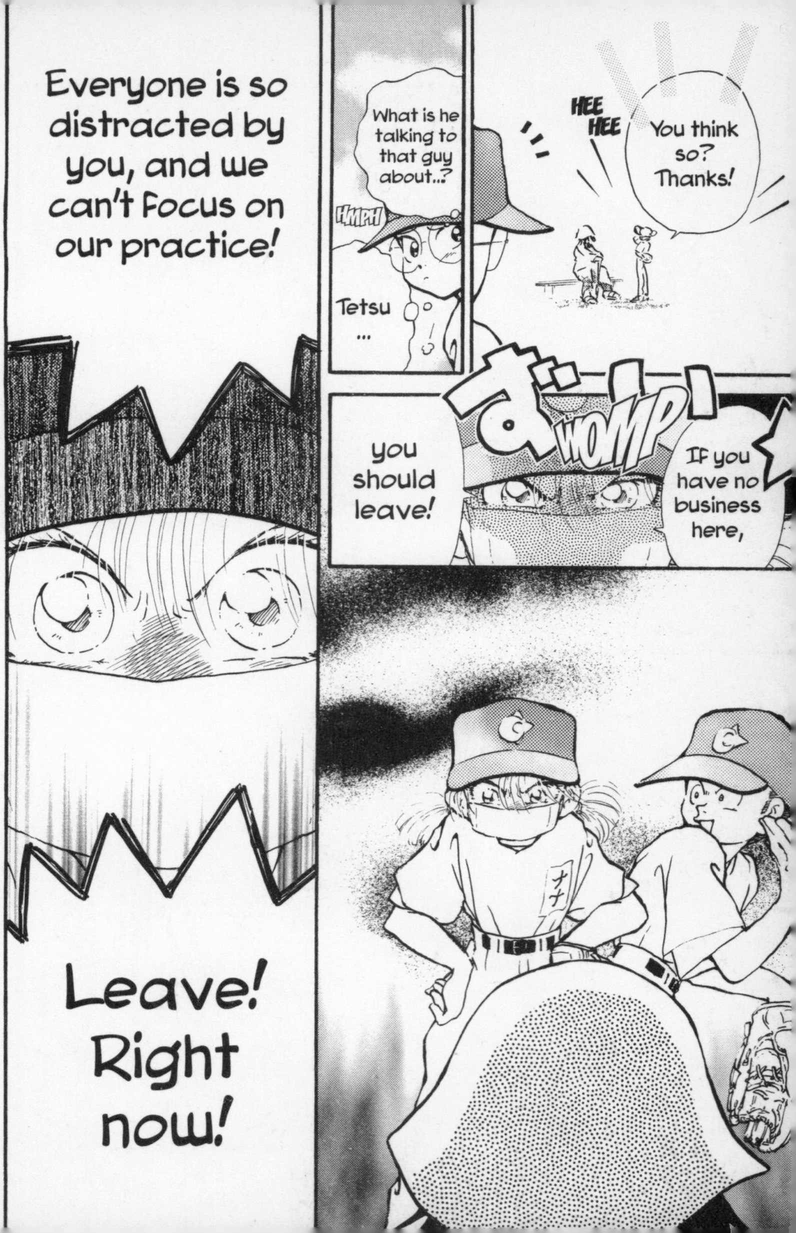
HEE HEE
You think so? Thanks!
What is he talking to that guy about...?
HMPH
Tetsu ...
WOMP
If you have no business here,
you should leave!
Everyone is so distracted by you, and we can't focus on our practice!
Leave! Right now!

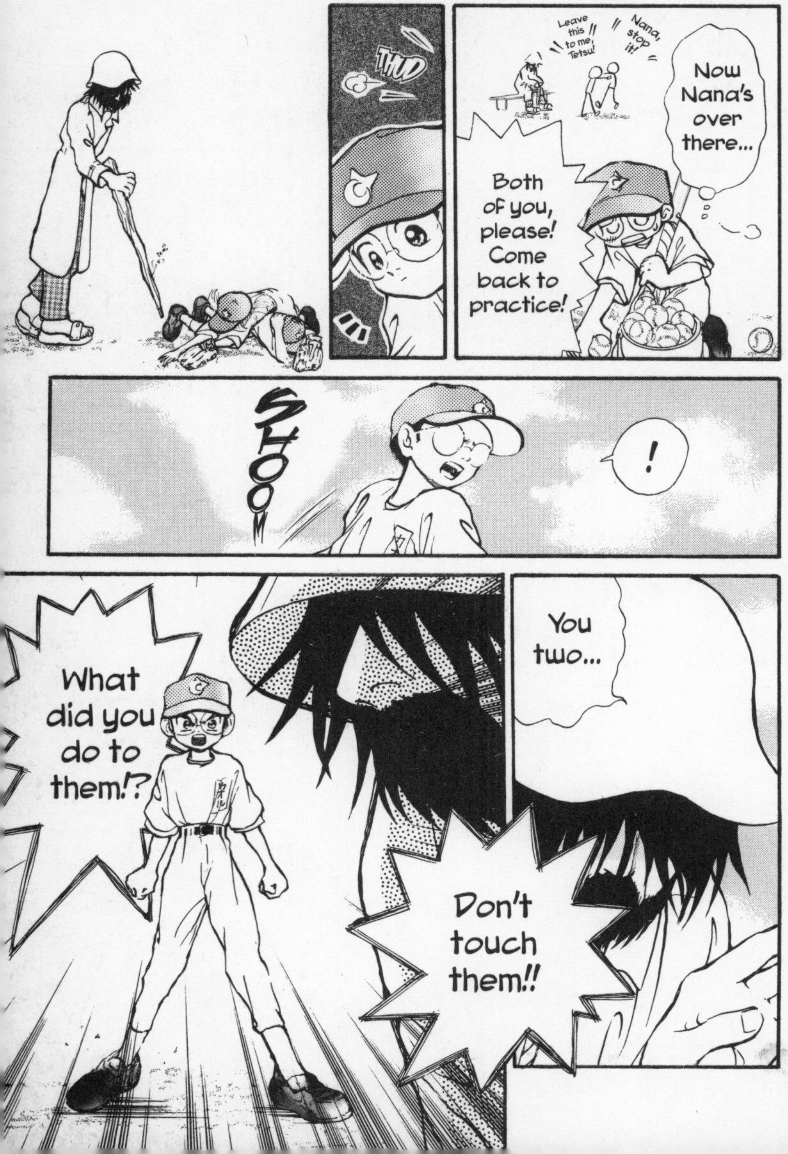
Now Nana's over there...
Nana, stop it!
Leave this to me, Tetsu!
Both of you, please! Come back to practice!
THUD
SHOOOM
!
You two...
Don't touch them!!
What did you do to them!?

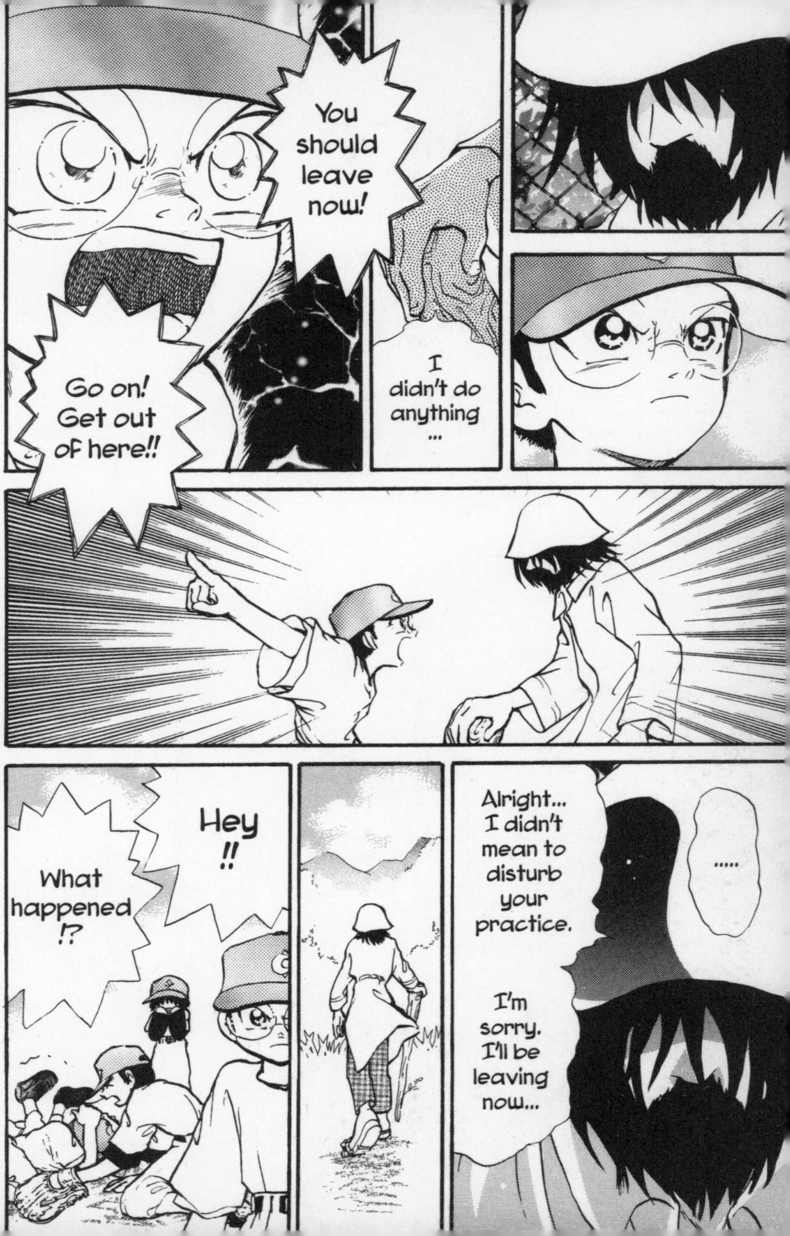
I didn't do anything ...
You should leave now!
Go on! Get out of here!!
.....
Alright... I didn't mean to disturb your practice.
I'm sorry. I'll be leaving now...
Hey !!
What happened !?

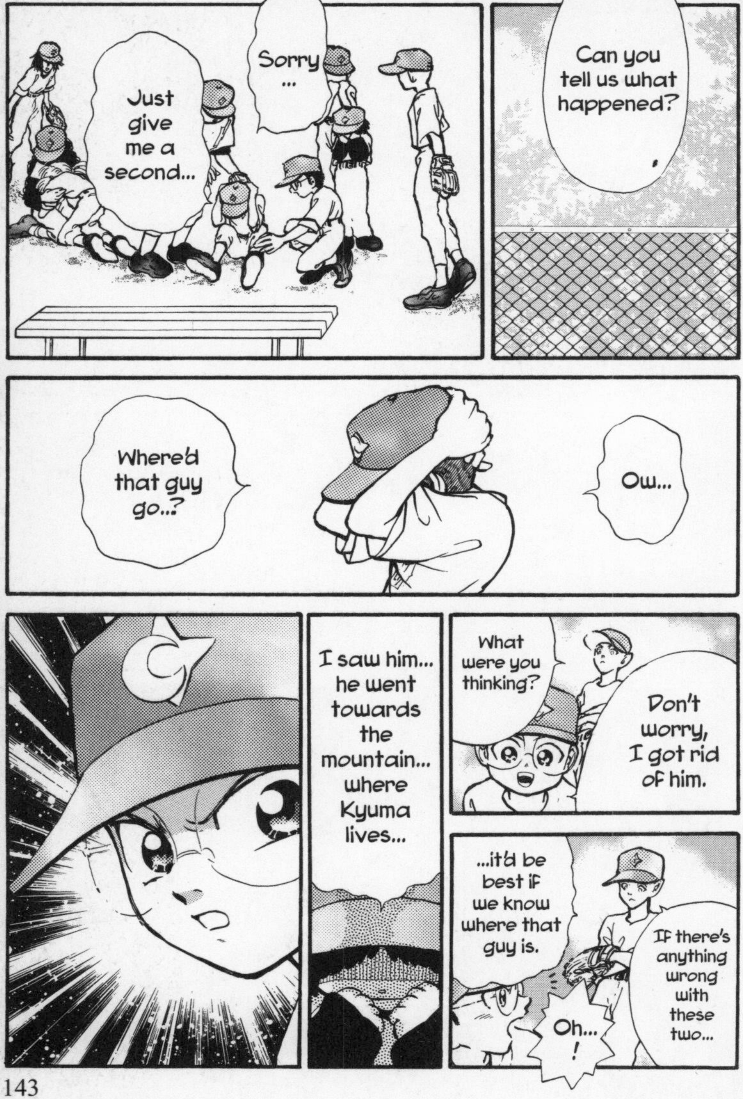
Can you tell us what happened?
Sorry ...
Just give me a second...
Ow...
Where'd that guy go..?
What were you thinking?
Don't worry, I got rid of him.
If there's anything wrong with these two...
...it'd be best if we know where that guy is.
Oh... !
I saw him... he went towards the mountain... where Kyuma lives...

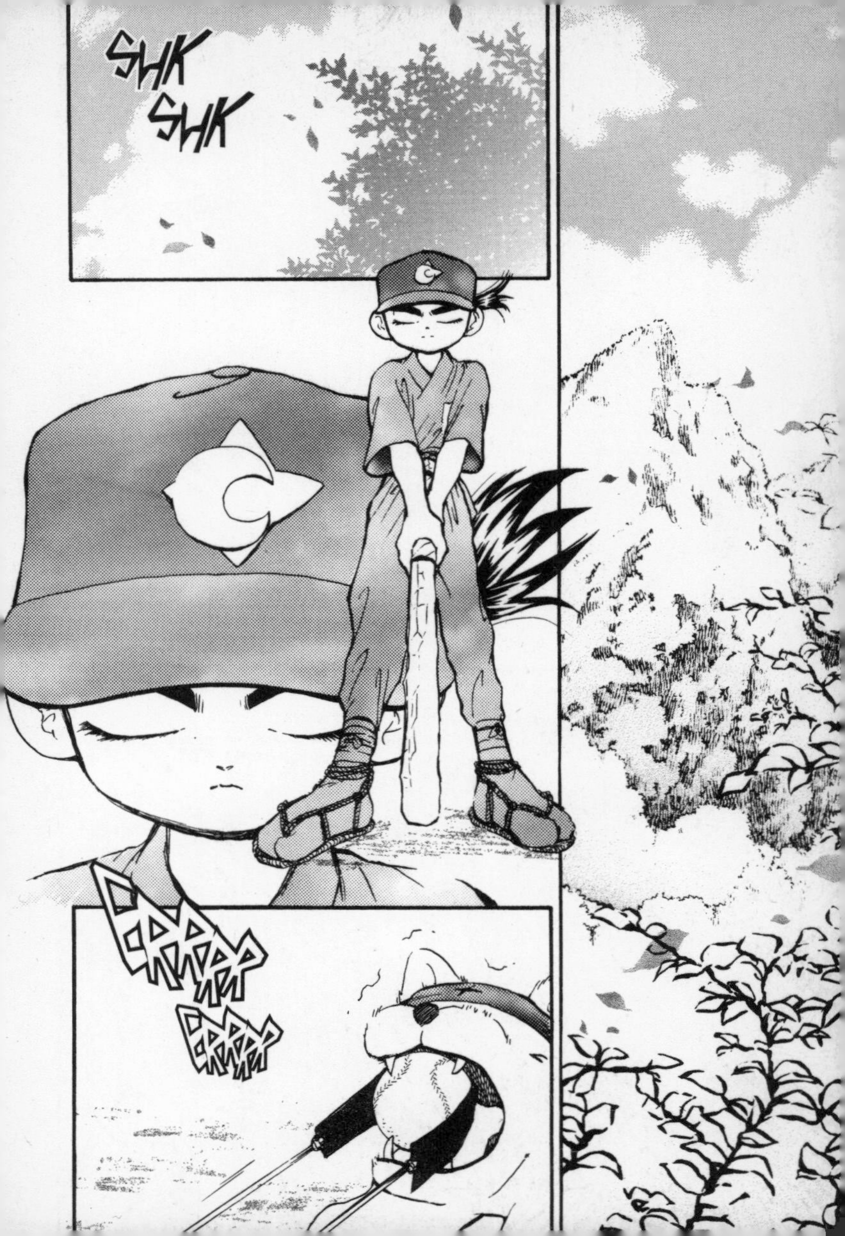
SHK
SHK

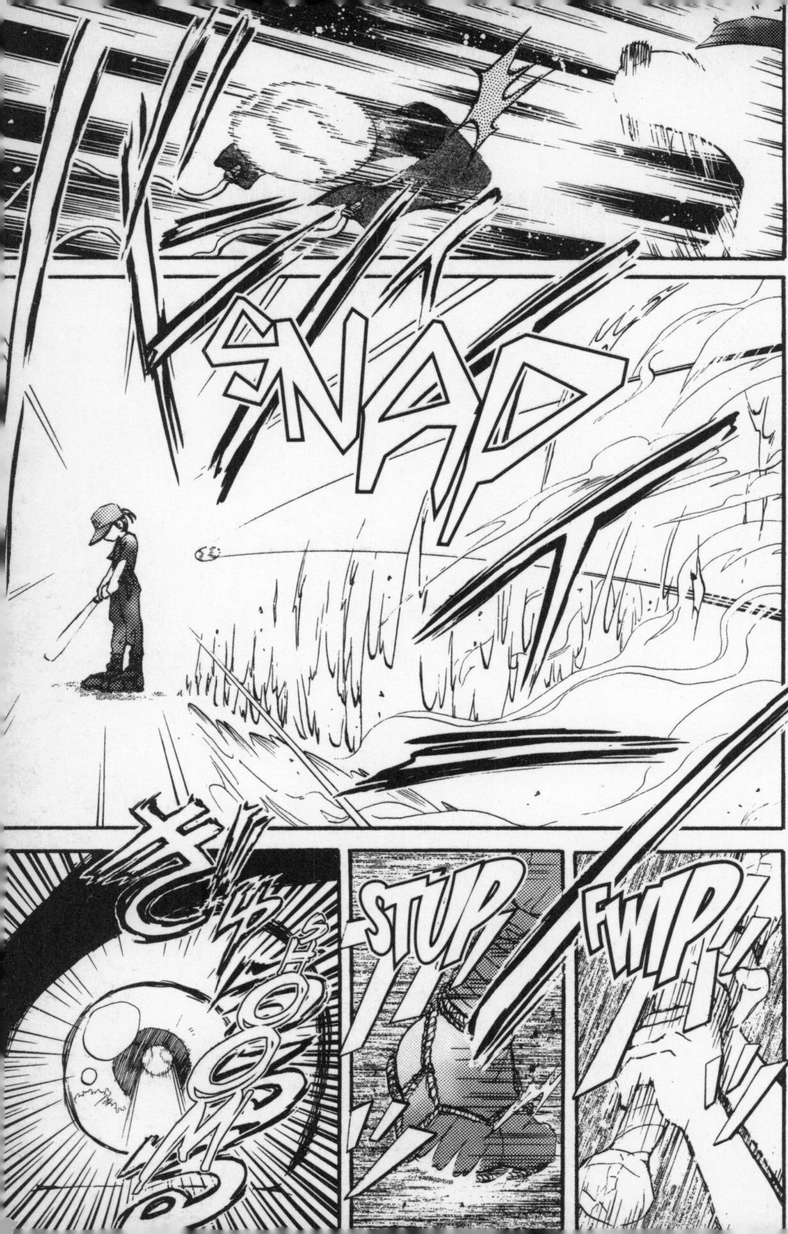
SNAP
FWIP
STUP

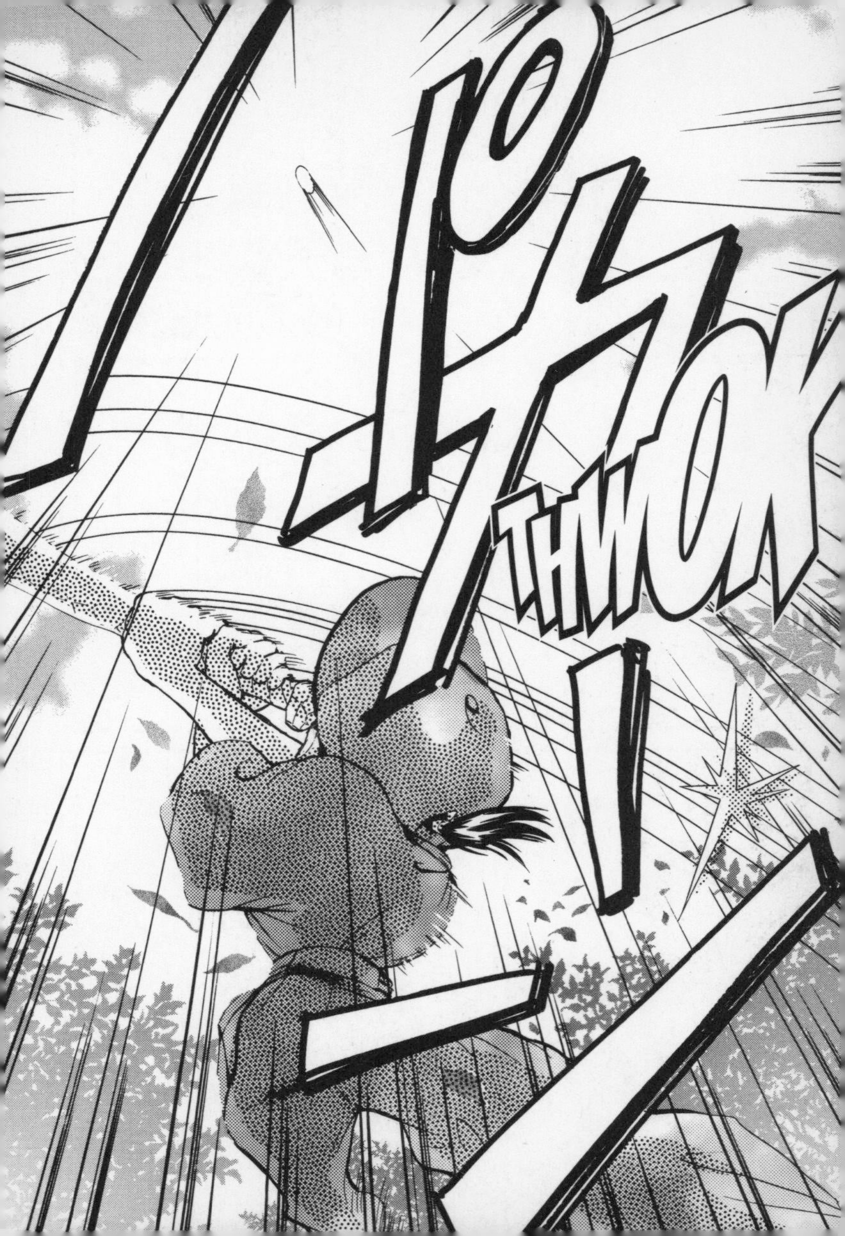
THWOCK

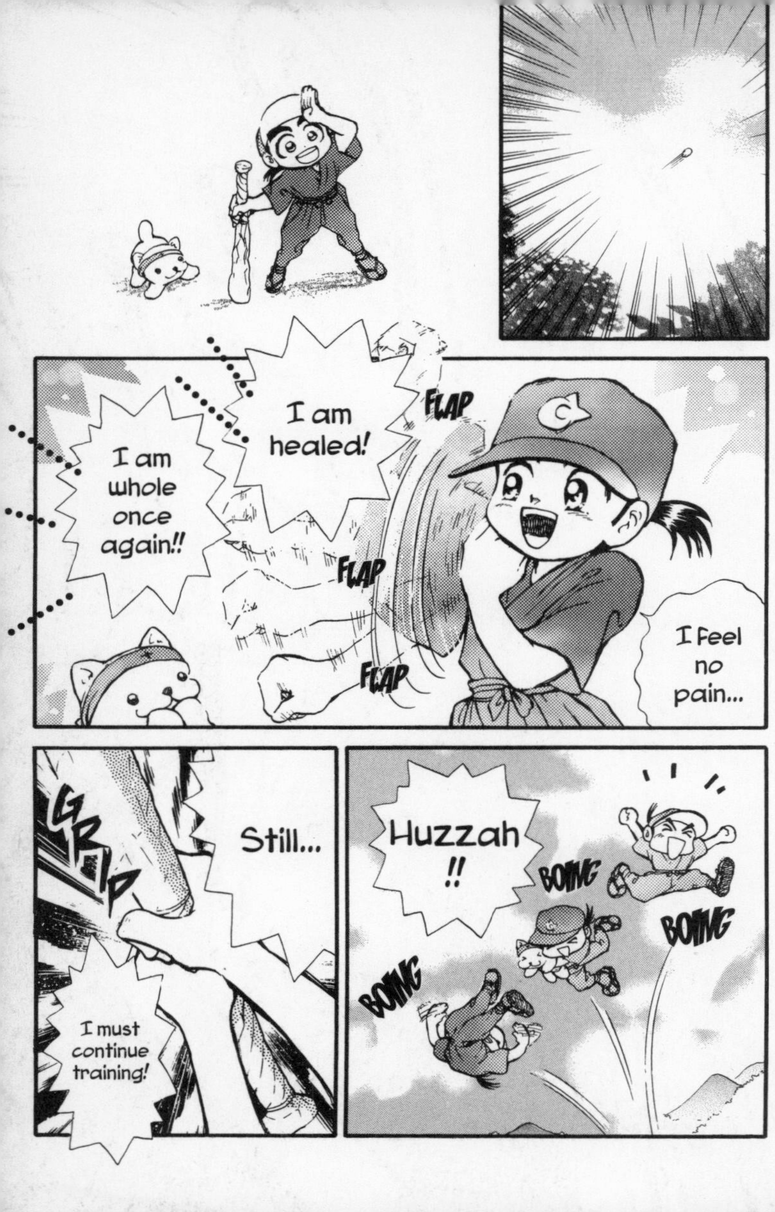
FLAP
I feel no pain...
I am healed!
I am whole once again!!
FLAP
FLAP
Huzzah!!
BOING
BOING
BOING
GRIP
Still...
I must continue training!

Read this way

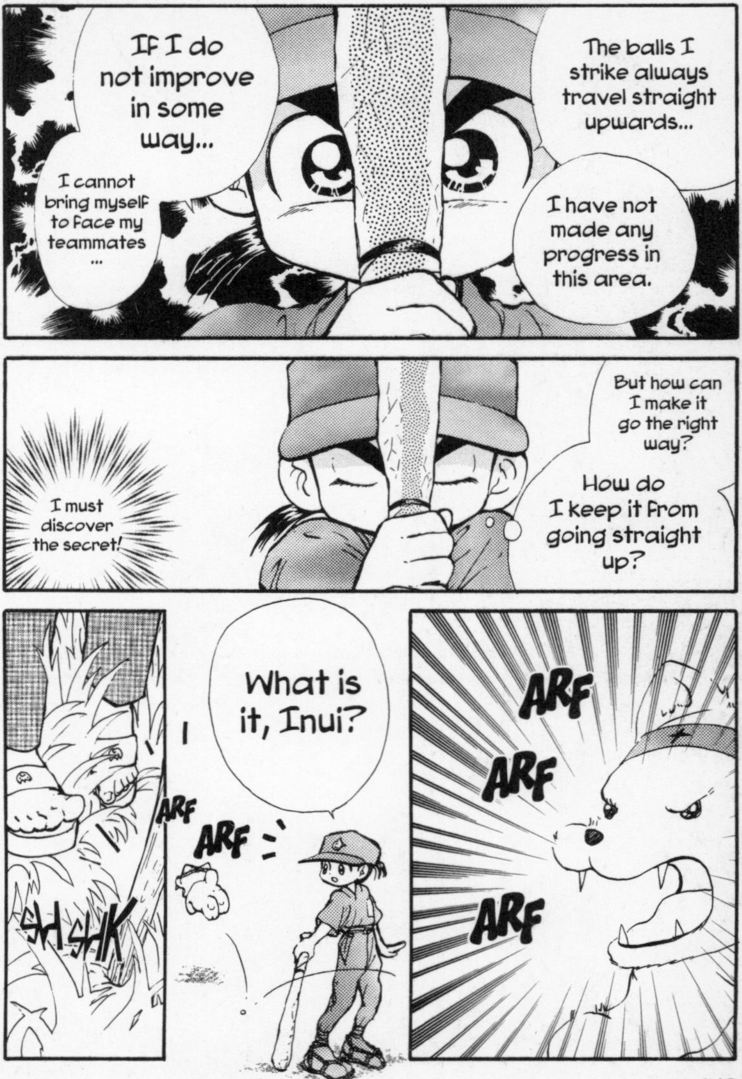
The balls I strike always travel straight upwards...
I have not made any progress in this area.
If I do not improve in some way...
I cannot bring myself to face my teammates ...
But how can I make it go the right way?
How do I keep it from going straight up?
I must discover the secret!
ARF
ARF
ARF
What is it, Inui?
ARF
ARF
SHSHK

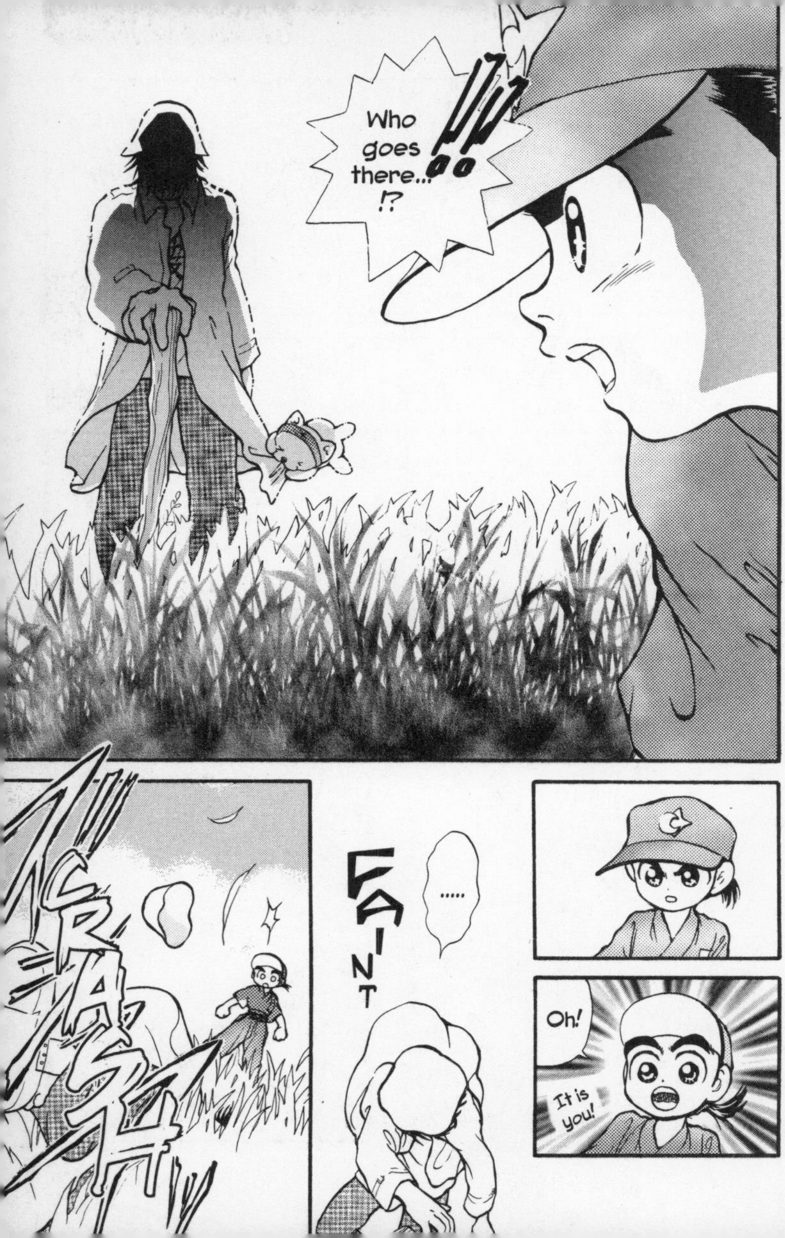
!!
Who goes there...!?
Oh!
It is you!
.....
FAINT
CRASH

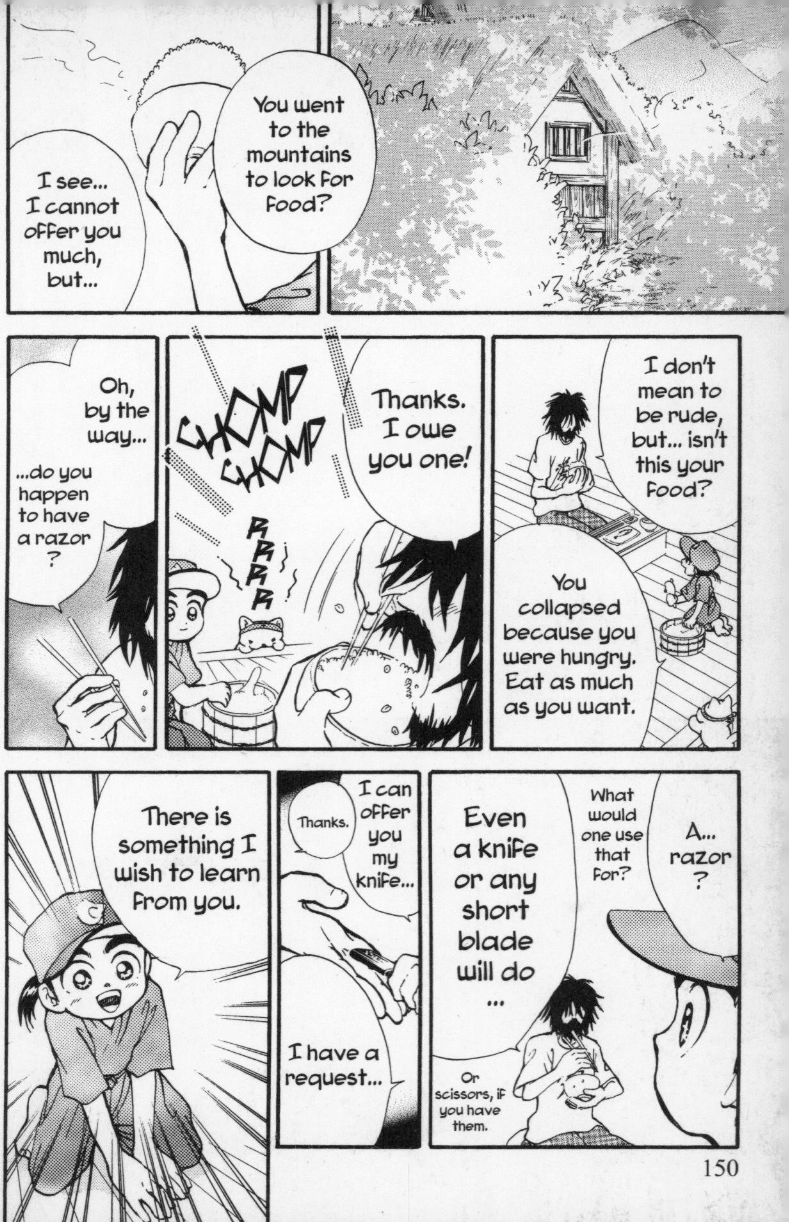
You went to the mountains to look for food?
I see... I cannot offer you much, but...
I don't mean to be rude, but... isn't this your food?
You collapsed because you were hungry. Eat as much as you want.
Thanks. I owe you one!
CHOMP CHOMP
RRRRR
Oh, by the way...
...do you happen to have a razor?
A... razor?
What would one use that for?
Even a knife or any short blade will do...
Or scissors, if you have them.
I can offer you my knife...
Thanks.
I have a request...
There is something I wish to learn from you.

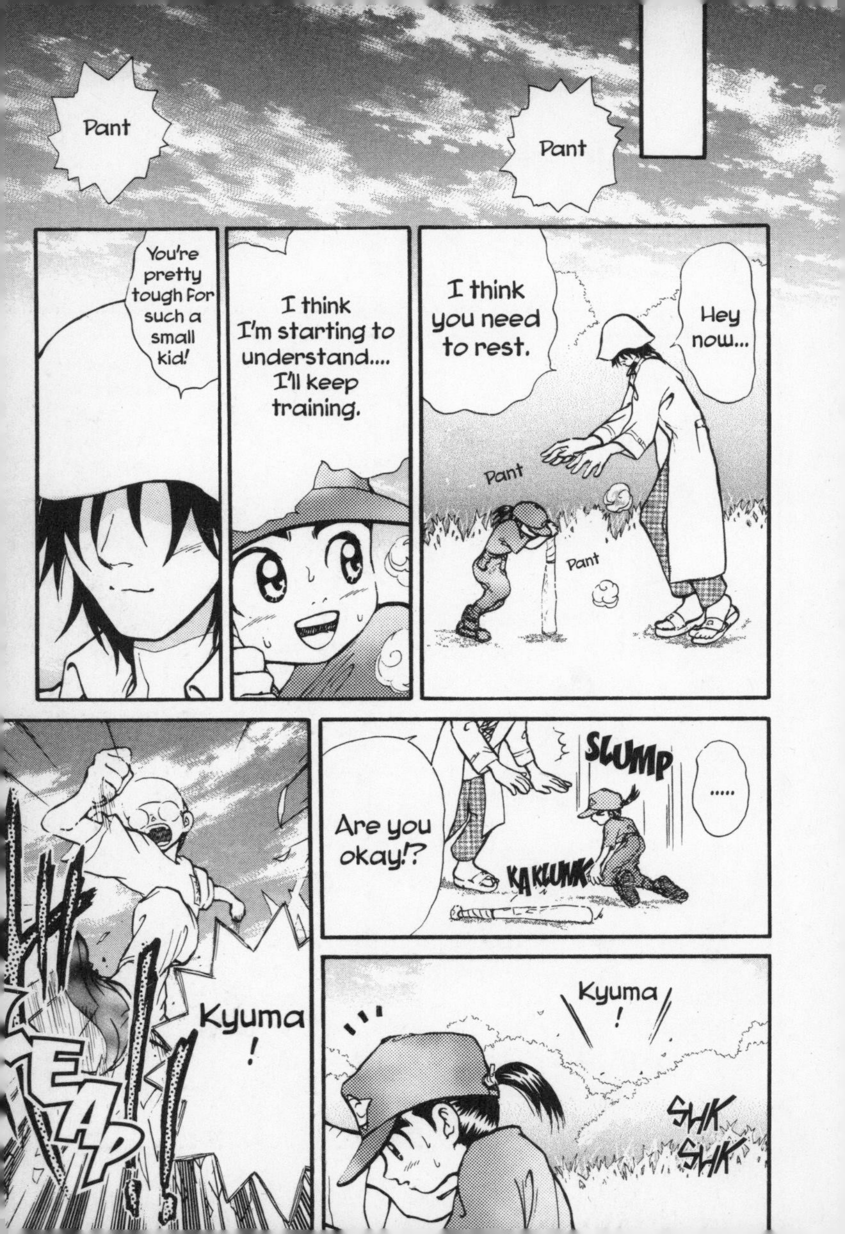

Pant
Pant
Hey now...
I think you need to rest.
Pant
Pant
I think I'm starting to understand.... I'll keep training.
You're pretty tough for such a small kid!
.....
SLUMP
Are you okay!?
KAKLUNK
Kyuma !
SHK SHK
Kyuma !
LEAP

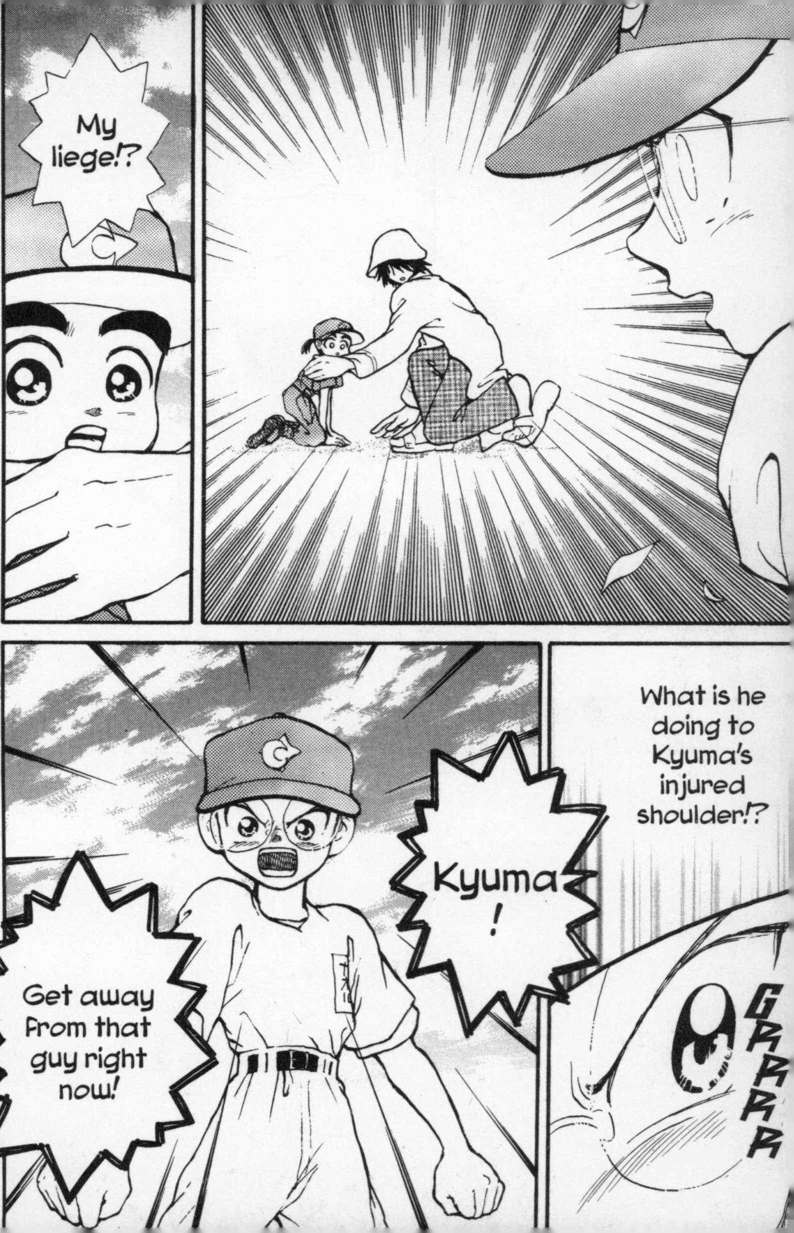
My liege!?
What is he doing to Kyuma's injured shoulder!?
GRRRR
Kyuma!
Get away from that guy right now!

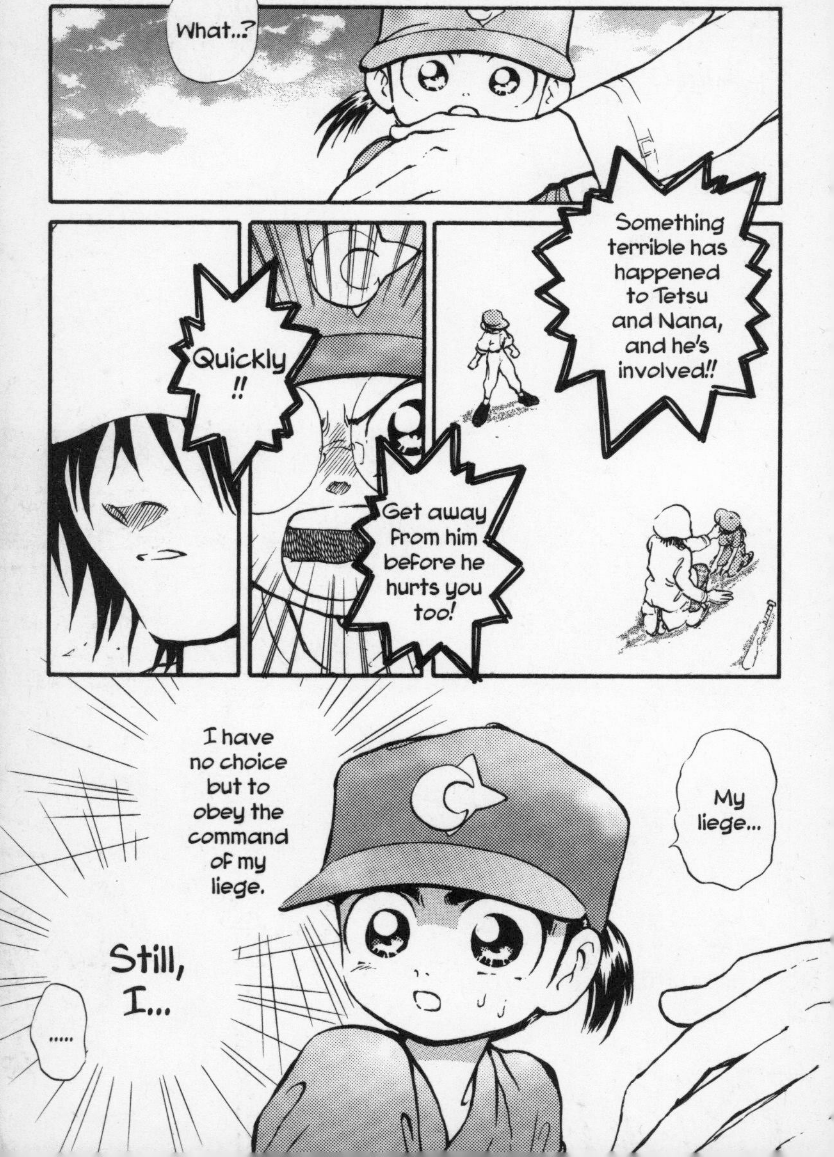
What..?
Something terrible has happened to Tetsu and Nana, and he's involved!!
Get away from him before he hurts you too!
Quickly!!
My liege...
I have no choice but to obey the command of my liege.
Still, I...
.....

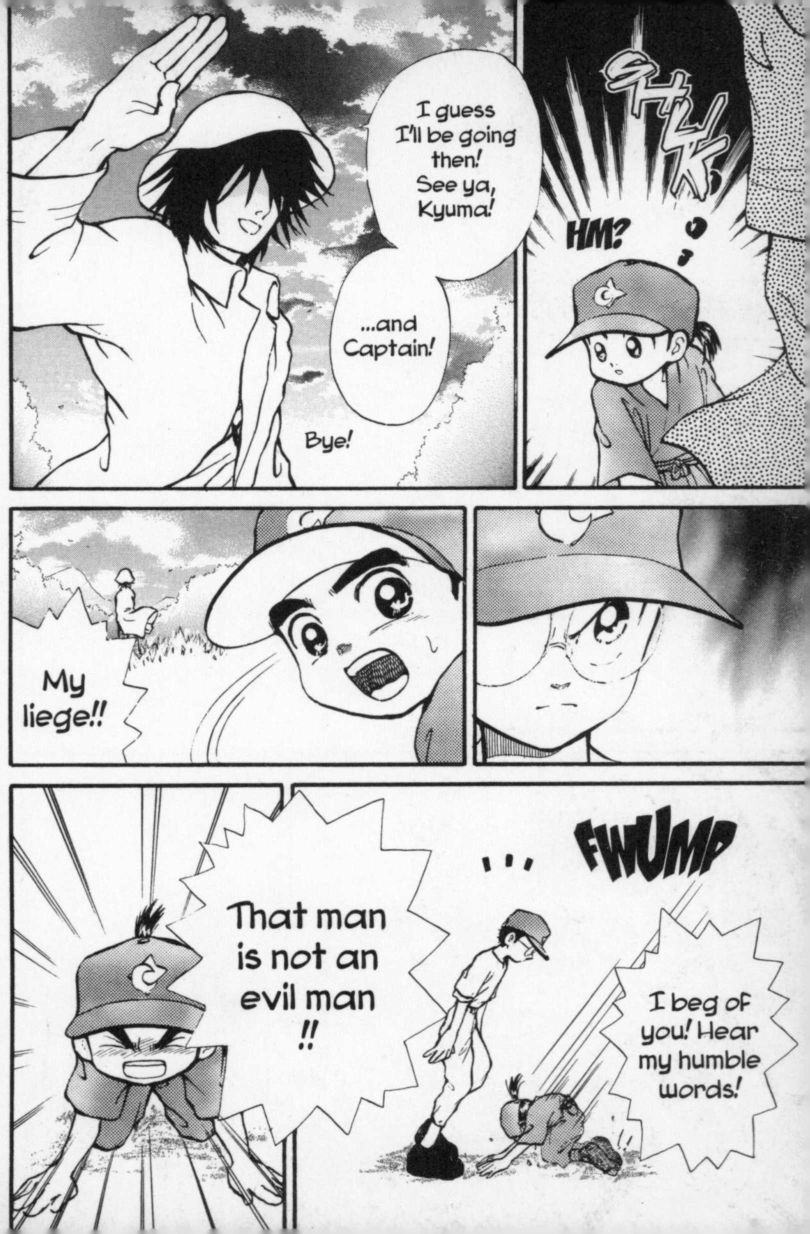
SHKK
HM?
I guess I'll be going then! See ya, Kyuma!
...and Captain!
Bye!
My liege!!
...
FWUMP
I beg of you! Hear my humble words!
That man is not an evil man!!

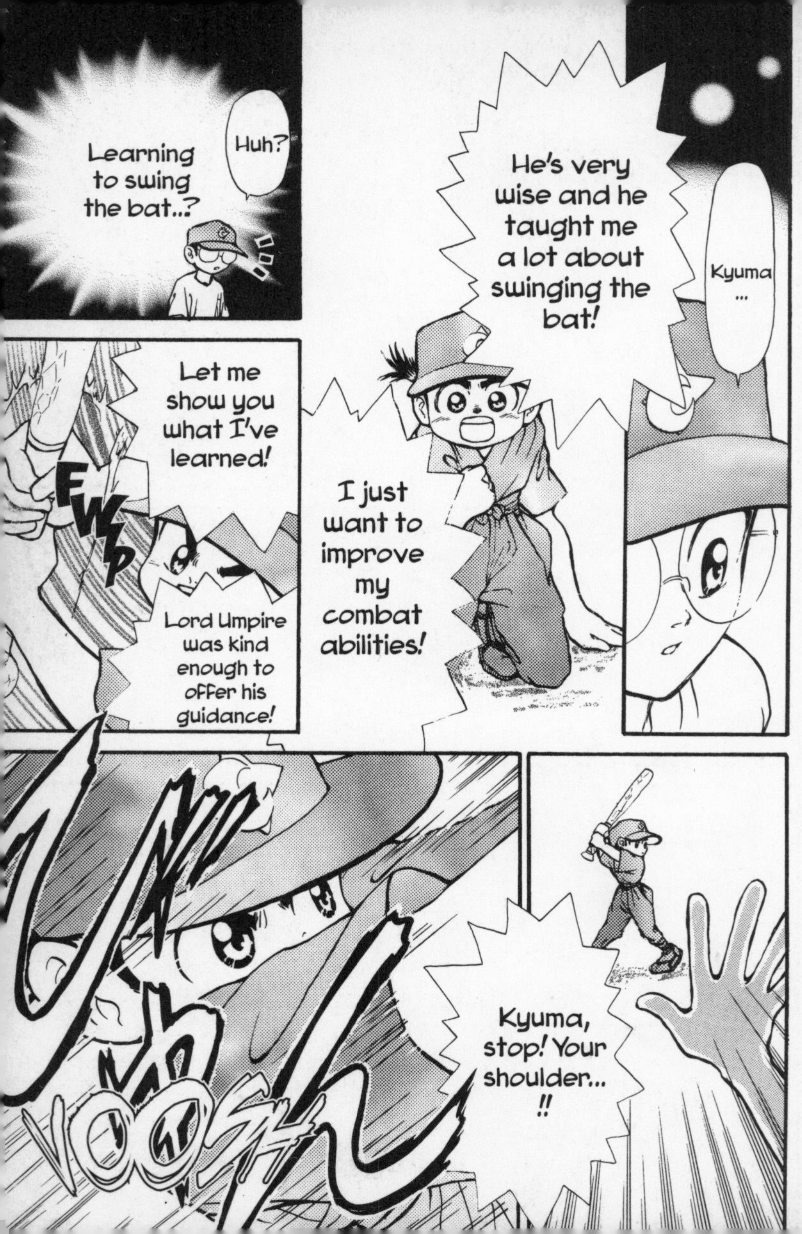
Kyuma ...
He's very wise and he taught me a lot about swinging the bat!
I just want to improve my combat abilities!
Huh?
Learning to swing the bat...?
Let me show you what I've learned!
FWSP
Lord Umpire was kind enough to offer his guidance!
Kyuma, stop! Your shoulder... !!
VOOSH

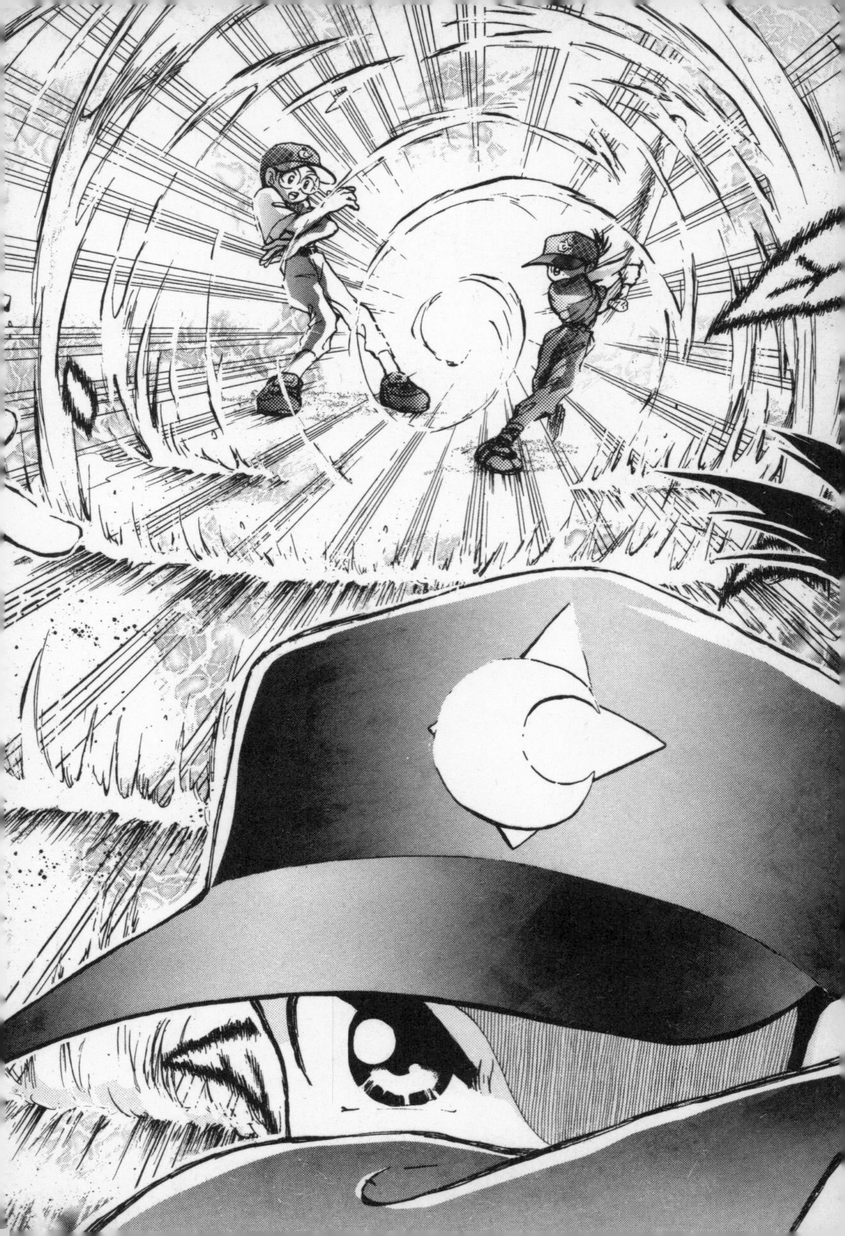

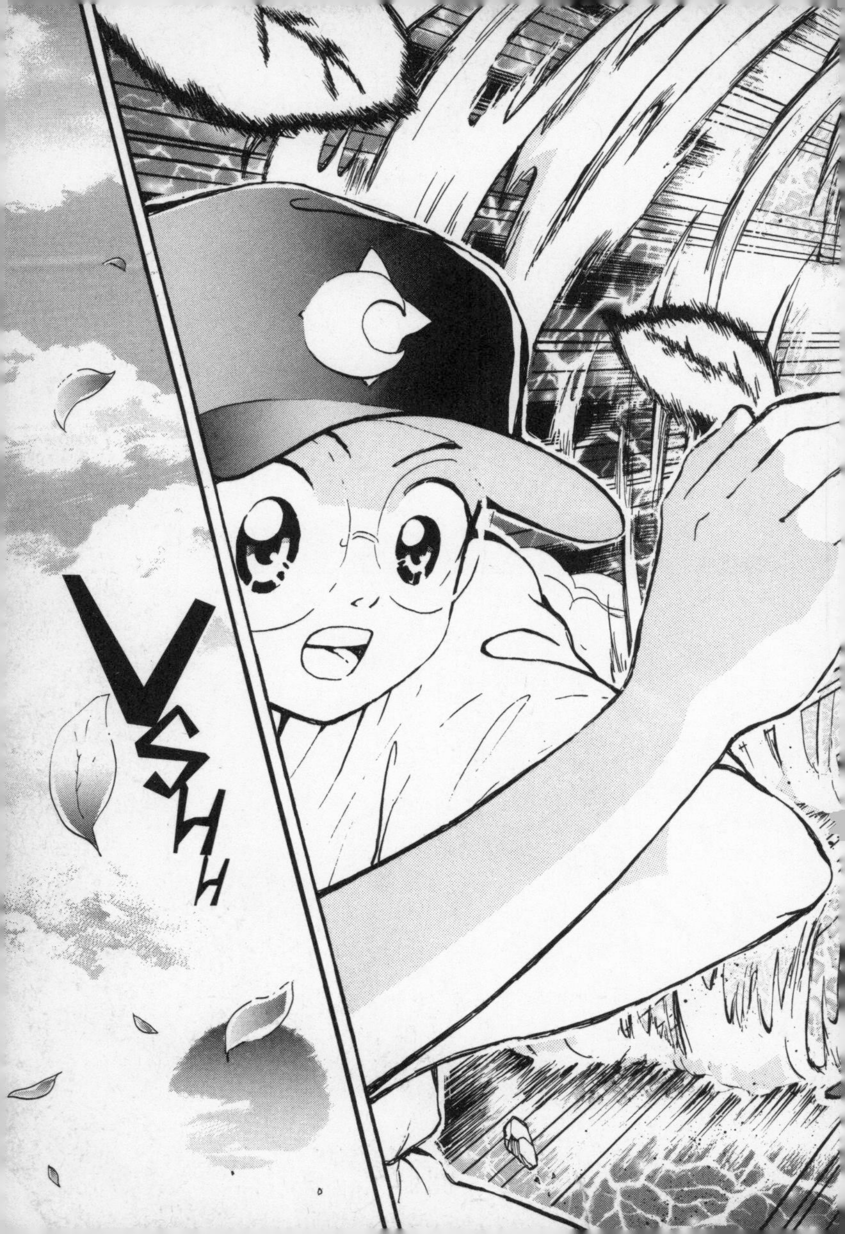
VSHHH

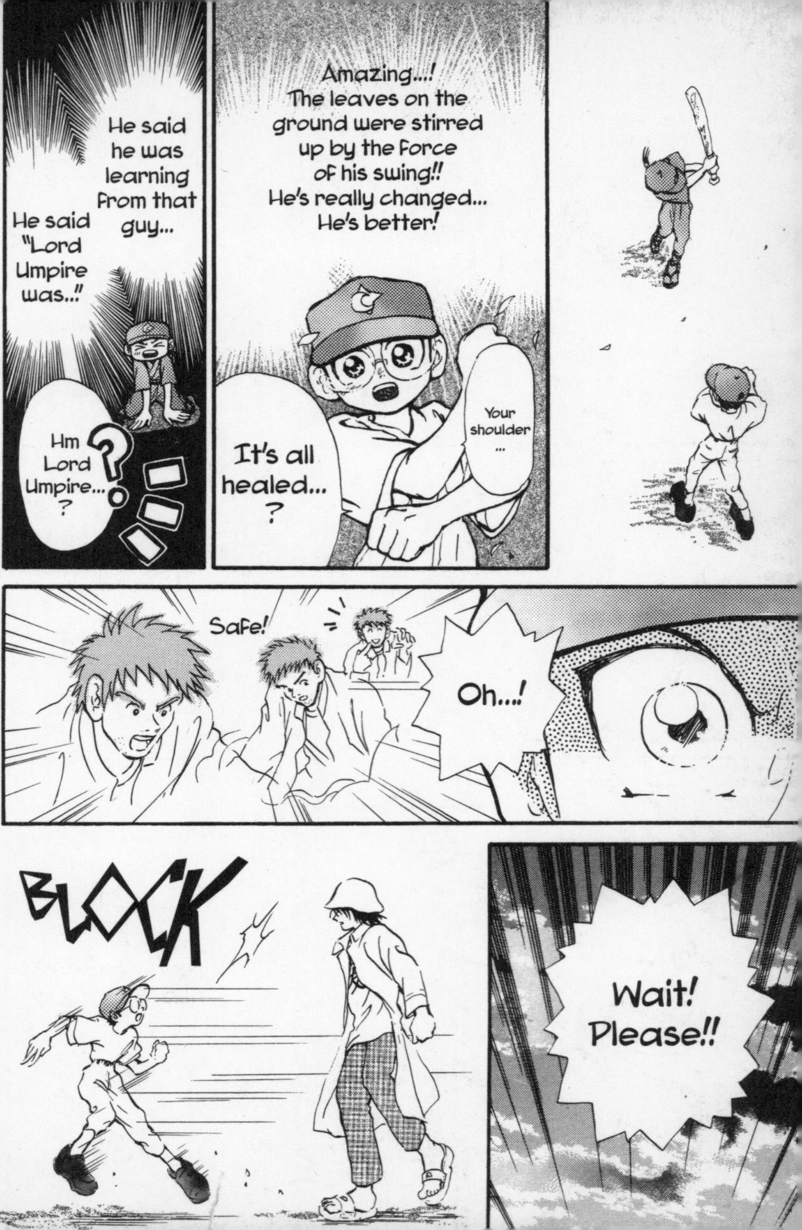
Amazing...!
The leaves on the ground were stirred up by the force of his swing!! He's really changed... He's better!
Your shoulder ...
It's all healed... ?
He said he was learning from that guy...
He said "Lord Umpire was..!"
Hm Lord Umpire... ?
Oh...!
Safe!
Wait! Please!!
BLOCK

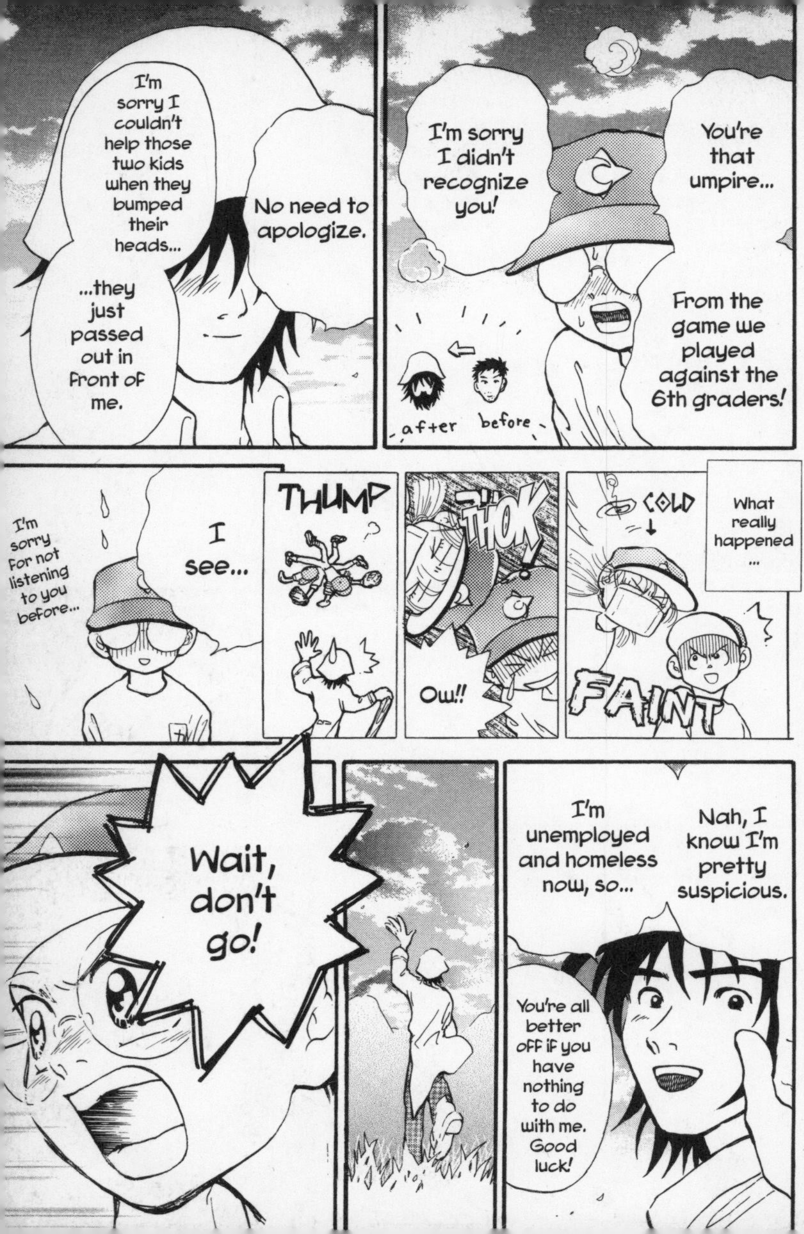
You're that umpire...
From the game we played against the 6th graders!
I'm sorry I didn't recognize you!
before
after
No need to apologize.
I'm sorry I couldn't help those two kids when they bumped their heads...
...they just passed out in front of me.
What really happened ...
COLD
FAINT
THOK
Ow!!
THUMP
I see...
I'm sorry for not listening to you before...
Nah, I know I'm pretty suspicious.
I'm unemployed and homeless now, so...
You're all better off if you have nothing to do with me. Good luck!
Wait, don't go!

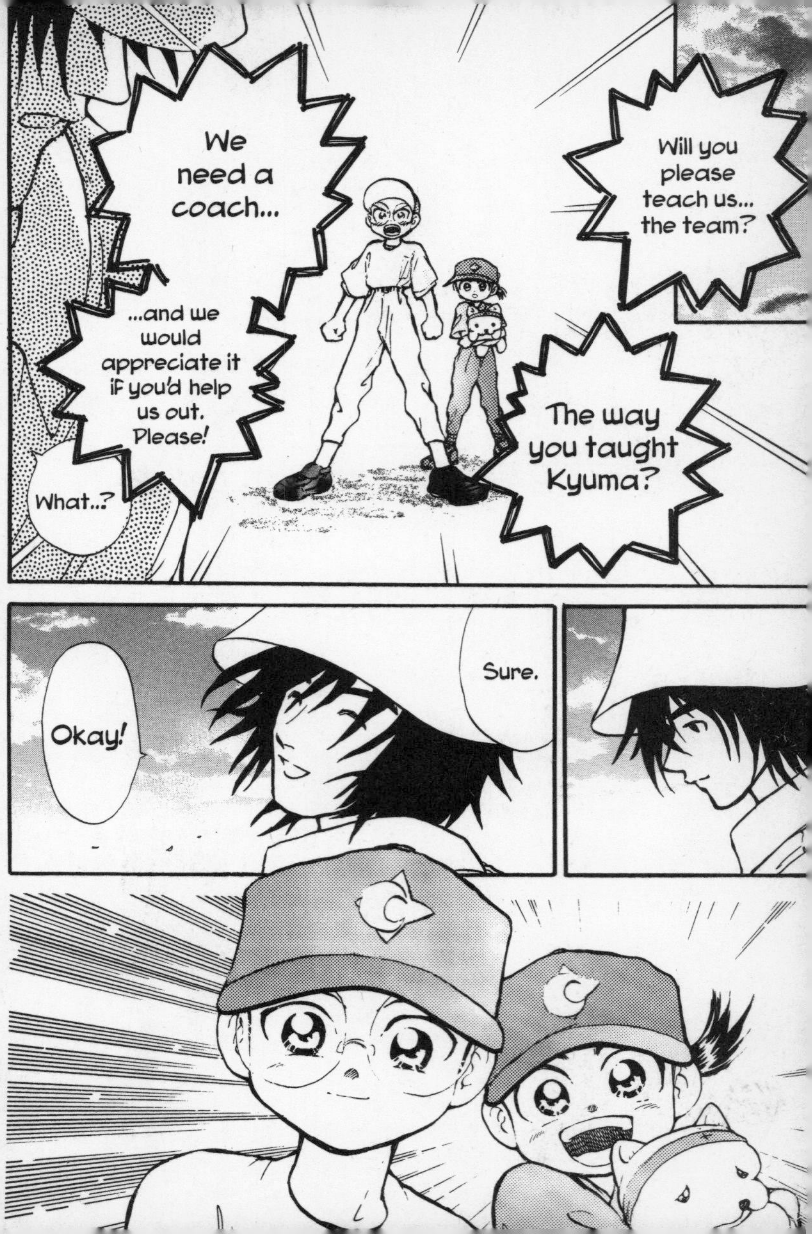
Will you please teach us... the team?
We need a coach...
...and we would appreciate it if you'd help us out. Please!
The way you taught Kyuma?
What..?
Sure.
Okay!

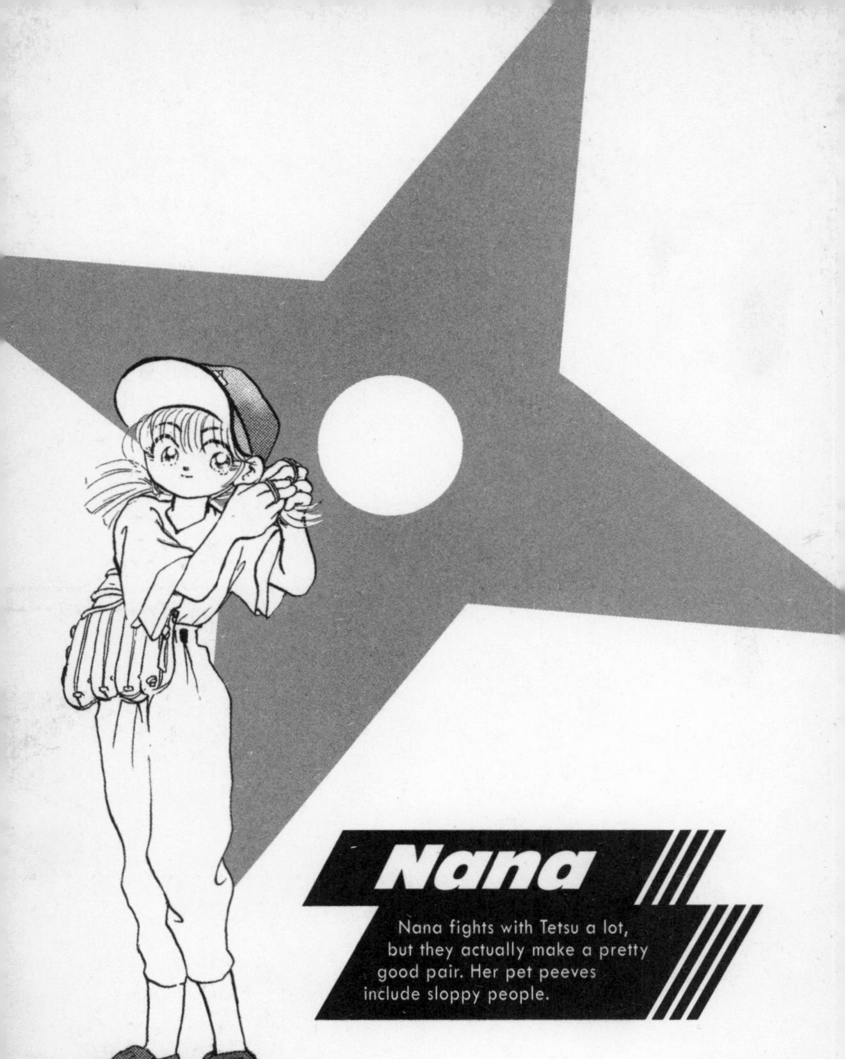

Nana

Nana fights with Tetsu a lot, but they actually make a pretty good pair. Her pet peeves include sloppy people.

Coach (to be) Tamori

Despite his shady past, Coach Tamori is extremely cheerful. Does he have what it takes to coach a baseball team?

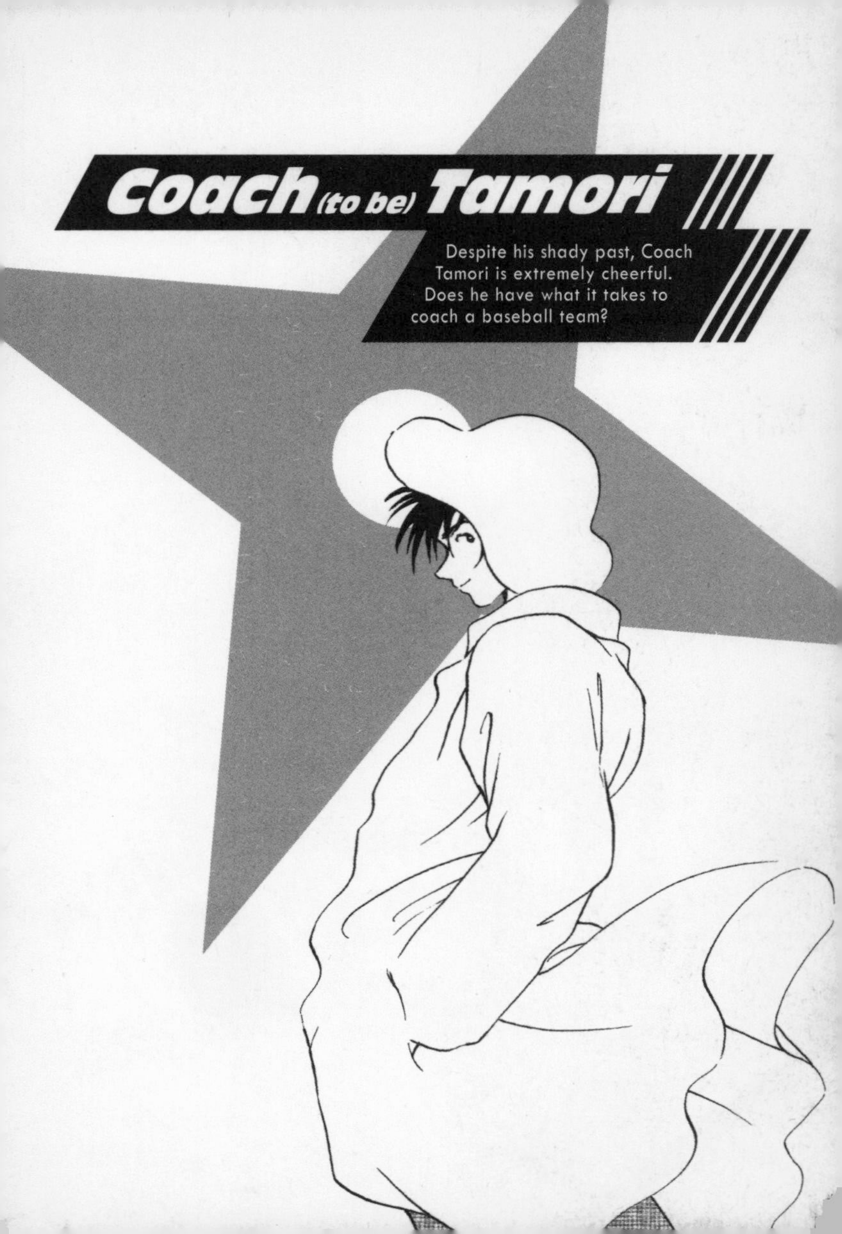

PITCH 7
IS KYUMA A NINJA?

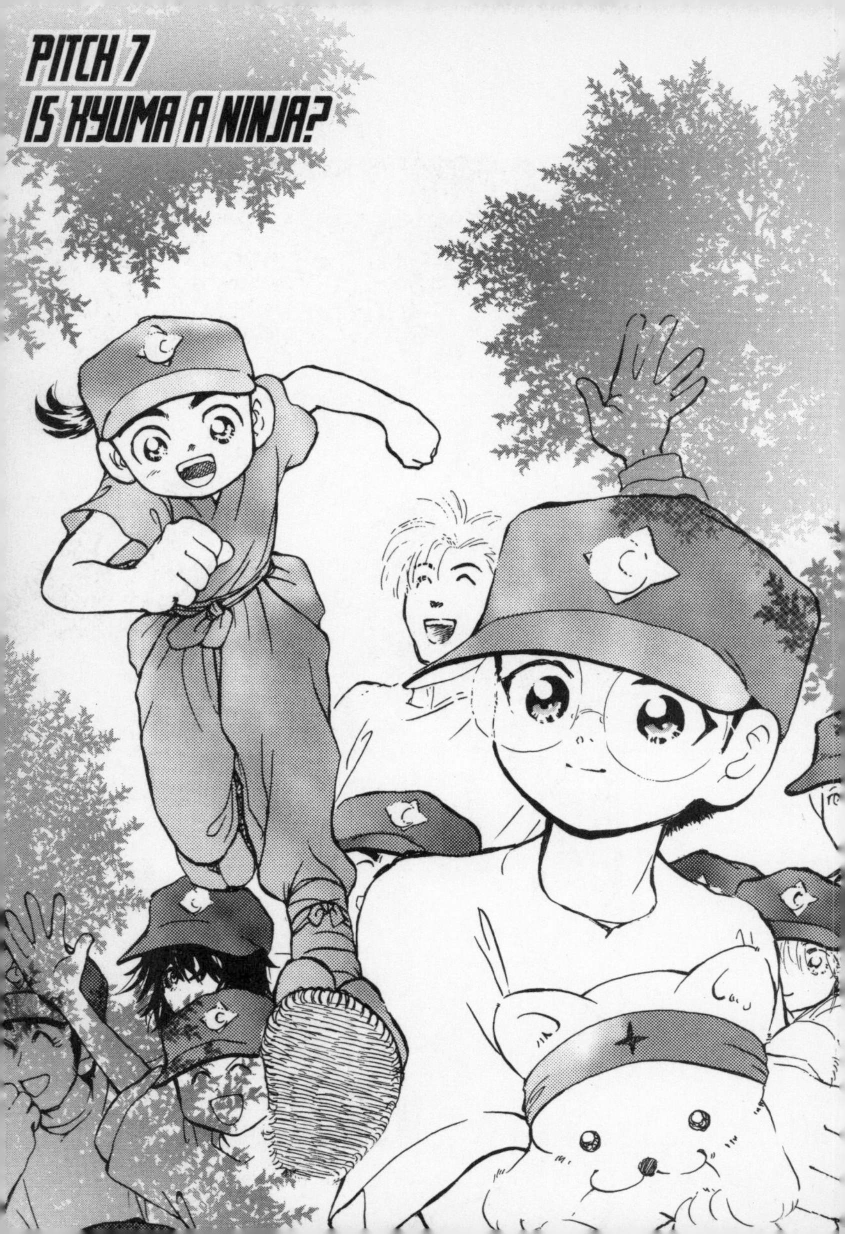

Read this way

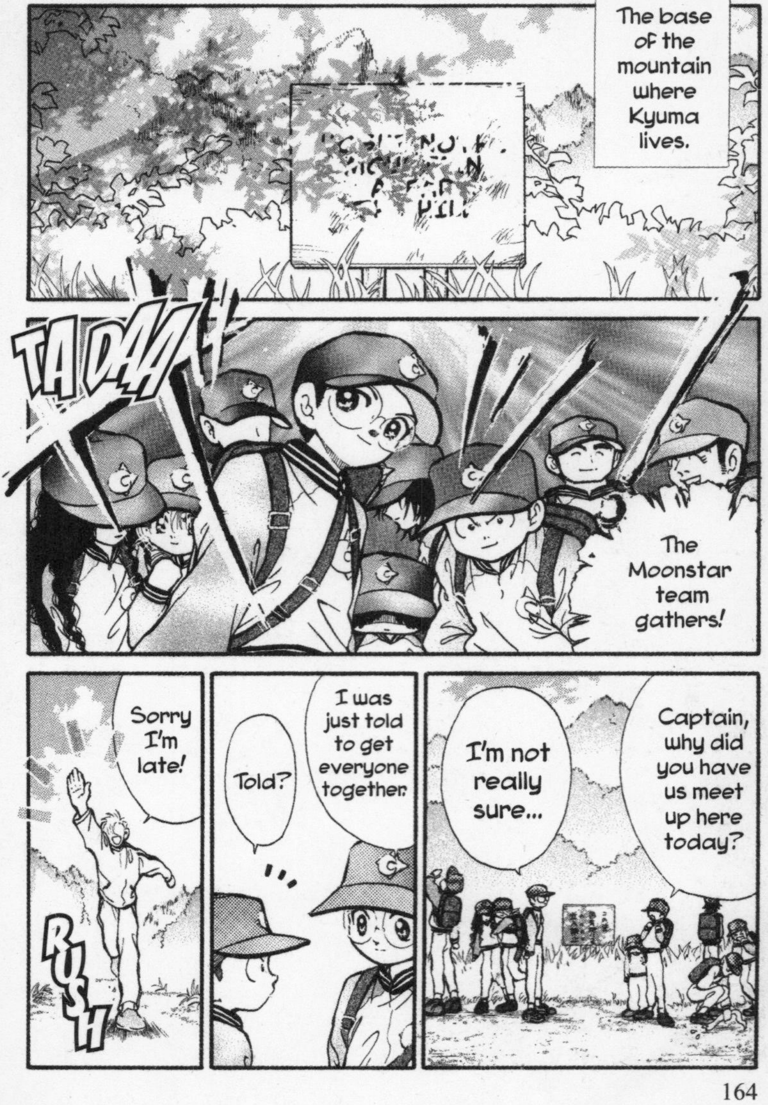

The base of the mountain where Kyuma lives.
TA DAA
The Moonstar team gathers!
Captain, why did you have us meet up here today?
I'm not really sure...
I was just told to get everyone together.
Told?
...
Sorry I'm late!
RUSH

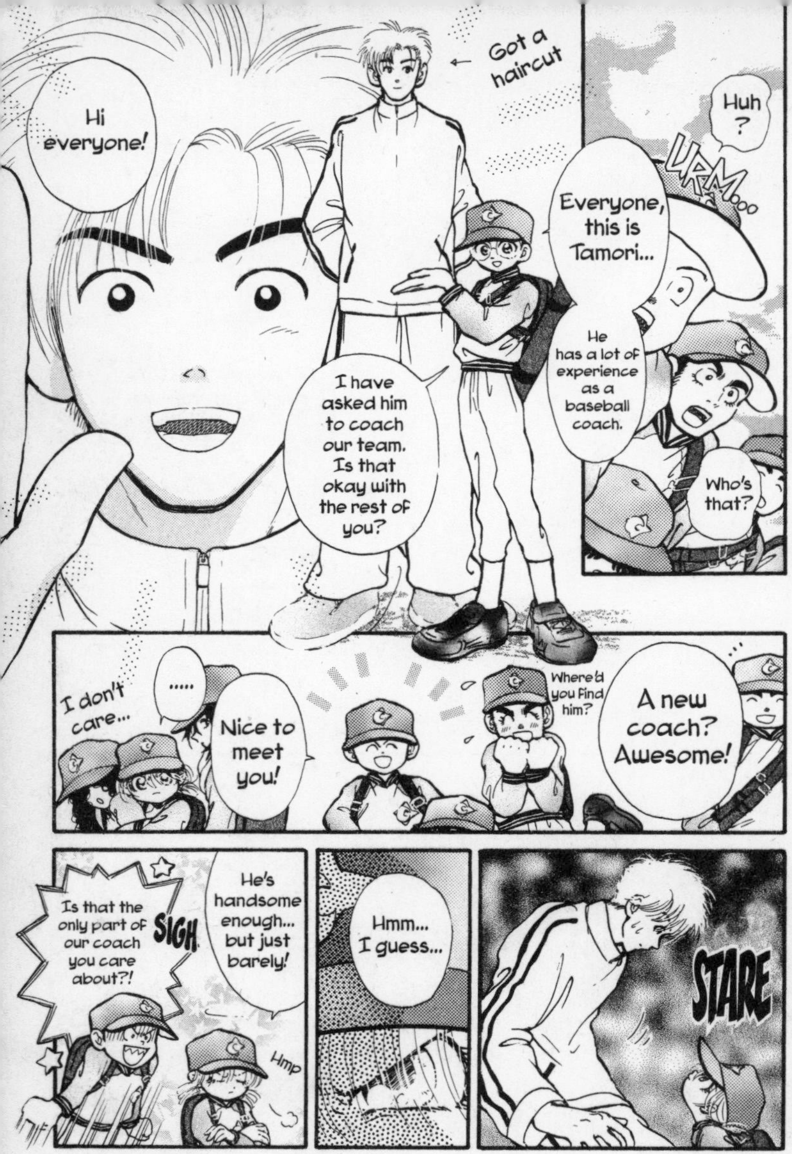
Huh?
URMooo
Everyone, this is Tamori...
He has a lot of experience as a baseball coach.
Who's that?
I have asked him to coach our team. Is that okay with the rest of you?
Got a haircut
Hi everyone!
A new coach? Awesome!
Where'd you find him?
Nice to meet you!
.....
I don't care...
STARE
Hmm... I guess...
He's handsome enough... but just barely!
SIGH
Is that the only part of our coach you care about?!
Hmp

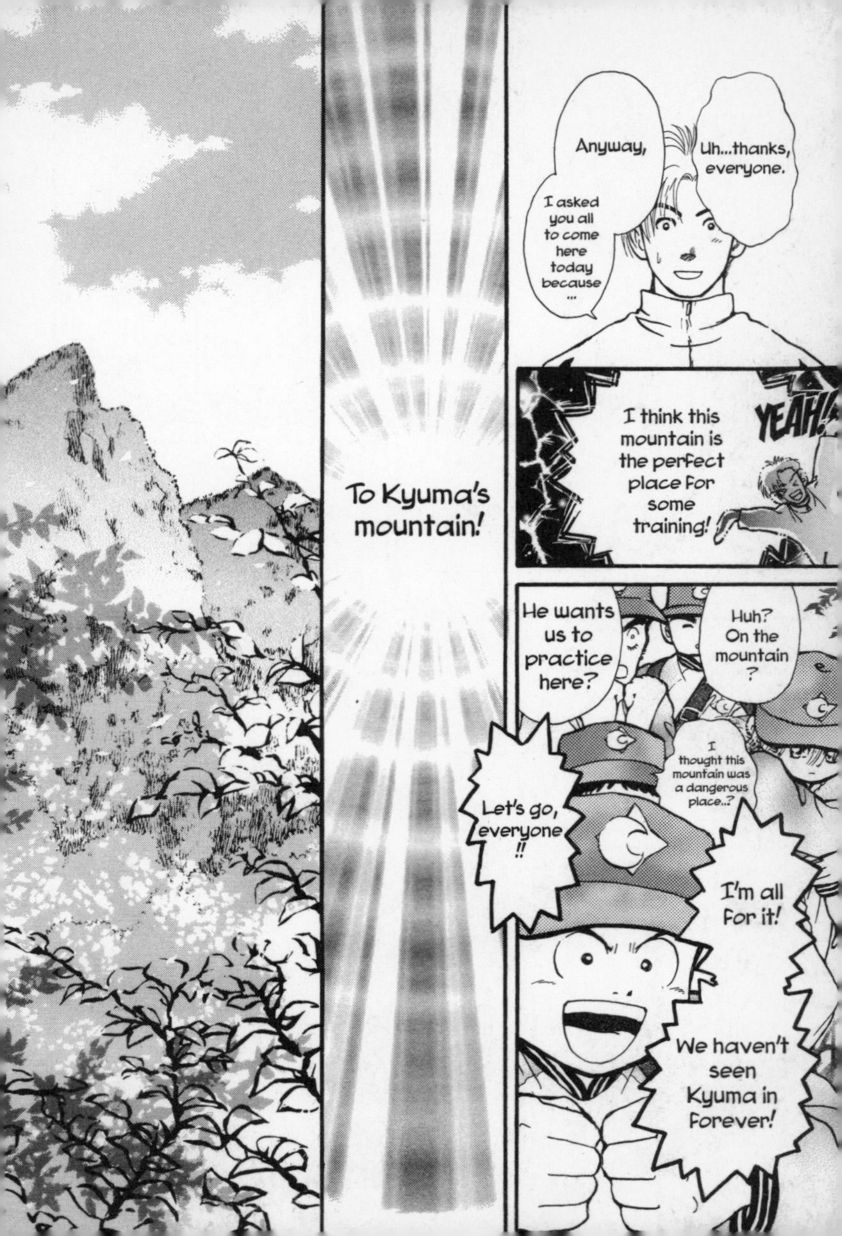

Uh...thanks, everyone.
Anyway,
I asked you all to come here today because...
YEAH!!
I think this mountain is the perfect place for some training!
Huh? On the mountain?
He wants us to practice here?
I thought this mountain was a dangerous place..?
Let's go, everyone!!
I'm all for it!
We haven't seen Kyuma in forever!
To Kyuma's mountain!

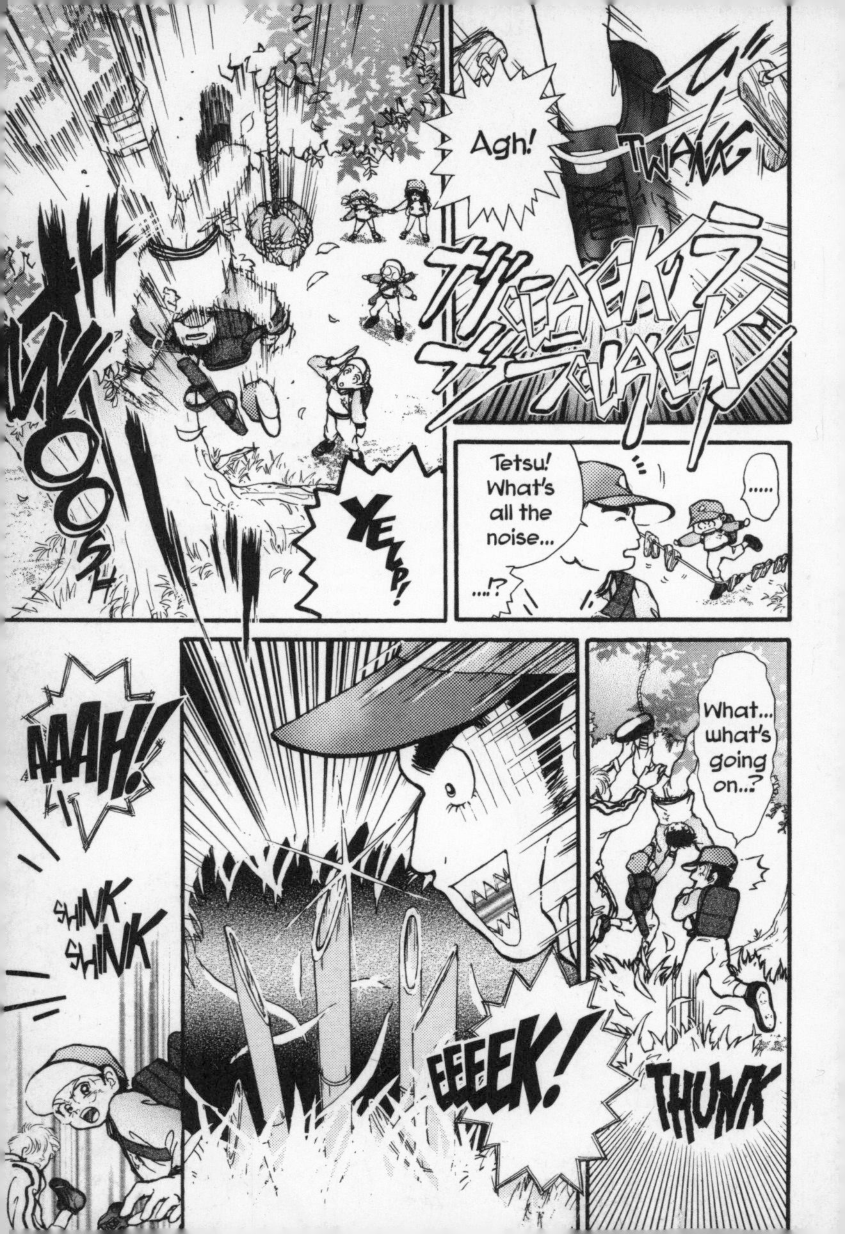
Agh!
TWANG
CLACK CLACK
Tetsu! What's all the noise...
......
...!?
WHOOSH
YELP!
What... what's going on...?
THUNK
EEEEK!
AAAH!
SHINK SHINK

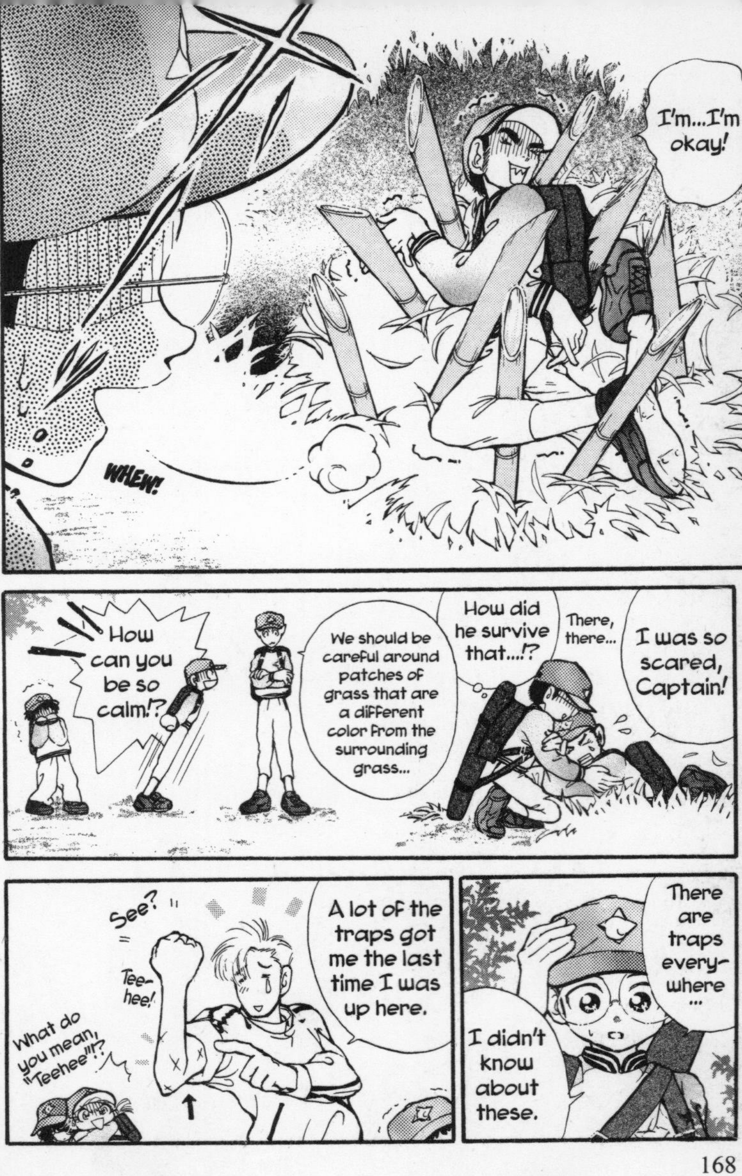
I'm...I'm okay!
WHEW!
I was so scared, Captain!
There, there...
How did he survive that....!?
We should be careful around patches of grass that are a different color from the surrounding grass...
How can you be so calm!?
There are traps every-where...
I didn't know about these.
A lot of the traps got me the last time I was up here.
See?
Tee-hee!
What do you mean, "Teehee"!?

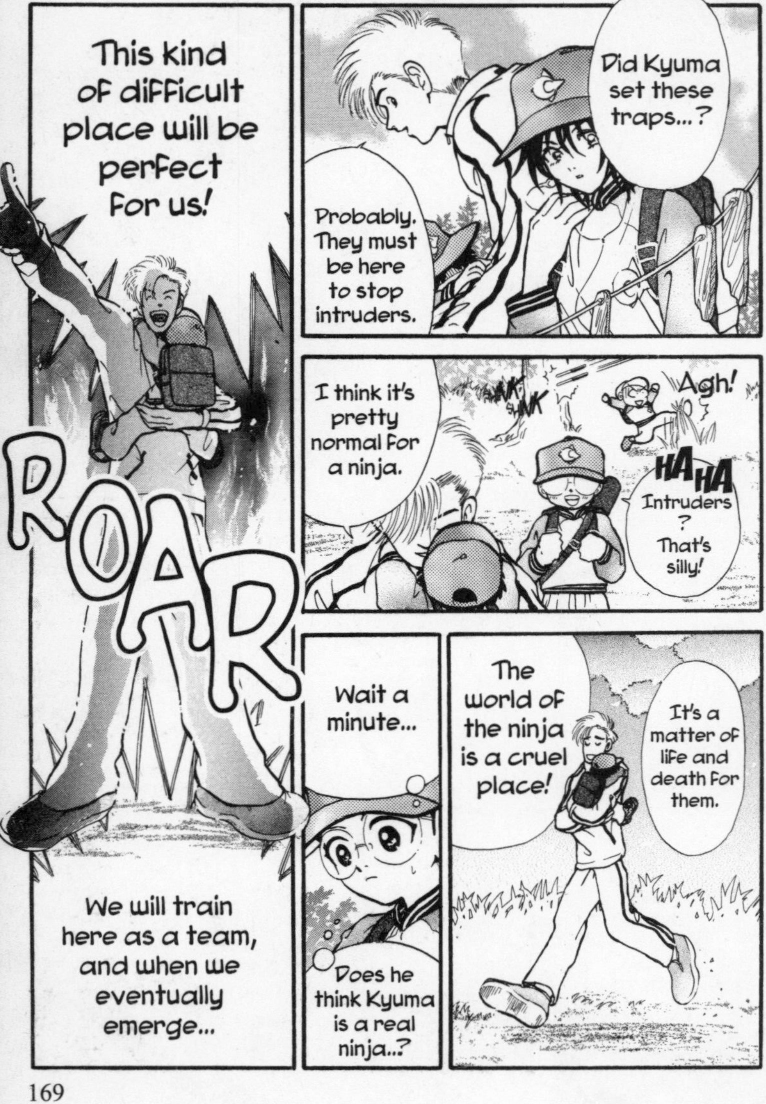
Did Kyuma set these traps...?
Probably. They must be here to stop intruders.
Agh!
SHINK SHINK
HAHA
Intruders? That's silly!
I think it's pretty normal for a ninja.
The world of the ninja is a cruel place!
It's a matter of life and death for them.
Wait a minute...
Does he think Kyuma is a real ninja..?
This kind of difficult place will be perfect for us!
ROAR
We will train here as a team, and when we eventually emerge...

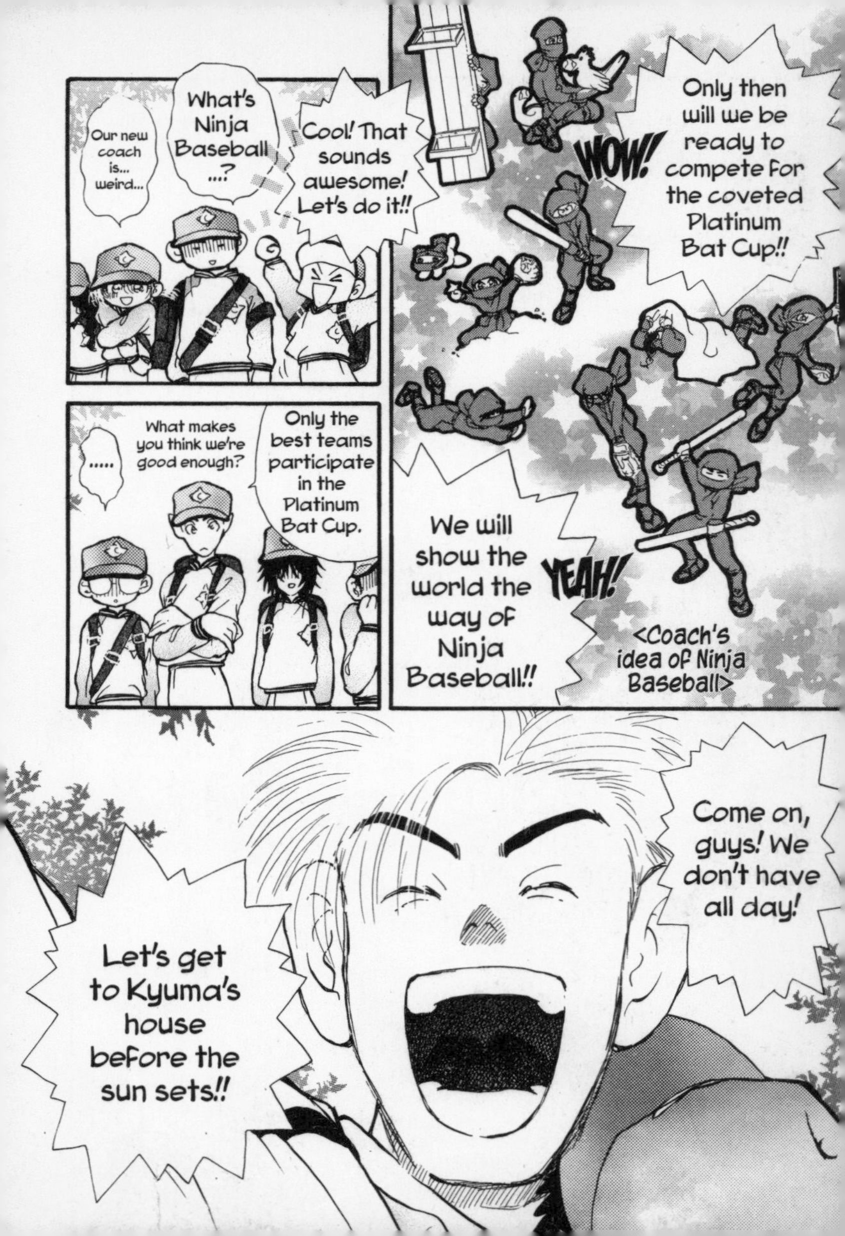
Only then will we be ready to compete for the coveted Platinum Bat Cup!!
WOW!
<Coach's idea of Ninja Baseball>
YEAH!
We will show the world the way of Ninja Baseball!!
Cool! That sounds awesome! Let's do it!!
What's Ninja Baseball ...?
Our new coach is... weird...
Only the best teams participate in the Platinum Bat Cup.
What makes you think we're good enough?
.....
Come on, guys! We don't have all day!
Let's get to Kyuma's house before the sun sets!!

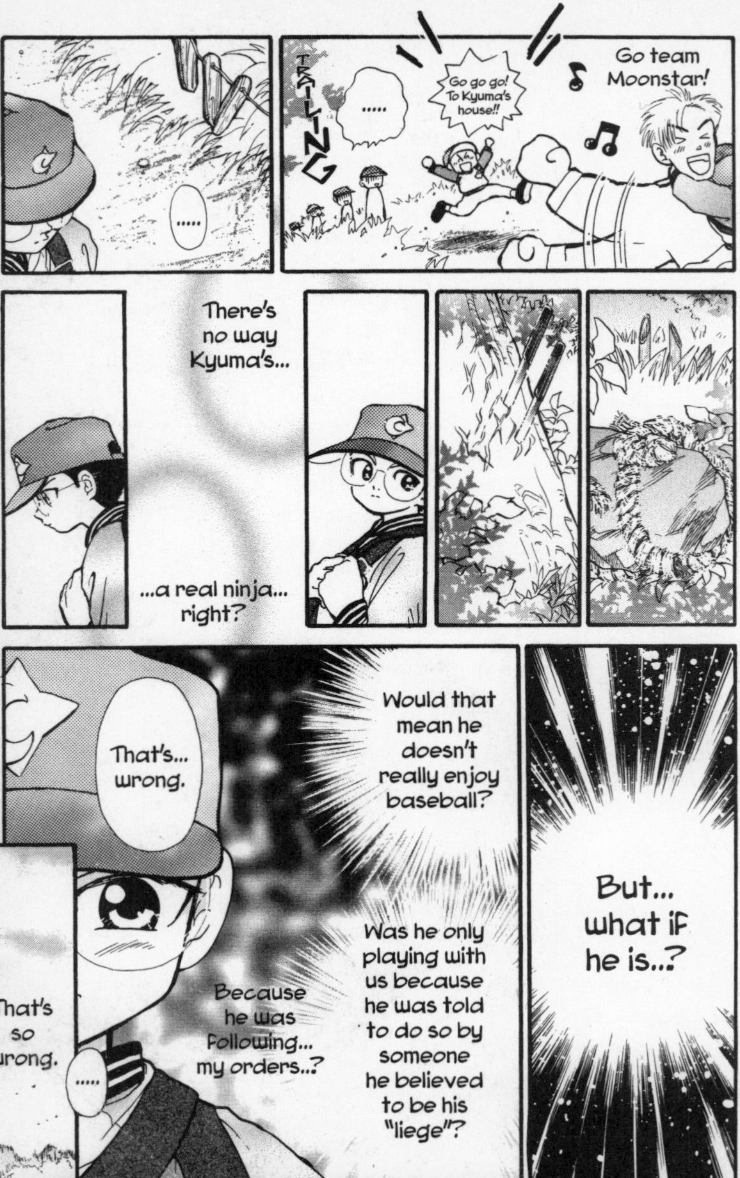
Go team Moonstar!
Go go go! To Kyuma's house!!
TRAILING
.....
.....
There's no way Kyuma's...
...a real ninja... right?
But... what if he is..?
Would that mean he doesn't really enjoy baseball?
Was he only playing with us because he was told to do so by someone he believed to be his "liege"?
Because he was following... my orders..?
That's... wrong.
That's so wrong.
.....

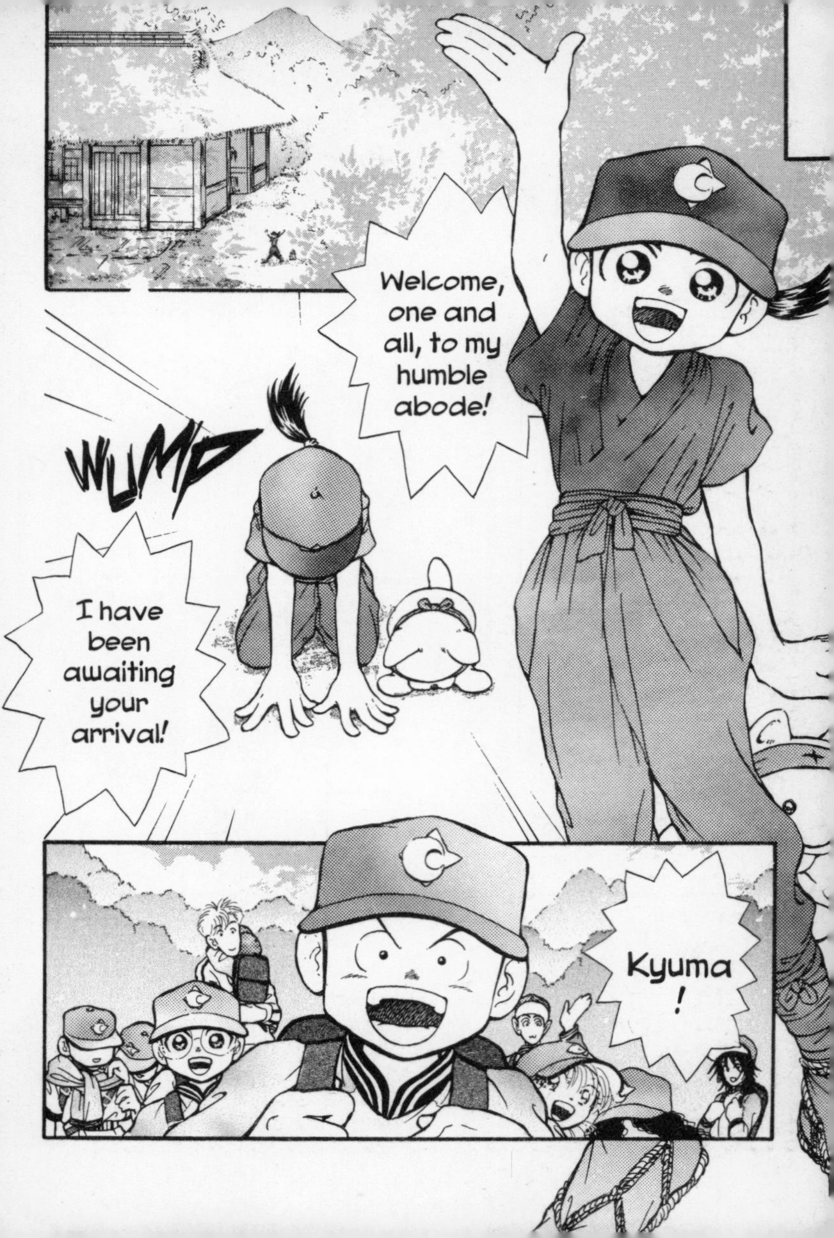
Welcome, one and all, to my humble abode!
WUMP
I have been awaiting your arrival!
Kyuma!

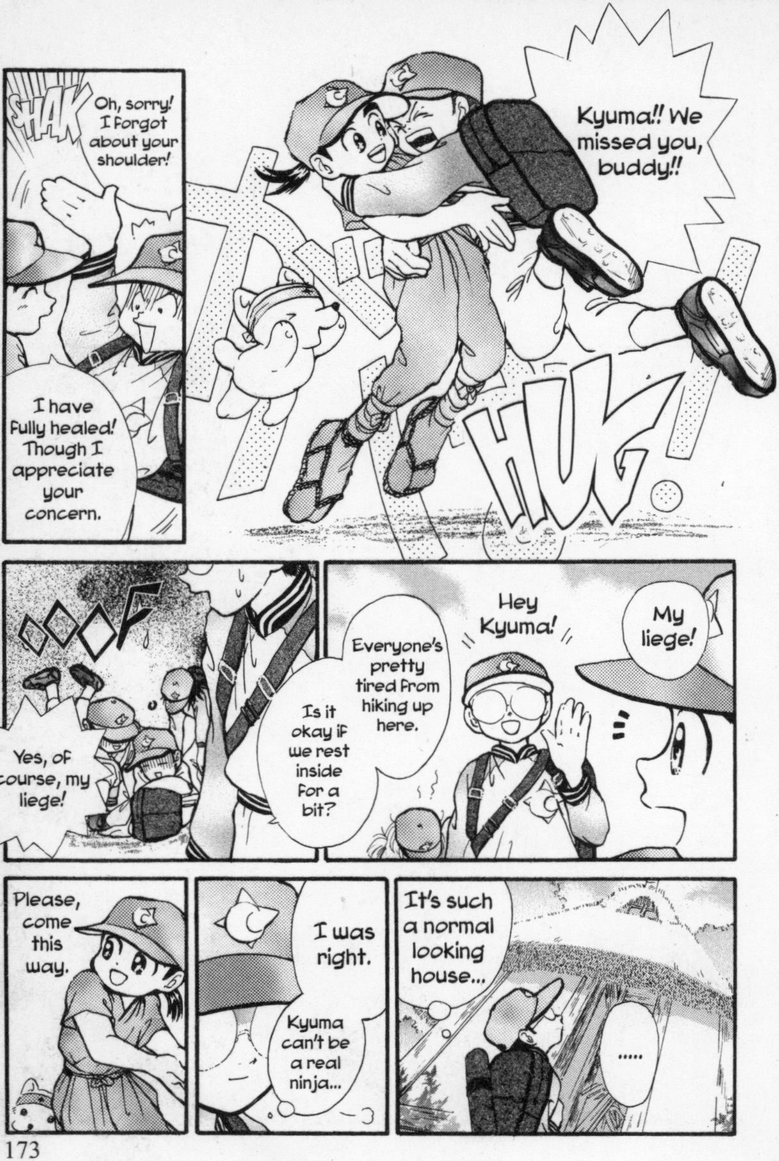
Kyuma!! We missed you, buddy!!
HUG!
SHAK
Oh, sorry! I forgot about your shoulder!
I have fully healed! Though I appreciate your concern.
My liege!
Hey Kyuma!
Everyone's pretty tired from hiking up here.
Is it okay if we rest inside for a bit?
OOOF
Yes, of course, my liege!
It's such a normal looking house...
.....
I was right.
Kyuma can't be a real ninja...
Please, come this way.

So this is your house, Kyuma?
How've you been?
Thanks for having us.
Yeah, thanks for having us!
Please, allow me to carry your belongings!
SWIPE
SWIPE
SWIPE
Whoa!!
Just a moment, please!
SCRUB
I'll make sure my home is all clean!
I shall take your footwear!
Huh!?
YOINK
Allow me to rinse your feet!
Cool, Kyuma. Can you do my feet too?
No! Kyuma! Stop!!

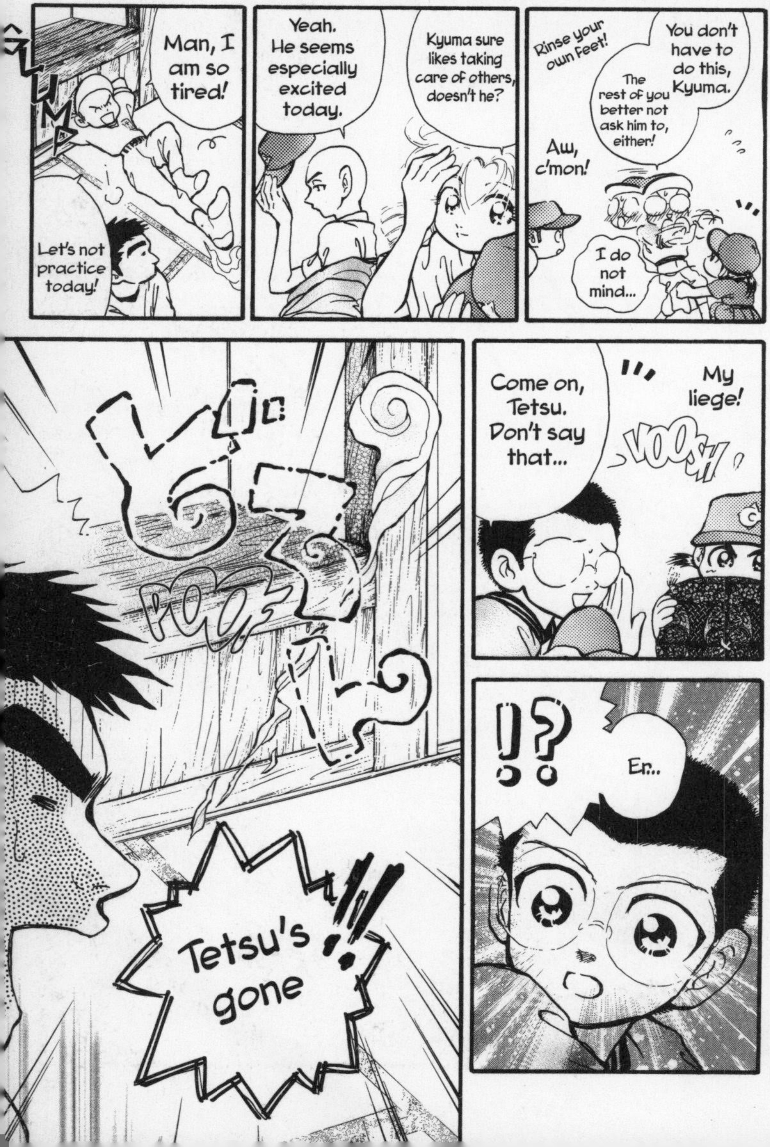
You don't have to do this, Kyuma.
The rest of you better not ask him to, either!
Rinse your own feet!
Aw, c'mon!
I do not mind...
Kyuma sure likes taking care of others, doesn't he?
Yeah. He seems especially excited today.
Man, I am so tired!
SLUMP
Let's not practice today!
My liege!
VOOSH
Come on, Tetsu. Don't say that...
!?
Er..
POOF
Tetsu's gone!!

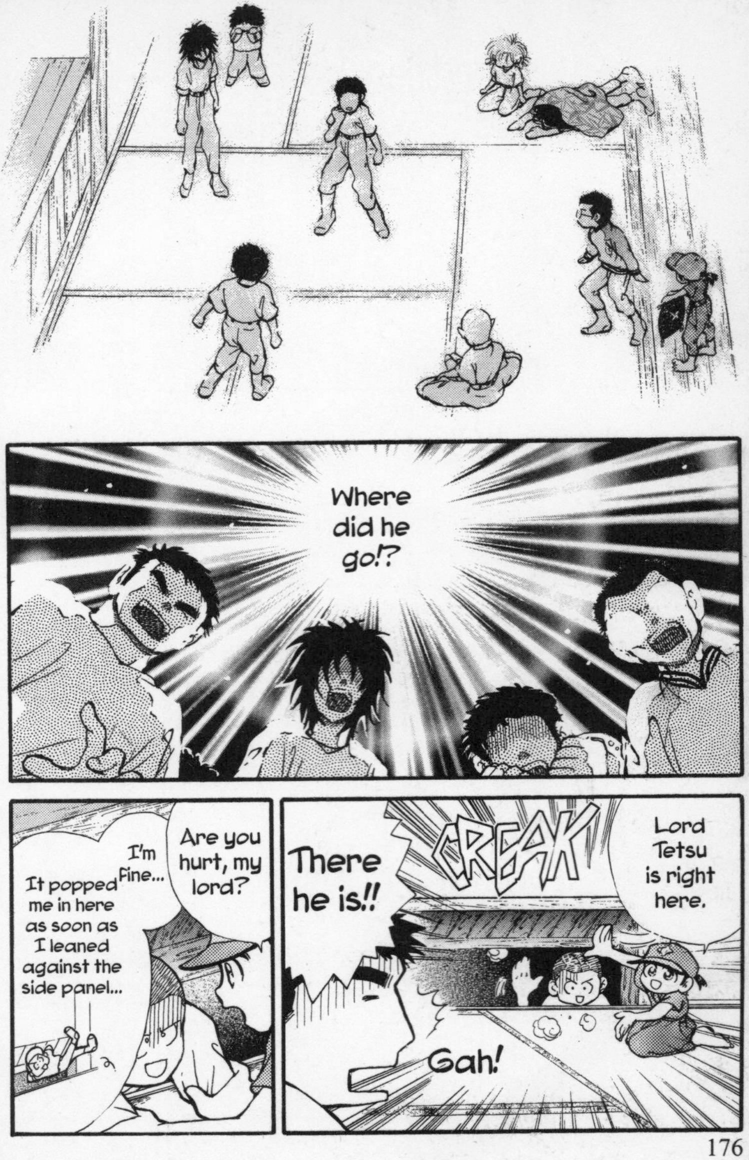
Where did he go!?
Lord Tetsu is right here.
CREAK
There he is!!
Gah!
Are you hurt, my lord?
I'm fine...
It popped me in here as soon as I leaned against the side panel...

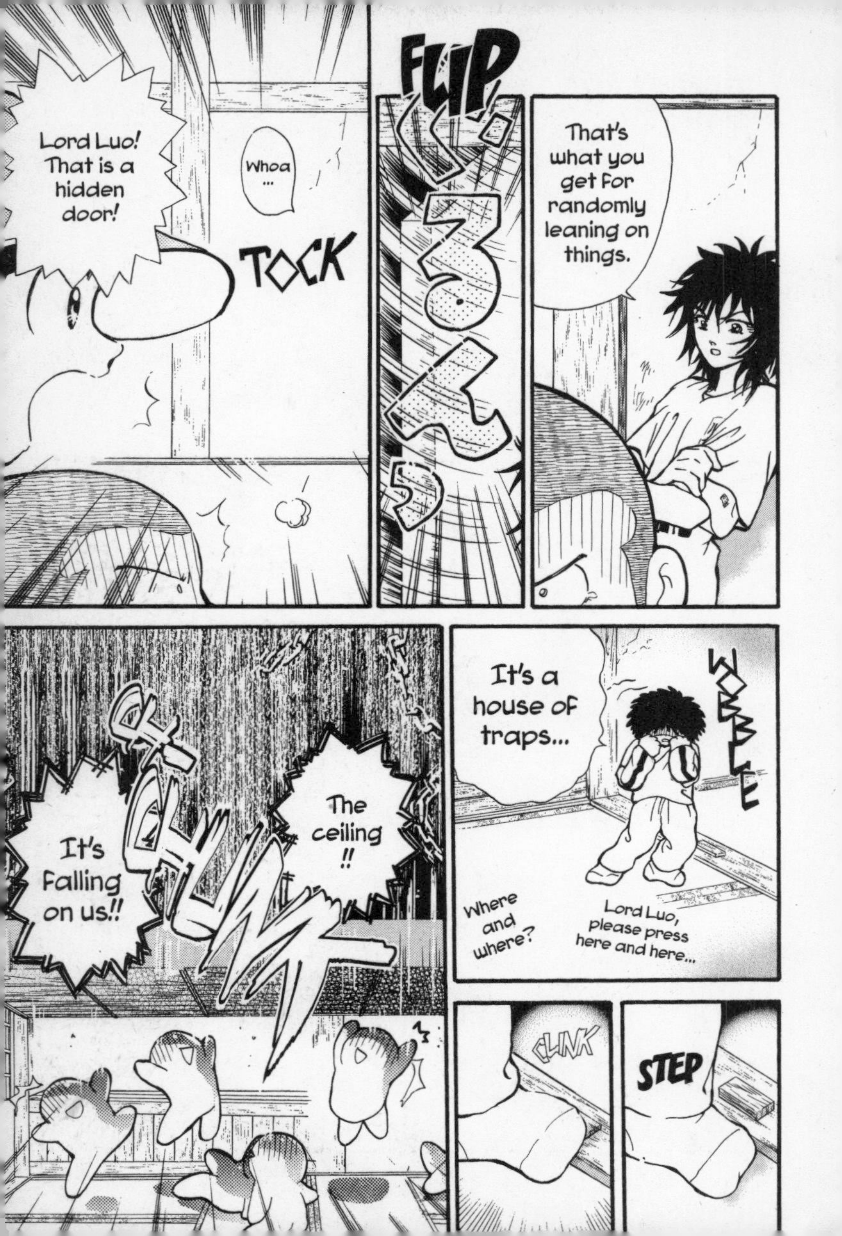

That's what you get for randomly leaning on things.
FLIP
Whoa ...
Lord Luo! That is a hidden door!
TOCK
WOBBLE
It's a house of traps...
Lord Luo, please press here and here...
Where and where?
STEP
CLINK
The ceiling !!
It's falling on us!!

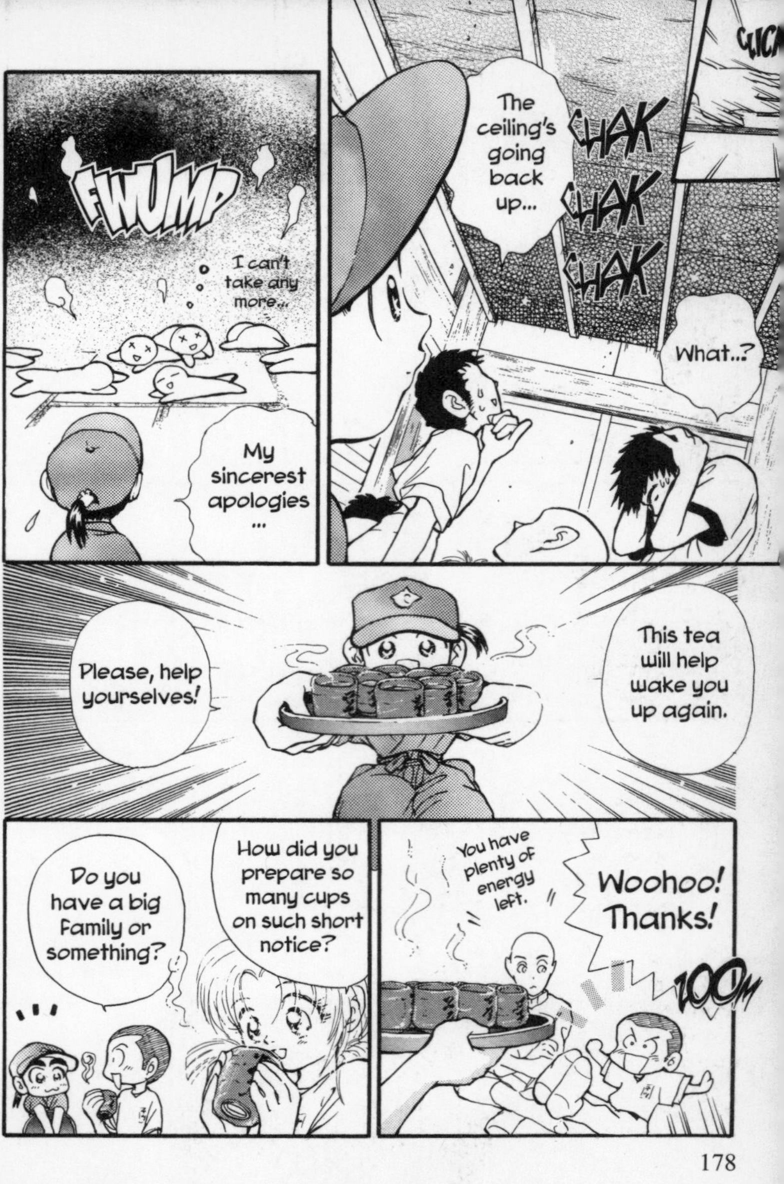
The ceiling's going back up...
CHAK
CHAK
CHAK
What..?
FWUMP
I can't take any more...
My sincerest apologies...
This tea will help wake you up again.
Please, help yourselves!
Woohoo! Thanks!
You have plenty of energy left.
ZOOM
How did you prepare so many cups on such short notice?
Do you have a big family or something?
...

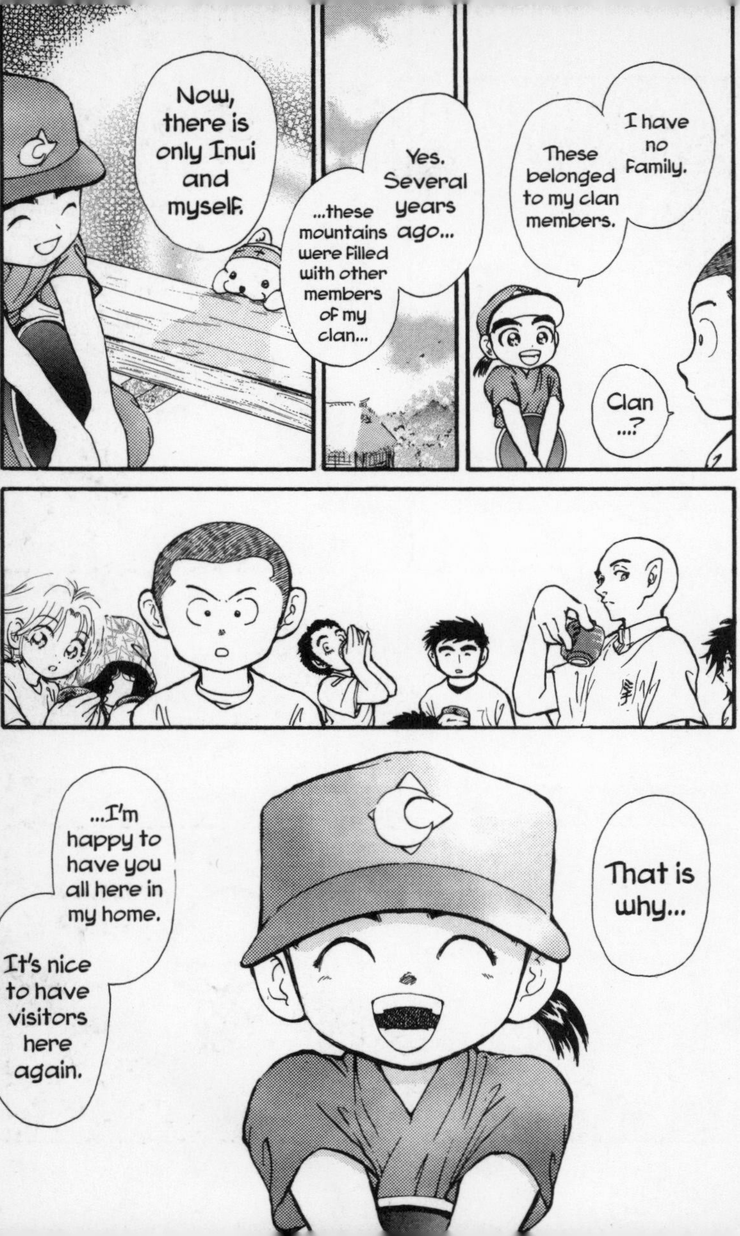
I have no family.
These belonged to my clan members.
Clan ...?
Yes. Several years ago...
...these mountains were filled with other members of my clan...
Now, there is only Inui and myself.
That is why...
...I'm happy to have you all here in my home.
It's nice to have visitors here again.

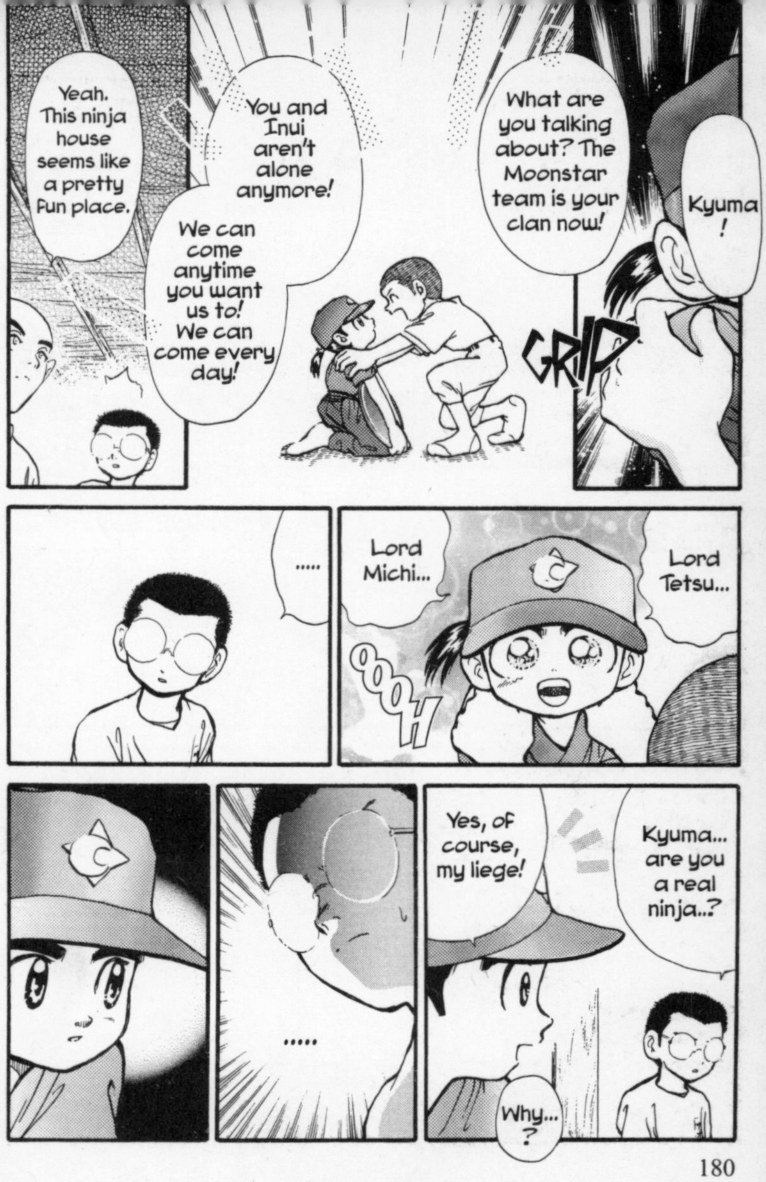
Kyuma!
GRIP
What are you talking about? The Moonstar team is your clan now!
You and Inui aren't alone anymore!
We can come anytime you want us to! We can come every day!
Yeah. This ninja house seems like a pretty fun place.
Lord Tetsu...
Lord Michi...
OOOH
.....
Kyuma... are you a real ninja..?
Yes, of course, my liege!
Why...?
.....

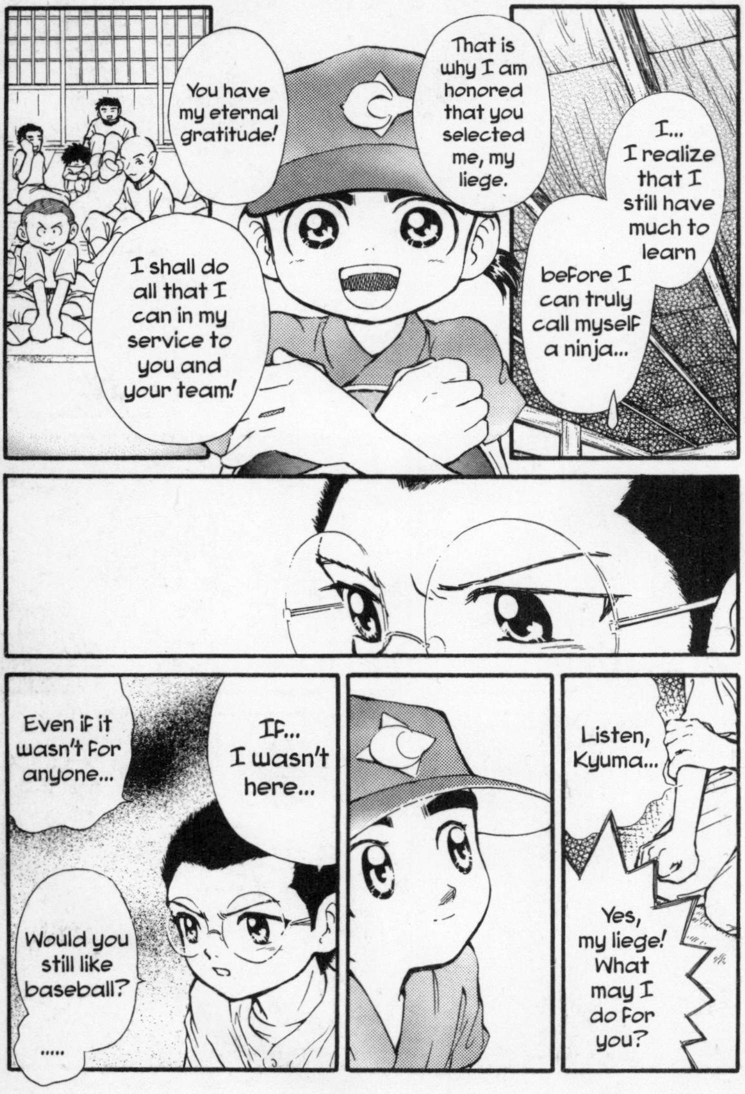
I... I realize that I still have much to learn
before I can truly call myself a ninja...
That is why I am honored that you selected me, my liege.
You have my eternal gratitude!
I shall do all that I can in my service to you and your team!
Listen, Kyuma...
Yes, my liege! What may I do for you?
If... I wasn't here...
Even if it wasn't for anyone...
Would you still like baseball?
.....

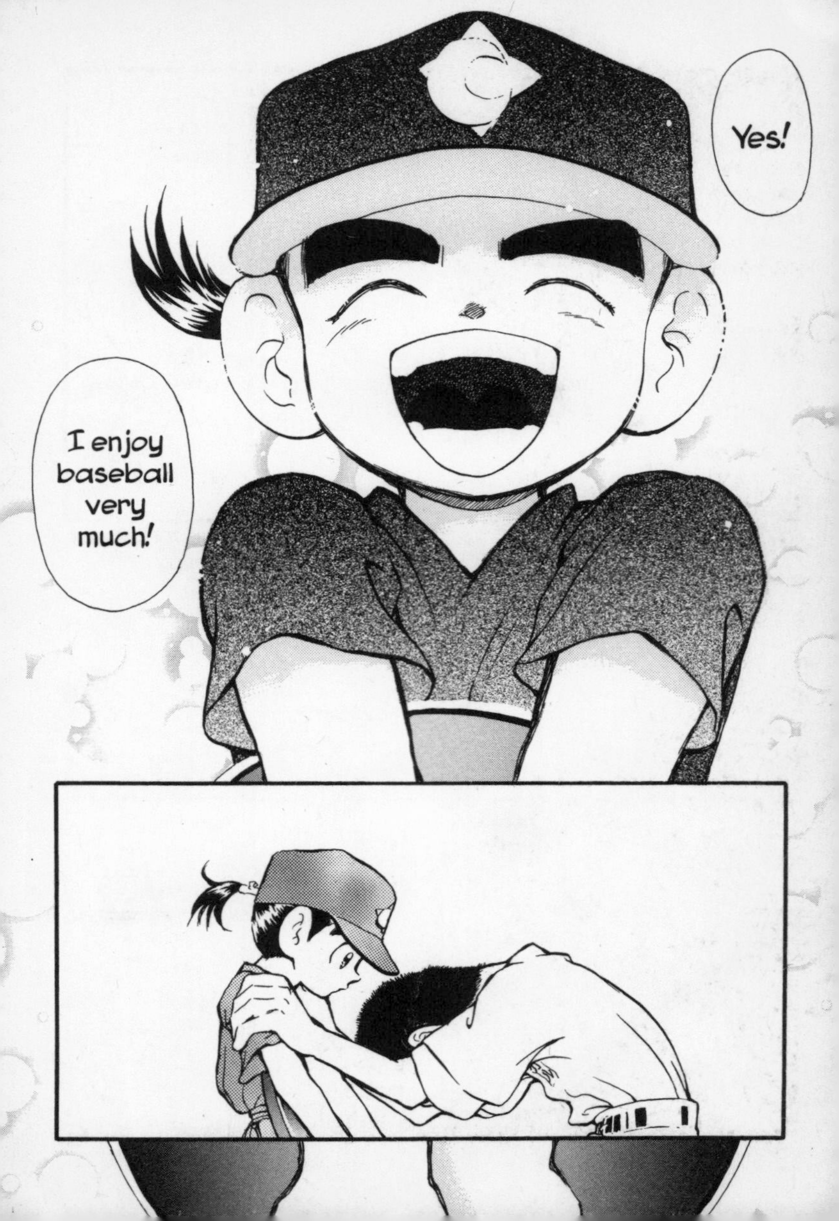
Yes!
I enjoy baseball very much!

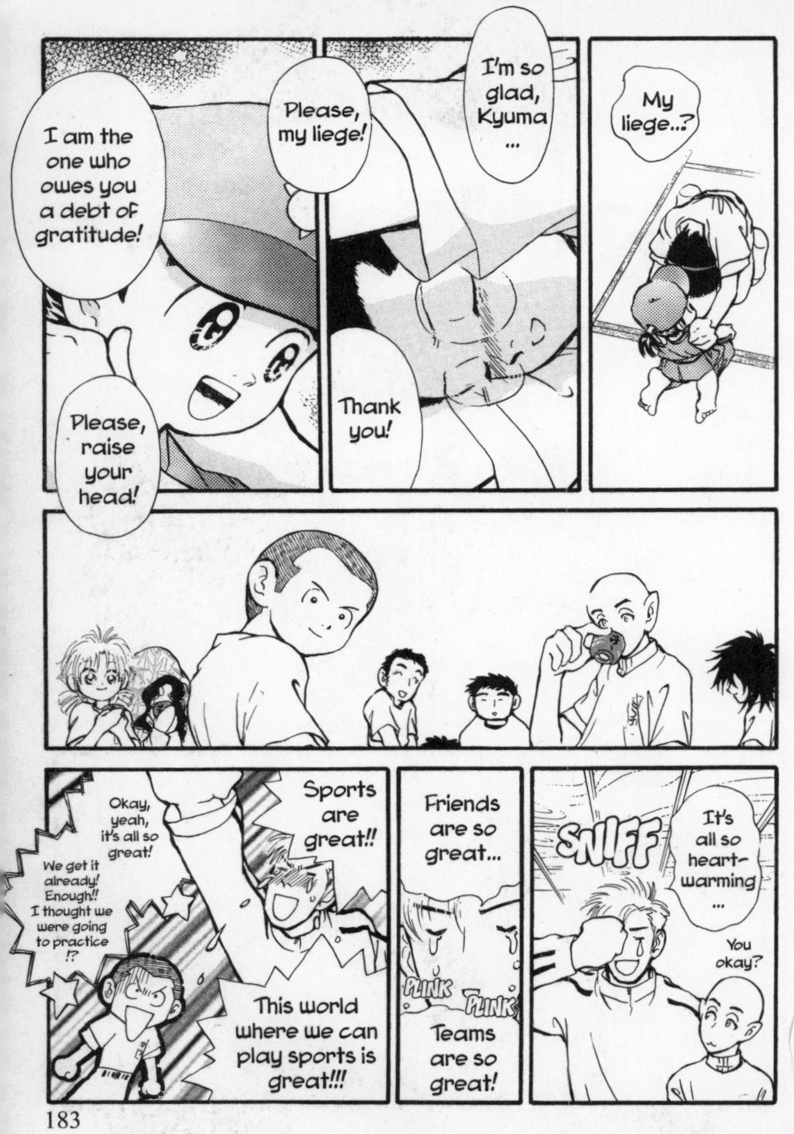
My liege..?
I'm so glad, Kyuma ...
Please, my liege!
Thank you!
I am the one who owes you a debt of gratitude!
Please, raise your head!
SNIFF
It's all so heart-warming ...
You okay?
Friends are so great...
PLINK
PLINK
Teams are so great!
Sports are great!!
Okay, yeah, it's all so great!
We get it already! Enough!! I thought we were going to practice !?
This world where we can play sports is great!!!

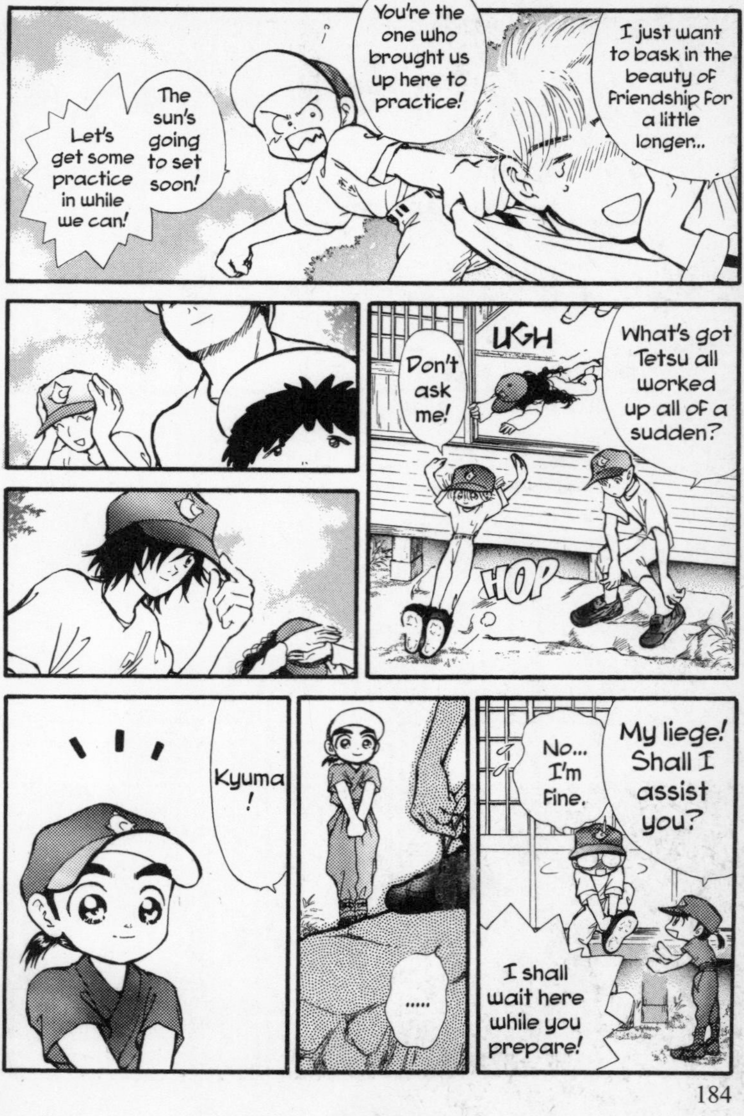
I just want to bask in the beauty of friendship for a little longer...
You're the one who brought us up here to practice!
The sun's going to set soon!
Let's get some practice in while we can!
What's got Tetsu all worked up all of a sudden?
UGH
Don't ask me!
HOP
My liege! Shall I assist you?
No... I'm fine.
I shall wait here while you prepare!
.....
Kyuma!

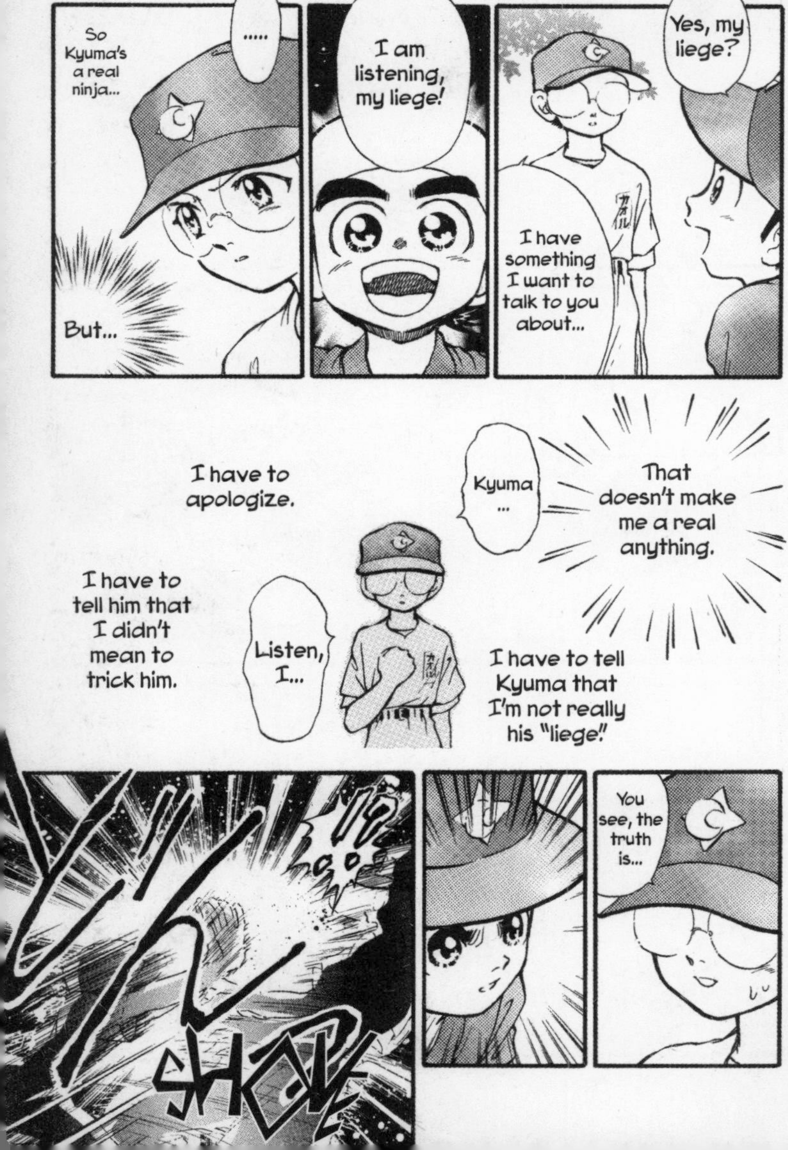
Yes, my liege?
I have something I want to talk to you about...
I am listening, my liege!
.....
So Kyuma's a real ninja...
But...
That doesn't make me a real anything.
Kyuma ...
I have to apologize.
I have to tell Kyuma that I'm not really his "liege."
Listen, I...
I have to tell him that I didn't mean to trick him.
You see, the truth is...
SHOCK

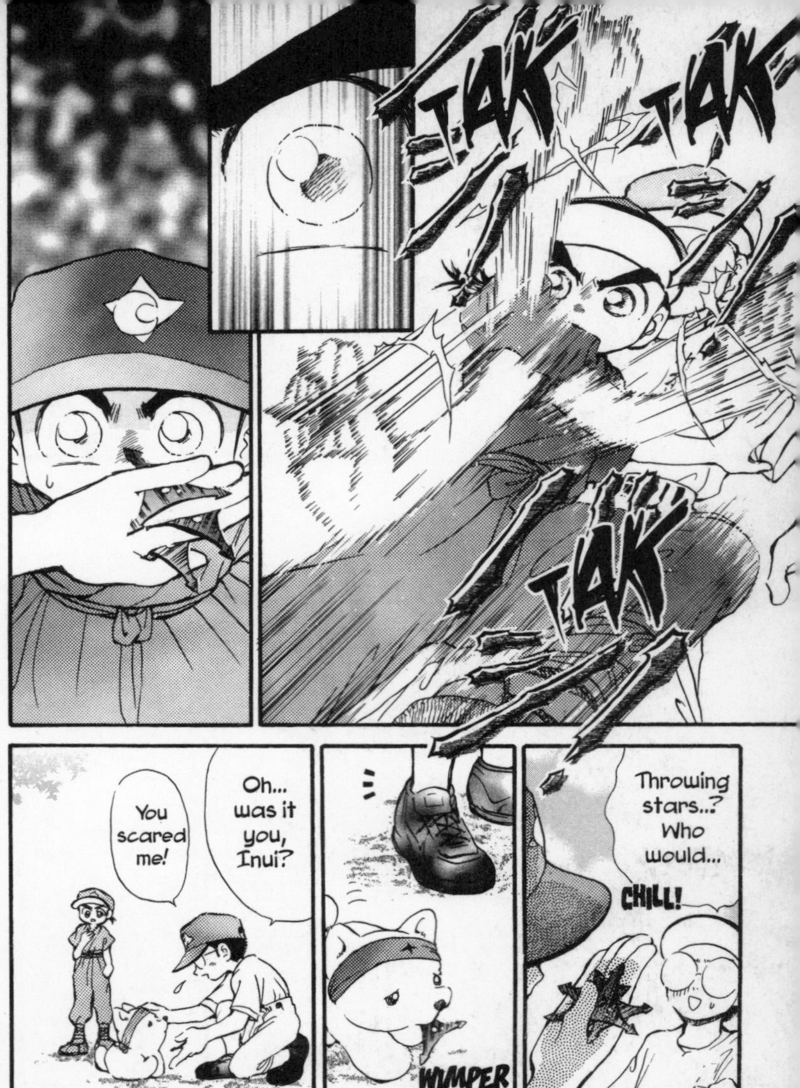
TAK
TAK
TAK
Throwing stars..? Who would...
CHILL!
WIMPER
Oh... was it you, Inui?
You scared me!

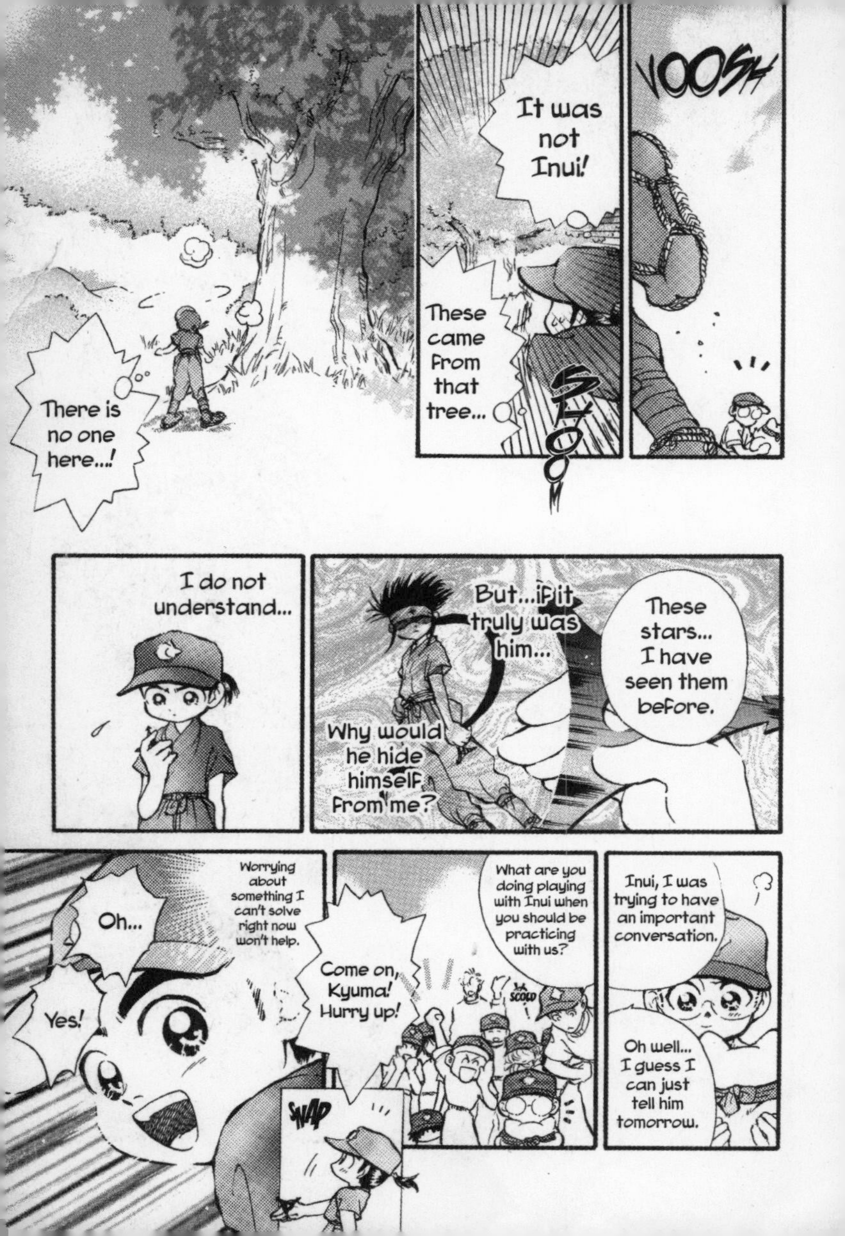
VOOSH
It was not Inui!
These came from that tree...
SHOOM
There is no one here...!
These stars... I have seen them before.
But...if it truly was him...
Why would he hide himself from me?
I do not understand...
Inui, I was trying to have an important conversation.
Oh well... I guess I can just tell him tomorrow.
What are you doing playing with Inui when you should be practicing with us?
SCOLD
Come on, Kyuma! Hurry up!
Worrying about something I can't solve right now won't help.
Oh...
Yes!
SNAP

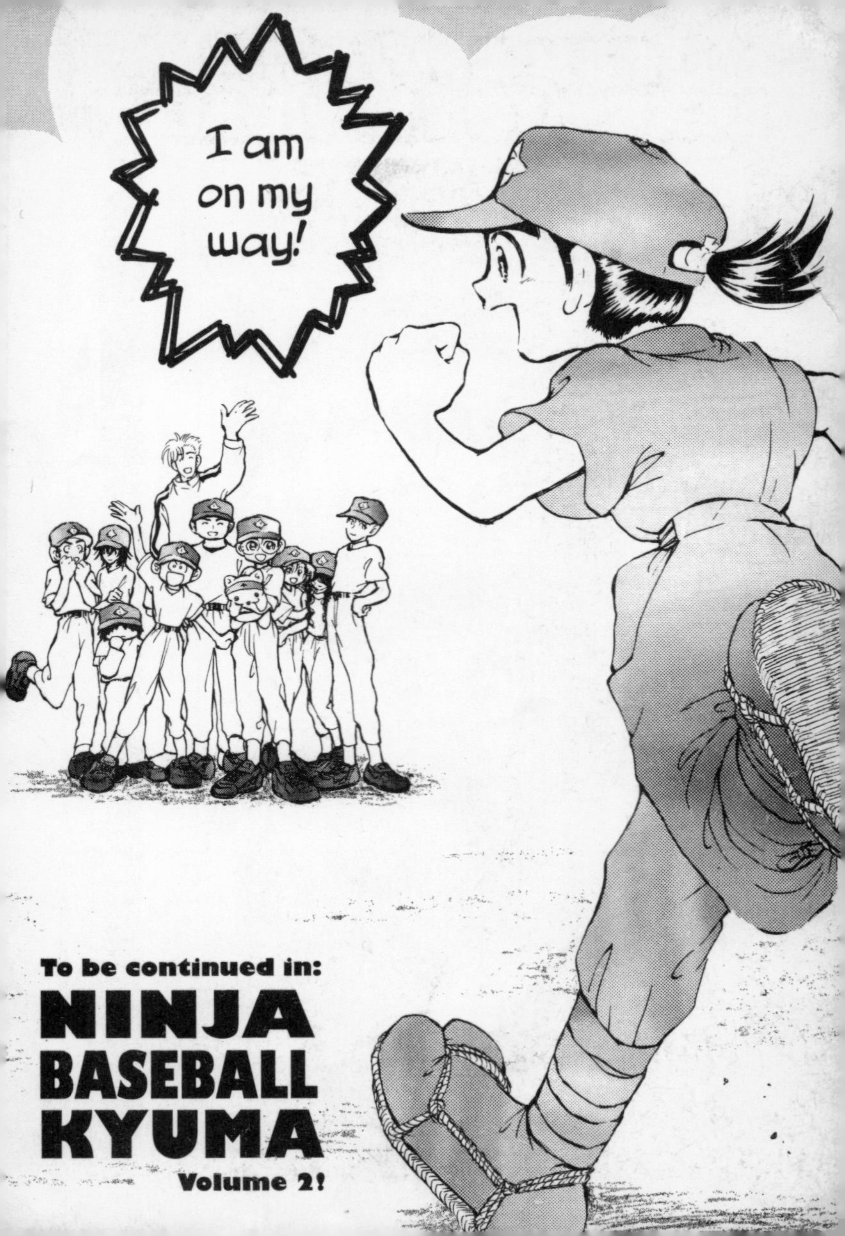
I am on my way!
To be continued in:
NINJA BASEBALL KYUMA
Volume 2!

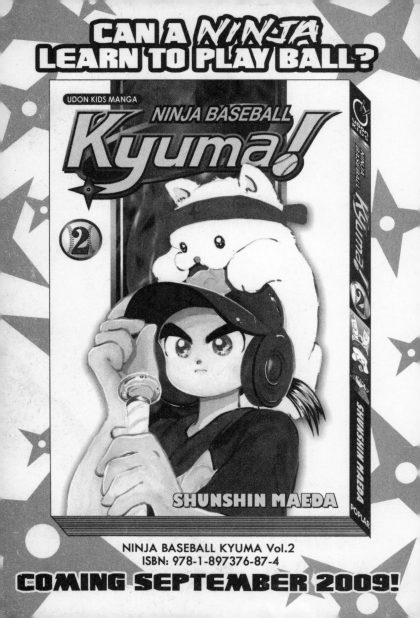

UDON KIDS MANGA
The Big Adventures of Majoko
1
MACHIKO FUJI

UDON KIDS MANGA
NINJA BASEBALL
Kyuma!
1
SHUNSHIN MAEDA

UDON KIDS MANGA
FAIRY IDOL
Kanon
1
MERA HAKAMADA

THE BIG ADVENTURES OF MAJOKO

Vol.1 *(APR 2009)*
ISBN: 978-1-897376-81-2

Vol.2 *(JUL 2009)*
ISBN: 978-1-897376-82-9

Vol.3 *(NOV 2009)*
ISBN: 978-1-897376-83-6

NINJA BASEBALL KYUMA

Vol.1 *(APR 2009)*
ISBN: 978-1-897376-86-7

Vol.2 *(SEP 2009)*
ISBN: 978-1-897376-87-4

Vol.3 *(FEB 2010)*
ISBN: 978-1-897376-88-1

FAIRY IDOL KANON

Vol.1 *(MAY 2009)*
ISBN: 978-1-897376-89-8

Vol.2 *(AUG 2009)*
ISBN: 978-1-897376-90-4

Vol.3 *(JAN 2010)*
ISBN: 978-1-897376-91-1

SWANS in SPACE
LUN LUN YAMAMOTO
1
SPACE PATROL
FULL COLOR MANGA!

SWANS IN SPACE

Vol.1 *(JUN 2009)*
ISBN: 978-1-897376-93-5

Vol.2 *(OCT 2009)*
ISBN: 978-1-897376-94-2

Vol.3 *(APR 2010)*
ISBN: 978-1-897376-95-9

MangaforKids.com

NINJA BASEBALL
Kyuma!
VOLUME 1

Story & Art: Shunshin Maeda

Translation: M. Kirie Hayashi
Lettering: Ben Lee
English Logo Design: Hanna Chan

UDON STAFF
Chief of Operations: Erik Ko
Project Manager: Jim Zubkavich
Managing Editor: Matt Moylan
Market Manager: Stacy King

Original Japanese edition published by POPLAR Publishing Co., Ltd. Tokyo
English translation rights arranged directly with POPLAR Publishing Co., Ltd.

English language version produced and published by UDON Entertainment Corp.
P.O. Box 5002, RPO MAJOR MACKENZIE
Richmond Hill, Ontario, L4S 0B7, Canada

www.udonentertainment.com

First Printing: April 2009
ISBN-13: 978-1-897376-86-7   ISBN-10 : 1-897376-86-3
Printed in Canada

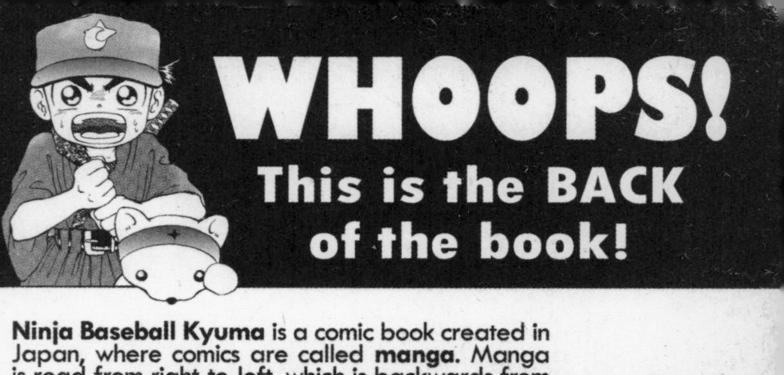

WHOOPS!

This is the BACK of the book!

Ninja Baseball Kyuma is a comic book created in Japan, where comics are called **manga**. Manga is read from right-to-left, which is backwards from the normal books you know. This means that you will find the first page where you expect to find the last page! It also means that each page begins in the top right corner.

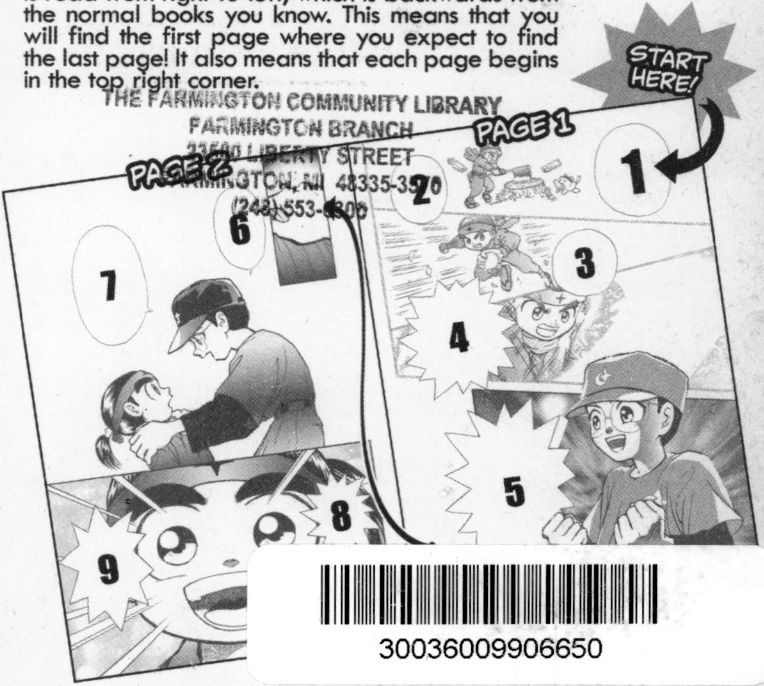
START HERE!
PAGE 1
1
2
3
4
5
PAGE 2
6
7
8
9

Now head to the other end of the book and enjoy **Ninja Baseball Kyuma!**